D0424575

Dear Reader,

We at Zebra would like to welcome you to a wonderful reading experience. From the publisher who consistently brings you the best in historical romance come two memorable, magical novels—*Masque of Sapphire* by Deana James and *Masque of Jade* by Emma Merritt.

There may be no relationship more demanding, more fragile, or more rewarding than that between sisters. Deana James and Emma Merritt capture the essence of such a relationship in their separate but interwoven stories of Judith and Laura—strong-willed, beautiful women who struggle to understand and trust each other as each learns what it means to love the man who has claimed her.

Separately, each book stands alone as a spectacular sensuous historical romance in the best-selling Zebra tradition. Together, *Masque of Sapphire* and *Masque of Jade* create an evocative and very unique tale.

In the prologues, interludes, and epilogues of the books, you will watch the sisters argue and agree as passionately as only sisters can. In *Masque of Sapphire*, you will discover Judith's secret thoughts and dreams; in *Masque of Jade*, you will see Laura's side. And when you have finished both, you will have a very special understanding . . . of sisters, and of love!

Happy reading!

Carin Cohen Ritter
Senior Editor and Product Manager
Zebra Books

MASQUE OF SAPPHIRE

DEANA JAMES

ZEBRA BOOKS
KENSINGTON PUBLISHING CORP.

ZEBRA BOOKS

are published by

Kensington Publishing Corp.
475 Park Avenue South
New York, NY 10016

First printing: February, 1990

Printed in the United States of America

For
Hona and Jane.
Memory is a rushing stream.
When it dries, then I shall be no more.

Prologue

1804
Harrestone, England

"I am not, and you can't make me." Judith Claire Talbot-Harrow noted with satisfaction the look of affront her sister tried to hide. Concealing her own grin, Judith watched as Laura's perfect features took on a slightly supercilious cast.

Looking down her nose from the superiority of her seventeen years, Laura Elyse Talbot-Harrow allowed her large green eyes to roam critically over her little sister's thin, bony figure. "All right, Judith, but you're cutting off your nose to spite your face."

Hot color rose in the nine-year-old's thin cheeks. "It's my face," she replied defiantly. "You go on and be what *Grandmère* wants you to be, but nobody can make me do anything." To cover the blush, she stamped across the room and flounced around, arms akimbo. "And don't think she hasn't tried."

Her nemesis pointed at the mirror. "Judith Claire, turn around and look at yourself."

Grinning impudently, she whirled around. When her light blue batiste dress swirled out like a tent, her grin faded somewhat. Before she could push the skirt down, Judith had revealed the draggling pieces of lace on her

7

pantalettes rucked high above her knees. They wer
almost as bad as her scabby knees themselves showin
through the holes in her stockings. A quick glance at th
reflection in the mirror showed that her sister ha
allowed a grimace of distaste to mar that perfect fac
Judith tossed her head. *Let her be disgusted. She'll g
away all the sooner.*

Laura put on a gentle smile. "Now tell me truthfull
you don't want to do something about the way you look.

For an answer Judith stuck her fingers in the sides o
her mouth and thrust out her tongue at the other'
reflection in the cheval mirror.

"Judith Claire, behave yourself." The voice wa
sharper.

Twitching her long red hank of hair over her shoulde
the younger girl dropped her hands. Then with Laur
watching, she deliberately wiped her fingers on her skir
"I think I look just fine the way I am."

"Yes, you do look fine." Laura's words came out on
weary sigh. Judith noted it and could not conceal
cheeky grin. People always tired very quickly of trying
cajole her into proper behavior. A few more minutes an
her sister would go away too. "That's what I'm tryin
to tell you. You're a beautiful little girl."

Here she comes. Almost close enough to kick. Judit
watched in the mirror as Laura approached. The slend
white hand slid into the pocket of the fine lawn walkin
dress and drew out a blue velvet box. Opening it, sh
pulled out a gleaming gold chain. "Hold still."

Her plan of action forgotten, Judith stared into th
mirror in open-mouthed amazement. Light glinted off th
fragile links that spilled from Laura's fingers like trickl
of water. A moment to undo the clasp, and the gold lock
hung suspended above Judith's tangled red hair. At th
center of the chain hung a small gold heart, and reflectir
its light from the center of the heart was a fiery blu
stone—a sapphire. Almost mesmerized, Judith stared
it descended past her eyes and came to rest at th

8

neckline of the faded blue dress.

Prickles of excitement ran up her spine and into her scalp as Laura's voice brushed her ear. "But you can look so much better."

A shiver vibrated through her whole slender body as she felt Laura's cool fingers fasten the necklace. Unconsciously, Judith raised her hand. It was too beautiful. She did not dare touch it.

A pleased smile on her face, Laura reached for the hairbrush.

Almost fearfully Judith studied her reflection from the toes of her scratched black patent shoes, past the grubby white stockings, to the faded blue batiste dress. The locket looked out of place amid the frayed lace trim. Above her face in the mirror she saw her beautiful, immaculate sister.

A feeling of angry helplessness held her motionless. From the top of her head to the tips of her shoes Laura was perfect. The Lincoln-green velvet spencer was made for her. The folds of material fairly glowed, and the wonderful red hair caught the light. Laura's white dress, made of finest lawn, was dotted with tiny leaves of the same green as the spencer. Around her neck she had tied a white velvet ribbon from which dangled a small phoenix of rare gold-shot jade.

Laura's perfection and beauty made Judith want to grind her teeth in rage and weep in pain at the same time. Taking a hold on her whirling emotions, Judith plucked up the sapphire heart between her thumb and third finger and pretended to study it critically in the mirror.

Behind her Laura moved closer. Her gentle smile had a distasteful quirk to it. Using only two fingers, she lifted a curl up to Judith's crown. "It's time to put your hair up when you come to dinner."

Does she really think that smile looks sincere? Or does she just think that I'm too stupid to know? "No!" With a twist of her head Judith darted away. Not for the world would she be bribed. "Cook doesn't mind what I wear." *Besides, I*

9

don't have any nice clothes to wear to dinner.

Taking a deep breath, Laura followed. Still smiling although not quite so much—Judith noted with satisfaction—she put her arm around her sister's waist. "You're not eating with Cook tonight. You're eating downstairs with the family."

And how is that supposed to make me happy, sister dear? I can't stand her a minute longer. Judith jerked away from the restraining arm and fled across the room toward the door. "I don't want to!"

Darting after her, Laura caught the trailing end of the blue sash inset in the waist of the dress. "Stop right there! You're going to eat downstairs if it's the last thing you do."

The indignity of being reeled in like a fish on a line made Judith furious. *I will kick her. I will!* "You let me go!" Judith kicked backward at Laura's shins, but Laura sidestepped the flying heels and managed to grab the other piece of the sash.

"Come back here." Laura transferred her grip from the sash to one of Judith's wrists.

"Ouch!" Her hand closed over the exact spot where Mistress Haycraft had struck her charge with a pointer for inattention. Judith began to struggle and kick in earnest. Tears started in her eyes.

"You're not getting away from me. I'm bigger than you are, and I know what's best for you."

"You're not my mother. You can't make me." Furious that she could not control her tears, and determined that Laura should not see them, Judith ducked her head and shoved hard at her older sister's body. Her ragged nails caught in the delicate lawn of the white and green walking dress. As Laura staggered back a step before the violence of the assault, the fine material tore away from the waistband.

In paralyzed silence the sisters stared at each other. "You little hellion! Look what you've done!"

"You made me do it! It's nothing but a stupid dress

10

anyway." Judith blinked frantically to conceal the tears of remorse.

"It was a Madame Bernice." Laura's voice vibrated with thinly controlled rage. *"Grandmère* chose this material and design especially for me."

The mention of their maternal grandmother by her obvious favorite put steel back into Judith's spine. Shrugging her shoulders with elaborate disdain, she lifted the hem of her faded blue batiste and paraded across the room toward the mirror, her left hand poised as if dancing the minuet. "Why, sister dear, she did this for me too."

In the mirror she caught sight of Laura's expression of disbelief. Bent on revenge, Judith darted back toward her sister, flapping the skirt like a flag. Her voice quavered, then escalated into a screech. "This was your dress five years ago!"

Laura could not quite conceal her embarrassed gasp. Her elegant white hands made soothing gestures in the charged air. "But I have one for you that is new. I had it made especially for you."

"You did?" Judith allowed her skirt to drop. *If this was a bribe, it was turning into an expensive one.* She could not remember when anyone had brought her a new dress. Perhaps she had never had one? Why should anyone bring her a locket and a dress? She stared intently at Laura trying to read her expression. "Is it a Madame Bernice?"

Laura took a deep breath. "Actually, yes, it is. Come and see." She held out her hand, making a coaxing motion that Judith recognized immediately. A frown creased her forehead. Her eyes narrowed. Her older sister was wiggling her fingers and waving her hand as if Judith were a pet dog.

There, arranging her skirts as though she were a queen on a throne, Laura patted the place beside her and lifted a large striped dress box onto her lap.

Torn between antipathy and curiosity, Judith allowed

11

herself to be lured to the divan of chased maroon velvet. It wouldn't hurt to look at the dress. Thinking back, she was sure she had never had a new one. Cautiously, she took a step as Laura opened the box. Glowing chintz with bright blue stripes drew her like a magnet. With one wondering hand she touched the soft folds reverently while the other sought the warm gold of the locket around her neck.

"Is this really for me?"

"Yes, it's really for you." Laura lifted the dress by the shoulders. "Don't you like it?"

The presentation of such a treasure made Judith feel dizzy. The chintz, its stripes the exact color of the heart of the sapphire, shone with a luster like silk. Around the low square neckline was a delicate ruffle of Irish lace. The high waistline was marked by a two-inch ribbon of sapphire blue silk. Tears prickled at the backs of Judith's eyes. She ground grubby fists into them, but the effort did no good. When she looked at Laura, she knew her tears would show. Keeping her head lowered, she asked in a choked voice, "Why?"

Her sister's smile was beatific. "I want you to meet George."

"Who's George?"

"Who's George?" Laura murmured. "He's the man I'm going to marry. He's George Beckworth, Viscount Chichester."

Judith stared at her sister. "Viscount! Humph! Is he made out of some more of *Grandmère*'s special material just for you?"

Laura bristled. "He's quite a famous whip of the *ton*."

Judith grinned.

"And I've known him for ages."

Judith's grin faded. "And you've never brought him to see me before?"

"Well . . . no . . ."

"Why?"

Laura spread the dress onto the divan. Her cheeks

12

flushed faintly. "You . . . you needed some time to grow up."

Suddenly, like a crash of thunder, Judith knew the reason. "You didn't bring him because I'm ugly." Even as Laura shook her head in protest, Judith backed across the room to the door. Her fists clutched the faded material of her skirt. She tried to speak, but hurt pride almost choked her. She was not being given a beautiful gift of love. Instead, she was being tricked out to parade for company like a coach horse with a plume on its bridle and a tight checkrein.

"No!" Her sister gathered up the dress and hurried after her. "You can be as pretty as anyone."

Judith shook her head wildly. "But not pretty enough for George!" Feeling as if her blood were boiling, she sought to gather her armor about her. Temper, hot and fierce, dried the tears. "And I don't want to be. George is probably just an old stuffed shirt anyway. Who'd want to meet him!"

"Judith . . . that's not the way . . ."

"Oh, yes it is."

"You don't understand . . ." Laura held out the dress. Its skirt draped across her outstretched arms in shimmering folds.

All the pieces of Judith's armor were in place. The tangled red hair tumbled and swirled as she threw a glance over her shoulder at the door. "I understand!" she screamed. "Take your old dress and go back to *Grandmère* and George and Madame Bernice."

Laura held out the beautiful new dress, her expression pleading.

Disappointment, hurt, and furious anger erupted. Judith dragged the dress off Laura's arms. One fist closed over the skirt and twisted. The other twisted in the bodice. Her face contorted by childish temper, she pulled with all her might. Fine lace and cotton could not stand against such anger. The dress split with a terrible sound. Its rending pulled asunder the more delicate fabric of

13

their momentary accord.

Laura's face blanched to the lips. She might have been turned into a marble statue.

With a harsh cry Judith threw the dress on the floor and stomped on it. "You leave me alone!" Whirling, she fled the room. The door slammed behind her with a resounding crash.

She dashed headlong down the hall. On the small landing, halfway down the backstairs, where she could be seen neither from the upstairs nor the downstairs halls, she crouched, trembling. In the shadows she waited, listening intently, hearing nothing but her heart beating so fast that it nearly jumped out of her throat. When a tight knot swelled there, she clutched at it and encountered the sapphire heart.

And suddenly she was crying, crying, crying. Her mind refused to function, so great was the pain and the hurt. She was so ugly. And so hateful. And Laura was so beautiful. And Laura had given her the heart. And she hadn't even thanked her. No matter that the reason was George.

The thought of Laura and her love for George only made her cry harder. She had no right to the heart. The heart symbolized love. She tugged on the chain, wanting to tear it from her neck and fling it down the stairs.

But it was the only piece of jewelry she had ever owned. Whatever the reason for the gift, she could not part with it. She threw a fearful look up the stairs. Suppose Laura should come after her and take it back? Since there would be no dinner with George, she might very well want to keep it for herself.

There would be no dinner. The thought of having to eat for the rest of her life in the kitchen with Cook set off a fresh storm of weeping.

She had brought it on herself. She had no one else to blame. Except why did Laura look so beautiful, like a princess in a fairy tale, while she looked like a witch in the same book? Her sobbing abated to an occasional snuffle. She pushed disconsolately at her snarled hair. If she were beautiful, someone might love her.

She caught the offending mop in her hand and tugged. In frustration she gritted her teeth. A sharp pain made her gasp and cover her mouth with her hand.

When she took it away, she stared in disbelief at the bloody object, then let out a piercing shriek. As if demons pursued her, she tore down the backstairs and out past the enormous cook, who made a grab but missed her fleeing figure. She ran until she was exhausted, then dropped down behind a hedgerow to weep. In disgust she opened her hand.

She had lost another tooth.

Chapter One

Winter, 1814
Harrestone, England

"Spiders! Spiders! Oh, God!"

Piercing shrieks echoed and reechoed through the little house. The crystal prisms hanging from the small sconces in the entry hall vibrated and tinkled against one another.

"Spiders!"

Porcelain shattered with a fearful crash.

The old man in a rusty black frock coat came out from the pantry behind the staircase and exchanged a helpless glance with Judith Claire Talbot-Harrow before she clutched at her dark skirts and hurried up the steps.

"Spiders! They're all over the sheets! For mercy's sake! Help! Somebody help me! Help!"

The bell in the kitchen set up a furious jangle.

At the door to her mother's room, Judith paused to take a deep breath. Not that she was tired from the narrow flight of stairs. She climbed it at least a couple of dozen times a day. She merely steeled herself for the struggle that faced her on the other side of the panels.

"Spiders! They're going to bite me! For pity's sake!"

The screams had given way to passionate sobbing.

Judith pushed the door open. Its edge dragged over the

17

shards of a tall vase, sweeping before it the larger pieces as well as the stems and shattered blooms of pink and cream roses. With a weary grimace she picked her way across the sopping carpet.

The pale golden light of late afternoon bathed the topsy-turvy scene. Cream linen sheets, pillows, and a spread with deep edgings of lace were all tossed helter-skelter about the floor. Books, sheets of notepaper, and envelopes lay on and among them.

"Mother."

The woman cowering against the walnut headboard managed to pull her eyes from the foot of the bed. Wildly, she struggled up into a sitting position and held out her emaciated arms. "Judith," she sobbed. "Oh, Judith, there were spiders crawling all over me."

Judith clasped her hands behind her back. "Mother, you've had another one of your dreams."

"No! No, no, no, no," the woman whined piteously. Her bony chest heaved above the fine lace of her nightdress. Her skeletal arms retracted beneath the wide sleeves. "I didn't dream them. They were there."

Judith bent over to gather up the bedclothes. Draping them over her arm, she came to the foot of the bed. "Mother, where is it?"

Shielding her face with one clawlike hand, the woman slid back down into a prone position. "Don't throw those nasty things over me again. They've had spiders on them." She began to moan as she pulled her sticklike legs up. With her other hand she tucked the edges of her gown over her blue-veined feet.

"Mother, where did you hide the brandy?"

The woman rolled her head in weary negation, ignoring the question. "They all ran away. Nasty scurrying . . ." Her eyes closed. "I . . . I'm so tired."

Plumping the pillow with both hands, Judith came to her mother's side. With practiced efficiency she slid one arm under the skeletal shoulders and eased the pillow into the space in front of the headboard. Her face was

18

nches from her mother's. The sick woman's breath made
her nostrils twitch. "Mother, where is it?"

The face's gaunt look was accentuated by the knot of
gray hair screwed at the crown of the head. It flopped
from side to side as Charlotte nodded wearily. "There
really were snakes."

"I thought you said there were spiders."

"Spiders? No, I never said anything about . . ." The
words trailed off into silence. The woman's head slumped
to one side.

With a sigh Judith stepped back. Presented in profile,
the face was a mixture of gray hollows and dead white
protuberances where the skin stretched taut over the
bones. Only the temporary flush induced by the alcohol
brought a bit of color to the cheekbones and the dry,
seamed lips.

With the faintest of shrugs Judith eased the torso into
a more comfortable position and straightened the
birdlike appendages. When the bed was decently remade,
she turned her attention to the broken vase.

As she so often did, she marveled at the transitory
urges that shot through the dying body. Where had her
mother found the flash of strength to fling one of her
books across the room and break the porcelain vase
heavy with water and flowers? Not that she had aimed the
book. In her insanity such conscious effort was
impossible.

It had been a beautiful vase, Judith thought with a
twinge of regret, one of a very few pieces remaining from
their former life. Had one of Beau's ships brought it back
from the other side of the world? She turned a fragment
of the base around in her hand, unable to decipher the
brushstroke characters. With another sigh she laid it in
the bottom of the trash receptacle.

Finally, when all the flowers and fragments were
collected, she carried them out.

The old man waited at the top of the stairs. "I'll take
that, Miss Judith."

19

"Thank you, Morris. I'll need a towel to mop up th water."

Silently, he handed one to her, then peered at th contents of the receptacle. "The Chinese vase, miss?"

"I'm afraid so. It . . . fell."

"Yes." He showed no emotion.

"She's asleep now."

"I'll have Mrs. Morris make some tea."

She smiled faintly. "I'll be down as soon as I'v finished in here."

"Very good, miss."

The sound of her mother's stertorous breathing an the sickening odor of the cancerous body combined t oppress her as she knelt beside the stain. How soon? Ho long? She hated herself for the direction of her thought:

As she turned the towel to absorb more of the wate out of the carpet, a sliver of glass lanced into the flesh a the base of her thumb. She gasped and sat back on h heels, staring at her palm, seeing nothing. She had turn her hand before her face until light glinted off th tiny spear. When she plucked it out, a drop of bloo welled after it.

A muscle jumped in her cheek as she gritted her teet Cradling her hand against her waist as if the tiny pric were some grievous wound, she hunched over. She wa going to cry. She could feel the angry tears starting.

She swallowed, and a guttural sound somewhe between a groan and a sob slid from between her lips

The snoring broke off with an explosive cough. For te seconds everything was still. Then a voice quaver weakly. "Who's there?"

Judith pressed her face into the skirt of her dress. H forehead touched the carpet. Teeth clamped tight together; she did not answer. She could not face h mother now, could not conceal the nausea, the disgus the pain.

The covers rustled. After a tiny pause the breathi evened, then became heavy again.

20

Judith climbed to her feet and slipped out onto the landing. Her hand still smarted, but the bleeding had stopped. And the wound was nothing. She struggled to catch hold of her temper, but her anger and sense of injustice flamed hot.

Wildly she stared around her, sapphire eyes blazing in her white face. The space at the top of the stairs could not be called a hall. It was only a cubicle with a railing running on three sides of the stairwell and three doors opening onto it. Not an ornament of any kind graced it.

Her whole body shook with frustration. How unfortunate that Mother had broken Beau's vase. *She* would have liked to break it—and more. She wished vainly for a whole sideboard of ornaments to fling to the floor one by one. A dozen vases would not empty the well of her rage.

She would write another letter to her sister. In it she would vividly detail their mother's brandy and laudanum dreams. That would fix Beau.

She knew Laura read her letters to him. He would write his own replies to be delivered every month when the purser from one of Beau's ships came with the money. And now he would beg her to come. But she could not. Would not. He had not taken her when she had begged to go. He had left her to live with this. She stared around her at the cold bare hall. She would not write to him. She never wrote to him. But Laura would know.

Her face composed, the color high on her cheeks, Judith stalked down the stairs. The tea was waiting below, but she did not drink it in the kitchen. While the anger burned bright, she carried it into the library, where she sat down to write the letter.

She could still see him—the most beautiful man in the world—her father—"Beau" Talbot—as he had looked on that last day. His eyes had been blue as sapphires. His skin, evenly tanned. His hair, in dark waves over his broad forehead. She had run into his arms certain of her welcome, certain of his love. His teeth had flashed in a smile of greeting.

21

It was the only time he had smiled throughout the entire interview.

She had been only thirteen years old. And even today, at nineteen, she hated him. To this very day she hated him. Shuddering, she stared at the blank paper in front of her.

He and Laura would go across the ocean to America. Laura's chances with George were ruined. Laura was crushed. Laura was unhappy. Laura would accompany him. But she, Judith, must stay behind. She must stay with her mother.

And he had promised nothing. Not that he would return. Not that she would come to see him. In the end she had screamed at him and flung herself against him, flailing her arms, kicking at his shins. When he had caught her in his arms to keep her from doing herself an injury, she had bitten his wrist.

Judith could still remember the taste of blood, remember the sudden stillness of his big body as he held her against him. He had waited, enduring the pain, his face white. She had twisted her face upward, a smear of blood on the corner of her mouth. Identical pairs of sapphire eyes stared at each other only inches apart, yet miles apart.

"I hate you," she had stormed. "I hate you. I hate you. I hope you never, never come back. I hope you die. Die! Die!"

"Miss Judith?"

She blinked. Morris stood before her, rubbing his hands. "Miss Judith, you have a visitor, a man."

A wild hope rose in her breast. She felt as if she were choking. "Who is it?" Her voice was hoarse.

"His card . . ."

Her trembling excitement subsided. She took the proffered piece of white pasteboard. "Randolph Carew, Lord Lythes."

A chill swept away all traces of her previous excitement. She handed the card back to Morris. "We are

22

not at home."

"Ah, but you are . . ." He stood in the doorway, peering at her.

Not for the first time did Judith think that Randolph Carew knew no other way to smile. "My mother is asleep."

He nodded as if he had expected nothing else. "I'd heard she was ill. Came to pay m' respects."

"How kind. I'll tell her you called."

Her pointed lack of enthusiasm discouraged him not a whit. "Here, m' man." He tapped Morris smartly on the elbow with his cane. "Take m' things and trot out the good brandy. The trip was devilish long."

Judith replaced the pen carefully in the inkstand. "There *is* no good brandy, Lord Lythes. I'm afraid you've made the trip for nothing."

He raised one pale eyebrow. Instantly, the droop of his eyelid was more pronounced. He thrust his cane and beaver into Morris's hands and swung his great cape from his shoulders. "Laura," he chided. "Will I catch you in a lie? What a naughty, naughty child you are!"

"Laura is my sister. I am Judith."

He paused in the act of passing his palms lightly over his graying temples. Again the eyebrow rose. The eye beneath it, a startling dark brown beneath his blond hair and eyebrows, stared at her appraisingly. One hand dropped to extract his snuffbox from his waistcoat pocket. The other stroked the mustache that lay on his upper lip. When he spoke, he matched exactly her earlier lack of enthusiasm. "Why, so you are? My. How you've grown."

"It has been six years. I should hope so." She paused to draw a deep breath. "Lord Lythes, my mother and I live very simply here on the sufferance of my grandmother and cousin. As you see, the house is very poor. I'm sure you'll be more comfortable spending your night elsewhere."

Her uninvited guest made a clicking sound. Judith

23

watched him with a sort of detached wonder. How coul
his tongue make that sound while the side of his mout
still leered? "Obviously, someone is going to have to tak
you in hand," he murmured. "Such behavior should n
go unpunished."

"Lord Lythes . . ."

He snapped his fingers contemptuously at Morri
"The brandy, m' man. And be quick about it."

"We have no brandy," Judith insisted, mentall
cursing the servant, who backed from the room like
cowed spaniel.

"Another lie, Judith. That's two." Leering again, h
crossed to a carved walnut highboy beside the fireplac
and pulled open its doors. His chagrin was obvious whe
he found it stuffed with books.

"I'm not lying," she said, gritting her teeth.

Without bothering to close the doors, he turned awa
"Ah, but you are," he contradicted her, his dark ey
scrutinizing the shabby room. "Remembering m' darlir
Charlotte as I do, I know there might be no food in th
house, but there would be brandy."

Judith positioned herself in front of him. "My moth
has been very ill."

He stared at her. The leer became more pronounce
"I suspect the red hair has something to do with you
untamed behavior. Such an unusual color. Don't belie
I've ever seen anything quite like it. Damme if I have

In irritation she ducked away from his hand. "We a
not receiving visitors."

"But I'm hardly a visitor, m' dear. Rather, an o
friend of the family. The eyes are rather too much,
course. That bright sapphire blue with all that red ha
does make for rather a startling picture." He brushed
her to stroll down the row of bookshelves along one wa
His eyes scanned the spines of the volumes intently.

"Lord Lythes . . ."

"I brought a change of linen with me," he assured he
as if that were the problem. "Instruct that semi-corp

24

to make up a bed in the guest room. . . ."

"There is no guest room."

He paused to stare pointedly at her figure. "Then I'll sleep anywhere."

She charged across to the door. "I suggest you sleep at the inn down the road in Harrestone. Or, better yet, in your own bed in London."

Paying her no attention, he pulled a large book off the shelf and grinned into the space behind it. "For shame, Judith. How inhospitable!"

"What?" She started forward as he pulled out a dark squat bottle.

"*The History of the World* by Sir Walter Raleigh," he chuckled. "One of Charlotte's favorite hiding places." He held it up to the light. "Almost full too."

"My mother has not been able to come downstairs in weeks."

He heaved a sigh. "Perhaps I have made my trip for nothing."

She crossed her arms tightly across her chest. "I thought you came to visit her because she was ill."

He frowned although the leer never left his lips. "And so I did. Now, Judith, please be so good as to get me a glass. Surely you won't force me to drink this out of the bottle."

"You cannot stay here!"

Bottle swinging in his hand, he crossed the room. Defiantly, she lifted her chin before his insolent swagger. Less than a yard from her, he stopped. "Perhaps your mother will instruct me to punish you while I am here," he suggested softly. He glanced toward the ceiling. "Charlotte!"

His sudden shout shocked Judith. "Lord Lythes . . ."

"*Charlotte!*"

Her hands fluttered placatingly. "Lord Lythes, you'll disturb her."

"Only think how disturbed she'll be when she finds out how rude you've been to me. *Charlotte!*"

"For heaven's sake!" She thrust herself forward, pushing against him, covering his open mouth with her palm.

He chuckled. His tongue moved against her sensitive skin.

As if he had brushed her with acid, she jerked her hand away.

"Where shall I spend the night?"

Furiously, she wiped her hand on her skirt. At the same time, she fumbled behind her for the handle of the door. "I'll have Morris prepare a room."

Outside in the hall Morris waited, his chin trembling, his eyes shifting nervously up the stairs.

Judith listened, too, but all was quiet. She let out her breath in a sigh. "Bring Lord Lythes a tray and glasses, Morris. And inform Mrs. Morris that we will have another for dinner. I will see to his room. He will be staying the night."

"The night, miss." Morris rolled his eyes doubtfully. "But where will he sleep?"

"In my bed."

"But, miss . . ."

"I shall sleep down here in the library on the chaise lounge."

Morris slumped, his relief visible. "Very good, Miss Judith."

"Now, hurry with the glass before he turns up the bottle and drowns his stupid self."

"So, little Judith, all grown up and locked away in this shabby old hovel like a princess in a tower." He ran his gaze over her thin figure as she entered the library.

"My mother is awake, Lord Lythes."

"Please call me Randolph, Judith. Let's not stand on ceremony. Lord Lythes is so formal. After all, I feel like one of the family." He rose from behind the desk and came to her side.

26

Hastily, she put the chair between them. "I'll take you up."

"No hurry." He put his hand on her arm. "What do you do, little Judith, when your mother doesn't need you? Does some village swain come calling from Harrestone? Does your taste run to rustics?"

Judith twisted her hand free and stepped back. "Lord Lythes."

He leered suggestively. "Or perhaps a handsome young footman takes your fancy? Strong back and broad shoulders."

"My mother is waiting."

He regarded her steadily. "Of course."

"I'll show you up."

"So good of you," he murmured. Matching her steps when she would have preceded him, he put his hand under her arm

Her skin prickled beneath his touch. When she would have pulled away, his fingers gripped her elbow with almost painful tightness. The tobacco and brandy mingled with the strong odor of his body. Her nostrils dilated as she wondered if Lord Lythes obeyed Beau Brummell's injunction to bathe and change his small clothes every week.

Fortunately, the narrow stairs forced him to drop his hand and come behind her. On the landing before her mother's door, she stopped. "You . . . you will find her much changed from what she was. She's been so ill." Her voice faltered to a stop. She did not look to him for sympathy. Her eyes remained fixed on the bare floor between his dusty shoes.

"No doubt." He shifted his weight from one foot to the other.

Stiffening her spine, she looked him full in the face. "Do not upset her."

He raised a mocking eyebrow. "Of course not," he murmured. "Especially after you ask me so nicely."

Her expression did not change as she opened the door

27

and stepped back.

"Rand . . ." Charlotte lay propped against every pillow in the house, her skein of hair artfully arranged over her shoulder and down her breast. With Judith's help she had applied cosmetics so that despite its dreadful thinness, her face managed to look patrician. "Oh, Rand. It's been so long."

"Charlotte." He crossed the room in a graceful sweep, his eyes scanning her condition although his leer remained intact.

"I've missed you so." She held out her hand. A small pearl and emerald ring glittered on her third finger.

He hesitated an instant at the sight of the knotted blue veins and brown spots.

Judith gritted her teeth. If he hurt Charlotte . . .

His smile widened. "My dear, you're looking lovely." He brushed his mustache across the back of the proffered hand.

"Oh, Rand." Charlotte's voice wavered, then strengthened. "I'm so glad to see you. We get so few visitors these days, here in the country. Not like Harrestone."

Lord Lythes replaced the fragile hand on the spread and stepped back. His nostrils twitched at the odor that rose from the bed. He shot a swift glance at Judith. "No." He swallowed hard, his leer stiffening. He stepped back and glanced around the room for the first time. "No. This is not like Harrestone."

"Please sit down, Lord Lythes." Judith indicated the chair beside the bed. It was the one she sat in during the times between dosages when she and her mother waited together for the laudanum to take effect.

He stared at the shabby object with ill-concealed loathing. His knees would be touching the edge of the bed. He took another step backward. "But surely that's your place."

"I thought I'd leave you two alone to discuss old times."

"No. Stay." His hoarse reply came swiftly.

"Please, Rand," Charlotte coaxed. "Please. Sit right here by me and tell me all the news. What about Amanda Darlington? Has she managed to bring Gregory up to snuff?"

Lord Lythes shot Judith another pleading glance, but she pointedly ignored him. Instead, she went around to the other side of the bed to lift her mother's back and thrust another pillow beneath it. From behind Charlotte, Judith shot him a murderous look.

Flushing slightly, he pasted his leer back in place and sat down. Instead of leaning forward, he leaned back and draped one arm across the chair back. "Amanda Darlington. Oh, yes. Gregory married her," he snickered. "But the word about the *ton* is that she truly trapped him. Set him up for a weekend on the old dirty acres and primed her father. At a given hour, outraged Papa bursts into bedroom. *Voilà! Flagrante delicto.* And Gregory's leg shackled for life."

A bit of natural color brightened Charlotte's cheeks. She laughed heartily as Judith had not heard her do in years. Perhaps she had been wrong about Lord Lythes. She gave him a grateful smile. The leer was now firmly back in place and broadened as he watched her move back to the end of the bed. "Shall I bring you tea, Mother?"

Charlotte looked from her daughter to her former lover. "Some tea would be nice, I think. And some brandy for Rand. He loves it so."

"It's quite early in the day—" Judith began.

"Nonsense. This is a celebration. The time is unimportant." Lythes waved his hand. "Right, Charlotte."

"Of course."

As swiftly as she fetched the tea and brandy, Judith was too late.

Lord Lythes met her on the stairs. "She's asleep," he growled. "Drifted right off in the middle of a speech."

"She does that. Usually, she wakes right up though. If you'll—"

He shook his head, his dark eyes blazing. "No! Damme! No! You should have warned me."

"I did." Judith retorted coldly. "I told you we were not receiving visitors."

"But that woman's dying."

"The doctors have diagnosed cancer. It is very widespread."

"God!" Snatching the brandy bottle off the tray, he brushed by her and thudded down the stairs.

Judith heard the library door slam behind him. A moment later Judith heard her mother.

"Rand!" The tone was imperious. "Rand, where are you? Judith . . ."

She hurried up the stairs and through the door Lord Lythes had left ajar. "Mother, I'm here."

Charlotte was sitting up in bed. Her eyes glittered. "Where did he go? Did you send him away?"

"Mother, he went downstairs when he saw you had fallen asleep."

"I was asleep just a moment. He could have waited," Charlotte whined.

Judith set the tray down. "I'm sure he'll be back when he knows you're awake. Lie back, Mother. I've brought you some nice hot tea."

"You sent him away," Charlotte accused.

"Mother, I assure you . . ."

"You hate him because I love him. He was so kind to me when your father all but deserted me." Charlotte hitched herself toward the edge of the bed. "Rand! Rand!"

"Mother, I'll get him."

"You won't. You hate him. You're just like your father. Neither one of you ever let me have any fun." She tossed back the covers.

"Mother!"

"Hand me my robe. Rand can't have gone far. Rand!

30

Wait!" She managed to get her feet over the edge of the bed.

"Mother . . ." Judith reached for her but too late. Sense of balance impaired by weeks flat on her back, leg muscles atrophied from lack of use, Charlotte pitched headfirst off the bed.

"Mother!"

On elbows and knees, Charlotte began to cry. "Rand! Oh, Rand? Where are you?"

Judith rang the kitchen bell for Mrs. Morris before she stooped to catch her mother by the shoulders. "Charlotte. Charlotte. You'll hurt yourself. Let me help you back to bed."

"No." Her body drenched in sweat, Charlotte managed to push herself up on her hands. With Judith's help she got her hands off the floor. Scrabbling clumsily, she managed to get one foot under her. "I can walk," she panted. "Just help me."

"Oh, Miss Judith . . ." Mrs. Morris hurried in.

"Help me get her to bed."

"No. Give me . . . robe . . ."

"Mother . . ."

Charlotte uttered a hoarse scream as anger gave her strength. "Give me my robe." She twisted herself out of their arms and took a couple of steps. Then the pain hit her. Another scream more terrifying for its shrillness reached every room in the house. She doubled over, clutching at her belly. Her body toppled to one side.

Petrified with horror, Judith heard the sharp snap of a bone.

Chapter Two

"Is she all right?"

Dazed with exhaustion, for a moment Judith did not recognize the man standing in the doorway.

"Is she all right?" he repeated, making his way carefully into the room. For once the leer was gone from his mouth. His pale skin had a distinct gray undertone.

His continued presence further ripped at the shreds of her self-control. "No. She is not all right," she snapped. "Don't be ridiculous. *Grandmère*'s doctor said her hip is fractured. She's in terrible pain. Even the laudanum is having only slight effect. Since her hip will never heal, she'll never walk again."

He dropped into a chair and rubbed a sweaty palm across the lower half of his face. "God!"

After a final disgusted look, Judith turned her face away. A tiny flame leapt among the lumps of charcoal in the grate. She allowed it to draw her in and close her mind to the horror of the past twenty-four hours.

"It wasn't m' fault," he groaned. "I just went downstairs to get m'self together. The shock of seeing her like that . . ."

"You're not to blame," Judith told him wearily. "It was the cancer. The doctor said that her bones are so weak that one of them could have broken when she turned over in bed."

"God!" He groaned again.

"Your being here had nothing to do with what happened."

A silence grew in the room. Judith turned her exhausted mind to what she must do. Tomorrow she would find the strength to write to her sister. If Laura ever intended to see their mother alive again, she must come immediately. Even then, Judith doubted that Charlotte would last the eight to ten weeks minimum time required for a letter to reach New Orleans and for Laura to return.

"I don't suppose there's any more brandy." A petulant voice interrupted her calculations.

The tone fired her anger. "Lord Lythes." Her voice grated out between her teeth. "There is no more brandy. You have seen my mother and upset her irreparably. Furthermore, your stay is inconveniencing everyone. I cannot be a hostess to you. I cannot think why you remain."

He stiffened in turn at her tone. "Are you asking me to leave?"

Her eyes, blue as Beau Talbot's had ever been, blazed with indignation. "No. I'm not asking. I'm ordering. Leave now. Morris will pack such things as you've brought with you. Although by the look of you, you can't have brought much. Not even a shaving kit."

His dark eyes narrowed dangerously. "I'll leave when I'm ready."

She shot to her feet. "Get out."

He leered then. "And who will make me? Those antique creatures that totter around at your beck and call?"

With an effort she brought herself under control. "Lord Lythes, you have paid your call on my mother with disastrous results . . ."

"It's not my fault. The doctor said so. She was practically dead before I ever—"

She gasped in horror at his abrupt volte-face. "She was

33

your friend."

He muttered a curse under his breath. "She was useful to me as I was to her."

"But . . ."

"She wanted to make Beau jealous. I wanted . . . other things."

Judith shook her head. "I don't understand. If she wasn't your friend, what did you come here for?"

"I thought she might be able to come back to London. People in society have short memories. The name of Harrow opens all doors." He rose and began to prowl about the room. "Charlotte was such a pretty little bit of fluff. Never a serious thought. Good connections. Accepted everywhere."

Judith cut him off with an angry gesture. "You've wasted your time. She'll never be accepted anywhere again. When she divorced my father for you, she lost everything."

He pulled out a particularly thick book to peer behind it. "She was weak. She should have stayed in London with me. Together we could have faced them down. It only needed that old witch, her mother, to have come round. And she'd have come round in time. They all do."

Judith shook her head, her tone mocking "*Grandmère* would never have 'come round.' There never was a harder woman than my grandmother. Charlotte had to stay here. She knew if she ever left here, she'd never get another penny of support."

He pushed the book back into place with a disappointed snort. "She's a woman, isn't she? Mother love and all that sort of rot."

Judith laughed mirthlessly. "You see around you 'mother love.' A shabby house rotting down around our ears, a pensioned man and his wife for servants."

He seemed to be mulling something. His head tilted to one side as he stared at her. "But you're her granddaughter."

"My grandmother doesn't care anything about me,"

34

Judith sneered. "She never has. Why do you think I'm living here as a housekeeper-nurse to my mother? Nobody cares a fig for me."

His expression wavered. He seemed genuinely amazed. "You're lying. Why are you lying?"

"I'm not. I was the failed experiment. They were going to break the entail with me. But I was a girl. A girl nobody wanted." She spread her hands. "Look around you. Do you see anything that would indicate that I'm important to anybody?"

"But you're a Harrow."

"Talbot-Harrow. The first name cancels out the second."

"Then drop the first."

"Never."

He made a whistling sound between his teeth. "You're not at all like your mother."

"Thank you for the compliment."

He ended his wandering around the room to drop into a chair some distance from the fire. The dim lighting cloaked his expression completely. "What will you do when your mother dies? If nobody cares for you, as you say?"

She had no desire to talk to him about her problems. She shook her head in intense irritation. "Lord Lythes. Please. I have many things to do before nightfall. And I don't expect to get much sleep. I don't have time for idle conversation. I'm sure you must be on your way."

"I could show you the rich life you were meant for."

"What?"

"I could show you the life of the *ton*. Society. The rides through Hyde Park. The teas. The music hall. The routs. The balls." His voice had taken on a seductive huskiness. "You could be the delight of the season. All that red hair. Those flashing sapphire eyes."

"You're out of your mind."

"Damme, if I am. I'm thinking for the first time since I came downstairs this morning."

35

She opened the door. "Leave."

He did not move. "Of course, I had hoped for some money too. Apart from Charlotte's name, there was all that money. Talbot money. Harrow money." He looked around him in distaste.

"I'm sure you see that there is no money here. This is not even the dower house at Harrestone. It's an old hunting lodge that doubled for the gamekeeper and his family."

"The doctor came swiftly enough."

"Oh, that's *Grandmère*. She sends a doctor when I send for one. But if not for the money Beau sends, Charlotte and I wouldn't have enough to eat."

"Your father sends you money?" Lord Lythes rose from his chair. Light fell across his face, revealing his eager leer. "How much? Even a small amount would—"

He had said too much. Anger trembled in every line. "Get out," she stormed. "Get out!"

Insolently he strolled toward her. "Why, Judith Claire, aren't you afraid you'll disturb Charlotte?"

She threw an involuntary glance over her shoulder toward the stairs.

His hand captured her wrist. Dragging her back into the library, he closed the door and leaned back against it.

Furious that he had tricked her, she flew at him. "Let me go. Monster. Get out of my house." With her free hand she struck at his head, landing a stout blow on the side of his jaw.

His expression turned ugly. He caught the flailing arm, twisted it behind her, and dragged her in against him.

She twisted furiously. "How dare you? Let me go."

"No, damme, I don't think I will." His grip tightened, punishing her deliberately.

Summoning all the strength in her right arm, she wrenched it out of his grasp and slapped his face.

He did not even flinch. Color rose instantly beneath the pale skin. With a nasty laugh he struck her back.

The blow snapped her head back on her shoulders, but

36

the pain was nothing compared to the shock. She had never been struck before. She could not believe that he had actually hit her. Her face only inches from him, her mouth fell open and her eyes widened.

He read her reaction. His lip curled upward. Deliberately, he swung the back of his hand across her other cheek. That blow was delivered with more strength. This time she cried out.

"Quiet! Not a sound, Judith. Not a sound." He wrapped both arms around her in a crushing hug. "We don't want that old fool breaking in on us. I'd have to hurt him and his old wife too." His foul breath so close to her face made her gag. "You don't want them hurt, do you?"

"Let me go. What are you doing? You can't do this. Let me go." She was panting now, breath hissing from her throat, twisting and writhing in his grasp. With her free hand she clawed at his face with her close-trimmed nails. A set of red furrows appeared as if by magic down his cheek.

"Vixen!" he snarled. He released her suddenly, purposefully, almost flinging her from him. She stumbled back. Before she could recover and dart away, he was on her, again seizing her wrists and shaking her viciously, as a terrier shakes a rat. "We'll have no more of that, m' girl. Oh, how I'll enjoy the taming of you."

Unintelligible cries of distress served only to drive him to be rougher. Using his full strength, he twisted her slender arms behind her. Stunned by his violence, and helpless in his grip, she offered no resistance. Deliberately, he used his weight to flatten her body against the door.

When she tried to speak, only a dry rasp escaped her.

"Now." His mouth was next to her ear, his teeth in her lobe. "Now. You'll do what I say. If you call for those old family retainers, I'll have to hurt them. And you don't want that, do you, Judith?"

She tried to push herself away from the panels, tried

37

to turn.

He leaned against her and bit the lobe of her ear. His eyetooth cut the skin. Blood trickled down the side of her neck. "Do you?"

"No." Her answer was a painful whimper.

He eased back a little, but kept his lower body hard against hers, grinding her slender frame against the hard wood. "You've been a haughty little minx the entire time I've been here. Sticking your nose in the air, treating me like dirt, guarding that whoring mother of yours as if she were the Virgin Mary. But you're stupid. Your kind always is. You think your rank protects you." He tightened his grip around her wrists, crushing the tender bones.

She whimpered again.

He chuckled. At the same time, he stabbed his hips forward against her buttocks. As her hipbones slammed against the paneling, she could not suppress a cry. "Careful," he remonstrated. "If you can't control yourself any better than that, you'll have to watch while I break up their old bones. I'm very good at that. Damme. No one better."

"No," she begged as he butted her again. "No. Don't hurt them."

"That's m' girl. That's better. Much better. Pain's nasty. And you're not going to let them know, are you? Going to protect them." He let her feel his weight and strength a moment longer, then released her and stepped back.

She clung to the panels for a moment, not certain what he was going to do next, trying to think what she might do. Contrary to what he might think, she was not afraid. Her anger boiled away her fear. All kinds of weapons were available in this room. Her mind tried to inventory them through the pain and fury. Tentatively, she flexed her fingers and turned to face him.

Their eyes locked, his triumphant, hers furious. "You'll do," he said. "You'll do nicely. I wanted

38

Charlotte, but why settle for an old mare when I can have a young filly. And the granddaughter of Old Harrow herself. Despite what you've told me, I'm sure your grandmother would do a great deal to protect her granddaughter's reputation from stain. You've been lying to me, Judith. None of m' girls get away with lying to me."

Judith pushed herself away from the wall. As he stared at her, she walked aimlessly toward the fire, her head drooping as if she were utterly defeated.

"You're young . . ."

Unfortunately, the poker was a short-handled affair hardly two feet long. The small stove needed no more, not even long-handled fire tongs. Beside it sat an unwieldy coal scuttle of heavy metal with a long wire bail. Her eyes flew to the wall, where a regimental sword and scabbard hung far out of reach.

He pressed close behind her, following the movement of her head, reading her thoughts. He shoved her toward the chair. "Sit down."

Reluctantly, she tore her eyes away from the wall and sank into the chair. Suddenly, she began to tremble. For the first time, she felt the smart in her cheeks where he had struck her. She clasped her hands tightly between her knees.

". . . done with you, you'll do very nicely in society," he was saying.

"I hate society," she whispered.

"What?"

"I hate society."

"That's because you've never been taught to look at it properly." He strolled away from her. "Damme! Are you sure you don't have any more brandy in the house?"

"I'm sure."

He grunted. "You hate society because all those bitches like your grandmother who control it have hurt and neglected you. But now, with me, you can get revenge. Wouldn't you like that?"

39

He came back to her side. She could smell the strong odor of his body. His exertions in trying to subdue her had worked up a sweat. He put out his hand to rest on the top of her shoulder. Angrily, she shrugged away.

"How old are you? Twenty-two? Twenty-five?"

She felt her temper rise. She knew she made a poor appearance, but the insult was too much. "I'm nineteen."

"Poor girl. So neglected. You need a good dressmaker and a hairdresser."

"I'm fine as I am."

"You need new clothes as befit your rank." He touched her cheek, this time with backs of his fingers.

"Leave me alone."

"You need affection. Love. I'll see you're taught all about love. A man would pay well to love you. Very well indeed."

She twisted around in the chair, lifting her face defiantly. "I'll never do what you want. You'd better leave this house as fast as you can. *Grandmère* might not care anything about me personally, but you're right. She does care about the Harrow name. She'll not let you drag it down into the dirt."

He laughed. "But m' dear girl, I've already done it. Poor Charlotte was feeling so neglected by Beau. Then I introduced her to several men who were willing to pay handsomely for her favors. She, of course, thought they loved her for herself alone. They were all paying me for the introduction." His eyebrows arched quizzically. "Now do you understand?"

"You're the lowest of the low."

"Damme. I'm not. I'm just a man trying to make a living in the only way he can. I'm not fit for anything else except the social round. But that takes money, and I've none. So I have to find ways to get it."

His voice had deepened, taken on a husky tone. He had strolled around behind her chair. Suddenly his arms came over its back. His hands laid hold of her shoulders and pulled her back against the worn leather.

40

"What . . . ?"

"Hush. Behave yourself. I won't hurt you. You'll like this." His fingertips slid downward over the swell of her breasts.

A thin, high-pitched scream escaped her. She tried to fling herself from the chair, but his hands were too strong. They grasped her breasts like claws and squeezed. Her scream became a shriek of pain. She kicked futilely as he laughed.

He slapped his arm up under her chin, all but throttling her. The other hand squeezed her breast, then closed over the peak, tugging at the nipple.

"You'll like it rough." He raised his voice to be heard over her cries. "I can tell. There's a man I know who'll be panting to have you. He'll pay hundreds. Thousands of guineas. Damme! He will!"

She screamed again as he ripped the cloth away from her front and bared the breast. Red marks from his fingernails appeared instantly in the white flesh. He laughed as her struggles increased.

"Settle down," he snarled. "Don't be a fool. Don't make me damage the merchandise."

She twisted her head and tried to bite his arm, but her teeth could not penetrate the folds of thick material.

He squeezed again. His thumb and third finger pinched her breast. The side of his fingernail cut her.

She screamed again. She did not hear the metallic thud. She felt only Lythes's grip tighten, then loosen. He staggered around. The next minute he cursed furiously, gasped, then all but strangled. Gray dust and ashes flew into his eyes and all over the room.

Judith stumbled from the chair, gathering the pieces of her dress together, choking in the acrid air.

Another metallic thud, and Lythes dropped to his knees. His gasp of pain sucked more dust into his nose and throat. He began to cough, batting the air with his arms. His eyes streamed blinding tears.

"Morris?" Judith exclaimed.

"Yes, miss," the old butler replied. His voice sounded only a bit more breathless than if he had been responding to an ordinary summons.

Lythes directed his blind eyes toward them. "I'll kill you, old man," he snarled. "And you, bitch. Just wait'll I get my hands on you."

Morris lifted the coal scuttle. "Perhaps you'd better run for the countess's footmen, miss. I don't know that I can hold him off much longer."

"Yes. Yes. I'll run." She sped to the door.

"Come back here." Lythes got one knee under him. "You come back here."

With an air of great equanimity, Morris stepped forward into the settling gray cloud and swung the heavy coal scuttle with all his might. It caught Lythes on the side of the head. He sprawled across the rug, unconscious before he hit the floor.

Judith managed a smile despite the tear stains and the gray ash. "Morris, I don't know how to thank you. I . . . I never expected."

"I wasn't always an old man, Miss Judith," he said with unruffled dignity.

"Thank God." Her teeth began to chatter as shock tore at her nerves.

"Just run, miss. We need help. He's only stunned."

Snatching her shawl from the hall tree, Judith sprinted out the door.

"She will be buried, of course, at Harrestone . . . in the church . . . with the family." The dowager countess's mouth pursed tightly at the unpleasant thought.

"Do you want me to prepare her now, or will you wait until she has stopped breathing?" Judith asked sarcastically.

The dowager's mitted hand tightened over the head of her walking stick. Her chin rose a notch. The green eyes were the only traces of color in the powdered face. Her

42

lips were so shriveled that they were only a mass of seams radiating out from a tight line. "Intolerable! I should have taken you in hand long ago."

"Ah, but you didn't. You and everyone else left me strictly alone."

The old woman tightened her seamed lips. "You are my granddaughter."

"How kind of you to remember after all these years."

"Perhaps there has been some neglect, but you have had tutors. Whatever you requested."

"Thank you."

"Now, see here, Judith Claire. I left you with your mother because you were young. A young girl needs her mother."

"As a model for behavior? I certainly know where to look for brandy bottles. I can carry trays and empty bedpans. I can change sheets without getting the patient out of bed."

The old woman's mouth twitched. She appeared to be chewing on some exceptionally tough morsel. At last she sniffed. "Fortunately, it's not too late. You shall have your come-out. Of course, it cannot be until next year, but we'll simply shave a couple of years off your age. No one will guess that you are . . . as old as you are . . . with the proper hairdresser and couturier."

Judith clenched her fists in angry pain. Her own grandmother did not remember how old she was. Worse. For the second time this week someone had commented on her appearance. Bitter with resentment, she lifted her chin. "I have no wish to come out in society."

"Don't be ridiculous. Of course you do." The countess narrowed her eyes and squinted at Judith. "You're not impaired in any way, are you?"

"Not at all. I simply do not wish—"

"Don't be obstinate. I despise obstinacy for the sake of false pride. You have a right to be angry. I admit it." She waited as if in hopes of a contradiction, then cleared her throat noisily. "You have been shamefully neglected. I

43

admit that too. But you should be overjoyed that we are ready to make amends."

"Roll over and lick the hand that wielded the whip."

"Stop that!" The countess struck the floor with her walking stick.

"Then you stop." Judith had dealt with her mother so long that older people and their imperious commands did not impress her. "Why don't you ask me what I would like to do when my . . . this responsibility ceases? I might have plans."

"Plans!" The countess's voice rose and fell in amazement. "Plans! You! You are a female of good family. You have no plans other than to be presented to polite society, where a young man of good family can choose you to be his wife."

In the back of Judith's head was Lythes's suave voice. *I'm just a man trying to make a living in the only way he can. I'm not fit for anything except the social round.* "No."

The countess stood abruptly. Again the walking stick struck the floor. "You will have time to think about this. I'm sure you will come to your senses."

Judith did not answer. Instead, she rose too. "I'll lead the way upstairs."

The countess cast her eyes toward the ceiling. "No. No. I don't think that would be appropriate. I would not wish to disturb her rest."

Judith had been about to open the door. She turned back in horror. "You aren't going upstairs to see your own daughter."

"Perhaps another time."

"There may not be another time."

The old woman came to stand before the door. Her eyes were now fixed firmly straight ahead.

Judith opened the door and curtsied mockingly. "As you wish, 'Your grace.'"

In the hall, the countess's footman sprang to his feet. "Ready, m'lady."

"Yes, Harkness."

A bell tinkled above them. All three involuntarily glanced up the stairs. "Judith . . ." came the wavering call. Again the bell.

Judith looked square into the faded green eyes. "Well, *Grandmère* . . ."

The old woman's eyes dropped. "Harkness. I will wait on the stoop."

"Judith Claire . . ."

"Yes, Charlotte. I'm here. Do you hurt badly?"

"Not too badly." The voice was hoarse from sobbing and wailing.

"I'm glad. Would you like a sip of water?"

"Yes, please."

When she had held the glass to her mother's lips and fluffed the pillows, Judith sat beside the bed.

"Did I hear my mother's voice?" The words were barely a whisper of sound.

Judith hesitated.

"I heard the sound of thumping. It made me remember her stick. Then I thought I heard her voice."

"*Grandmère* was here." Judith wondered if she should have lied.

A rueful smile played around Charlotte's thin lips. "And she did not come up to see me?"

"She thought you might be resting. She did not want to disturb you. But she was really concerned about your health. She sent her own doctor when you fell."

The figure on the bed lay silent. Judith thought she had fallen asleep. Then she spoke again. "How strange that you should be the only one to care for me."

Judith shrugged. "Not strange at all. Without you I wouldn't be here at all."

"You were to have been a boy."

"I've heard the story," Judith assured her dryly.

Again the silence. "I don't suppose Rand will come back."

45

"I don't think so. He felt terrible that he had somehow caused your fall."

"But you told him that I forgave him . . ."

"Of course."

The figure on the bed heaved a sigh. "I don't have a single person except you."

"I've written to Laura. She should be here next month."

Charlotte looked her daughter full in the face. "Then I'm dying."

"Charlotte, I didn't say that."

"You sent for Laura. Did you send for Rand and for Mother? I'm not dead, you know?"

"I know you're not. You're very much alive."

"Indeed I am." She coughed then. "I need some laudanum. The pain is getting worse."

"It's been only an hour."

"I need it. And put it in brandy. Brandy washes away the taste."

"Charlotte . . . brandy is so bad for you."

"You don't call me Mother anymore."

"I'm sorry. Mother. The brandy would be bad for you."

Charlotte's gaze was unusually direct. "Nothing will be bad for me ever again." She coughed in a futile effort to clear her lungs.

Some minutes later Judith bent over her mother with the medicine in brandy.

Charlotte's green eyes looked up at her daughter. "I'm sorry you're here," she whispered. "I doubt if I would have done this for you."

"None of us knows what he'll do until the time comes."

Charlotte lay back on the pillow with eyes closed. She might have been a corpse if not for the breath that rattled faintly as it slipped in and out of her distended nostrils and the flush the brandy induced in her cheeks. Thinking her mother asleep, Judith prepared to tiptoe out.

46

"Stay with me."

"All right."

The sick woman waved her hand limply. "I didn't mean to sound like that. Please, stay with me."

Judith sat down again in the chair beside the bed.

"What have you done with yourself this past six years?" Charlotte asked suddenly.

Judith shrugged, thinking her mother was only making idle conversation. "Oh, a little of this. A little of that. Grown up mostly."

"You didn't go to school, did you?"

"No. But *Grandmère* sent a tutor. He was quite a knowledgeable man."

"A man? What did you study?"

"Oh, all sorts of unsuitable things. Numbers, mathematics, business, counting."

"How amazing! Whatever for?"

"I don't know." Judith looked away uncomfortably. No use telling her mother at this late date that the studies were to impress her father. No use telling of the rudiments of seamanship and navigation.

Seething with desire to show her father what a mistake he had made in leaving her behind, she had planned to claim her share of the Talbot Shipping Line. She could still remember struggling with the difficult mathematical problems and encouraging herself by picturing her father's amazement when she revealed her knowledge.

Her mother, too, lay silent. At last she spoke. "You've never been to a party?" A tear trickled down her cheek. "I should have arranged for your come-out two years ago. You would have been so beautiful."

"Mother, please. That's all over. It's too late now. Don't upset yourself."

"You should have gone with your father."

"He didn't want me."

"He didn't want me either, but not for the same reason." Charlotte held out her hand. She looked directly into her daughter's eyes. "I can't imagine how anyone

47

could have been as stupid as I was."

"Everyone does stupid things. He left you, after all."

"Still, you look so much like Beau. I can almost convince myself that by looking into your eyes I can see him."

"I certainly don't look like you. Or *Grandmère*," Judith murmured in agreement.

Charlotte's eyes glazed. She blinked. "I wonder what Laura looks like now. She was so beautiful as a young girl." She touched her other hand to her cheek. "I'd hate her to see me like this. I almost hope I die before she gets here."

"Mother!"

With a shake of her head Charlotte let the hand fall back to the bedsheet. Her eyes closed; her breathing seemed to even. Judith thought she had drifted off. Then suddenly her lips moved. "Beau," she whispered. "Beau. I love you. I'm so sorry."

Tears in her eyes, Judith squeezed her mother's hand. "Are you ready to go to sleep, Mother?"

The eyelids flickered, then opened. By some trick of light the eyes seemed greener than ever. "I'm so sorry, Judith. I never meant any of this to happen the way it did."

"I know, Mother. Go to sleep."

The clawlike grip tightened fractionally. "If your grandmother comes tomorrow, tell her that I demand to see her. She must make right what's been done to you."

Judith rose and kissed her mother's forehead. "I'll tell her. Lie back now and go to sleep."

The messenger unwrapped his woolen scarf and handed it with his hat to Morris. He flexed his stiff fingers inside his gloves.

At the sound of the door opening, Judith had come out on the landing. Now she hurried down the stairs.

"Milady." He stepped forward to meet her.

48

"What is it?"

"I'm sent ahead to tell you that Miss Talbot is on the road from Portsmouth."

Judith felt a thrill of gratitude. "Then she is only a few miles behind you?"

The man shook his head regretfully. "The roads are bad, milady. I misdoubt a coach could be through."

"Oh, no." She glanced upward. "When will she arrive?"

"I cannot say. Man and boy, I've never seen the like of such weather so early in the year."

Judith clenched the newel post, her knuckles turning white with her grip. "When did she dock?"

"Yesterday morning."

She sighed heavily. To Morris she said, "Prepare a meal and give him a warm bed."

She turned and hurried back up the stairs. Charlotte lay like a dead woman, so still, so skeletal, she did not appear to breathe. Judith put her mouth inches from her mother's ear. "Laura will be here in the morning, Charlotte."

No sign that she had heard.

"Charlotte. Charlotte. Mother!"

The eyelids flickered. A gasp. A sigh.

"Mother, Laura is coming. She's in England. She'll be here in the morning." Judith spoke the lie with perfect ease. Charlotte had been conscious for only a few minutes a day for over a week.

"Mother, can you hear me? Laura's on the way. She'll be here soon."

The eyelids flickered up. The green eyes brightened with tears. "My . . . ba . . . by."

"You must hang on. Don't give up."

Silence. A shuddering breath.

"I'll wait." The eyelids flickered closed.

Interlude I

"You have to come to New Orleans." Her distaste obvious, Laura looked around her at the shabby furnishings of the library. "With Charlotte gone, you have no reason to stay in England by yourself."

The gamekeeper's lodge had never appeared more dismal, but Judith lifted her chin proudly. "I am an Englishwoman and England is my home."

Through the thick panels of the library door could be heard the grunts and thuds made by two burly footmen. At Judith's request, *Grandmère* had graciously loaned them to supplement Morris's frail strength. Now they labored to bring down the bedding and utensils from Charlotte's room. Everything would be disposed of. The soiled mattress, pillows, and sheets would be burned; the pans, trays, and other paraphernalia donated to the parish hospital.

One of the men cursed as he struggled to maneuver the cumbersome bundles down the narrow stairs. Judith shrugged away a tiny shudder that threatened to envelop her whole body.

"You call this home. Open your eyes, Judith, and look around you." Laura's soft voice pulled her back into the room; at the same time, a wave of a soft white hand dismissed the house and all its contents.

"It's not so bad." Perversely, she sought to defend the

51

home she despised. For Laura's benefit and to occupy her mind against nervous tremors that racked her, she made a show of rearranging a couple of the leather-bound volumes on the shelf. The inch of space in front of the spines was dusty, she noted. Morris had been worse than dilatory even before the funeral.

Conscious of Laura's eyes on her, she obstinately refused to turn around. She had no wish to face the gentle censure. Laura sighed. "It's not so good either. Papa and I divide our time between the town house on Calle di Conti, and *Ombres Azurées.*"

"How nice for you, sister dear. But I prefer a cottage in England to a mansion on a primitive frontier." *And that should tell you what I think of America.*

"New Orleans is hardly a primitive frontier. Besides, what will you do? Charlotte's allowance ceases with her death." Did Laura's voice contain a hint of pity? How dare she? How dare she?

Judith hugged her paisley shawl more tightly around her thin shoulders. "I'm sure the earl will see fit to extend it to me. Besides, I have my own money coming quarterly from Beau."

"That doesn't make any difference. The allowance is a mere pittance. You can do no more than exist on it, as you're doing now." Laura moved behind her. Suddenly Judith felt her sister's hands on her shoulders. The warmth startled her. No one had touched her in such a long time. "Is this all you want for yourself?" came the soft voice. "If you come to New Orleans, Papa will—"

Nerves tingling, Judith pulled abruptly away from Laura's gentle hands. "Don't tell me what Beau Talbot will do. I know. I remember well what my father did for me."

Surely Laura could not have lived all these years without knowing what had passed between her and Beau that day. Judith smiled grimly. *But perhaps she knew a different version?*

"Judith, you didn't—and still don't understand."

52

Sick to the teeth of hearing people tell her she did not understand, Judith dodged across the room. With her back to the fire, she spun, fists clenched, rusty black skirts disturbing the gray ashes. "I think we've had this conversation before, Laura. The content hasn't changed even after ten years."

"Papa was doing only what he thought was best for you, Judith. If you'll remember correctly, you didn't go out of your way to endear yourself to anyone. You were a . . ."

"*Hellion* was the word I believe you used." Judith pronounced the word with satisfaction. If she had been a hellion then, Laura had best beware of her now.

"Exactly." Laura's hands were hidden in the folds of her skirt, but Judith would bet that her fists were clenched.

"And you were a superior prig, and still are. You haven't changed one bit." She flung the words down like a gauntlet between them.

Laura's eyes narrowed and chilled. The green-ice look reminded Judith all too strongly of their grandmother at her most disapproving. The dowager had bequeathed that rich, regal color to her daughter and to her eldest granddaughter. *Laura should have been a countess. Grandmère would have been so proud of her.* Why did that knowledge make her more resentful than ever?

"Judith . . ."

The younger daughter of Beau Talbot drew herself impossibly straighter. "You've always tried to manipulate my life. And you're still doing it. You're trying to tell me what to do. What are you going to buy me with this time?"

A speculative look came into Laura's eyes.

Hastily, Judith looked away. *I'll not tell her that I still have the necklace. If she asks me about it, I'll lie.* The fire hissed and spat on the hearth. Eager for something to do to forestall questions, Judith tipped a couple of lumps from the coal scuttle. Her hands were shaking, the

53

fingers stiff and icy. What would her sister say if she knew that the sapphire locket was safe upstairs in her treasure box? More likely, she had forgotten its existence. Anyone who divided her time between a town house and a plantation wouldn't be likely to remember a trivial gift.

Laura came over and held out both hands to the fire. Side by side, the sisters stared intently into the glowing heart. "Judith," Laura murmured softly, "Papa left you with Charlotte because you were so young. He thought she could do more for you than he could. He had to give all his time to recoup his fortunes. After he'd gotten on his feet, he was willing to take Charlotte and you, but she wouldn't go. And he believed that *Grandmère* would offer you your rightful place in society."

"But he took you with him." *Damn!* Her voice had quivered. *I'm not going to cry. I'm not.* The pain in her chest and her throat was making her eyes water.

"Yes, I was older and able to care for myself. After George renounced me, there was no chance for me in England. Not until the scandal had died down completely."

Had Laura really suffered more than minor inconvenience? Somehow Judith didn't think so. Frantically, she steadied herself, whipping up her anger. When she found her voice, her tone was bitterly accusing. "If you cared about me as you say you did, why didn't you insist that I come with you and Beau, sister dear?"

Laura sucked in her breath sharply. "I could have. But I didn't. You rejected everything I'd ever tried to do for you. How did I know you wouldn't reject my efforts again?"

"I was just a child," Judith flung out.

Laura shook her head in exasperation. "You were a child. And a mistake was made with you. But you've got to put that behind you. You can't let our mistake lead you to make a bigger one."

54

A mistake, sister dear, being anything you and Beau don't want me to do. "I won't make a mistake."

Suddenly, Laura began to shiver. Hugging her arms to her body, she sank into the chair nearest the fire. From its protection she stared at her sister. "See that you don't. This is the most important decision of your life."

Looking at the huddled form, Judith acknowledged that England must seem terribly cold and barren after the lush warmth of New Orleans. In that case Laura would leave all the sooner. Why did that thought bring her no pleasure? Barely controlling her own shivers, Judith returned to scanning the library shelves.

At length she found another few books to arrange. For a long time neither sister spoke. Finally, Judith asked the question that was uppermost in her mind. "You're asking me to come to America, but what about Beau? I don't see him over here asking me to leave the only home I've ever known."

Laura shrugged in her turn. "You didn't ask him to come, Judith. You wrote your letter to me. You've written all your letters to me. But still you remember how many times he's asked you to come to America."

Here Judith was on firm ground. "I couldn't leave Charlotte. You saw the condition she was in when she died. That didn't happen overnight."

"No, and you never told me how bad she was," Laura accused. "Why didn't you, Judith? I would have come and helped you with her."

Judith left off replacing the volumes and sat down behind her desk. "I didn't want to be whining and complaining all the time. Besides, I was handling it fine by myself."

"But didn't you ever consider that I would want to be here? Judith, no matter what Charlotte had done in the past, she was my mother too."

Acknowledging the justice of that question, Judith hung her head. Somehow she had never thought that Laura would have been really concerned about Charlotte.

55

The years and the miles that had separated them had surely made the tie too tenuous to be more than a formality.

Still, Laura would not let the subject rest. "You did wrong. You should have told me sooner that my mother was as sick as she was. You've kept me from her when she needed me. I'm only thankful that I was able to see her before it was too late."

Judith studied her hands, now concealed behind her desk. They were rough and raw from the never-ending tasks required by a patient of her nurse. She sighed. "I didn't think you'd care about either one of us."

"Of course I care. Charlotte was my mother and you're my sister. I love you both."

The unfamiliar word snapped Judith's head up. Bitterness twisted the pale features. "What is love?" she asked.

Laura was taken aback. She shook her head, frowning as she struggled to answer a question that she had never needed to answer before. At that moment Judith felt an emotion closely akin to contempt for the pampered romantic her sister had become.

At last Laura swallowed visibly. When she spoke, she ignored the question. "I understand why you didn't come, particularly in the last year or so. And you didn't let me know how bad she was. But don't you see? I've got to forgive and put all that behind me. And I am. Judith, you need us. You don't have anyone to protect you in England. You have to come to America with me."

Judith sat up straighter in her chair. Purposefully, she laced her fingers together in her lap. "I can apply to the earl. *Grandmère* said that she would introduce me to society."

Laura stared at her baby sister with calculating eyes.

Suddenly conscious of her shabby, unprepossessing appearance, Judith could feel an embarrassed flush rising in her cheeks. Her mouth tightened mutinously.

At the sight Laura hurried into speech. "You're

56

nineteen years old. I was engaged when I was seventeen to George, a man I loved and respected. *Grandmère* has ignored you for years. She might bring you out after all this time, but you can bet that you'll have to do exactly as she says. And marry when and where she wants you to."

The truth made Judith shift uncomfortably. "At least I'd be in England."

"And Lord Lythes would still be around. Neither *Grandmère* nor the earl protected Charlotte very well. Do you think they'll do any better for you?"

At the mention of Charlotte's tragedy, Judith rose from her chair and moved to stare out at the snow on the path that wound through the garden. The stone bench was clearly visible through the naked branches. Chills slid down her back at the memory of his touch. "I don't know," she admitted tonelessly.

"Yes, you do."

As if the words were dragged out with a windlass, Judith began to speak. "The night Lythes attacked me was the most frightening, humiliating experience of my life."

Laura walked over to stand behind Judith. This time Judith did not shrug away. The fear was too real—and too long unshared. If she had not found the coal scuttle . . . Judith shivered, and Laura rubbed her arms. "Believe me, Judith," the soft voice continued, "I understand how helpless a woman can feel when a man exerts his strength."

"You can't understand!" Judith bowed her head, shuddering. "No one can understand how horrible, how totally helpless a woman is when a man abuses her like he almost did me. You, least of all, sister, can understand how I feel."

"I of all people *most* understand how you feel," Laura whispered.

"You? How could you?" Judith's voice rang incredulously.

"The incident and the man may be different, but the

57

feelings of helplessness are just as real. Even though your bruises are physical and mine are emotional, the men still took advantage of us."

Judith glanced back across her shoulder. Laura's skin was white as the snow in the garden, her jade-green eyes the only color in her face.

"For heaven's sake, Laura . . ." Judith turned in her sister's arms to offer comfort.

"Oh, I know you think I'm in control. And most of the time I am, but when I'm around this man—this gambler—the most terrible feelings take control. For the first time in my life, I feel—helpless and afraid. Just as you did. Except that with emotions it's ten times worse."

Judith shook her head, unable to comprehend. Emotions were things she did not understand. "Oh, Laura. How could it have been worse?"

"When your emotions are involved, Judith, your very soul is touched." Laura pulled out of Judith's hands. Her jaw clenched to still her chattering teeth, she made for the fire. "I don't care a flip about the loss of my virginity," she flung over her shoulder.

Judith gasped at the defiance that made her sister's voice strange and unnatural. Laura was actually upset.

"I really don't," she continued. Nervousness, anger, and disgust rang clear in her voice. "After all, I'm twenty-six years old. What I care about is the loss of control. He destroyed my composure. He destroyed my confidence in my ability to be in control. He made me feel—"

She dropped down in the chair, drawing her feet up under her. Her eyes locked with Judith's.

Why, she's afraid! My sister's afraid. But why? She has Beau to help her. "Oh, Laura." Judith held out her hands helplessly. The silence grew between them.

Laura shrugged her shoulders as if to throw off a heavy weight. Carefully, she eased her feet out from under her and arranged her skirts neatly over her knees. When she spoke, her voice was once again smooth and controlled.

58

She might have been relating the most mundane of anecdotes. "So you see, Judith, if you remain here, sooner or later Lord Lythes is going to drag you into his world just the way he dragged Charlotte. Just the way Clay Sutherland dragged me into his. He made me doubt myself. And I'll never forgive him for that. I really think I despise men."

The contrast between the tone and the sense of the speech horrified Judith. "Oh, sister, you don't. Remember how much you loved George."

Laura tensed, then forcibly relaxed again. With studied care she arranged her hands gracefully over the chair arms. Judith had never seen anything like her sister's performance. Suddenly, she wanted to help her. *How odd to want to help Laura. I never thought of her as needing help.*

"George has never married. I suspect he still loves you," Judith suggested gently. "Why don't you see him again. Maybe it's not too late."

Laura shook her head slowly and definitely. "If he loved me, why did he turn his back on me when I needed him? No, I'll never be able to forgive him for that."

Judith made a rude sound. "You *can* forgive him. He's a victim of the same society. He's bound by the same laws that bind you." She grinned. "Why would you want me to enter that society? I don't want to have anything to do with it."

Laura lifted her chin. "The laws may be binding, but everybody's life needs structure. I'm smart enough to know that there are wonderful things to be gotten from pleasant society. In New Orleans you'd have a chance for a new life."

"The sort that you are having with Clay Sutherland?" Judith scoffed.

Laura's hands clenched on the chair arms. "Not at all," she said furiously. Then deliberately she forced herself to relax again. "Now we're talking about you and your problems. Leave Clay Sutherland alone. He's got no

59

part in this."

But Judith would not stop. "Oh, but he's very much a part of this, sister dear. You're offering protection to me? You can't protect your own self."

"I've put him out of my life, and I'm going to put him out of my mind." Forcibly, she relaxed her hands again.

Judith rolled her eyes in an exaggerated plea for strength. "Brave words, sister dear."

"At least I can call on Papa if I absolutely have to. But I won't have to call on Papa about this because I'll have everything under control."

"How very nice to be so nearly perfect."

"I'm surely not perfect. I'm just in control."

Sure that her sister was not so controlled as she pretended to be, Judith dropped to her knees in front of Laura, forcing the cool green eyes to lock with her own. "Must you always fight so hard for control? My God! You're human, Laura. And human beings have feelings. You'll suffocate if you don't allow them to come out. Break something! Scream! Cry! I'd suffocate if I had to live as you do."

Laura dropped her eyes before her sister's angry words. "Clay Sutherland is a thing of the past. I confided in you because I wanted you to understand that I have had my problems. And have solved them."

"Oh, for heaven's sake!" Judith sprang to her feet again.

Laura ignored her sister's irritation. "Forget about all that. We're talking about your future. And you have a future, Judith. Believe me. You've honestly never been given the chance to see if you could live in society." Her voice brightened with real enthusiasm. "Now Papa and I want to give it to you with no strings attached. Papa would never tell you whom to marry. And you'd be safe. You'd be foolish not to take the opportunity. Or are you going to cower here until Lord Lythes comes for you?"

Judith winced as Laura's question unerringly found a vulnerable spot. The silence grew between them. At last

60

Judith asked humbly, "How can I believe you?"

"Judith, I've bared the inmost secret of my soul to you. You have to believe me. And you have to accept help from me. Because you really have no alternative. I promise that you'll have a chance."

Judith clenched her hands in front of her as if she were tearing fabric.

Instantly, Laura reached out to cover them with her own. "Judith, please. Let's give ourselves another opportunity to know each other as sisters should."

Gradually, Judith's hands relaxed. The angry flush faded from her cheeks. Taking a deep breath, she managed a half smile. "I can't go with you to America when you leave next week. I want to believe you, Laura. And I do. But I need more time to think about this."

Laura returned the smile. "Of course you do. Just don't think about it too long. Lord Lythes is only postponing his plans. Don't think he'll respect Charlotte's death any longer than a fortnight. He wants you, and if you remain within his reach, he'll have you—fair means or foul. You have to get away."

Judith regarded her sister thoughtfully. "You know, Laura, I'm luckier than you are. At least I have a place to run to. You have to run back to the place that you came from—and face your nemesis head-on."

Laura shuddered. She deliberately drew her chair a bit closer to the fire and spread the palms of her hands to its warmth.

Judith remained at the window. Slowly, she turned to face the frosted panes. The blue sun had melted the snow on the dark bench. It stood a stark contrast to the purity of winter.

Chapter Three

London sights and sounds confused Judith. The clang of ironshod hooves—monstrous hooves of dray horses—against the stones made her hunch her shoulders and step a little closer to the wall of the building.

Marching behind her, arms laden with parcels, the countess's footman allowed his lip a cynical twist. He could always spot country green, and this one was about the greenest ever. He shot a knowing glance at the lady's maid chaperoning the shopping expedition. She grinned faintly in response.

With a feeling of relief Judith hurried up the steps of the town house on Sheffield Terrace. The dimness of the entry hall offered her a cave where she could rest and recuperate from the stresses of dealing with London tradesmen who haggled and protested and bullied her.

Grandmère's injunction that Judith buy herself a "suitable" wardrobe had been eagerly embraced. However, since the money spent was Beau's, she had gone shopping alone, determined that she should be the one to buy the very first new clothing she had had since the onset of her mother's illness.

In her room alone for the moment, she pulled open the boxes, lifting out each garment with pride and pleasure. They were all so beautiful, so new. Not patched, nor worn, nor fashioned by some back-country seamstress.

Standing in front of the mirror, she draped her shoulder in her particular favorite, a dark forest-green of heavy raw silk. With her free hand she plucked the pins from her hair and shook it out. The dark green made her skin look whiter than ever and her hair redder. She stared at herself critically. A shiver ran through her.

Had Lythes been right? Was she too brightly colored? The thought of his appearing suddenly before her on a street or in a shop to take his revenge caused her stomach to knot in apprehension. A light tap on the door made her start.

"Her ladyship wishes you to come down to tea, miss." The maid smiled helpfully. "I'll be pleased to unpack those things for you."

"Thank you." Judith smiled in her turn. She could learn to love having servants take care of her every wish even before she thought it. Such a pleasant change.

"You are still determined on this foolish visit to New Orleans?" The Dowager Countess of Harrestone poured tea with studied care. The harsh edge to her voice was the only evidence of her anger.

Judith reached to take the cup and saucer. "Yes, *Grandmère*."

The countess poured her own but set it aside. "You'll regret this, Judith Claire. You cannot expect to be welcomed into the family of a man who has had no contact with you for six years. If Laura has told you that you will, she is leading you along a primrose path, my girl."

Judith managed to set the tea down without sloshing it. "They have sent for me," she reminded her grandmother softly. "Beau has arranged passage for me on the *Portchester*."

The old woman sniffed contemptuously. "One of his oldest ships, I might tell you. Oh, you don't need to look surprised at me. I have kept up with my erstwhile son-in-law. Laura has written me faithfully. Such a good girl. And I have other ways. I am not without influence in the world."

"I'm sure," her granddaughter murmured.

"If you are so sure, then you must know that your place is here. You can never have any business in that savage country."

"I want to see for myself."

"Stubborn. Filled with detestable false pride. A place—an important place—could be made for you in society. I . . . I would like to have some member of my family with me. I am growing older." Her lips formed a tight slash in her wrinkled, powdered face.

Judith picked up the cup and saucer again. "I must make this visit."

"Perhaps next year," *Grandmère* snapped impatiently. "At this stage in your development, you can't help but fail. You know nothing about society. Nothing about proper behavior. It's true you'll be among parvenus of the worst sort. They'll despise you for your ancient lineage. And they'll be watching your every move. You'll embarrass yourself and them."

"Thank you, *Grandmère*."

"Stop that! No sarcasm, please. Sarcasm doesn't become a young woman. That's exactly what I'm talking about. I understand that your father has married a Frenchwoman." Her nostrils pinched more tightly together. "She won't want you around. You mark my words. She'll be eager for you to fail so she can throw you up to your father."

"Then you'll be glad to see me coming home sooner."

The old spotted hand crushed the fine Madeira napkin. Blue veins stood out on the back. "I'm telling you that you should not go at all. Not at all. Your place is here. I am willing—" She paused, relaxing her grip, smoothing the napkin across her lap. "I am eager to begin your education so that you can be introduced to society. I tell you, your place is here."

65

"I will go only for a visit. Laura was most insistent."

"And don't think your sister will be welcoming either. She's been the only chick for too long. She won't thank you for taking some of the attention away from her. And you, my girl, can't hope to compete with her on the social level. She's too experienced by half again."

Her words pelted Judith's self-esteem like hailstones. She could feel the tears prickling at the backs of her eyes. Her grandmother was certainly right about competing with Laura. But Judith's debut into society here would be the same. A whole bevy of magnificently beautiful young girls would quite put her in the shade. She blinked the tears back. "I won't be competing," she announced firmly. "I tell you I am merely going for a visit."

The *Banshee* aimed a burst from its forward cannon to cut across the bow of the *Portchester*.

"She's reefin', Cap'n." The first mate supplied the needless information as the flute's sails came rattling down.

"Right, Mr. Archer. Bring the *Banshee* around and give the order to board."

"Aye, sir."

Tabor O'Halloran lowered the spyglass; a feral grin bared even white teeth in his tanned face. "I'll lead the party, Mr. Archer. You take command."

"Right, sir."

The captain of the *Banshee* leapt down the steps to main deck. A dozen men stood poised, grappling hooks swinging gently from the lines held in their hands. Another dozen waited behind and above them, ready to swing aboard once the brigantine came alongside the lumbering flute. Instead of taking a place beside them, O'Halloran stepped into the cabin.

Only a moment later he emerged with a bright red kerchief bound around his temples. The wind tangled the ends with the thick locks of his black hair. To his

66

ordinary seaman's garb and black jackboots, he had added a red silk sash around his waist. Into it he had thrust a couple of horse pistols.

Flashing Mr. Archer a cheeky grin, he received an answering nod. The second mate emitted a derisive whistle between his teeth. Tabor lifted one black eyebrow in mock warning. "The captain's rank requires a certain style, after all. The flag, Mr. Pinckney. Let 'em know who we are."

"Aye, aye, sir."

The mate stepped to the masthead and pulled on the lines. A cheer went up from the men on the decks of the *Banshee* at the same time that a groan arose from the ten men on the deck of the flute. The black flag of the brigand fleet, feared from the Amazon to Nova Scotia, slithered up the mast and snapped open in the wind. But against this black background stood out a sharp white profile and stream of tangled red hair.

"Jesus Mary," the mate of the *Portchester* breathed. "The screaming skull. 'Tis the *Banshee*."

"It can't be," muttered the captain. "I'd heard he was dead."

As Tabor—very much alive—swung down onto the deck and pulled one of the horse pistols from his sash, the *Portchester*'s captain held up his hands and stepped back. "Take whatever you want. You'll not get much more than the trouble of hauling it away."

Tabor swung the bore across the man's body and pointed toward the cabins aft. "Your cargo doesn't interest me, Captain. It's your passengers I came to see. The list, please."

The captain hesitated. His eyes darted toward the door that led to the companionway below deck. "Nobody of any importance," he muttered nervously.

"Perhaps I'm the best judge of that." Tabor motioned with the pistol to the second mate. "Fetch the books from

67

the cabin, Pinky."

"I'm telling you, we're just carrying—"

"Save that for someone who'll believe you." Tabor grinned again, this time without mirth.

In a minute Mr. Pinckney returned. Tabor found the list. "Only three passengers," he noted. "One, a woman traveling alone. Two, a man and wife. Very interesting. Roust 'em out, Pinky, and let's see who we've got."

A woman screamed as Pinky pulled open the first door at the foot of the narrow stairs. The mate stepped back, glancing upward at his captain for reassurance. At a nod he drew his own pistol. "Would you please to step out on deck, ma'am?"

"No." The voice was punctuated with hysterical sobs. "Oh, no. Please. Edgar, save me."

"For God's sake, man," Edgar pleaded fervently. "I'll come out, but let her alone. She's had a terrible crossing. In the family way and all."

Pinky threw another quick look up at Tabor, who came partway down the steps. When the black head inclined fractionally, the mate nodded. "I guess that'll be all right."

The man called Edgar came out, his mouth twitching nervously. His face was white as chalk. "Don't shoot. I beg you, sir. Please. I have a little money." Watering eyes immediately spied Tabor, tricked out in sash and jackboots. He held up a leather purse. "Take it. Don't make my child an orphan. Don't make me walk the plank, sir."

From behind him Mr. Pinckney made a wry grimace. Tabor's eyebrows rose, then drew together in a frown. The passenger gave a squeak and fell to his knees. Tabor stared disgustedly at the groveling figure.

"Get on to the next cabin, Pinky. Don't waste any more time."

The mate tried the knob of the door across the companionway. "Locked, Captain."

"Knock."

68

No answer came when the mate reversed the butt of his pistol and hit the heavy slab of mahogany. He looked questioningly at Tabor.

"Break it in."

The captain of the *Portchester* came down the steps. "Captain, there's just one lady in there, and she's most likely fainted from fear. She's not a wealthy one. No jewelry. Just a little old lady." His next words reached Tabor's ears only. "She's a poor relation of some people in New Orleans. They paid for her passage, but she's got no money otherwise."

"I'll be the judge of that. Break it in, Pinky."

Bracing his back against the opposite wall of the narrow passage, the mate lifted his bare foot, its sole hard as any leather. With the full strength of his body he slammed it against the door just beside the lock. Metal spanged, wood splintered, and the door burst open.

No sound came from within the cabin. Tabor put a hand on the mate's arm when the man would have entered. "I'll handle this 'little old lady.'"

"Aye, Captain."

A couple of strides took him into the center of the tiny cabin before she struck. Judith Talbot-Harrow leapt from her place of concealment behind the narrow upright locker and swung the heavy pitcher with all her might.

The weighted crockery from the washstand caught Tabor across the side of the head. Had he not instinctively thrown up his shoulder, she would have knocked him unconscious. Only the scarf he had knotted at his temple prevented her blow from breaking the skin.

Nevertheless, the force staggered him. He pitched forward into the bunk, black spots swimming through his vision.

Judith whirled away from the fallen man. The hallway beyond her broken door was empty. Would no one come to help her? Would other pirates come through? On the bunk behind her, the man muttered a curse. Whirling again, she found him pushing himself slowly up. Without

69

hesitation she swung the pitcher.

If her blow had landed as intended, he would have been knocked unconscious. Tabor ducked completely as the heavy utensil arced toward him again. This time it smashed on the bunk frame above his head. The thick pottery shattered in all directions. Shards littered his thick black hair, his shoulders, the bunk, the floor.

Both fists ready to do battle, one clutching a brass-tricked horse pistol, he sprang at her.

Judith screamed in terror.

Lunging for her was a nightmare figure out of her imagination. So this is how the infamous pirates of the Spanish Main must have looked. Out of the history books and the headlines of old newspapers he leapt to kidnap her and sell her into slavery in Barbary. He needed only the eye patch and wooden leg to be Captain Kidd or Blackbeard.

As she darted for the door, he caught her by the shoulder. She screeched again as he pulled her backward. "Here, now. Settle down. Settle . . . umph!"

Judith drove her shoulder into his midsection as he tried to turn her around. Pain jolted through her body. He was solid as a tree and as heavy. Although she had managed to knock the breath out of him, she had hurt herself more. Tears started in her eyes as she reeled away, tearing herself out of his grasp and stumbling for the door, where she thudded into Mr. Pinckney's chest.

"Grab her, Pinky," Tabor called, righting himself. "She's a tiger."

Obediently, the mate's arms, heavily muscled from years of hauling on lines and reefing in sails, closed around her in a bear hug that pinioned her so she could not move.

"Let me go. Damn you! Let me go," she spat out.

Tabor stepped up behind her so she was imprisoned between two male bodies, both much heavier and taller than she. "When you promise to stand still."

She twisted her head, the only part of her she could

70

move effectively. "Monster! You'll be sorry for this."

He sank a hand into the fiery wreath of hair that fairly bristled about her head. "I'll make you sorrier than I'll ever be, lady, if you don't get some sense in your head." For emphasis he tugged roughly.

Judith's breath hissed through her teeth at the pain. "Bully."

"Will you stand still if Pinky releases you?"

She set her teeth stubbornly, but he yanked again. "Yes!"

Tabor nodded to Mr. Pinckney, who moved back into the companionway with an obvious expression of relief.

Instantly, Judith stepped back only to blunder into Tabor's body. He caught her shoulder at the same time he slowly released his hold on her hair. The fiery strands seemed to spring after him. He had to shake his hand free of them. His grip on her tightened as he realized his pulse had accelerated. "Where is it?" he growled into her ear.

"Where is what?" She ground out her question through teeth clenched against the pain in her bruised shoulder.

He shook her roughly. "Don't make this hard on yourself. You know what I mean."

She cupped her hand around her elbow and flung back her head. "My money? I don't have even a pound. My jewelry? In the bottom of my trunk." She pointed to the large camelback of morocco, studded with brass. He looked at her doubtfully, but she met his expression with a scornful toss of her head.

The pain in her shoulder was growing steadily worse. She must have really hurt herself slamming into him that way. Whereas he appeared none the worse for her best efforts except for chips of pottery in his dark curly hair, she was feeling distinctly nauseated. She watched miserably as he turned the key she had left conveniently in the lock and threw the lid back.

The contents—dark, neatly folded garments—were unprepossessing in the extreme. Impatiently, he plucked out the first and tossed it aside.

71

"Wait!" She sprang forward to catch it before it billowed to the floor. It was one of her new dresses, purchased with money sent by her father. Indeed, the entire contents of the trunk, all she owned in the world, were her new clothes. Furthermore, they were more than she had owned in years. Of course, they were all black and dark colors, as befitted her mourning state, but new materials in the new styles.

As she had selected the materials, she had sternly turned her back on her favorite colors—the sapphire blues, the emerald greens, the aquamarines—as well as the soft yellows and more daring pinks. But when she had tried on the dresses for her fittings, she had found they looked well enough. The blacks especially had toned down her red hair and high coloring. Her eyes looked bluer than ever against the white of her skin.

While her clothes were not what she would have chosen had she been free to choose, they were fresh and crisp. No threads were broken in their seams. No frequent washings had dimmed their colors. No stench of the sickroom clung among their folds. Furthermore, they numbered more garments than she had had at any one time in her life. And they were new.

"Don't!" she cried as a second dress followed the first. "I'll find the jewelry for you."

His lips curled back from his white teeth in a feral grin. "And pull a loaded pistol out from among those rags. Not a chance." He tossed out another garment, this time over his other shoulder.

Her temper flared again at his insult to her clothes. "Stop it, you idiot. I don't have a loaded pistol. I swear." She winced as the dress of darkest forest-green fluttered down half on, half off the bunk.

Ignoring the rising heat in her voice, he rudely shoved the other garments aside until he came to the jewel box. Lifting it out, he regarded it with suspicion before flipping open the lid. One glance at its contents and he contemptuously cast it aside.

The lacquerwood box with its delicate Chinese scene broke apart when it hit the cabin floor. With a cry Judith went down on her knees among the scattered pieces of her mother's jewelry. Long before the divorce, much of Charlotte's collection had been pawned to pay gambling debts. After dividing with Laura, Judith had only these few simple pieces.

Desperate to save the only things of value she had in the world, Judith fell on her knees. Her hand closed over her mother's favorite piece, a tiny gold ring set with a pearl and an emerald. She was too late to save her own gold locket with the sapphire in its heart. His heel crushed it as he turned. Only with anger could Judith control her pain. "Monster!"

If Tabor had hoped by his action to shock her into revealing the whereabouts of the payroll, he was doomed to disappointment. Blue eyes almost black with anger lanced at him. Fierce color had risen in her cheeks. Her lips looked hot and slightly swollen.

For a moment his original intent was forgotten. At the sight of her kneeling at his feet, his role of pirate of the Caribbean took possession of him. Tabor felt a sudden perverse stirring in his loins. His black eyes focused on her beautiful angry mouth. Down he dropped to one knee, his tanned face with its red kerchief banding the forehead only inches from her.

Instant awareness leapt between them. Even as she shrank back, his right arm whipped around her waist, lifting her to him. Their eyes locked. She raised her chin a notch. He kissed her. He did not have to force her. Her gasp of fright opened her mouth for his tongue to thrust into, filling her, penetrating her, making her his.

Only for a moment did she succumb, numb with virginal shock. Then memory flooded her consciousness. She was helpless in the grip of Lord Lythes. Her fighting blood surged through her veins. Her jaws clamped together hard.

He jerked his head back, snarling as her sharp teeth

73

scraped his tongue. With an unintelligible curse he cuffed her on the shoulder. She fell backward, sprawling on the floor, her legs doubled under at the knee, her lower body arched. Though he knelt between her thighs, he could only glare at her, his hand clapped to his mouth. From behind it came an expletive, succinct but unintelligible

She glared back, then scrambled away.

Swallowing hard, his tongue scraped and raw, he had to grate the next words out. "You'll save us both a lot of time if you'll just tell where it is."

"Where what is? I don't have anything except what you've destroyed." Her voice broke as she scanned the floor trying to locate the cherished pieces before they were trodden underfoot.

"That's trash," he observed. "Where's the real stuff?" He pushed back on his heels and stood up.

Angrily, she scooped up the large part of the jewelry and held it up to him. It did not fill her hands. "Will you please take this and get out? You're wasting time." Her voice was heavy with contempt. "Isn't there someone rich you ought to be robbing?"

Ignoring her, he looked around him with a frown. "Where's the payroll?"

"The what?"

He turned back to her trunk. Hoisting it by its handles, he lifted it and turned its contents out on the floor of the cabin.

"Stop! Don't!"

He paid no attention to her frantic pleas. The trunk felt no heavier than a normal empty trunk, but he could not be sure. "Pinky!"

"Aye, Captain."

As the mate entered the cabin, Judith scrambled to her feet. "Leave my things alone. Get out of here."

"Break it up."

"No. Oh, no."

Mr. Pinckney looked doubtfully from one to the other.

74

"That, sir. I don't understand."

Tabor slid the trunk toward him. "Knock the bottom out of it. Let's see what she has stashed away."

"I don't have anything. Nothing." Judith flew at Tabor, who caught her wrists.

"Don't. It's new. I just bought it. Oh, don't."

At a nod from Tabor, Pinckney pulled the trunk half off the floor. Holding it by the handle, he smashed his foot down into the bottom of it.

"No! For heaven's sake. No!"

"Nothing there, Captain."

Her face contorted with rage, she doubled up her fist and swung it at Tabor. "Monster."

He caught her easily, twisting both hands behind her. "She's taken it out, then and hidden it in the cabin."

"No. I haven't. I don't know ..." She twisted impotently in his grip.

"Get Eben in here to help you. Turn this room upside down if you have to, but find it."

Tears trickled down her cheeks. "I don't have anything."

He pushed her into the narrow space between the bunk and the washstand. His broad shoulders partially obstructed her view, but she struggled furiously, managing to see around him as the men tore the bedding from the bunk, pulled open the locker and the doors of the washstand, and sifted through her garments, tearing the hems and the linings.

The new blue dress Laura had given her caught on the hinge of the locker. Judith's cry of agony echoed the ripping cloth. At that she could no longer hold back the tears. "For pity's sake," she moaned. "Those clothes are all I have in the world."

Staring down into the brilliant pleading eyes, he half raised his hand to halt the devastation, then clenched it into a fist. No matter how beautiful she was, she was still the enemy.

He hardened his heart. He had an honest man's

75

contempt for spies. If she managed to carry the special payroll through to New Orleans, valuable information could and would be purchased. The war would go on and on to the detriment of the struggling new United States.

He cleared his throat uncomfortably. "I'll give you this. You're a great actress. The War Office sure picked a good one when they made you the courier."

She hooted at the suggestion. "A courier! Me? For what? I've never even been to London until this month. I'm on my way to New Orleans to join my father and sister."

"And your father is?"

Her lips framed Beau Talbot's name. Then she clamped them shut. "Oh, no. I'm not going to tell you. Not you. You want to hold me for ransom."

At that he shrugged. She looked around her at the wreck of the cabin and pressed her fist against her mouth to hold back her distress. His eyes followed hers around the cabin. His forehead wrinkled in a frown. "Mr. Pinckney."

"Aye, Captain."

"Take a hard look at the cargo manifest. What about baggage in the hold?"

"I don't have any baggage in the hold." Bending carefully, as if in pain, Judith retrieved one of her mother's pearl earrings. Where the mate lay, she had no idea.

"Captain." Mr. Pinckney appeared in the doorway. "I think you'd better come hear this."

Relieved at the interruption, Tabor left her.

Pinckney stood aside for his superior to pass out into the companionway. When he would have motioned the sailor away from the door, Tabor remained where he could see Judith. As he watched she picked up another shiny object from the floor. Something dangled from it, then fell with a tiny clink. She mopped at her cheek.

"Captain O'Halloran," Pinckney muttered sotto voce. "I been thinking." The mate cleared his throat. "And if

76

I'm right, you're not gonna like this."

"Somehow I'm not surprised."

"I've seen that Edgar somewhere's before."

Tabor's eyes narrowed suspiciously. "Are you sure?"

"Not much doubt. I'm thinking he was on board the *Halifax*, that day they took me and Roberts off the *Narragansett*. He was one of them fancy cadets."

"What!"

Pinckney winced. "He was a big jasper even then. He's still too big to be crawling around and licking ever'body's boots topside. I'd stake my share, he's a naval officer."

The color drained from Tabor's face, leaving it waxen under the skin. His dark eyes flew from his mate's doleful countenance to the red-haired girl who sat on the bare box of the bed. He could not see her face. "Holy Mother," he muttered. Shoving Pinckney back, he stepped into the companionway and closed Judith's door firmly behind him.

The screams of Edgar's "pregnant" wife quickly changed to curses as Tabor and his crew discovered the hiding place of the payroll. Taking the two into custody was a matter of minutes.

Screwing his courage to the sticking place, Tabor came back into Judith's cabin.

She looked up at him with dull eyes, the pieces of the jewel box in her lap. Her tiny store of treasure lay beside her on the bare bunk.

"I . . . er . . . that is, we found the . . . er . . . payroll."

She managed a defiant sneer. "Pardon me if I don't give a hearty cheer."

The tear stains on her cheeks made him sick. He came toward her, picking up her garments as he came, draping them over his arm. The black pelisse, its silk lining ripped out, he left lying on the floor. He looked around for the camelback trunk, then a dull flush rose in his face. It, too, lay in pieces, the bottom knocked out by Mr. Pinckney's foot, the lining ripped out of the top of the curved back.

Wordlessly, he draped the garments along its side so they no longer touched the littered floor. Pulling a heavy leather purse from his pocket, he turned to face her.

The hatred in her sapphire eyes drove him back a step. He swallowed. "I'm sorry for the damage we've done."

"You're sorry. Wonderful. That makes it all right." Bitterly, she dropped her eyes to the shattered pieces of wood in her lap before raising them again to his face.

He tried to rake his fingers through his tangled black hair, encountered the red scarf, and jerked it off angrily. He hated to be in this position.

"Well," she sneered after a moment. "What did you come back for? Rape?"

He sighed heavily. "Here." He shoved the purse into her hand.

She looked at it as if it were a dead rat. "What's this?"

"Money. There's ten twenty-dollar gold pieces."

She hit him in the face with it. "Get out!"

He staggered back. "Hey, just a minute!"

The pieces of the jewelry box clattered to the floor as she sprang up and strode to the door. "Get out of this room this instant. The very sight of you makes me sick."

"I was only . . ."

She flung open the door. "I've got a lot of work ahead of me and you're in the way. If you've got what you came for, leave me and this ship in peace and sail off over the horizon to new adventures."

He stooped and picked up the purse. Her attitude made him more than a little angry. If she couldn't be gracious about this . . . "Now, listen here. The captain told me that you're the poor relation of some people in New Orleans. You'll be needing this money." He took her hand and pressed the purse into it.

She looked at it and then back at him. Her eyes sparked fire as she spun and hurried out into the companion-way. He followed her heels as she ran up the stairs to the deck. In front of the crews of both ships she flung the money down at his feet. "Will you get off this ship?"

78

she demanded.

He thought he had never seen anything more beautiful in his life. The red hair shone in the sun. Her heavy black dress, rather than dimming the auburn color, made it all the more striking. Her eyes were blue as the sea and the sky. He picked up the purse for the second time. "Take it. Take it and I'll go." He stared deeply into her eyes.

She lifted her chin. "Never!" Whirling, she flung it as far and as hard as she could.

A concerted groan went up from the watching men as it arced out across the blue water and fell like a stone into the waves. Tabor could do nothing but gape at her.

Hands on hips she faced him. "Give me another purse and I'll throw it overboard too. I promise you that. What would I use stolen money for? I wouldn't touch it."

Tabor staggered slightly and passed a hand over the lower half of his face. His eyes drank her in—her red hair, her flawless skin. More wonderful than her beauty was her spirit. Never had he expected to meet a spirit as wild and proud as his own. Heedless of the crews who stared incredulous at the pair, he advanced on her.

As a tremor racked her body, her eyes dilated, but they never faltered.

His big hands clasped her shoulders. Roughly, he pulled her forward. From thigh to mouth she was held hard against him. Then he bent his lips to hers.

The kiss was meant as a salute and a pledge, but her mind was too unsophisticated to comprehend it as such. To her it was an insult, punishing her as Lythes had punished her, fueling her hatred, torturing her sensibilities in ways she could not identify. Finally, when she thought her control would break, when she feared she would give him the satisfaction of some kind of movement, he let her go.

His expression enigmatic, he sketched her a quick bow. "Let's go, men."

The remaining crew of the *Banshee* scrambled up the lines and swung over onto their own deck. Last to go was

79

Tabor O'Halloran. He leapt to the railing, one strong tanned hand clasping the line. "I'll see you again," he promised. "This is just the beginning."

She shuddered visibly. "I hope and pray I'll never see you again."

He grinned and swung onto the brigantine's deck as the last of the lines was cast off. Immediately, he leapt up the ladder to the quarterdeck. From its vantage he faced her as wind swelled the sails and the ship moved ahead of the flute.

Her temper reasserted itself. She ran to the rail of the flute. "If I ever see you again," she shouted, "I'll manage to find a pistol."

He raised his hand in farewell. "I would expect no less."

Chapter Four

Nervously, Judith clutched the rope railing at the head of the gangplank. Now that the time had arrived for her to actually disembark in New Orleans, she was trembling so hard she could scarcely stand.

All the long sail up the Mississippi River and for six years before, she had dreamed of meeting her father again. Before her mirror she had rehearsed the cool inclining of her head in greeting. She had recited the emotionless words she would utter. Now she could remember nothing.

She glanced anxiously over her shoulder at the captain of the *Portchester*. He paid her not the least attention, being involved in a serious conversation with the mate.

Sternly, she ordered herself to descend calmly and steadily. The way seemed incredibly long. The life of the cosmopolitan city teemed before her, but she had eyes only for the tall man who stood at the foot of the gangplank.

His hair was darker than she remembered and his sideburns were silvery gray. His face, too, was darker with little lines around the eyes and deep parentheses around his smiling mouth.

He teetered forward as if he could not restrain himself, then held out his hands. She put her own into one of them, at the same time keeping a tight grip on the rope.

"Judith." His voice was hoarse. "Little Judith."

She had been determined to call him Beau, but her resolve fled. "P-papa."

With a groan he caught her in his arms, dragging her in against him, hurting her against the buttons of his vest. "My baby girl. You're . . . you're a beautiful young lady."

The lump in her throat hurt so badly that she felt strangled. "Papa."

"Six years. Six long years. Oh, my baby."

She felt him shiver. Then he held her off at arm's length. His cheeks were wet with tears. His eyes, as blue as her own, searched her face eagerly. "You've grown into such a beauty," he murmured shakily. "I can't believe it."

Her carefully rehearsed scenes fled her mind. She was a child again and this was her father. "Papa. It's been so long."

"I know. Lord, do I know." He caught her to him again. Beneath her cheek his chest heaved with the force of his emotion.

"I missed you so much," she mumbled, then clamped her lips together tightly. Strong emotions had literally forced those words from her.

"Let me see you," he murmured. His hand trembled as he slipped it under her chin and tipped her head back. Her face, framed by the rim of her black bonnet, was only inches from his. He swallowed hard as he scanned her features. "I'll go to my grave regretting . . ."

He left the last words unsaid. Wordlessly, they stared at each other. His arm tightened around her waist. Tears started in his eyes.

At last he pulled himself away from her. "Your sister and your stepmother are waiting in the carriage," he said hoarsely. "You'll like your stepmother. And she's eager to meet you." He slid one arm around her shoulder and hugged her against him while he pulled a snowy handkerchief from his pocket and wiped his face.

Her own emotions in turmoil, Judith hung back against his arm. "Give me a minute. I need to stop just a minute. I'm all red in the' face." She fumbled in her reticule for a handkerchief.

"Don't you worry about that, baby. You look just fine. Just fine. You look so beautiful. So damn beautiful. I can't believe it. You were just a little, skinny . . ."

His words, and particularly their rhythm, sounded strange to her ears. After the accents of England, he sounded foreign. The profound emotion began to subside. All around her she became aware of people speaking English but not English—French but not French—as well as languages she could not begin to recognize. Almost everyone was male, their deep, strong voices vibrating in her ears.

And they were of every color in the world—white and black and all the shades in between. Some were dressed as well as any aristocrat; some had no shoes. And everyone sweated as they went about the business of transporting goods. They eddied around her and her father as he led her across the docks to the carriage.

Her own skin was hot. Perspiration dampened her black dress. She felt an uncomfortable pinch and looked down at the back of her hand. A mosquito had driven his proboscis under the skin. Frowning, she brushed the insect away.

The top of the landau had been folded back. From the shade of a lace-trimmed parasol Laura waved gaily, her smile bright with welcome. Beau laughed aloud as he hugged Judith against him again. "It's just about too good to be true," he called. "But she's here, Celeste. She's really here."

The woman sitting across from Laura tilted her own parasol to one side and turned around in the carriage. She smiled warmly and lifted a lace-gloved hand. "Welcome, *chère* Judith."

A black man clad in tricorne and tan livery opened the carriage door and unfolded the steps.

83

"In you go," Beau directed heartily.

"Sit by me, Judith." Laura moved to make room. Gratefully, Judith sank onto the leather squabs. Beau climbed in beside Celeste. The driver fastened the door and bounded onto the box. The carriage moved slowly away through the crowd.

"My luggage?"

"Emil will already have started for the town house with it," Beau assured her. He beamed happily at her. "You don't ever have to worry about anything again, baby."

"No, indeed," Celeste put in. "It is my dearest wish that you become my daughter too."

"You are too kind . . ." Judith began.

"We shall take care of everything." She looked at Judith critically but not unkindly. "Until you become accustomed to our heat, we must keep you out of the direct sun. I can see that with your complexion, *ma chérie*, you mustn't stay out in it ever."

Beau threw his arm across the back of the landau behind his wife. "I can already see you girls are going to get along fine."

The sun was indeed causing her head to reel. Judith could feel it beating down, the black bonnet absorbing its rays. Her hair had to be soaked with perspiration already. Her stepmother and sister were shaded by their parasols. Her father wore a lightweight suit, pale fawn in color, his head protected by a broad white hat with a curled brim.

The crowd she had noticed with such trepidation became infinitely more terrifying. All around her were strangers engaged in strange activities. Massive shoulders of black men all but jostled the carriage as it threaded its way along the dock. Drays with huge jute-covered bales of cotton, and wagons with loads of hundred-pound sacks of sugar granulated in Monsieur de Boré's new refining process lumbered by on both sides.

She threw her father a pleading glance which he failed to catch. At that moment he was beaming fatuously at her

84

stepmother. Hastily, she dropped her eyes to her black-gloved hands. They were trembling slightly and cold despite the heat.

"My two girls together!" Beau exclaimed. "Aren't they beauties, Celeste?"

"Even as you said, *chèr* Beau."

Nauseated as she was, Judith could scarcely keep from wincing. She shot a quick glance at her sister. Laura was certainly exquisite. Today she wore pink, a pale muslin creation over a deeper blush underdress. The empire waist was banded in Chantilly lace. A pink parasol the same shade as the underdress leaned against her left shoulder, its deep lace ruffle fluttering in the breeze. The overall effect with her red hair was breathtaking. She looked supremely beautiful as well as supremely cool.

Celeste, for her part, looked only a few years older than Laura. Her dress in the very latest style was a knee-length lavender tunic, scalloped and heavily embroidered at hem and neckline, over an underdress of identical material.

Judith tried in vain to smooth a wrinkle from the lap of her black wool. She looked like a crow. No. Worse than a crow. No crow would allow its feathers to go unpreened. Her new clothes even before they were despoiled by the pirates were pitiful next to her sister's. Terror set her fingers a-tremble. Instantly, she clenched them before anyone else could see.

Desperately, she sought to compose herself. She had known all along that she could not compete with the magnificent Laura. Likewise, she might have guessed that her stepmother would be a beauty. She would not try!

She was an Englishwoman. Her blood was of the very finest; her tutors had praised her mind. She could make her own place if she could just keep her emotions under control. She swallowed once more, concentrating on being an Englishwoman of *bon sang*. The nausea and terror abated somewhat.

The horses turned into a narrow drive beside a brick house. The landau stopped beside the flight of some ten steps that led up to the veranda. Another black man in the same tan livery as the driver descended rapidly to open the landau door. Beau stepped down and turned to help Celeste.

Only with an effort could the woman rise and then her stance was obviously unsteady. For the first time Judith realized that her stepmother was less than five feet tall. The hand that she extended to Beau for support was tiny as a child's and very thin.

With practiced efficiency Beau brought his wife down safely and began to help her up the steps. "Now, Beau," Celeste protested. "I can make this just fine. Don't forget your manners."

Judith shot Laura an uncertain glance, but the older sister was in the process of furling her parasol. "Go ahead, Judith. I can't get this thing to close properly."

Beau held out his hand again and Judith stepped down onto damp gray stones with bright green moss growing between their edges. Their eyes met. His were full of love and pride. "Welcome to your new home, baby."

"We'll have such fun together," Laura declared, patting Judith's knee lovingly. "We'll go shopping together and attend the opera and all the parties. And when we're together at *Ombres Azurées*, we'll keep each other company."

Celeste nodded her agreement from the chaise lounge where she reclined, a Kashmir shawl draped across her limbs. "I know both my daughters will be such a help to me. I'm so fortunate, Beau. You've made me so happy by giving me a ready-made family." Her eyes took on a haunted expression. "For a woman like me, your two beautiful daughters are the answer to my prayers."

Beau put his hand in hers and smiled down into her eyes. "We're your family, sweetheart."

86

Judith felt tears prick her lids. She glanced around the room, taking in the beautiful appointments and the rich comforts he had provided for the woman he loved. From a silver tray offered by yet another servant in the tan livery, Judith accepted a glass of cool lemonade with a sprig of mint.

Deep wells of resentment stirred within her at the evidence of wealth and graciousness. She could not help but remember the shabby gamekeeper's lodging where she had spent the past nine years of her life.

Her hatred of Beau Talbot's desertion flamed white hot, but her expression was as reserved as *Grandmère's* had ever been. "I have looked forward to this visit for a long time," she said, emphasizing the word *visit* with a lift of her chin.

Beau and Celeste exchanged startled glances. Beau frowned uneasily. "Now, Judith baby, this is your home. We've been planning for you to come and live with us for a couple of years now."

Ever since Laura told you that Mother had cancer. His answer made her even angrier. *You still left me there to handle it all alone.*

"We've got a beautiful room just waiting for you in the house on Bayou d'Ombres," Beau continued. "It's a lot prettier than the one upstairs. Both of them are yours, just waiting for you."

Just waiting for Mother to die.

"That's right, Judith," Laura interceded. "I chose all the decorations myself. After you rest a couple of weeks and get used to this climate, we'll have a party to introduce you to society."

The lemonade slopped against the side of the glass. For an instant Judith thought she was going to spill it in her lap. Rather than take the chance again, she set it down hurriedly. "I'm in mourning, Laura. I can't attend any parties for a year. Besides, I don't want any parties."

Celeste leaned forward, her smile a masterpiece of gentle understanding. "Well, of course you don't, *chère*

87

Judith. You have only just completed an exhausting trip. I cannot imagine an entire month on a rolling ocean."

Judith seized upon the opportunity to change the subject. "Not only did the ocean roll, but we were attacked and boarded by pirates."

"Pirates!" Celeste fell back in consternation.

"Pirates?" Laura stared at Judith and then at their father. "Pirates attacking a Talbot ship. How can that be?"

Beau frowned heavily. "Are you sure about this, Judith?"

Judith raised her eyebrows. "Well, of course I am. They came on board. The captain of the *Portchester* struck sail immediately."

Beau took a hearty swallow of his lemonade and set the glass down. "And so he is instructed to do. We can't have passengers injured."

"Well, it seems to me he could have offered more of a fight."

At the word *fight* Celeste made a pitiful sound and collapsed back against the chaise. Beau was instantly at her side patting her shoulder reassuringly. Laura shot her sister a warning look.

Everyone sat in silence while Celeste recovered her breath. She took Beau's hand. "How kind you are," she murmured. Then her attention returned to Judith. "How terrible for you. How frightened you must have been."

"I was—especially when he came into my cabin."

Celeste gave a sort of moan. "Oh, how horrible." She looked up at Beau. "Every time we talk of visiting France, we hear of something like this."

He bent to brush his lips across her forehead, then straightened. "It's unfortunate that this happened to you, Judith."

"But now you must put this behind you, sister," Laura interposed. "We don't want to discuss topics like that, especially at teas and parties."

They were all staring at her with faintly accusing

expressions. Judith bit her lip. "No one need be concerned. I shan't be going to teas and parties to speak of it."

Beau left his wife's side. "Of course you will, sweetheart."

She looked at him squarely. "Papa, I won't."

Her stepmother gasped at the brazen contradiction. A muscle ticked in the side of Beau's jaw. Judith would remember that movement till her dying day. She had seen it last when he had adamantly refused to take her to America with him. The sight of it strengthened her resolve.

Beau held out his hand. "Would you excuse us, Celeste? Laura?"

"Of course, Beau."

The sitting room was cooled by a huge fan being gently swung back and forth above their heads by unseen hands. Likewise the jalousies opened all along one side of the room onto a deeply shaded inner courtyard. A stream of water bubbled placidly from a fountain in one corner.

With Laura looking on, a troubled expression in her eyes, Beau left his wife's side to offer Judith his arm. "Shall we walk in the garden, baby."

The garden was warmer than Judith was used to but more comfortable than the room. Her black wool dress was stifling, but she had nothing else. She had not had sufficient time nor materials to repair the damage done to her wardrobe by the *Banshee*'s crew. Had she all her clothes, however, she would still have had nothing suitable, for the simple reason that she had never been able to imagine a climate like New Orleans's.

On a bench of black wrought iron, Beau seated her. "Now, baby, tell me what's bothering you."

Despite the heat, she shivered. How could she tell him the tumult of feelings? He was practically a stranger. She took a deep breath. "Papa, I'm not Laura."

He shook his head in some amazement. "I never thought you were."

His simple statement hurt when he had meant it to be reassuring. "I'm sure you didn't," she replied coldly. "The fact is that I don't want the same things she wants."

He smiled broadly in the face of her denial. "You just don't know what she wants. Why, with the right clothes and your sister to guide you, you'll be the belle of New Orleans. We'll find you a husband before you know it. You've been out of touch with society."

She shuddered hard at the memory of her mother's unhappiness. This man had left Charlotte alone and neglected until she had been seduced by a monster. Her marriage had ended; society had scorned her; and she died alone. Though resentment rode Judith hard, she tried to disguise it. "Papa, please try to understand. I've never been in touch with society. And I don't want to be. I don't want parties." She took a deep breath. "And I particularly don't want to get married."

He looked at her strangely, seeing for the first time the tight lines around the mouth, the cynical expression about the eyes. He reached out to cover her tightly knitted hands with his own big warm one. "You've got a lot of forgiving and forgetting to do, baby."

She shrugged. "Maybe so."

He sighed heavily. "Let's go back in and finish our drinks. Then you go up to your room and rest. Tomorrow we'll go to *Ombres Azurées*. I want you to rest there for a while. Do nothing but be waited on. You'll come to change your mind."

"And if I don't?"

"Then we'll have another conversation. I'll listen to whatever you want to do. If it's within my power, you'll get to do it."

She looked at him suspiciously. "Is that a promise?"

His expression became graver than ever. He bowed his head, seeming to contemplate the highly polished toe of his shoe. "Yes."

*   *   *

In spite of the mosquitos, the trip down the Bayou of Shadows had been a pleasant outing for Judith and Laura. For Celeste the whole thing was quite exhausting. Immediately upon reaching the house, she took to her bed. While Beau called for his horse, she lay in a darkened room.

Laura led Judith onto the back veranda, where they sat in white rocking chairs of woven wicker. Bright-flowered cushions padded the seats as well as protected their dresses. Dispatching a servant to bring cool lemonade from the spring house, Laura passed Judith a fan made from a trimmed palmetto. "The only place to be at this time of the afternoon is right where we are with our feet up."

"Is it always this hot?" Judith asked, opening the top buttons of her black dress. To her body, still acclimated to the cool English summer, the heat and dampness made every breath she drew feel as if she were drowning.

Laura chuckled sympathetically. "You'll get used to it. Come winter, you'll think that it's cold when the temperature drops barely twenty degrees."

Judith shook her head in disbelief at the semitropical climate.

The great water oaks heavily bearded with Spanish moss shaded the deep verandas on both sides of the house. The jalousied windows and doors were left open to allow the breeze to blow through. Still, an occasional mosquito sang about their heads to be wafted away by the palmetto.

As she sat fanning herself, Judith began to fidget. The trip down the bayou had not tired her, and the work habits of the past few years were too deeply ingrained. She felt guilty with nothing to do.

Berthe, the housekeeper who was also Celeste's personal maid, had been sent to unpack Judith's things. Since Judith possessed only the one damaged trunk and very little clothing intact, Berthe had only a few items to press and hang. The black woman had indeed completed the task in a little over an hour and had taken Judith's damaged garments away to be repaired.

Judith looked out over the water of the bayou. "What do you do all day long?"

Laura tilted her head to one side and smiled. "There's lots to do. For instance, tomorrow morning I have to make the rounds of the workers' quarters to be sure that everything's in order there. Someone might have hurt himself or been taken sick. There's also a load of clothing to distribute. It was in those boxes that we brought from town."

Judith sat up straighter. "Could I go with you?"

Laura hesitated. "I suppose you could, but I think Papa and Celeste want you to rest and be with them. Besides, I'll be back in time for the visit."

"The visit?"

"It's just a little surprise. I won't tell you now." Laura smiled as she lifted the glass of lemonade to her lips.

The first surrey arrived at five the following afternoon. Two couples—one young, one old—climbed from it, the ladies completely swathed in veils and masks to protect their complexions from the sun. Celeste called delighted greetings. Once under the veranda roof, they doffed their coverings and accepted glasses of lemonade. Laura whispered to Judith that they were the Villehardins, who owned the farthest plantation down the bayou.

Madame Villehardin embraced both girls with easy familiarity. "We've been waiting for so long to meet you, Judith. Nicolette is just your age. And my son"—she waved the youth forward—"Reynaud is but one year younger."

Judith smiled faintly in answer to Celeste's nod and expression of encouragement. Reynaud was a handsome youth, but half a head shorter than she. He could not have stood more than five feet tall. His sister was even shorter and so slight that she could hardly have weighed

92

eighty pounds.

Reynaud stared up into Judith's face, gulped, then began. "So you're just arrived from England?"

She smiled at his effort. "Yes, just within the week."

"Do you like it here?" Nicolette asked. Her voice was as tiny as her body.

Judith hesitated. "I find it very hot," she said. "But I suspect I'll get used to it."

"Yes."

Celeste then embraced Madame Villehardin, and the two seated themselves on a wicker swing, where they began to converse in French. Monsieur Villehardin sat on the veranda rail to smoke a thin rolled cigar.

"I suppose the weather is much colder in England." Reynaud observed after a lengthy pause.

"Yes," Judith replied.

"Does it ever get warm?"

"In the summer."

"Oh."

The silence became embarrassing among them. Judith stared at her hands and wished for Laura, who had gone to inform Berthe to bring more chairs and more refreshments.

The sounds of horses announced the arrival of a second family. A woman and two little girls came in a wicker governess cart drawn by a pony. Three men rode beside them on handsome horses. They were the Fontaines, from the plantation adjoining *Ombres Azurées*.

The two sons Lucien and Antoine were instantly attentive to Nicolette and Judith. For the first time in her life, she enjoyed the company of three young men who chatted and laughed. Lucien teased her about her hair as the setting sun matched its color to flames.

As the afternoon shadows lengthened, Beau rode up on a bloodbay stallion. Immediately, the men switched to whiskey. The talk turned to crops and the weather and the problems of shipping produce to world markets. The women retired to one side of the gallery with Madame

93

Fontaine's children.

For Judith it was one of the most pleasant evenings she had ever spent. When dinner was served and she was escorted in to the long table by Lucien Fontaine, she felt more relaxed than ever before. If life in America was like this, she could see herself living pleasantly.

Unfortunately, the talk at the dinner table turned to balls and society. A thread of excitement ran through the women's voices. Their eyes sparkled as they discussed clothes, dances, entertainments. The names of people, mostly French, pronounced in heavy nasal tones, confused Judith. She could not separate the words. Frequently, the guests switched back and forth from French to English in the middle of a sentence.

Unable to contribute, much less hold her own in the conversation, Judith began to push her food around on her plate. She was sure that everyone had forgotten her presence, when Lucien leaned toward her.

"It's very rude of us to carry on this way," he murmured. "Do you not speak French?"

His concern warmed her. She smiled at him shyly. "Not very well." Why did she lie? She had not had a French lesson since she was thirteen years old. "I really don't speak it at all. Just a word here and there."

"I shall say something." He started to tap on his glass with his knife handle.

She put her hand over his. "No. Everyone is having such a good time. Don't bother about me."

He looked at her uncertainly, then sank back. "You will learn it after a very few months," he promised. "I will undertake to teach you."

She nodded, smiling vaguely. Her lack of facility in French was one more reason that she should plan only a visit, but Lucien's offer warmed her heart.

"*Chère* Judith, will you please bathe my temples with florida water? My head aches something fierce."

94

Judith wrung out a cloth and whirled it around in the air to cool it before she folded it and laid it across Celeste's forehead. As she straightened, a mosquito sang by her ear despite the citronella candles that burned in alcoves about the room.

"You're such a good girl." Celeste sighed dreamily. "Did you enjoy meeting all the young men?"

"They seemed very nice. Particularly Lucien Fontaine."

"Ah, yes. Lucien is engaged, to Ammie Trinignant. Her family has sent her to Natchez for the summer." Removing the cloth from her forehead, Celeste sat up. "But Reynaud is not engaged."

"He is younger than I am, Celeste." Judith did not think it kind to mention his height.

"True," Celeste smiled as if she were picturing the slight youth. "He would probably not be appropriate for you. You shall meet many such eligible young men when we return to town. I merely thought to give you a taste of what wonderful attention you will receive."

"I appreciate your efforts, but I don't have to be entertained."

"Ah, but when Laura would read us your letters, I knew you must be very lonely. And you were a good girl to your mother. You took such good care of her in her illness. You never went away and left her alone."

"No. I never did."

They sat silent for a moment. Then Celeste reached over and patted Judith's hand. "But now all that is behind you, *chérie*. Your father wants you to be the girl you were never allowed to be. He wants to make up for your pain."

Judith lifted her chin a fraction. Her hands clenched in her lap.

Celeste raised an eloquent eyebrow. "Do not maintain your stiff silence when I wish to explain your papa to you. He is a man like any other. He is not all good, not all bad. But mostly good. He would have brought your mama here. He told me the whole story before we married. I

95

knew he was divorced. I had to marry him outside my church, but I did so because he undertook to save me and give me the life I am fitted for."

"So he saved you and let my mother die," Judith said from between stiff lips.

"She chose that he should leave her," Celeste said softly. "He did not cause her cancer. He came to me an unhappy man, lonely, with an unhappy, lonely daughter. I loved him at once, but he came to love me. Perhaps he married me because your mama would not let him save her?"

A rumble of hoofbeats drew Judith to the top of the veranda steps. Beau on a fine bloodbay gelding galloped along the river road. When he caught sight of her, he waved and reined the horse aside. "Judith baby."

"Papa." She put one arm around the cool column and waited while he dismounted.

"Is Celeste feeling any better?"

"Berthe is with her now giving her a *tisane*."

"Good. Good." He dismounted, handed the reins to an omnipresent servant, and mounted the steps.

"Would you like something cool to drink?"

He put his arm around her waist and led her to the white wicker chairs and table. "You don't need to be the hostess for me, baby."

As if to demonstrate the truth of his statement, Berthe came to take his hat and stick. Another servant, at Berthe's direction, appeared and disappeared to fetch refreshment for them both. Then Berthe reported that Madame Celeste had gone to sleep.

Throughout the entire ritual of greeting and reporting to the master, of seeing to his creature comforts, Judith studied her father. Had she been here at *Ombres Azurées* long enough to satisfy him that she would never want to live here? Would he allow her to return to New Orleans? She curled her fingers in tightly against the palms of

96

her hands.

"The house is lovely, Papa."

He leaned back, one booted ankle crossed over the top of his knee. "It surely is. I'm a lucky man."

"The fields that lined the bayou. Were those yours?" she commented in wonder at the tall stands of blue-green cane rippling like silk along the shore.

"Yes. *Ombres Azurées* belonged to the Devranches, Celeste's family. They came with Bienville in the early 1700s. But she'd love to tell you all about the family history. When I fell in love with Celeste, I never had any idea that she had a possibility of owning this. I just knew that I wanted to marry her and take care of her. Then her brother died, and Blue Shadows just sort of fell into our hands."

Judith looked out across the gently sloping expanse of lawn to the dark green waters of the bayou. Blue Shadows. Bayou of Shadows. Somber names. She shivered. "What did he die of?" she asked at last.

"A fever. The doctor wasn't sure what it was. A lot of different things around here. Diseases from Africa that turn meaner than ever in this humid climate."

"How can you be so complacent about it?"

"Death's everywhere, Judith. On the high seas. In India. In England."

"Yes." She shivered.

Beau was instantly apologetic. "I didn't mean to resurrect unpleasant memories, baby."

"You didn't," she assured him. "The shiver was for the idea of death, not for the fact."

He leaned forward, elbows on his knees. "Was it hard, baby?"

She pressed her fist against her mouth and swallowed hard. "Just about as hard as anything could possibly be."

"I'm sorry you had to go through that."

"There was no one else," she reminded him coldly. All her barriers suddenly swung into place. As suddenly, she knew her course.

97

"But surely Amelia . . ."

"Two months before Mama died, *Grandmère* came to visit for the last time. She begged off going upstairs to visit her own daughter. She sent her regrets, but grief and a terrible cold kept her away. She could make her appearance only at the funeral. When I stopped to stay with her in London on my way here, she demanded that I stay there so she could marry me off to someone of importance in society."

"Damn the old witch to hell."

"My own feelings exactly."

They stared at each other silently. The servant brought the drinks in handblown glasses. When they were alone again, he raised his to her. "Let's drink to the end of all that."

She smiled grimly as she took a sip of the cool lemonade.

"Laura and Celeste want to have some sort of a party to introduce you to their friends."

Judith took a deep breath. "I can't have that, Papa."

He shook his head. "Of course you can."

How could she make him understand? "Papa, look at me. I'm your ugly duckling."

He grinned. "You've never been an ugly duckling. You're as pretty as a picture. With a new wardrobe, we'll turn you into a swan."

She did not believe him. "I'm in mourning."

"This is New Orleans. Nobody knows the details of what happened back in England. If we don't tell everyone we meet, no one will know. You can discard those black things in another month. No one will *ever* know."

"I would know."

He let out his breath in an exasperated sigh. "What do you want, baby?"

She leaned forward, her hands pressed tightly together. "Papa, you've never once asked me what I did for the last six years when I wasn't carrying trays and plumping pillows."

He looked at her suspiciously. "What did you do?"

"Oh, nothing bad, I assure you." She chuckled a little at the irony of that thought. "I studied."

He set the glass down, his relief evident in the way he seemed to relax.

"I studied mathematics and accounting and navigation and—"

"Hold on." He held up his hand, incredulous.

"I did," she insisted.

"What did you study all that stuff for?"

She hesitated, trying to decide how best to tell him. If only she knew him better . . . "You and Mama both wanted me to be a boy, didn't you?"

He shrugged. "Your mother wanted a son. She had some scheme about getting your great-grandfather to agree to break the entail. But we didn't make a boy. I think that was the beginning of the end. Your mother was furious." Suddenly, his jaw clamped to. He glanced uncomfortably at his daughter, thinking he might have revealed too much.

She correctly interpreted his look. "Don't be concerned about hurting my feelings on that score. I've heard the story. I'm the disappointment, the death of hopes, the 'reason we're living in this dead-and-alive hole . . .'"

"For heaven's sake . . ."

". . . at least once a month for the last six years."

His face almost funereal in its solemnity, he straightened in his chair. "What do you want, Judith?"

She noted with some hope that he did not call her baby. She took a deep breath and clenched her teeth. "I want to work for your shipping line."

He did not shake his head. He did not draw back in horror. Nor did he laugh and try to pat her knee. "What could you do?"

"What would you employ your son to do?" she countered.

He looked at her appraisingly. "If you were a young man . . ."

"Think of me as one."

99

"That's impossible."

"What would you have a son do?"

"I'd send him to sea, first as an observer, then perhaps as a third mate." His sapphire eyes narrowed as he thought.

"I don't suppose that I could . . ."

"Don't even think about it," he warned.

"But the business itself. The books. The maintenance. The orders. The loading and unloading. The ticketing of passengers."

"We're primarily a cargo line," he protested weakly.

"I'm prepared to learn," she replied simply. "Anything."

He looked out across the broad expanse to the dark green waters of the bayou. The sun turned the ripples into a glinting silver mirror. "Your sister and Celeste had such plans for you."

Sensing his weakening, she sat forward eagerly. "I'll make a deal. If I can go back to New Orleans and go to work for you every morning, I'll go to the parties and the opera with my sister at night."

With a wave of his hand he capitulated. "I need to return to the city at the end of the week. I'll take you back with me and introduce you to my partner. If he has no serious objections, I should think you can start work immediately."

"And if he does?"

"I'm the senior partner," he replied meaningfully.

Cynical understanding, tragic on one so young, flashed across her face. It lifted one corner of her soft lips, hardened the expression in the blue eyes. She nodded. "Thank you, Papa." Her shoulders back, she turned and walked back into the house.

For many minutes Beau stood alone on the back veranda. Celeste walked out to join him. She leaned her cheek against his shoulder and stared with him at the darkening water of the bayou. "Such an unhappy girl," she mourned. "So afraid to trust. So determined never to be young."

"It's my fault," he rejoined, his voice hoarse. "I should have brought her with me."

"You should not blame yourself. You did what you thought was right, what any reasonable person would have advised you to do should you have asked. It turned out badly. Had you taken her with you, she might have been more unhappy than she is now."

He sighed heavily. "She wants to work for me. To work for me. When I want to carry her around like a princess."

She slid her arms around his big body. "Remember you must give her what she wants, not what you want."

He turned to her and bent to take her mouth. "At least I have one princess."

Interlude II

From her bedroom window Judith saw the black groom guide Laura's gig out onto the road from the stables. He was her signal to hurry out to confront her sister and remind her of her promise to tour the plantation.

Laura Talbot paused on the veranda to pull on her fine kid driving gloves. She took a deep breath, inhaling the rich scent of rain-washed flora. The morning was already warm enough to make a tiny mirage shimmer across the end of the road. The legs of the high-stepping mare and then the wheels of the gig broke through its sinuous ripple.

The door opened behind her, and Judith hurried out. "Good morning, sister. You promised to take me on a tour of *Ombres Azurées*. I'm ready to go."

Laura hesitated, then smiled. "Not quite." She stepped back into the house and called to her personal maid. "Jeanette, please get Maîtresse Judith the proper coverings to protect her skin."

Smiling acquiescence, the servant opened a huge wardrobe in the upper hall and produced a wide-brimmed hat, veils, mask, and duster.

While Judith stared in horror, Jeanette descended with yards of gauzy material billowing from her arms. She spun around. "Laura, surely all of that isn't necessary. My bonnet and parasol will do well enough."

Laura struck what Judith was sure was a pose of cool detachment. "You're not accustomed to the heat, Judith. I insist that you wear it. I know Celeste would agree with me."

"She probably wouldn't want me to go at all." Judith lowered her voice rather than take the chance of her stepmother's finding out. "She's a great one for lying down in the middle of the day."

Laura shrugged, her expression faintly disapproving. "Judith, Celeste has never worked a day in her life. She does what is expected of her and likes it."

"But you don't. You told me that you had to go around to visit all the workers' quarters and distribute food and clothing." Judith looked pointedly at Laura's neat, suitable style. "You don't wear all that protection."

"No. But I'm accustomed to the heat," Laura pointed out with the voice of sweet reason.

Unwillingly, Judith pushed her arms through the cream-colored duster that the maid held for her. She glared at Laura, who smiled back equably. While Jeanette handed her white cotton gloves to protect her hands and wrists, Judith studied her older sister's dress.

Unfortunately for her sense of rebellion, she had to admit that Laura's dress was eminently more practical than her own forest-green wool. The broadcloth riding habit was of pale taupe cotton. It absorbed the sun to no great extent, nor would it easily show soil. A broad-brimmed straw hat was tied under the chin with a swatch of pale green lawn that complemented her eyes.

Judith sighed, then protested desperately as Jeanette began to arrange the veils from the brim of her own hat. "If you swathe me from head to toe in muslin and linen, I'll pass out before we've gone a mile. I'll bet no one can breathe under all that."

"If you want to go, you'll have to figure out a way to breathe," Laura said brusquely.

"You sound just like *Grandmère*."

"That's right. And I'm the Countess of *Ombres*

104

Azurées." Her tone changed abruptly. "You can be Countess of the Talbot lines."

Judith smiled just before she adjusted the cotton mask over her face. "On land and sea. Right, sister dear."

"Right."

Laura's two-wheeled Stanhope gig bounded smoothly along the bayou road. After perhaps a mile they turned inland, driving through fields of sugar cane higher than the horse's head and impenetrable as a blue-green wall on either side of the road. When they trotted into the clearing, Judith felt a distinct sense of relief. The mill and the workers' quarters were unprepossessing structures backed up to a smaller bayou. From a dock, small black children dived and splashed in the warm green water.

Past the quarters they drove through another field of cane and finally into a wood unlike any Judith had ever seen. Lush, green, spreading, trees with every branch festooned with gray-green Spanish moss. She opened the veils and tugged the mask down to admit the soughing wind.

She felt a sharp stab of homesickness. Halfway around the world from Harrestone and England, she was suddenly afraid. Louisiana was too far away from everything and everyone she knew. Its strangeness appalled her. Quickly she clasped both hands around the arm rail, holding tight to her courage.

Laura brought the gig to a skillful stop in the circle drive in front of what Judith could see was a cottage, but so strange. The center of the house was cut out in an architectural design to offset the ever-present heat. A smiling servant came hurrying out to take the horse's head.

Bright pink flowers, exotic and delicate, clustered thickly across the front. Together the sisters mounted the steps and entered a lovely sitting room. Through windows on the other side of the breezeway, the odor of baking bread identified that section as the kitchen. Steps scaled one interior wall to the rooms above.

Through casement windows flung wide, Judith stared at an oak tree. Instead of Spanish moss, it was host to magnificent purple wisteria. Its sweet scent perfumed the air in the room.

Laura swept off her hat and took a deep breath. "Isn't it beautiful?"

Judith managed to push all the veils, hat, and mask off in one motion and drop them into the arms of the waiting maid. She took a deep breath, then moved to the window to place her hands on the sill. "It's all so wild. It's not like any garden I've ever seen. Certainly not like an English garden."

Laura came to stand beside her and lean her shoulder and temple against the casement. "Perhaps that's why I love it so much. It's a challenge to keep it all under control."

Judith shook her head. "And they must grow so fast. I would think cutting back the same plants over and over would get awfully boring."

Though the sun shone brightly above them and bees hummed about the tumbling purple flowers, thunder rumbled distantly. Judith could not see the approaching storm beyond the wall of lush vegetation.

Laura made a wry face. "I can't think of anything more boring than sitting in a stuffy office moving figures from one piece of paper to another. The land is never boring."

"How can you say that? It's always the same." Judith stared at the panorama before her.

"Oh, no. It's constantly generating new life. Crops are planted, they grow, they're harvested. A wonderful cycle—which I control." Laura sat down in her favorite chair. A smile of pleasure made her face beautiful as a madonna's. Turning back from the window, Judith could not suppress a wince of envy. How wonderful to have something that you loved so much that your face would light up at the very thought.

She shook her head with a sigh. "Just as I said. Boring."

106

Laura's smile never faltered. "It's mine. And I'd do anything I had to to keep it."

"Are you sure you're not heading for disappointment? I understood the plantation was Celeste's." Judith was surprised to find that she cared about the possibility of her sister's being hurt. How her attitude had changed since her arrival.

"In point of fact, it's in Papa's name now. She insisted when they married." The maid entered, bearing a silver tray with teapot and cups. While she arranged the tea things, the sisters were silent. When she departed with a smile, Laura leaned forward in confidence. "She had so many outstanding debts that she was about to lose it."

Judith's eyes widened. "What kinds of debts?"

Laura hesitated briefly. She extended the cup and saucer to her sister. "Celeste likes to gamble."

Judith sat back with a shrug. "So did Charlotte."

The small silence increased until Laura said with more than her usual firmness, "I don't like to gamble."

"I don't like to drink," Judith responded instantly.

They finished the tea in perfect accord. Then Laura asked, "Would you like to see my retreat?"

Judith stared around the room appreciatively. "Yes, I'd like to very much."

"I come here when I want to be alone. From here I can walk out to the fields. I can hear the Negroes singing. I can see the bayou from my bedroom window. Here I read and work without making Celeste unhappy. I don't have to live my day on a social routine. I can leave that to her."

Judith grinned at that last comment. "I know what you mean. I've worked hard for the past few years. I don't enjoy sitting around doing nothing. That's why I want to be part of the Talbot lines. I've planned on it. That's why I had my tutors instruct me in accounting and mathematics instead of watercolors and French."

Laura took Judith's hand and turned her to view the picture over the fireplace. "I'm quite proficient at watercolors and French," she said archly.

107

"Why, Laura, that's the plantation house to the life."

Laura smiled.

Judith turned away restlessly and walked again to the window. She stared out for minutes at the magnificence. Its colors were almost overwhelming. Besides the purple of the wisteria, she could see dogwood trees, their delicate limbs dotted with wide white blossoms. Pink honeysuckle ran wild along a fence. She turned her back abruptly. "I want to live in town, Laura. I don't want to live here. I've been stuck in the country all my life. I don't like it." Both girls remembered the shabby gamekeeper's cottage in the woods on the back acres of Harrestone.

"But if you go back to town and work for the Talbot lines, you'll have to stay in a cramped little office. How can you stand that?"

Judith came to her sister with palms outstretched. "It's what I'll be working with. Figures and the tangible objects that they stand for fascinate me. They're the exact sciences." She crossed her arms tightly across her body. Her chin lifted proudly. "I think I'd like to make money on my own."

Laura stared at her sister. "Why is money so important?"

Judith smiled ruefully. "All my life I've lived hemmed in on all sides by the wealth of Harrestone, but I've been a pauper. I want to make money. Wealth makes a person strong and respected. I want to be wealthy. I want that respect."

"I never thought we were anything alike. And yet we are. The land is everything to me, the way money is to you. For me it's an exact science."

Judith stared at her beautiful sister. Suddenly, she was seeing Laura as not just a beautiful woman who filled the eye of every man she encountered, not just as the darling of their father and their grandmother as well as the rest of the family and probably the English *ton* as well. Suddenly, her sister was a real person with a brain and

108

ambition. Did Laura dream the same dreams Judith did? The thought was incredible. "Why, Laura, I never realized . . ."

The beautiful green eyes flashed emerald fire. "The land I should have had was taken away from me. I want this. It's my wealth and my power."

Judith smiled in admiration. "And you know who you sound like? *Grandmère.*"

Laura looked insulted. "Papa!" she declared.

Judith shook her head in disbelief. "We are sisters after all."

Chapter Five

"Absolutely not. Never. *Jamais de la vie. Non.* No, my friend. This is a place of busines. Women do not understand business." Dark as Beau was fair, short, and heavily muscled, Maurice Dufaure bounded from behind his desk. His face worked; his pock-marked cheeks flushed with indignation.

"Come now, Maurice," Beau protested mildly, backing up against the counter. "This is my daughter. She'll inherit this place someday and—"

"Then find a husband for her and he can come into the office. But a female in a place of business. *Non. Impossible.*" Veins strutted and throbbed beneath the skin of Dufaure's temples.

Beau cast a hopeful glance over his shoulder at Judith. She swallowed with difficulty but held her ground. With a shrug he returned his attention to his partner, who was now stomping back and forth across the office, gesturing toward the file boxes and voicing a steady stream of protests. Since he shouted in French except for an occasional English word, Judith could not understand him.

"That's enough, Maurice," Beau said finally. "I've promised Judith that she can try her hand here."

"Try her hand! This is a place of—"

"I know. I know. And she does too. She's not going to

111

want to interfere in business." He stepped forward a little diffidently. "You understand. She just needs something to fill her time."

Judith opened her mouth, but her protest was drowned by Maurice. "Fill her time! *Le diable!* Get her *petit-point* or watercolors."

Beau pulled a spotless white handkerchief from his pocket and wiped perspiration from his upper lip. "She wants to work in the office."

"In the office. In here? With me. *Impossible!* Let her work anywhere but here. On the docks if she wants to work so badly. But not in here. My desk . . . My accounts . . ." He hurried across the office and slammed a ledger closed. His face was so dark that Judith wondered if he was about to have an apoplectic seizure.

Evidently her father thought the same thing, for his forehead creased in a worried frown. Jaw tight, he hunched his shoulders. "Maurice," he said loudly. "That's enough. Calm down. You've had your say. Now I'll have mine. My daughter is a Talbot. If she wants to work for the Talbot lines, she will work for the Talbot lines."

Maurice quieted somewhat. His voice took on a pleading tone. "But, my friend, she will ruin everything. Women have no head for business. No. The ledgers. The accounts."

"Perhaps I *could* work on the docks," Judith suggested mildly.

Beau whirled. "Impossible."

Maurice's mouth flicked up at one corner. "I'm glad you finally see sense. Of course she cannot work there. Nor anywhere."

"I *could* work on the docks. It would be the logical place for me to start." Judith's voice gained strength. "I assume you mean that I would take some kinds of cargo lists down to the docks and inventory the shipments as they were loaded and unloaded."

At the word *inventory* Maurice's black eyes narrowed.

112

Beau shook his head. "You can't work out there. It's impossible."

"Why?"

"Because you'd be the only woman out there except for a few passengers. You'd be out in the blazing hot sun and the rain and the cold. You couldn't stand it."

"She should not work at all," Maurice declared from behind Beau's shoulder.

"You promised," Judith reminded her father even as she approached Dufaure. "I am very serious about this, sir. I can understand that you would not think I am. But if you'll just give me a chance . . ."

"*Non. Jamais.* Never. Never." Dufaure retreated, shaking his head stubbornly. His hands came up as if to ward her off.

Beau came up behind Judith's shoulder. His eyes were flinty. "Maurice, she's going to work for us and that's the end of it."

The father and daughter faced the partner.

Dufaure opened his mouth to protest, but thought better of it. When he spoke, he sought to regain some measure of dignity. "She will not work in the office."

"No," Judith agreed.

"Yes," Beau insisted.

"No. I'll work on the docks." When her father glared at her, she caught his hand between both of hers. "Wouldn't that be where you'd send your son?"

"But you aren't a boy."

"That doesn't mean I can't do the job. Just let me try. I'm not afraid of hard work. Please, Beau." Her eyes were shining with hope.

He heaved an unhappy sigh. His eyes sought Dufaure, who was shaking his head. "She'll work on the docks," Beau said with an air of finality.

"You have not made a great mistake, *chère* Judith?" Celeste asked uncertainly. "The docks are very dangerous. Huge bales of cotton. Sweating workingmen. The language you would hear . . ." She made a clicking noise with her tongue.

"I'll just have to get used to it," Judith replied.

Celeste sighed. "Ah, you modern young women. In my day . . . but never mind. The first thing tomorrow we must take you to the dressmaker. There is so little time to select suitable materials and make your new dresses."

Judith stared in amazement at her stepmother. "I can't go, Celeste. Surely you see that I have to be at the docks early in the morning."

"But how will we have your clothing made? Don't you care about the selection of materials? That is something that every woman should enjoy." Celeste looked at her pointedly. "And I would think that you have not had many opportunities to select beautiful clothes."

For a moment Judith was sorely tempted. Dufaure would undoubtedly be glad when she did not appear. What would one more day hurt? Sternly, she shook her head. "I can't. I have to go to work."

Celeste threw up her hands. "But the dresses. You cannot go in those drab old things."

"Then I suppose I won't be able—"

"No." Celeste held up her hand peremptorily. "No. Do not even say such a thing. There must be a way." She paced around the room. The exquisite Chantilly lace wrapper swept the floor behind her. Deep ruffles of lace fell from her throat and wrists. Her long dark hair had been brushed and braided up over her ears with satin ribbons. She looked beautiful, even in dishabille.

"I really don't—"

"I have it." Celeste turned with a smile. "It is not the best solution, but it will suffice." She opened the door to the wardrobe. "Which is your favorite dress?"

Without hesitation Judith pulled out the forest-green wool.

"And it fits you well?"

"It was made for me in London just before I sailed."

"*Bon.* I will take it to the dressmaker. She will take

114

your measurements from it."

Judith smiled. "Oh, Celeste. You really are a wonder."

"Of course. With clothes and things domestic. After all, I am old enough to be your *maman. N'est-ce pas?*"

Judith spread her hands as she tried to offer an explanation. "I know it seems hard for you to understand, but I have to do this thing."

Celeste caught hold of Judith's hands and turned the young woman to face her. "It is hard, but it is not impossible. You have much to prove. To Beau."

"I suppose I'm going about it the wrong way."

"Not at all. He will be very proud of you if you do well. If you decide that you do not want to do this thing, then he will be glad that you gave him the chance to say I told you so." She chuckled softly.

"He'll probably be disgusted with me if I fail?"

"He is a little bit disgusted with you now, but he will not be then—if you fail."

"Oh, I'm sure he's furious with me, but I—"

"Only because he is a spoiled baby sometimes himself."

"Beau Talbot?"

"Of course. He is a man, as I told you, *chérie*. I spoil him terribly. I give him his way in everything, because why should I not? His way is always good for me. For you, his way is not always so good."

"I suppose that Laura spoils him too."

Again Celeste chuckled softly. "Oh, Laura. No. She would have her place. She would have her own gig. She would ride out and oversee the crops. The overseer threatened to quit. I told her she would ruin her skin. Beau told her his daughter would do no such thing."

"And she did."

Celeste patted Judith's cheek. "It is a great trial to him to find he has sired two daughters as obstinate as himself."

Judith blinked once—twice—but still the tall figure

115

came on. Alarm changed to anger as she stared fixedly at the man who strode toward her along the Bienville Street wharf. His hair might be neatly trimmed and combed. His seaman's garb with red sash and jackboots might have been exchanged for a more conventional blue tailcoat above buff nankeen trousers. But he was surely the pirate captain of the *Banshee*.

Before she considered the consequences, Judith sprang from the landau. "Emil! Georges! Hurry!"

Assigned by Beau Talbot to guard and protect, the driver and the footman exchanged looks of alarm. Even as Emil was looping the reins around the brake, the footman sprang down from his place at the back and followed his mistress.

"Stop! Stop right where you are!"

"Maîtresse!" Georges loped after her, waving his hands frantically in protest.

Tabor stopped in his tracks. His face registered amazement, then apprehension as she halted in front of him.

"Pirate," she snapped. "Georges. Emil. Grab him."

Georges, who had stopped behind her, made no effort to come forward. The man he was being ordered to grab was bigger than he with broad shoulders and a straight-backed, commanding carriage. Moreover, he was well dressed, obviously wealthy. A black footman could be whipped merely for laying his hands on a white man whether at the order of another or no. Emil, too, stopped a step or two behind Georges. The men exchanged uneasy glances.

Seeing the men's hesitation and knowing himself to be in command of the situation, Tabor swept off his hat and bowed low. "Good day to you, m'lady. I am fortunate beyond measure to have met you again."

"I would say that you were unfortunate," she snapped. "Emil! Georges! Grab him, I say. He's a pirate. He belongs in prison."

Neither man moved to obey her.

116

Emil removed his hat and bowed humbly. "Maîtresse, maybe you should tell your father . . ."

"My father wanted you to protect me." She pointed an imperious finger at the grinning man. "He's a pirate."

"I don't suppose you'd believe me that I'm not a pirate."

"You're Tabor O'Halloran of the *Banshee*. The captain of the *Portchester* told me all about you after you robbed me."

Tabor managed a hurt expression. "I did not rob you."

Her eyes spat blue fire. "That's true. You didn't. After your men were finished with my belongings, I had nothing left to steal."

The humorous expression faded. He inclined his head, his face sober. "I regret the whole incident more than I can say, m'lady. If you remember, I offered you reparation."

"And you remember what I did with your reparation. Emil! Don't stand there with your hat in your hand. If you can't bring yourself to lay hands on him, run for the magistrates."

Tabor turned to the men. "Your mistress is obviously upset. Perhaps if you'd step back a bit, I can explain to her satisfaction."

Emil might have been unwilling to lay hands on Tabor, but he was not willing to abandon his office. Alarmed at the man's suggestion, he shook his head. "Maîtresse, come with me and Georges. We'll all go together to M'sieur . . ."

So furious with both men that her voice shook, she tried once more. "I can handle this myself if you two will only do as I say. You were told to guard and protect me. This man is a pirate. Grab him, I say!"

"Maîtresse," they pleaded.

She swung back around to face her nemesis, who hastily smothered his smile. "You'd better scuttle back to your ship and head it downriver. My father will have you in the Cabildo before nightfall."

117

At last he would find out her name. Purposefully, he grinned, taunting her beyond caution. His voice was tense with expectancy which she was too angry to notice. "And who is your father that he can snap his fingers and put a man in the Cabildo?"

"He's the Honorable Howard Francis Talbot, a nephew of the Earl of Teigh, and owner and president of the Talbot Shipping Lines."

The grin slipped from his face as if it had never been. "You're Beau Talbot's daughter?" His eyes raked her, searching for some sign that she was lying. "Impossible."

"Why impossible? Do you attack and destroy only the poor and helpless?"

"His daughter's older than you by half a dozen years." His eyes slid over her black dress and white bonnet and parasol trimmed with black rosettes. "And . . . and . . ."

Hectic color blazed from Judith's cheekbones. "She's eight years older, as a matter of fact. And prettier. Much prettier. She wears beautiful dresses in lovely colors. And she stays on the plantation like a lady. But he has two daughters, and I'm the other."

"I didn't mean that she was prettier," he contradicted himself quickly. "I just meant that Beau never mentioned anything about you."

"Why should he discuss his family with a pirate?"

"Why indeed?"

"Maîtresse, please."

"I'm coming, Emil." She turned on her heel and strode back to her carriage, her skirts swishing from side to side, her red hair fairly bristling from beneath the bonnet.

Tabor O'Halloran wiped his hand across the lower half of his face. The expression in his blue eyes was bleak. Unknowingly, he had insulted and injured the daughter of one of his best friends. Remembering the terrible scene, he cursed himself for not leaving her in peace.

How easy now to account for the hot temper, the fierce resistance, the furious pride that had heaved a purse of

118

gold into the ocean rather than excuse his vandalism. She was an aristocrat to her fingertips, but why the black garb? Why had she been traveling on the old flute when she could have had a stateroom beneath the flying sails of the *White Hound*, the flagship of the Talbot lines?

He shook his head as he remembered with awful clarity his sneers and jibes, the destruction of her clothing and possessions in what subsequently proved a mistake. When he explained to Beau, he'd be lucky to be allowed to leave New Orleans unscarred.

Suddenly, he smiled. Her lips had been warm and sweet, her fury exciting. He had thought he'd never meet her again. But luck or fate had brought them together here in New Orleans.

He needed to contact Beau Talbot immediately.

"What? Back so soon, Miss Talbot-Harrow." Maurice Dufaure rose from behind his desk. "I cannot believe—"

"I did not finish supervising the unloading of the *White Stag*, M'sieur Dufaure. Doubtless the goods will be unloaded in proper order without me. Something most pressing . . ."

A muscle twitched in Dufaure's pock-marked cheek. It drew his mouth upward into what might have been a mirthless smile. "Already you find your job too taxing, Miss Talbot-Harrow? It is as I suggested to you when you persuaded your father to take the company's time . . ."

Judith closed the door behind her with a sharp slam. "I did not find my job too taxing, M'sieur Dufaure. Quite the contrary. I find the job most stimulating. I returned here for a very good reason. I need your voice added to mine."

Dufaure cocked his head to one side. His slightly protruding black eyes looked upward as he sighed faintly. "How can I be of service, Miss Talbot-Harrow?"

Judith clenched her fists with the effort required to stop herself from sweeping up the model of the *White*

Hound on the shelf before the window and flinging it at him. "You can stop calling me Miss Talbot-Harrow in that vicious, mocking tone and listen to what I say."

Maurice coughed unconvincingly to cover up his chuckle. Pulling his coattails around in front of him, he dropped down into his chair. "Very well. I shall listen attentively."

"I have seen a pirate here on the dock."

"Oh, is that all?"

"Is that all?"

"It's of no consequence, my dear Miss . . . er . . . my dear. There are pirates all over the docks practically every day."

"No. No. I mean a real pirate. One that I actually saw rob a ship. One of our ships, in fact. The *Portchester*."

Dufaure raised one black eyebrow, then seated himself again at his desk and made a show of opening a ledger and running his finger down the page. "The *Portchester* came into New Orleans with her cargo intact."

"My luggage was all but destroyed, and a man and his wife were taken off that ship. Just because no company cargo was destroyed—"

"Why haven't you reported this before?"

"I assumed the captain would handle all that."

"He made no mention of any such incident."

Judith put her hands flat on the desktop, attempting to read the upside-down columns of numbers. "Then he should be called to account for what is obviously a neglect of his duty."

Dufaure closed the ledger with a rude snap. "He has unloaded his ship, picked up his new cargo, and set sail."

Judith's eyes narrowed. Her father's partner had been unequivocally opposed to her coming to work. Furthermore, his antipathy was palpable every morning when she reported for her assignments and collected the cargo manifests. Only her unusual upbringing that had thickened her protective shell enabled her to face him with aplomb.

120

Still, she was puzzled. Why was he not eager to arrest someone who had attacked a Talbot ship? "M'sieur Dufaure. I am telling you what happened. The captain should have reported the incident. It involved the boarding of one of my father's ships."

Dufaure looked up at her. A muscle ticked in his cheek, pulling up the corner of his mouth. "Obviously, the master of the vessel did not consider it important enough to report. I'm sure you misinterpreted the situation, if indeed the situation was as you say at all. Frequently, ships meet in mid-ocean to exchange letters."

"This was not an exchange of letters. The pirate captain came into my cabin and tore my clothing to pieces."

Dufaure's face instantly split in a nasty grin. "Indeed."

"Damn you." She swung away, her face flaming as she realized what she had said. Behind her Dufaure chuckled. "Why won't you take me seriously? He's getting away."

Dufaure rose and strolled insolently around the desk to stand behind her. "If I were you, Miss Talbot, I would not mention to anyone else that the pirate came into your cabin and tore your clothes off."

"My name is Talbot-Harrow. And he did not come into my cabin and tear my clothes off my body," she snapped. "You are being purposefully obtuse. Why? Why are you doing this? Saying these things?" She swung around to find herself face-to-face with Dufaure. Their eyes locked.

His were opaque, allowing no light to enter, hard and cold as stone. "Perhaps you should return to the duties you so eagerly wanted to assume," he suggested after a moment's icy silence.

She lifted her shoulder as if to shrug him off. "I'm not going to let pirates roam the streets. I'll go to the law."

"Go to the governor for all the good it will do you. He's an American through and through." Dufaure made the nationality sound like a dirty word. "Jefferson appointed him and Madison left him in. For a while he had a few of the Barataria pirates in the Cabildo. But he's really not

121

interested in pirates. Taking the land and privileges from the French Creoles is more to his liking."

Frustrated and upset, Judith was only dimly aware of the bitterness in his voice. "But this is infamous. I knew America was a barbarous frontier, but this is ridiculous. That man's a pirate. He should be locked up in prison, where he can't board ships and steal from innocent women." She started for the door.

Dufaure stepped in front of her, clapping his hand to the door facing. "Miss Talbot-Harrow."

She kept her eyes sullenly trained on the cypress panels. "Mr. Dufaure."

"I need not tell you that when your father brought you in here to work, I objected most strenuously. I thought that you would be inattentive and dilatory at best. At worst I thought you would be ignorant and cause errors that would slow down office efficiency."

She sucked in her breath. "I knew that you were angry," she acknowledged.

"Now I find that you are worse than I imagined. You were given the simple job of counting the items in the cargo as it is unloaded, something a young lad should be able to do with ease. Instead of tending to the business at hand, you leave your job to come running in here with a senseless fairy tale."

"I'm not telling a fairy tale," Judith cried indignantly. "The pirate captain Tabor O'Halloran was strolling along the dock. He robbed our ship. He robbed the *Portchester*."

"The captain reported nothing of this."

"You don't believe me," Judith gasped incredulously.

With a shrug he turned back to his desk. "I believe that you are finding work more difficult than you had first thought it would be. Perhaps you thought it would be a lark. Perhaps you thought it would be a way to meet a certain type of man . . . *n'est-ce pas?*"

Too insulted, too furious to listen longer, Judith stalked from the office and slammed the door behind her.

*   *   *

"For God's sake, Beau, I had no idea who she was. I'd cut off my right arm rather than harm your daughter." Tabor paced the length of the room, then back again.

"Relax, old man. I know you didn't mean to hurt her. It was just bad luck that the British War Office happened to pick the old *Portchester* to travel on and that Judith happened to be on her rather than on one of the 'white fleet.'" Beau smiled reassuringly at his friend, who stopped his pacing to thrust his hands into the pockets of his nankeen trousers and stare moodily at the carpet.

"I destroyed her clothing," Tabor said bleakly.

Beau laughed. "No great loss there, if what survived was any sample. Judith's insisting on observing strict mourning for her mother. The darkest, drabbest stuff I've ever seen. Don't worry. We're buying her new clothing. Celeste is getting ready to order gowns for the coming balls."

Tabor stepped forward eagerly. "Let me buy them."

"Nonsense, man. They're expensive. A couple of times in the past when I've gotten the bills for Laura and Celeste, I've had to sit down and hold my heart." Beau chuckled to himself.

"Then let me buy them."

Beau waved him away. "Absolutely not. It's not done, old man."

"That's under ordinary circumstances. These are extraordinary. Society be damned. I want to do this. I have to do this." He turned away, driving his fist into the palm of his hand. "If you could have seen her face . . . I've been haunted by it. The men tore every garment apart looking for papers. We even ruined her trunk looking for a false bottom."

Beau stared for a minute at the broad back. "You're certain you want to?"

"It would give me the greatest pleasure in the world."

The hour was late, the shadows long when Judith returned to the house on Conti. Shaking with fury, she

123

had returned to the dock where the unloading of the merchantman had indeed proceeded without her. With an effort she had calmed herself and taken back the manifests.

She had discovered ruefully that Dufaure had been right in one respect. Only by doing double work was she able to locate all the cargo already unloaded from the forward hatch at the same time she kept track of that coming out of the rearward. By the time she had caught up, the dockhands were almost finished. Another half hour found her able to sign the manifest and send it by Georges to the shipping office.

Nearly exhausted from the heat and dampness, she leaned back and allowed Emil to thread the landau through the teeming narrow streets of the *Vieux Carré*.

Beau Talbot frowned as she hurried in and immediately mounted the stairs. "Baby?"

She halted halfway up. "I'm sorry I'm late, Papa."

"No problem. I'm not hungry yet anyway. Just take your time and come on down when you get ready."

Judith closed her eyes in relief before taking the last five or six steps in a flurry. Without a bath and a change of clothing, she would not be able to face another human being, much less her father. In her own room she rang immediately for the servant to fetch cool water for the slipper bath.

When Judith finally came to dinner an hour later, she presented a cool and serene countenance.

"Will you have a sherry, baby?" Beau asked, pouring himself a whiskey.

She shook her head. "I'm not fond of any kind of liquor, Papa. After watching Mama for all those years . . ." She shrugged, leaving him to put whatever *finis* he pleased to the thought.

He sighed heavily. "I'm sorry, Judith."

Taking a small straight-backed chair, she arranged her black skirts around her with more care than was necessary.

"How did it go today?" he asked after a short silence.

She hesitated, having discovered a crease in the material. Her index and third finger smoothed it out. "Well," she said at last.

He looked at her narrowly. "No special problems crop up? Nothing unusual happen?"

She hesitated. Here was the perfect opening. She could place the entire problem of Tabor O'Halloran in her father's capable hands. But hadn't she done that with the captain of the *Portchester*? And he had done nothing, evidently not considering the boarding from the *Banshee* important enough to report.

Another consideration was the fact that Dufaure had not believed her. Would her father also think that she was making up a fairy tale for some unfathomable reason? She had never had anyone disbelieve her before. The lack of confidence shook her. "Oh, no. Emil and Georges are most protective. The longshoremen always recognize the landau anyway."

"Really." He seemed amazed. "Er . . . you and Maurice hitting it off all right too?" he probed.

"We're working together. Why shouldn't we be? After all, we're both working for the Talbot lines. Actually we don't have to like each other, do we?" She looked him full in the face, then, her back straightened perceptibly, her chin rose.

He blinked. "You surprise me."

"Papa, believe me, it's all right. M'sieur Dufaure didn't want me to work in the office. I'm out on the docks most of the time. That way we don't see each other very much."

"Maurice is a good enough man," Beau continued. "Old French. Came along at a time when I needed money to expand. Shortly after I married Celeste. *Ombres Azurées* needed repairs, some pretty expensive. This opportunity came along to buy a couple of merchantmen. He was there. *Voilà!* I have myself a partner."

"He works very hard."

125

"So do you," Beau complimented her roughly.

"The work is interesting. If I were your son, it would be a good place to start me learning."

"And so you had a good day?" he probed softly.

"A good day," she agreed, flashing him a bright smile. "I got behind a little once. But that was all."

He seemed to relax. "Your sister will be coming back to town at the end of this month."

Judith resumed her attention to the crease in the material. "Oh?"

"Celeste is planning a ball and a night at the opera for the two of you."

"It all sounds wonderful," she commented in an even voice.

"It will be." He warmed to his subject. "Baby, even if you'd been to a rout in London, you wouldn't have seen anything to compare with a masquerade ball in Old New Orleans. In New Orleans the masquerade is everything."

"Beau, I don't think . . ."

"For a hundred years the French celebrated before Ash Wednesday with masquerades. Then the Spanish came and no one could wear masks at all. Now the rule has been amended. No one can wear masks in the streets." He was grinning from ear to ear. "You'll have the time of your life. Dancing till dawn. No worries. No cares. Just free to be what you want to be. Do what you want to do."

"I'm in mourning."

"The ball will be a masquerade. You'll have such a good time. You'll have a beautiful dress. Last year Laura's was emerald green. She said it had a hundred yards of taffeta in the skirt."

For a minute Judith was tempted. A dress of taffeta with a hundred yards of material in the skirt. Sternly, she put the thought aside. "I'm still in mourning."

"Dammit, Judith." Beau set his drink down with unnecessary force. "Your mother's been dead for half a year—"

"Five months."

"No one in New Orleans has any idea about when she actually died."

"Laura went to England to visit her," she reminded him stubbornly.

"Laura went to England to answer a death message. For all anyone knows, Charlotte could have been dead for months when she arrived. It could have been for a gathering of the heirs to read the will. What's more, no one really cares."

"I care."

"Do you?"

She flushed.

"Your mother was the most shallow, self-indulgent person I have ever met. When I married her, she was a great beauty. We were both young and shallow. I *had* to grow up or be ruined, but she never did. And what's more, she never wanted me to grow up. The first thing I heard about when my ship docked at Portsmouth was her affair with Lythes. When I got back to London, men couldn't wait to corner me in my club and give me all the details about her and him and all the others."

"Papa." Judith held up a restraining hand.

"But I was still willing to take her with me. I'd come back for her and you girls, and she was your mother. I had my mind made up to forgive and forget. I swear I had. I asked her to come with me to New Orleans. To be my wife in America. She wanted to go on dancing at Almacks forever."

Judith bowed her head before the anger and disappointment in her father's voice. Instinctively, she realized that Beau Talbot was telling her secrets that few if any other people knew. She had never considered that he might have regretted the dissolution of his marriage, the loss of his first wife and younger daughter.

He took a deep breath and tugged impatiently at the high collar bound by the stock to his neck. "I hadn't meant to say all of that to you," he murmured by way

127

of apology.

"I'm glad you did."

"I'm glad too. Because maybe it'll help you. Baby, your mother wasn't a saint, but neither was she a black sinner either. She was just a girl who couldn't see anything else except the life she thought she had been born to."

"In the end she knew it, Papa. Not long before she died she mentioned your name."

"Did she?" He tipped his head back to finish the sherry. She could not see the expression on his face.

"She said she loved you."

He set the empty glass down a bit harder than necessary and put his hands on his daughter's shoulders. "I'm sorry she was in pain before she died. I'm glad you were with her. But I want you to put all that behind you and come to love us. Believe me, I want you to be happy. Now, shall we go to supper?"

Madame Estelle boasted of her training with the finest modistes in Paris before the Terror. Her shop on Royal Street in the *Vieux Carré* catered to the very wealthiest and most powerful among the city's social circles.

When Tabor O'Halloran pushed open the door, Madame regarded him with a jaundiced eye. He grinned engagingly as he picked her out easily from the two shopgirls clad in drab black costumes.

Madame was clad in crimson velvet with a high neckline hugging her wrinkled throat. Her fine white hair carefully pinned to the top of her head still managed to escape in wispy tendrils to soften her severe face. She looked the debonair young man up and down. "I am very expensive," she announced.

"But well worth every penny," he rejoined, bowing elegantly.

"That is true."

"Every seamstress that I employ is fully engaged until Easter."

"I'm sure that one or two might be persuaded to work overtime if the payment were sufficient."

"It would be very expensive. Very."

He regarded her steadily, a light in his bright blue eyes. She did not relent. "If one or two were to be persuaded to do this work—I do not say that they can be—what type of dress would you want?"

Tabor thought a minute, concentrating on a vision of hair red as cinnabar and eyes bluer than the sky or the sea. "A dress for a masquerade ball. A special dress."

"Ah! And the color?"

"Blue. Sapphire blue."

Madame snapped her fingers. The girl in the starched black dress rustled away. "This woman—is she short? tall? thin? plump?"

"Of medium height. Waist narrow. Slender." His eyes took on a faraway look as he recalled the feel of her in his arms when he had lifted her from the floor of the cabin to steal kisses from her mouth.

Madame Estelle allowed herself a tiny smile as his face softened. "My dear young man, I wish that I could help you, but how can one make a dress for a woman with blue eyes of medium height with a narrow waist? It is impossible."

"I have one of her dresses."

The dressmaker's eyebrows shot to her hairline.

"Provided by her father," he hastened to add. He held out the box. "To take her measurements from."

The eyebrows returned to their normal location on the narrow face. "Ah, very well." She opened the box and placed the dress on the counter. The sight of the black stuff made her wince.

Tabor was watching her closely. "It must be done immediately. This dress must be returned without her knowledge."

"Why would anyone want this back?" Madame Estelle sniffed. "Still, the measurements can be done immediately." The shopgirl returned at that moment, her arms full of bolts of material. "Indeed, here comes Marie. I feel

129

sure we will have something you will like." The modiste drew one from beneath the stack. "This velvet is sapphire blue. Very modish. The latest from France. Very expensive."

Tabor looked at the delicate stuff. The light glimmered among its folds. He could almost see Judith, the white skin of her neck and shoulders framed by this beautiful stuff, her red hair shining beneath the lights. "It's beautiful, Madame. Exactly right."

"Ah!"

He grinned again. "I must have it by next Tuesday."

"Impossible."

"And a mask of the same material stiffened."

"Impossible. You do not understand the time required to make these garments."

"And slippers to match."

Madame threw up her hands. "You are a madman."

He drew a purse from his pocket. Opening it, he counted out ten twenty-dollar gold pieces into the old woman's hand. "To begin the work."

The thin, clever fingers wrapped around the coins. "We will begin, but I cannot promise."

He counted out five more. "I shall return Friday to check on your progress." He bowed low.

She inclined her head. "I'm sure you will be pleased."

Chapter Six

"You were a great success, *chère* Judith. Madame Beauvaliet was quite, quite enchanted. She assured me that you will be invited to Violette's *bal masqué*."

Judith heaved a great sigh of relief, although not from the assurance of the invitation. With a great show of exhaustion she slumped back in her chair. "I thought working all day on the docks counting cargo was hard. It's nothing compared to the strain of making polite conversation with ladies over tea."

"Well, of course, it was a strain the first time," Laura interposed, seeing Celeste's expression of concern. "You were nervous. When you become accustomed to everyone, you'll look forward to seeing your friends and hearing all the latest news."

Judith shaded her eyes with her hand. Better to pretend that she had a slight headache—a condition Celeste could well understand—than to admit that she had been bored to tears. Sitting bolt upright sipping a pale, lukewarm liquid and listening to an old woman make pronouncements in an incomprehensible accent were not her idea of fun or profit. "Madame Beauvaliet reminds me of *Grandmère*," she murmured.

Laura flushed, but Celeste clapped her hands in delight. "The countess! How wonderful! I shall tell her that you remarked on the resemblance. She will be so pleased. She is of the nobility. A portion of her family, the branch that did not emigrate to New Orleans, was assassinated in the Terror. Now their title is lost forever. She is most regretful."

"Judith." Laura hastily changed the subject as her younger sister sat up straight, the beginnings of a grin on her face. "You look lovely in your new dress."

Pleased at the compliment, Judith plucked wide the sheer batiste of her scalloped overskirt to admire it. "It's lovely, isn't it?"

"Indeed it is," Celeste agreed with a smile. "The pale blue with just the barest hint of green is your color. I am so pleased that you have worn your veils and carried a parasol on . . . that is . . . whenever you go out. Your skin has not been damaged as I feared."

"I have been careful," Judith acknowledged. "That was one of Beau's stipulations."

"Still, you must have an application of cucumber lotion tomorrow afternoon before your bath." Celeste turned to Laura for confirmation of the efficacy of this beauty regimen.

Judith made a warning face at her older sister. "I'm not sure that I'll have time for a lotion treatment tomorrow, Celeste."

"But surely . . ."

"Judith's skin looks lovely without anything," Laura insisted.

Under Celeste's doubtful scrutiny Judith rose to excuse herself. "I have some work that must be done for Talbot Shipping. Remember I told you, Laura. The *White Cloud* is in the river south of Fort St. Philip. She should be docking sometime tomorrow."

"But surely Beau will make arrangements . . ."

Laura caught the stubborn set of her sister's jaw. "I don't think—"

"I will make the arrangements. It's part of my job, not his," Judith interrupted them both. "I'll be back by the middle of the afternoon, in plenty of time to bathe and change." She sketched a brief curtsy before her stepmother. "Now, if you'll excuse me, Celeste, I have time to go over some figures before dinner."

Celeste shook her head as Judith hurried from the room. "Are all English girls like your sister, Laura?"

Laura smiled wryly. "I don't think Judith is like any other girl, Celeste, English or otherwise."

"What a peculiar country that must be. But how did the lessons progress with M'sieur Braudet?"

Laura sighed. "She didn't do as well as I had hoped. Despite enjoying the music, she didn't like having a man put his arm across her back at the waist."

"How very peculiar!"

"She is very shy," Laura improvised hastily.

"How dear! But she did learn to dance?"

"After a fashion."

Instantly, Celeste flashed a smile. "I shall tell *cher* Beau. He will be enchanted." She leaned back against the chaise lounge. "Would you please draw the Kashmir across my limbs, Laura? And ring for my *tisane*. I must be quiet now for an hour."

"Celeste," Laura began uncertainly, "are you sure you don't need to see a doctor?"

"Of course not, *chérie*. I am merely fatigued. The weather here in the city is so oppressive."

The little man's spectacles slid forward on his nose. He pulled Tabor down the aisle to the counter at the back of the store. Although the place was empty, he spoke in a whisper. "Report."

"Nothing," Tabor whispered back, then cleared his throat self-consciously. "That is"—he resumed his normal tone of voice—"New Orleans is going about her business without a thought to war, either in Europe or on the Atlantic."

The shopkeeper shook his head. "Listen. Listen. On the docks. In the streets. In the markets. The talk is—"

"Gossip." Tabor shook his head. "Old men exchanging war stories, some as far back as Queen Anne's War."

The shopkeeper looked disappointed. "That will change very soon. Very soon indeed." He nodded his head sagely and dropped his voice a tone.

Tabor had to bend forward to hear. "Is something about to happen?"

"Oh, yes. Yes. Very soon. Very soon."

"What?"

"Don't know yet. Not yet. But I'll be informed in time to pass it on."

Tabor straightened again. His skepticism grew. "The *Banshee* can't stay in port indefinitely."

"To be sure. To be sure. New developments very shortly. The British've just about got Napoleon whipped. After Leipzig he's been a sinking ship. Rats jumping from every side."

Tabor doubtfully regarded his contact. Reynolds, or whatever his name was, certainly looked and sounded like a shopkeeper. His dry goods store at the corner of a tiny alley facing Canal was shabby and dusty. Certainly no one with any information would enter. "The British payroll?" he prompted.

"Where it will do the most good. Good job. Good job." The man pushed his spectacles into place and measured Tabor's tall length.

"And what about other agents here?"

The shopkeeper's eyes shifted to the scarred countertop. His fingers drummed once. "Stepping up efforts everywhere. Everywhere. The minute Napoleon's safely tucked away, Britain will turn her attention to America."

"The payroll on the *Portchester* was to pay spies," Tabor reminded him.

"Oh, to be sure. To be sure." The shopkeeper held up his hand suddenly. His eyes darted to the shop door. Tabor straightened alertly. Footsteps sounded on the stones outside. Booted feet walked on past with no hesitation.

"Can't be too careful," Reynolds snapped between set teeth. "Spies everywhere. Britain wants to know everything about New Orleans. She particularly doesn't want the Corsican ogre to come here. Loyal Frenchmen would welcome him. Nobody wants that. Not British. Not Americans."

"No." Tabor acknowledged the first thing he had heard to agree with.

"Your information regarding shipping is most valuable. Most valuable. When the British come they'll come by sea. Probably through Ponchartrain."

Tabor gaped at the man's lack of knowledge. "A British frigate in Ponchartrain is impossible. The Rigolets is too shallow."

Reynolds's spectacles slid forward on his nose. His fingers drummed once on the countertop. "Good. Good job. Know your stuff, don't you? Valuable man. Listen and look along the docks. Report new people in key jobs. Anyone, British sympathizer, who might be slipping information out of New Orleans."

"And those are my orders?" Tabor's voice was flat.

"Right. Come back when you've more to report."

Shaking his head over the strange shopkeeper and his enthusiasm for information that could be gained from any passing seaman, Tabor strode into the tavern.

In the late afternoon several gentlemen already leaned against the bar. At one end a pair whose deeply tanned faces and broad-brimmed hats labeled them as planters drank dark beer. At the other, townsmen, pale by comparison, lifted tiny drams of poisonous green absinthe.

Recognizing no one, Tabor strolled slowly through the smoky atmosphere to lean his elbows on the polished cypress surface. He thought briefly about sidling in the direction of one group or another as he took a sip of beer, but with a mental shrug dismissed the shopkeeper's injunction. These men were not going to be discussing anything of any importance in that lazy shady interior.

He turned his thoughts to Judith's gowns, congratulating himself that he had selected the most beautiful fabrics in the dressmaker's well-stocked shop. She could count herself a lucky young lady that a pirate had gotten rid of those dark, dowdy things. Her bright hair and eyes needed shining fabrics and jewel colors to set them off.

He would see her in the Orleans Ballroom. Masked—as they both would be—he could ask her to dance. From behind the mask those brilliant blue eyes and red lips would smile at him as she danced in his arms.

He took another sip of beer and shifted from one foot to the other. God! Thoughts in that direction would be getting him into trouble in another minute. He took a deep breath and turned halfway around, leaning one elbow on the bar and surveying the room. ·

". . . fooled her father so completely that he does not see what she is."

"But, Maurice, *mon ami* . . ."

"*Non! Non!* You will not persuade me otherwise. Do I not see it every day? Talbot left her too long with her mother. Infamous woman. Notorious. I have heard the story many times. The apple does not fall far from the tree."

The men nodded sagely, mumbling agreement.

The one named Maurice lifted his glass and drank deep of the yellow-green absinthe, rolling the bittersweet syrup on his tongue.

Tabor clutched his drink tighter. At the mention of the name Talbot, he had stiffened. Now, as he listened, he felt his temper rising. They were talking about Judith.

The man continued, holding out his glass for the bartender to refill. "If you want proof, I ask you. Why does she work at the docks?"

His audience shook their heads in amazement at the temerity, the unnaturalness of such a female.

136

"Why does she walk where no female of good character would walk unescorted? I will tell you. She looks for lovers. She says she wants to work." Maurice's face darkened in anger. He fairly spat the word from his mouth. "Work! Does her father—that *parvenue* Englishman—not make more money than anyone of us? Work. *Sacre Dieu!* Not that one. A couple of hours and she comes running back with stories of pirates so she does not have to work. The captain himself of the *Portchester* reported how men were in her cabin during the voyage. They offered her money."

"But does Talbot know of this?" asked one of his rapt audience.

"*Non.* And he will not listen. I have tried to tell him. I have hinted. But he is my partner. I do not want to damage our friendship. How can I tell him that his daughter is no better than a woman of the streets?"

The others agreed that such a tale would turn on the teller.

"Pity the man who is taken in by her," one remarked.

The man who had spoken first laughed bitterly and tossed off half the liquid in the tiny glass. He paused as the wormwood seered his gullet. Then he slumped morosely against the bar. "He will be a great fool," he sighed, more than a little intoxicated by then. "But he will learn soon enough that others have been there before him."

The group nodded as one and patted him on the back. None noticed the man beyond their circle, leaning against the bar as if he had been turned to stone.

The waist of Judith's dress clasped her rib cage like a lover. Its décolletage—quite modest in comparison to Celeste's—seemed so low that she had gasped with shock the first time she caught sight of herself in the cheval glass.

When the hairdresser had finished with Celeste and

137

Laura, she had stared at Judith and at her dress for several minutes. Then she had gathered all her hair at the back of her head and let it fall in rippling waves from combs of silver filigree like that of her mask. The effect was as if she wore a fanciful helm of delicate silver and blue velvet.

Her final appearance before the cheval glass had somewhat relieved her shyness. Instead of poor, plain Judith Talbot-Harrow, she saw an exquisite stranger.

Now the expression on Beau's face as she descended the stairs made her blush hot and then cold.

"Judith!" He came forward to take her hands and kiss her cheek. "You're more beautiful than I could have imagined."

She turned her cheek to accept his kiss, then smiled shyly. "The dress you bought me is so beautiful, Beau." She smoothed the skirt lovingly. "Do I do justice to it?"

He hesitated fractionally. Now was not the time to talk. He stepped back to view her magnificence. "The dress is nothing compared to the wearer."

She smiled brilliantly. "Thank you so much for buying it for me." She turned to Celeste. "And thank you so much for insisting that I go to the ball. I . . . I'm quite looking forward to it."

Celeste smiled a little stiffly. Beau glanced nervously at her, then cleared his throat and took the cloak from the butler. "Judith," he said as he put it around her shoulders, "don't think about thanking people tonight. Just be happy."

"Indeed, *ma chère*," said Celeste. "Be happy. *Sans souci . . .*"

On the city line the Orleans Ballroom was ablaze. Branches and tiers of candles shone from sconces with mirrored reflectors that doubled and redoubled their power. Crystal prisms dripped from the chandeliers and reflected the flames from a hundred different angles.

Below, in the ballroom, the brilliantly gowned and bejeweled couples whirled and dipped through the patterns of shifting light. Fantastic masks covered the upper halves of their faces. Masks of papier-mâché painted with brilliant enamels. Masks of leather, of velvet, of silk. Masks of iridescent feather, incandescent scale, and opalescent pearl. Masks that swept up into magnificent antlers, back into flaring wings, and down into flowing mantles.

Judith sat by herself in the central tier of loges built on each side of the ballroom between the French doors. Not at all upset to be a *bredouille*, she had been relieved when Laura had told her of the arrangements made for the girls who came without escorts, and the chaperones. As a wallflower she could see everything without having to have a man's arm around her or try to perform intricate steps that she was sure to botch.

From her perch she watched, completely dazzled. Nothing in her life had prepared her for the splendor of this scene. Concealed behind her own mask of sapphire velvet trimmed with silver filigree, she swayed in time with the reeling, scraping fiddles that characterized American music.

Time and again she glanced down at the magnificent skirt that belled around her. Yards and yards of sapphire velvet shimmered and rippled over the horsehair petticoat. Surreptitiously, she slid her hand down the side of the skirt, luxuriating in its rich texture.

The gown was so different from the black dresses that had been her garb for so long. In it she felt like a different person. She took a deep breath and sat up straighter, smiling around her. For tonight she could be someone else, someone *sans souci*, as Celeste advised. "Without care."

The fiddles struck a waltz and she began to sway in her seat, trying to see everything at once. A figure threaded his way through the dancers. His body was cloaked in a silver-gray domino in the Italian style. Likewise, the upper part of his face as well as his hair was concealed by a tight-fitting cowl of silver-gray satin. In some surprise, Judith realized he was coming in her direction. Unsure, she looked to the right and left. No young and beautiful woman sat near her.

As the music came to a close, he bowed low before the rail of the loge and extended his arm. "May I have the pleasure?"

Judith stared down at him, trying to discern his features beneath the smooth-fitting cloth. She could not. The diamond patterns woven into the material created an optical illusion of shifting color. Only the lower half of his face and the strong column of his throat were bare. When he repeated the question, his voice low and deep, she felt a warm blush rise in her cheeks.

He noted it, his smile broadening, baring his white even teeth, a contrast to the bronzed skin. Patiently, he endured her scrutiny.

She did not recognize him, but since she knew almost no one in New Orleans of the male sex except sea captains and bosses of cargo gangs, she was not surprised. She had not planned to dance. The unpleasant memories evoked by the dancing master's touch had convinced her that she would never dance for pleasure. "No, thank you, m'sieur."

He swirled the corner of the gray satin domino over his arm. The silver tassel swept the floor as he bowed again. She could not help but notice that the enveloping domino was not for the purpose of concealing a corpulent figure. Slim waist and hips were clad in sleek-fitting small clothes of palest gray buckskin. Gray silk stockings covered a well-turned, muscular calf as he made a leg. "You must do me the honor, mademoiselle, or I die," he said, his voice mournful.

She chuckled throatily at that. "I beg to doubt that, m'sieur."

He took her hand and drew her toward the floor. "Aye, well, perhaps not die. But certainly fall very sick. Perhaps fade away to a shadow of my former self."

"M'sieur," she protested.

"Only a measure, m'lady. A bar or two. I beg you."

She shook her head, twisting her gloved fingers in his, finding them trapped. "I don't . . ."

He caught her other hand and turned her to face him, smiling coaxingly beneath his mask. Around her the dancers were forming their squares for the quadrille. He had led her straight to a place. The others were looking at her expectantly. "Have no care, m'lady. I promise you'll not be disappointed."

The orchestra leader raised his baton.

She had no time to puzzle the peculiar lilt to his speech. Hideous nervousness made her hands icy within their gloves. Her mouth was dry.

Smiling encouragement, he turned her to stand beside him. His silver-gloved hand slid across her back and clasped her at the waist. Faintly, she could feel the heat through the velvet and the silk chemise. She had steeled herself momentarily for his touch as she did with all men, but when it came, she did not find it unpleasant. Probably the clothing made a difference.

The orchestra struck the introduction. For an instant she froze, certain she would forget the variations Monsieur Braudet had tried so earnestly to impart.

"Relax," he whispered into her ear. "There's nothing to it."

She did not think why he would know she had not danced before. Her whole mind was directed to matching the proper steps to the rhythms. Beneath the mask her forehead creased with concentration. Then she was honoring him with a curtsy as he bowed to her.

It was easy, she decided. Her partner was a graceful dancer who led her confidently through the steps. After the first time through the pattern, she began to relax. Gradually, she became aware of a heady sense of fun. It was quite easy. She could see why people might indeed spend the night at a ball.

She had barely tolerated the dancing master's touch even though he was a man of some sixty years. When he

141

held both her hands over her shoulders for the schottische, she had disengaged herself with unmannerly swiftness and refused to learn that particular step at all. Why—when this man was no elderly dancing master—could she allow him to touch her without a quiver? Curiously, she studied the elegant figure as he danced with the lady on his left.

When the music ceased, he took her arm and kept her pressed to his side.

"Shouldn't you . . . that is, shouldn't we . . . ?" She looked questioningly around her. Many couples were indeed quitting the floor, but just as many remained where they were while new ones stepped into the places vacated.

"Do you have the next dance taken?" Her companion glanced down at her, a smile in his voice.

"Well, no . . ."

"Not that it matters one whit to me," he continued. "Let him find himself another partner. I have found mine for the evening."

She felt a bit of uneasiness at his possession. Rebellion stirred. "I thought that a gentleman never danced more than once with a lady. If he danced twice with her, then he was serious. If he danced three times, they were engaged."

"Not at a masquerade. That's the beauty of one. Nobody knows who is dancing with whom." A liveried waiter eeled through the crowd, bearing a silver tray of wineglasses. The silver domino took one and passed it to her.

"I never drink spirits," she protested.

"Wine isn't spirits. It's the stuff of life."

Stubbornly, she shook her head.

"A sip only," her companion insisted. "Surely, you'll not be disappointing me, m'lady?"

She stared at him hard for an instant. Where had she heard that turn of phrase before? Then the candles reflected in the blue light of his eyes and she lost her will to resist.

He held the wineglass for her and tipped the golden liquid into her mouth. When he took it away, he turned the glass so his lips found the spot and drank from it himself while she watched.

A tiny shiver ran through her—at the unaccustomed taste, she assured herself.

The orchestra began another introduction. Couples began to form two lines for a reel. The silver domino pressed her wrists together to brush his lips across the tender skin. Unaccustomed heat slid through her veins. While she curled her fingers in confusion, he bowed low, smiled, and took his place opposite her.

Midnight came and one o'clock and two. They ate together, a late supper of oyster pâté, of succulent pink shrimp and filets of trout from the waters of Lake Borgne, of tiny veal cutlets in a demi-bordelais sauce, of creamy white asparagus and mushrooms, of Roquefort and Camembert, of *gateaux* in the Parisian style.

Although she drank very little, her brain was spinning with the heat and nearness of him. Suddenly, the candles shimmered and dipped in front of her. She stumbled and caught at his arm. Glancing down, he saw her slide her gloved hand up under the temple of the velvet mask. "Faint?"

"Yes."

He guided her away from the floor, through the couples, and out onto the balcony to take the night air. When she shivered, he swept the domino around her shoulders.

She did not realize she was pressed against his body until she felt the entire length of him clad in silk and leather. Suddenly alarmed, she tilted back her head while her hand came up to thrust against his chest.

Quick as thought he kissed her. When she tried to protest, his tongue flicked across her lip and into her mouth. She pressed hard against his chest, doubling her fist. When he did not stop, she struck him once. The kiss deepened. When she struck again, she could muster even less force. The third time her hand slid up over

143

his shoulder.

"Beautiful, m'lady," he whispered against her mouth. "Sweet as honey."

"Please. I can't think."

"You shouldn't be thinking, you know. Only feeling. Isn't this what you want, after all?" Still keeping his arm about her shoulder, he moved until he faced her. Leather and silk against velvet pressed the skirt against her legs until it billowed out against the wrought iron grillwork of the balcony railing.

The music faded beneath the rush of blood in her ears. "I've never . . ."

"Shhh." She felt a quick light brush of his lips on her lips. A touch of fire. Another on her cheek. Another on her forehead.

"Wait." Her protest sounded weak, meaningless. The heat grew in her head and spread down her throat and across her chest. Her heart pounded. Suddenly breathless, she inhaled sharply. Her breasts pressed tightly against the bodice of her dress, the soft silk of her chemise suddenly rasping against her taut nipples.

"Why? Sure 'tis what you've been wanting since you came to New Orleans." He had found her earlobe, sucking on it, tracing the shell of her ear with his tongue.

She squirmed uncontrollably. "I don't understand."

When he spoke, his words were equally spaced, his voice hoarse. "I think you do. I know you do. Come on. Let's find someplace where we can be more at ease."

Go with him. Where? She could not leave the ballroom. "I don't think so," she protested. "I don't know you."

"Ah! But I know you, m'lady. It's you I've been waiting for all my life." In some dim recess of his mind he realized it was true. No matter what she might have done. No matter what they said about her. He shuddered with the force of his desire.

Her mind whirled. She had heard that distinctive lilt somewhere before. Where? Desperately, she tried to stiffen her body to resist its treacherous weakness. She pushed against him. "I really think we should go back in."

"And deny us both what we're mad to have?" He was incredulous.

She shook her head helplessly. "I don't know what you're talking about."

He turned up her face, staring into her eyes in the depths of the mask. "You've no need to pretend. I don't . . ." He swallowed heavily. "I don't care about any of that."

The chilly night air flooded her throat, her bare shoulders. But more chill were her words. She shivered convulsively, setting her teeth to keep them from chattering. "What are you talking about? Any of what?"

Her protestations of innocence disappointed him. He would have preferred honesty. He turned away with a swirl of his domino. The tassels at the hood and corners shimmered in the lantern light. "As you wish, m'lady. I did not think you were a cruel tease."

"I am not cruel," she denied. Darting after him, she caught at his arm. "How can I be cruel? And a tease? What do you mean?"

"To dance and drink and kiss all night long and not . . ."

"Not what? You asked me to dance with you, and I danced with you. I told you I didn't want to drink, but you insisted. I didn't ask you to kiss me."

"Quite an actress," came the bitter comment.

She blinked at the appellation. Once before she had been accused of acting. But she had not. She never had. "Who are you?" she demanded suddenly. "You searched me out, did you not? You wanted to dance with me. Who are you? You call me an actress and a tease as if you knew me. But I'm newly come to New Orleans. Perhaps you've mistaken me for someone else?"

"Oh, I know you all right, m'lady."

She shook her head slowly. "Perhaps you've mistaken me for someone else. I'm masked. You're masked. I don't recognize you. How can you recognize me?"

"I've seen you often." He leaned against the rough

145

bricks, his face hidden in the shadows, his arms crossed repressively in front of his body.

Her hands dropped to her sides, where she clenched them into tight fists. Was Laura correct? Had she ruined her reputation by working for the Talbot lines? A few hours ago she would have scoffed and said she did not care. Now, suddenly, she cared very much. She hung her head. "You've seen me working on the docks."

His voice was mocking. "Doing a man's work. Among men."

"I do what I have to do."

"You deal with dockhand and ship's captain. From the Talbot landau. Pardon me if I don't believe you have to do it. You do what you *want* to do? Am I right?"

She thought of her hard-won independence. Of her mother's shameful poverty. "No," she insisted. "I do what I must." She raised her chin defiantly. "Who are you that you know so much?"

"I know that you know things that no lady should know. Certainly, no young lady."

She stepped forward angrily. "I do an honest day's work. I will not be dependent on anyone."

He frowned. Perhaps his information had been incorrect. "Has someone imposed this on you? Do you have no one to protect you?"

How dare he impugn Beau. "I could have protection if I wanted. I simply do not want or need someone to take care of me. I can take care of myself."

He paused, nonplussed, then reason asserted itself. No woman would want to work in that environment. His mouth curled up at the edges in a sardonic smile. Her tastes must run to the rough and ready. "I'm sure you can, but you must realize it's not right."

She stamped her foot. "Who are you to judge what is right? I know what is right. What is right for me is to know about business matters."

He gaped at that. "Business matters."

"Of course. I shall learn all about . . . my father's business."

146

He relaxed somewhat. The man he had overheard had said she pretended to want to work. "And still you claim to be a lady?" His tone was regretful.

She stared into the shadows, trying to see him. He must be a scion of one of the old Creole families that Laura had spoken of. Proud, aristocratic, conscious of their place in society, they would want a lady by society's standards. And she was none.

Why did that bother her so much? Until this night she had wanted no man's approbation, except perhaps Beau's. But this man in the silver domino made her uncertain, uneasy, made her yearn for his smile and his approval. To be honest, she wanted more. She wanted to be kissed again. The night had turned cold when he had withdrawn himself. Could this be the desire that Laura had spoken of when she had told her how Clay Sutherland had kissed her and made her his?

Judith had no desire for society, but she desired this man. Were these the same kinds of feelings that Laura had described? She had certainly felt the loss of control a few minutes earlier when he had kissed her.

While she longed to return to his embrace, she was proud of the work he disparaged. She lifted her chin. "Since you despise me, I will leave you."

When she would have stepped into the light, he forestalled her. His voice was deep. "I don't despise you. I did not say that. I merely said that a lady would expect certain treatment. But a woman. She would know what she wanted."

She shivered beneath his touch. "I . . ." Her voice was a dry whisper. "I know what I want. At least I think I do."

"That takes a strong, experienced woman—to know her own mind."

She thought of the battles she had fought with her mother, her family, Lythes, and O'Halloran. She had had to fight her father and her father's partner to get to the docks. She shivered. "Do you want a woman like that? Or do you want a lady?"

He gathered her tightly against him. His face hung

147

above her, their mouths only a few inches apart. She felt every ripple of the muscular torso through his silken costume. "I want you," he murmured huskily, his breath commingling with her own. "And I think you want me."

What had Laura said? She did not care about her virginity so long as she could remain in control.

A loud laugh from one of the masquers close to the French doors made her turn her head. Inside was warmth and beauty. Outside was the man in the silver domino, a shimmering figure in the moonlight, with black shadows where his eyes were. Everything was happening too fast. And yet he said he wanted her. She could scarcely believe him. "Say that again."

He straightened away from the wall. "I want you."

A tiny frisson of trepidation made her clasp her arms. "And what about tomorrow?"

"Tomorrow? The masks come off."

"What does that mean?"

"You discover who I am." He loomed over her.

She took a deep breath. "Do you promise that I will?"

He placed his gloved hand over his heart. "Oh, yes, I promise. If not tomorrow, then very soon. There is another ball tomorrow and another."

"And we will be together at each one?"

"If you desire me."

A fire burned in her. She had thought she feared and hated men, but this man's touch set her aflame. No one could love her and she could not love anyone. She had accepted that. But she was not so naive that she had not dreamed of the sensual pleasures.

Taking a deep breath, she lifted her lips to his. He opened his mouth and received the tip of her tongue, questing, tasting him. Through her velvet he felt the heat like a brand on his own body. As she kissed him, one gloved hand caressed his cheek. The other slid around the back of his neck to press him down to her. He groaned deep in his throat as she withdrew her tongue, and his followed. Locked together, they stood for a long time,

148

drinking from each other, imprinting themselves on each other.

Finally, he raised his head, shuddering and sucking in a great lungful of the night air.

"I do desire you," she whispered.

"My God," he breathed. His hands, strong, warm, gloved in silver silk, cupped her shoulders, one brushed across the tops of her breasts, down over the peak, ruffling the sapphire velvet.

"What? What are you . . . ?" Beneath his touch her nipple hardened. She inhaled sharply, seeing that he could feel its response. A tiny whimper of sensual excitement slipped from between her lips.

"You're a wonder," he whispered, sure now that he knew what she craved.

She shivered at the compliment, not understanding what he meant at all, knowing only that she burned. Her legs trembled beneath her, forcing her to lean against him.

"Feel what you do to me," he whispered, brushing his thumb over her breast. "You make me hurt with wanting you."

"Hurt?" she queried dazedly. "How? I'm sorry. What did I do?"

The man in the silver domino was silent a moment. When he spoke, he gave a little chuckle. "I'm sure you know."

Dazed, she shook her head, but he caught her chin with his hand and kissed her. Deep, hot, without restraint, his tongue plunged into her mouth as his hands shaped her to match him. She moaned helplessly as shiver after shiver ran through her.

At last, for want of breath, he raised his mouth from hers and gave his head a quick shake as if to clear it. The enveloping silk of the domino had long been too hot for them both. "Come with me."

"Where?"

"You'll see."

Chapter Seven

An outside stairway led down into a small courtyard. Nerves prickling, blood racing, Judith allowed the man in the silver domino to draw her beneath his cloak and lead her across the damp stones.

A knock at a door, an exchange of money for a key, and in a moment they stood in a small, dimly lighted room. With swift impatient movements he stripped off his gloves and tossed the domino over a chair.

She stood behind him, poised for flight. "Where are we?"

Rather than answer, he caught her in his arms and brought his mouth down firmly over the last word of her question. His hands slid over her back to lift her to him. He smiled as he felt her arch, pressing eagerly against his body. Her lips, already parted, invited his caress. He kissed her long and thoroughly until she made a faint sound of pain or ecstasy. He could not tell which, for his own blood was pounding in his ears.

At last, breathless, he raised his head. Her eyes were closed; she swayed, dizzy with passion and excitement. As his hands caressed her waist and then slid upward to the slopes of breasts, she clutched fearfully at his wrists.

He kissed her brow. "So beautiful. You are so beautiful."

She shook her head, tears standing in her eyes. He was

150

lying. These were the lies of love that men had told Charlotte. But they sounded so wonderful. For the first time she could feel sympathy for Charlotte.

He kissed her eyelids then, and her cheeks, and the tip of her chin. His lips nibbled down her neck, then across her shoulder, all to the accompaniment of her tiny mews and sighs of pleasure.

"You love to be kissed, don't you?" he murmured.

"Yes." She was barely conscious that she spoke. "Oh, yes. I didn't know it could be like this."

He smiled cynically at her words. She knew exactly the right thing to say to make a man want her, to make him believe he was the only one. He kissed her again, then ran a long, strong finger across the top of her gown. Startled at the sensation, her eyes flew open. She opened her mouth, but he laid the same finger across her lips. "Wait. You'll like this even more."

He kissed her eyes closed again before tugging the sapphire velvet down. Even in the dim light he could see how white her breasts were. Her skin was fairer than he had ever imagined possible and so delicate that faint shadows of blue veins showed. For a moment he could only stare, dazzled by the purity of shape and color.

When he took one pink nipple between his lips, she moaned, then moaned again when his hand fondled the other. Helpless to still the fire in her blood, she writhed beneath the first touch of a man's hand and a man's mouth on her breasts. "Oh," she breathed. "I can't believe . . ."

He raised his head. His lips were flushed and moist from giving her pleasure.

She trembled at the sight. *Oh, Charlotte. Was this what it was like? No wonder you were lost.*

"You are so beautiful," he said. "I can't believe it either. And so responsive. I've never known a woman to enjoy this the way you do."

His words chilled a tiny corner of her fevered brain. "Have you known many women?"

151

"Not so many. Probably more women than you've known men." He planted a kiss between her breasts, then eased down on one knee. His hand dipped beneath her skirt, sliding up over the silk stockings, the delicate silk pantalettes.

She gasped and tried to step back, away from the unfamiliar sensation. To forestall her, he slipped his hand around the back of her thigh. The single layer of thin silk pantalette did not shield her from the heat of his palm. "I . . . I've never seen a man."

The caressing hand paused for an instant only. Then his fingers slid around her thigh and in through the slit in the pantalettes. "If you say so." His voice sounded faintly sarcastic.

She could not think what he meant. She could not think at all because he parted the curls and the hot flesh beneath to touch a spot so sensitive that she cried out. Her hands clutched at his shoulders, her velvet gloves seeking a purchase on the slippery silk. "What? What are you doing?"

"Shhh! It'll be all right. I promise. You'll like this. You'll like everything." His thumb had found the spot he sought. Now he rubbed it in a circular motion. At the same time, his mouth moved to her ear. "Is that right?" he murmured. "Does that feel right?"

Blood pounded in her temples. She felt as if she were one huge blush. "It feels wonderful," she managed to choke. "Oh. Please. Please." Her teeth set against the tide of sensation.

No woman in his experience had ever been aroused so easily. Perhaps that explained her searching for lovers. Perhaps men seldom satisfied her. With the countenance of a man performing a mission, he redoubled his efforts. Feeling her near to her climax as she writhed and twisted ecstatically against him, he steadied himself and grasped her more tightly.

"What are . . . you . . . ? I feel . . . sssso . . ."

He plunged his tongue between her gasping lips. The

heel of his hand circled hard where his thumb had been before, and his fingers parted the throbbing flesh and slid into the well of her body.

She would have screamed had she not been so effectively silenced by his mouth. As it was, a high, keening sound, inaudible beyond the walls of the room, set the blood singing in his veins. Clamping his jaw tightly, he steadied her spasming body. In the aftermath of unbelievable pleasure she hung paralyzed in his arms except for a quivering of muscles that would have let her collapse.

Once her climax was reached, he was afire with his own need. He held her impatiently until her breathing steadied. When she could get her feet under her, he turned her in his arms to unlace her garments at the back. With more than his usual efficiency, he dispensed with the fastenings of gown, petticoats, chemise, and pantalettes. Before she could make a protest of maidenly modesty, he lifted her out of the welter of her clothing and swung her up into his arms.

Setting his teeth to keep from exploding at the exquisite feel of her skin in his hands, he stretched her on the bed. His manhood—already stiff—leapt at the sight of her in the candlelight. Her mask was still in place, as were the blue velvet gloves that covered her arms. Her legs from the knee down were clad in pale blue silk stockings. Like some exotic creature of fantasy, she stretched before him, awaiting his pleasure with moist lips and swollen breasts, each peaked with a hard pink rosebud.

A bolt of lust erected him unbelievably to the hardness of metal. If he did not have her immediately, he would explode. With a groan he stripped off the rest of his own clothing. Leaving the cowl mask in place, he bestrode the bed and lifted her knees to his shoulders.

Her eyes flew open. "What are you doing?"

"Taking my own pleasure, m'lady," he gritted out with hoarse urgency. "You've had yours, but I'm not averse

153

to your enjoying me a second time."

"What do you mean?" Her voice was nervous, fearful, shrill with embarrassment. "No. You mustn't." She pushed herself up on her elbows and tried to pull herself away.

His jaw set, his nostrils flared slightly, he positioned himself between her legs, probing at the moist entrance. "Just lie back, m'lady. No need to continue the game. You do like it rough and ready, I surmise."

"Wait! What . . . ?"

He drove himself forward, greedy to sheathe himself to the hilt. Her question ended in a shriek of agony.

His mouth dropped open as the membrane split. His mind insisted that he must be mistaken, but the tightness of her passage contradicted him. Aghast, he withdrew, staring down at the bright smear of blood. He shuddered, his eyes flying to her face.

Her eyes were shut beneath the shadow of the mask. She groaned through colorless lips. Her breasts so swollen before seemed shrunken now, the nipples flat and pale with shock. Her mind whirled helplessly, unable to direct her brain or to summon up resistance.

Tabor knew he should rise and leave her now. He knew that certainly a gentleman would. One corner of his mouth curled up. But he was no gentleman. He was a bloody pirate. And she—she was a teasing fool. She had come so willingly, had kissed so passionately that she had indeed fooled him completely.

Well, this time she had gotten her comeuppance. The man Maurice had said she had had men with her in her cabin. She must have teased men for years. Promised much but given nothing. His eyes narrowed behind his mask. She was certainly no lady, leaving the ball with him, allowing him to touch her.

He glanced down at his throbbing shaft, a mindless instrument that demanded satisfaction. He could not pull away. Drawing a deep breath, he pushed into her again, this time encountering no resistance except the

154

delicious tightness.

She shrieked again and tried to drag herself away, but her shoulders came up against the headboard that boxed her neatly. Eyes closed, teeth gripping her lower lip, she lay in helpless submission while he bore down on her again and again.

He was finished in only a few thrusts, her hot, tight sheath exciting him unbearably. With a groan that reverberated through them both, he stiffened, then collapsed, pushing her thighs so tight against her breasts that she could scarcely breathe.

Though the time was blessedly short, Judith wished she would faint. Why could she not faint?

The man in the silver domino opened his eyes to see tears glistening on her cheeks. Instantly, he slipped her legs off his shoulders and stretched her out on the bed again. "Sorry to hurt you," he muttered. "But you were so good. So good. I lost control."

She tried to push herself away but found her muscles too weak with shock. The best she could manage was to turn on her side and draw her stiff legs up toward her chest.

He slumped over on his back, one arm over his eyes, trying desperately to think through what had happened. He had made a mistake, but of what proportions? Talbot's partner had been wrong in part, but perhaps not in principle. After all, Beau Talbot had left her in England, away from the family for all those years—with his divorced wife, for God's sake. A faint suspicion entered his mind. Was she really Beau's daughter?

Instantly, it was dismissed. Talbot would not have sent for her and allowed her to associate with his family had she not been. He shook his head. Still incredulous, he slipped his hand down to touch himself. The reddish-brown smear that came away on his fingers confirmed and accused him in grim silence.

As her breathing evened, Judith became aware of the chill. The sheets on which she lay had a clammy feeling.

The tears of pain had dried on her cheeks. She slipped her gloved hand down between her legs. The wetness she found penetrated the thin velvet of her glove. Unable to suppress a faint whimper of revulsion, she began to shiver violently.

Rousing himself, Tabor pulled the covers up from the foot of the bed and arranged himself in spoon fashion behind her. When she would have hitched her body away toward the edge of the bed, he put his arm across her waist and drew her warmly against him. "I'm sorry," he whispered for the second time. "I didn't mean to hurt you."

"You should be," came the quavering reply. "I didn't know it was going to hurt so much."

"You were a virgin," he muttered, his tone faintly accusing.

"Y-yes . . ." She fixed her eyes on the candle. "Couldn't you have been a little gentler or something?"

"I didn't . . . that is, I wasn't expecting you to be untouched. I thought . . ."

"That I wasn't a virgin."

"Well, you do work at the docks every day." His voice was stronger now that he felt himself on safer ground.

She stretched one leg experimentally. Evidently, she would survive. "I work at the docks," she said evenly, "for Talbot Shipping. I check the manifests with the captains and assign the loading to the gang bosses. None of that has anything to do with . . . what we did tonight."

"Evidently not," he agreed ruefully. "But a woman just doesn't do those things."

"I do," she interrupted coldly.

He sat up. The conversation was making him uneasy. "Evidently. But you really can't blame me for getting the wrong idea. Good God, I even heard your name discussed in a tavern. You got what you deserved." He rose and reached for the silk shirt. He turned his back to her and drew the garment on with fearsome haste.

Stunned, she lay still as his words sank in. So her

156

reputation was ruined as she had been warned it would be. And he was right. She had only herself to blame. She rolled over and sat up, crossing her gloved arms before her naked breasts. Her voice was low and humble. "I don't."

"What?"

"Blame you."

He spun around suspiciously. "What!"

"I was warned about working there. I was told that people would think I wasn't a lady." She smothered a sob.

Suddenly he wanted to take her in his arms. She was so small and vulnerable and so incredibly desirable—the mask, the gloves, the incredible whiteness of her skin, and the redness of her hair spreading like silk over her shoulders.

He shook himself sternly. He dared not. He had to think this through before he compounded his error. "Get dressed," he barked crossly over his shoulder. "I've got to get you back to the ball."

"What are you so angry about?"

"I'm not angry. I'm concerned."

"Just because I work on the docks doesn't mean I'm a . . . a woman like you think I am." The utter misery was apparent in her voice.

"Get dressed!" Roughly, he tugged his small clothes and silk stockings on, hopping on one foot and then the other rather than sit down again on the bed.

Judith slid her legs from beneath the covers and got her feet on the floor. With only a little light-headedness she stood. "You'll have to help me," she murmured. "I'm not able to fasten that dress myself."

"All right." He held the chemise over her head and pulled it down wrong side out. Numb as a doll, she allowed him to dress her, not even protesting when he hiked her up on his hip and stood her inside her petticoats. When the tapes were tied, he dropped the dress over her head and pulled the laces tight. "That

157

should do."

"My pantalettes . . ."

"Forget them." He made a wad of the soft garment and thrust it into the interior pocket of his domino. Facing her, he caught the glitter of fresh tears in her eyes behind the mask. With a curse he pulled her into his arms and began to kiss her. "Don't cry. Don't cry, damn you."

"I . . . I can't help it. I'll stop in a minute. It's just reaction. I always do it when I see b-blood."

"God!"

"I'm already stopping."

He held her out at arm's length. "Next time it won't hurt at all. I promise."

"Next time," she whispered. Her heart leapt. "Do you really want to see me again?"

Her voice, desperately hurt yet so pathetically hopeful, twisted his gut. "Of course I do. Why should you think that I wouldn't?"

"You said my reputation . . ."

"Shut up." His rough words belied the tenderness with which he pulled her back against him and began to stroke his fingers through her hair. One of the silver filigree combs dislodged. Holding her face between his hands, he kissed her softly on the mouth. When he had finished, it was a minute before either of them could open their eyes. Finally, he sighed. "Now, I really must get you back to the ball."

"My hair?" she protested faintly.

"It looks fine. Everybody's too drunk to notice anyway."

"My comb." She tried futilely to reinsert it.

Shaking his head, he took both of them away from her. "Don't bother."

"Give them to me."

"You don't need them."

"I want them. I'll tell anyone who asks that I took them out of my hair because they gave me a headache."

He shot her a strange look, then practically shoved the

158

combs into her hands. "You're so quick to think of a lie."

"Pinky, contact Reynolds. Find out all he knows about Talbot Shipping."

"They've been sailing out of New Orleans for ten years, Captain O'Halloran." The second mate shook his head doubtfully.

Tabor stood on the quarterdeck of the *Banshee,* his spyglass trained on the harbor. Specifically, he followed the movement of Judith Talbot-Harrow as she moved to the foot of the gangplank of the *White Cloud.* "Their new clerk on the dock is newly come from England. And the owners are British and French."

"Everybody's British and French that isn't Spanish. And Irish, of course." Mr. Pinckney crossed his arms over his chest and stared in the same direction. A faint grin lifted one corner of his mouth.

Judith with Georges at her shoulder stalked up the gangplank, a ledger in her hand. The captain of the *White Cloud* shook the hand she extended to him, then bowed her down the deck toward the forward hold. The party passed out of O'Halloran's line of vision. Disappointed, he lowered the spyglass and slid its parts together. "I'm an American now, Pinky," he said half to himself.

"And John Paul Jones was a Scot. And a nastier fella I never hope to meet again. And this Jean Lafitte is as French as they come. But they say he's claiming he's an American."

"Your point, mister?"

"From what you've told me, I misdoubt that Reynolds'd know a thing that's of any use to anybody. Especially if he spends his days in that dusty shop. If you want information about that pretty little red-haired girl, you're going to have to get it yourself."

"Dammit, Pinky. She dresses up in mourning during the day but goes to a masquerade ball at night." A stiff breeze ruffled Tabor's hair. He swiped it back from his

159

forehead with an impatient hand.

"Aye, in a dress you've bought her and wearin' a mask."

"Nothing about her makes sense. Maybe she could afford to throw the gold overboard because she was getting funds from someplace else."

Judith came back into view. Instantly, Tabor whipped out the spyglass and trained it on her again.

Mr. Pinckney sighed.

"And no woman would work down here on the docks. It's hot and dirty. And hard. It's hard work. Man's work."

He lowered the spyglass as Emil unfolded a small traveling desk at the foot of the gangplank. Judith seated herself on a folding stool and opened the ledger. She spread several papers that both men knew to be the cargo manifest on the desktop beside it. Georges raised an outsize umbrella and held it to shade her from the sun. "She's risked so much." He cleared his throat uncomfortably as Mr. Pinckney cocked an eye in his direction. "She has to be doing it for a very important reason."

"Money's a powerful important reason."

Tabor did not hear his mate. "America can't have the British sailing up the Mississippi River on Talbot ships. New Orleans so far has been out of the war, but she's a target. The British could sit on our backside and squeeze us into submission if they controlled the Mississippi."

"Yes, sir."

"And Napoleon wants her too. Montignac limps around rumbling and a group of people listen."

The mate snorted. "An old half-blind man with one foot can't have much of a following, Captain."

"What? No, Pinky. You're wrong. He was one of Napoleon's best. A general. Lost his eye and his foot in Russia."

"That girl down there ain't French."

"But Maurice Dufaure is. And Napoleon is on his last legs. He's got to have someplace to run to." Tabor

160

clenched his fist around the spyglass. "Damn! The plots are all too easy to see. Too obvious. There can't be anything to them. And yet, there's got to be something. New Orleans is too vulnerable and too valuable. The British War Office is staffed by a pack of fools, but sooner or later someone has to look at a map and come up with a bright idea."

"Not likely," Pinckney muttered.

"She could be collecting information for them right now."

The second mate stared as longshoremen wheeled crates down the gangplank. Each one paused in front of Judith, who made notes and marks in her book.

"Reynolds is right about one thing. If there's anything important, it's going to happen here at the docks. That's where the information is. The rest of them are just sitting around spouting off and waiting for the information to arrive just like we are."

Pinckney fixed a meaningful eye on the younger man.

Tabor grinned suddenly. "Miss Talbot will have an escort now, one that'll dance attendance on her. If she's spying, I'll know about it."

Judith felt a warm tide of relief flood her as she looked down from her seat on the top of loges. The man who the night before had worn the silver domino was staring up at her with hand outstretched. Tonight he wore black, unrelieved except for the stark white stock around his neck. The upper half of his face was covered by a black velvet mask. His own hair, she noted, was black and wavy.

With a tremulous smile on her face she hurried down to put her hand in his. "I didn't see you at first. I was beginning to be afraid that you hadn't come."

He bowed low over her hand. His lips brushed it. "I beg your pardon. I was delayed unavoidably."

She had thought about him almost constantly since he

had escorted her back to her seat in the ballroom and disappeared into the crowd of revelers. A riot of emotions had come between her and her work, her sleep, her food. She had steeled herself to accept his disappearance from her life forever. Now, with his hand holding hers, she felt exalted. "I'm so glad you're here now."

He led her to a spot on the dance floor where a quadrille was forming. "Your dress is different and most beautiful."

She held out the skirt of rose-pink tissue silk shot with gold threads, and smiled lovingly down at it. "Isn't it lovely? It arrived in the middle of the afternoon. I was planning on borrowing one of my sister's, but then this one came. This must have cost my father a fortune."

The orchestra leader tapped on the music stand for attention.

"But what better way to spend it?" he smiled.

She sank into a low curtsy to honor him. He crossed one arm at his waist and bowed. Her sapphire eyes shone brilliant with happiness through the slits in a gold mask that swirled out from the sides of her head in fantastic tendrils.

Each turned to honor the lady and gentleman at the corners of the quadrille.

When they stood up together side by side, she spoke again. "You don't think it's a complete waste of money?"

"Never. Never. Money well spent." He took her hand and they came together, then stepped back apart. In truth he had never seen anything more beautiful than her hair. Vibrant as cinnabar, it framed her face and tumbled down her back.

At the end of the dance he kept her in her place as he had done the night before.

"I've never had a dress like this," she admitted shyly. "Nor like the one I wore night before last."

"It's about time, then." He stared down into her face, fairly glowing with happiness and expectation. He felt a stab of guilt.

162

"I told my father that I did not care for balls. I fought against going. I would not have fittings for the gowns. I didn't even know they were being made for me until they started arriving."

"And how do you feel now?"

"I have never been so happy."

He cleared his throat and glanced around him. The other couples in the quadrille appeared to be equally engrossed in each other. "Even though I hurt you last night?" he murmured for her ears alone.

"It had to happen," she replied philosophically, a hot blush rising in her cheeks.

"You are a most unusual woman," he observed after a moment. "You must tell me all about yourself."

She flashed him a smile as the music began. "Not until we have danced this. I never thought I'd love to dance. And I don't. Except with you."

When the set was finished, he led her in the direction of the refreshment table and waited while they were served a glass of *bière douce*.

"Is this another kind of spirits?" she asked suspiciously.

"Only very mild," he promised. When she had tasted and found it to her liking, he prompted her again. "You're only recently arrived in New Orleans."

"How can you tell?"

"Your accent. It's British."

"That's right. I'm from England. I'll return there someday." She smiled at the costumed couples that danced by in a lively round dance.

Instantly, he was alert. "You're planning on going back to England?"

"Yes. I'm learning the shipping business from my father. I suppose I'm not telling you anything you haven't already figured out. My father is Beau Talbot. You said you'd seen me riding around in the Talbot landau."

"I've seen you," he admitted, his mouth tight.

163

"He owns a merchant fleet. When I've learned the business, I'm going to return to England and manage the line from that end." She paused. Her tone took on a pleading note. "I suppose I'll make my home in Portsmouth. I don't suppose you ever get to England, do you?"

"Sometimes," he replied repressively. "Does your father approve this plan?"

She shook her head. "I haven't even told him about my plans yet. I have to prove myself."

"You are most unusual for a woman. But it takes money to open an office. Even a branch. Are you rich?"

She laughed. "No. Everything I have, my father has given me. But I hope he'll see the sense of having an office in England as well and finance the venture until I can make enough money to pay him back. I'll work hard. Night and day if I have to."

"What about love and marriage? Surely your husband" —he gulped over the word—"would have something to say about that."

Her mouth went very tight. The smile disappeared. She looked directly into his face. "No one is ever going to love me. The only person who might want to marry me would be someone who wanted something I had. There's no such thing as love."

His mouth dropped open. He took the glass from her hand and set it down on the table beside his own. Taking her arm, he led her out through the French doors. "What do you call what we had last night. And what we're going to have later on this evening?"

She felt the blush begin to rise in her cheeks. Nevertheless, she did not allow her eyes to drop. "I don't know. What do you call it?"

He dropped her hand and turned away to brace himself against the rail. Why did her question provoke him so? "If you didn't believe you were in love, you should never have let me touch you."

She joined him, looking down into the dark courtyard.

164

"Love, so I'm given to understand by those who claim to have experienced it, grows out of mutual respect after long acquaintance. We had known each other only a few hours. It could not have been love."

He ran his hand through his hair in frustration. "It . . . it was a form of love."

"You said I am not a lady. And you then certainly are no gentleman. You should not have wanted to touch me. A gentleman should not want to know a woman he could not respect."

"Dammit! I respect you."

"Do you really? Well, I respect you too. You've been very honest with me. Except you haven't told me who you are?"

He suddenly felt guiltier than ever. He gathered her into his arms and began to kiss her forcefully. "Damn you. You are the most exasperating female."

She responded by clasping him around the waist and hugging him to her. Her frank pleasure in the kiss excited him. This was all going too fast. She set his mind to whirling. He could not argue with her. He could not think of words to refute her arguments. He set her away from him and stepped back.

She sighed, her eyelashes fluttering up. She smiled dreamily.

"Why did you come to New Orleans in the first place?" he asked, his voice hoarse.

She looked at him with some trepidation. "Are you a friend of my father's?"

Instantly, he was alert. Had she been hired by the British government without her father's knowledge? Perhaps he was going to learn a secret. "Of sorts."

"You know so much about me. I hope you won't tell my father."

"God, no." *But I might tell Reynolds.*

"When will you tell me about yourself?"

He felt a need to confess, but not before he found out her political leanings. "I'll make a bargain with you. You

165

tell me about yourself tonight and I'll tell you about myself tomorrow night."

She shrugged. "There's so little to tell."

"We'll have that much more time for dancing."

"My mother and father divorced after he came here to America. It was a great scandal. She kept me because I was too young to go with my father. The thought was that I would be better guided by my mother."

"Evidently, she did a good job," the man in black grinned. "Look at you."

She shook her head. "None of what you see before you can be attributed to my mother's influence."

"Who else influenced you?"

"I suppose all my relatives did. But not in the way intended. My mother drank to excess. I can't stand the taste of spirits. My grandmother wished I'd never been born. But here I am alive. She wanted me to marry immediately and become dependent upon my husband, but I refused. My father didn't really want me here in New Orleans. But here I am anyway. He didn't want me to work on the docks. But that was the only place his partner would allow me to work."

A deep frown creased the middle of his forehead. He stared grimly at her. "And his partner is . . ."

"Maurice Dufaure. He hated me on sight."

"Surely, you're exaggerating."

She looked at him squarely. "I'm not in the slightest."

"And that's all? You haven't told me why you came to New Orleans."

"No, I don't suppose I have told you the actual reason that brought me here." Lythes's shadow flitted through her mind, but she did not even tremble. He was far away. "Nor do I want to discuss it anymore. I'm tired of talking. Let's dance. Then when the music has soothed my mind, we can come back out here on the balcony and kiss and kiss."

He shook his head in amazement. "How can you say there's no such thing as love?"

166

Laughing, she took his hand to lead him back into the light and the music.

"You may be too tender," Tabor protested as he raised his mouth from hers. One hand caressed the silken inside of her thigh. "I don't want you to have a single bad memory about tonight. I want you to be completely happy."

"I have never been so happy." Judith stared up at him, her eyes luminous in the candlelight. She had removed her mask and set it aside. Then he had lovingly removed each piece of her clothing, kissing her as he did so. When she lay nude on the bed, he had stripped off everything but his mask and come to her.

"Yes," he breathed. "But I'll make you more."

She pressed her thighs together as his skillful fingers traced intricate patterns on the soft skin.

"Don't," he whispered against her ear. "Let me go where I will."

"But it's unbearable."

"Good." He trailed his kisses across her cheek to the corner of her mouth. "Good. You'll die of pleasure."

"Die?" She arched her back, thrusting her breasts into prominence. Her breath came out of her throat in a gurgle of pleasure as he slid lower to cover one of her nipples and take it into his mouth.

His tantalizing fingers continued their play. She sought to pull her thighs together again, but this time he put his knee between them, holding them apart, a prey to his touch.

"Please," she sighed. "Oh, it's too much."

"Is it?" He raised his head. His face beneath the mask was dark with passion.

"You know it is," she managed to say through set teeth. A faint film of perspiration gleamed on her forehead.

"I know." He kissed her cheek, then her breast, the

167

cup of her navel, the nest of red curls at the base of her belly.

She gave a startled cry.

"Shh," he cautioned. His fingers gently parted the soft nest of hair to find the moist velvet skin beneath.

"What are you . . . ?"

The tip of his tongue stroked across the center peak.

She cried out and raised her thighs, trying to bring them together. Instead, she clasped his broad shoulders.

"You're . . . you're . . ."

"Shh. It's pleasure I'm giving you."

"But . . ."

"I'm only kissing you, m'lady. Only kissing." He dropped his mouth again and sucked gently.

She caught her breath of a sob. Her fingers clawed at the sheet, gathering up handfuls of it in the frenzy of shyness and pleasure. She could only think such feelings must be terribly wrong. Then she could not think at all.

His clever mouth drove her to the top of a peak, then over its edge into an abyss where her whole body seemed to shatter into a million bodies, each feeling unutterable delight.

He paused only a minute to give her time to float gently back together. Through slitted eyes she looked down to see his face, his eyes glittering through the holes in his mask, his mouth glistening with moisture. As she stared, he grinned like a devil, then dropped his face again.

"No," she whispered. "You'll kill me. You mustn't."

But he did. This time the attention of his mouth was rougher—his tongue, his lips, his teeth, delicately excoriated her sensitive flesh until she was sobbing in her frenzy. Her nails bit into his shoulders, holding him closer until with a scream of furious pleasure her climax came again.

He hoisted himself up on his knees and hauled her spasming body onto his thighs, hauled her closer still until their bodies joined. The wildness that had possessed her was as nothing compared to the exquisite sensations that rippled all along her sheath. Climax after climax crashed upon her until she fell spinning into oblivion.

He threw back his head as his own climax began. Blood, breath, and bone joined together, then rent apart, in a contraction of superhuman effort followed by an explosion that sent his consciousness whirling away.

They lay as they had fallen, joined together, one body, limbs wrapped around each other, hands clutching, gasping mouths open to drink the nectar of sweat-salt skin.

Chapter Eight

The ledger was not in its proper place.

Frowning, Judith lifted the hinged top and came behind the counter. Cautiously, seeking to avoid criticism from her father's partner, she lifted several stacks of papers on the open shelves.

Maurice Dufaure looked over the top of his spectacles, his black eyes glittering like jet. "My dear Miss Talbot-Harrow. Did you have a good time at the ball last night?"

His raspy snarl startled her. She snatched back her hand and turned half around. "Indeed I did, M'sieur Dufaure. The . . . er . . . ledger has been misplaced."

"I have it here." His fingers tapped the black and red leather cover. The long, darkly stained nails made clicking sounds. She reached for it, but he did not move his hand. "And your sister, did she have a good time at the Golden Fleece?"

"The Golden Fleece?"

He nodded solemnly. "The Golden Fleece. The most notorious gambling casino in New Orleans. How regrettable for poor Celeste. The last of the Devranches, one of the finest of French families. To be so disgraced."

"My sister did nothing disgraceful."

He grinned maliciously. "She has long made a fool of herself over the gambler Sutherland."

Judith shook her head obstinately. "You are mistaken,

M'sieur Dufaure. She despises Clay Sutherland."

Dufaure's shrug was a masterpiece of Gallic insolence. "We of the old blood say that the Americans and English are all the same—no breeding. What a pity that the gossip will reach Celeste." He made a clicking sound with his tongue. He leaned across the desk. "Your sister—in a fit of jealousy over her lover—attacked the voodoo priestess Jena Benoit."

Judith stared at him aghast, then drew herself up coldly. "You're mistaken. My sister would never do such a thing for the simple reason that she would never lose control of her temper."

He laughed unpleasantly. "Of course she will deny it. But you may ask her yourself."

"I shall do no such thing."

He nodded, still insolent. "A good idea. She might turn on you and ask you about your behavior."

"Mine." A frisson coursed up her spine. "M'sieur Dufaure, give me the ledger and let me be on my way. I don't intend to stand here and listen to you malign my family any longer."

"*Certainement.*" He extended the book, but when she took it, he held on to the end. "I sincerely hope your pleasure was worth the shame of consorting with a common pirate."

"A pirate?"

His malice a tangible thing, he watched the color drain from her face. "Tabor O'Halloran of the *Banshee.*"

"Tabor O'Halloran?" A cold pit opened at the bottom of her stomach. She clenched her hands tightly around the book and rocked back on her heels.

"The very one who removed your clothes on board the *Portchester.*" Dufaure's grin was diabolical.

She could feel the color draining from her face. "You must be m-mistaken."

Dufaure ignored the stammered words. His eyes never leaving her white face, he removed his spectacles. "How fortunate for your social life that you did not have him

171

thrown into the Cabildo as you threatened to!"

"T-Tabor O'Halloran."

"*Mais oui*," he chuckled humorlessly. "The pirate himself. Did I not tell you that New Orleans was full of pirates? I do not doubt that Jean Lafitte, too, was at the Orleans Ballroom."

Each word was crystal clear despite a ringing in her ears. "At a ball attended by the best families in New Orleans?"

"When everyone is wearing masks, what can anyone expect? It was for this reason that the Spanish forbade the balls and the Mardi Gras. No one can tell whom she is dancing with. Unless, of course, an assignation is arranged."

"An assignation?" She tottered back against the wall, every last vestige of reserve wiped away in her horror.

"*Naturellement!* Is it not the same in England as in France? One must pay for the gowns that one wears. It is expected." Pitilessly, he leaned forward, his left palm flat on the desk. He thrust the ledger toward her as if it were a rapier.

She straightened at that accusation and snatched the ledger from him. With an attempt at hauteur, she stalked to the door. "My father buys my gowns for me as he does for my sister and my stepmother."

"So strange that he does not buy them all from the same modiste."

Judith did not flinch. The pirate she might have met, but her father would never allow such a breach of good manners. "I would not repeat such slanders if I were you, M'sieur Dufaure. My father would be extremely angry to hear them, and know they came from you."

The Frenchman rose lazily while she was speaking, almost as if he had become bored with the whole conversation. Thrusting aside the edge of his frock coat, he consulted his watch. "If they were slanders, he would have a right to be angry. However, since they are not, he can have no complaints." He looked pointedly at her.

172

"You will be late, Miss Talbot-Harrow, if you do not hurry on your way."

She clutched the doorknob tightly, making no move to turn it. "I have not allowed a pirate to pay for my gowns."

"Oh, perhaps you did not know?" His sneering voice denied such a remote possibility. "But everyone else did. How sad to be so ignorant. It smacks of . . . *je ne sais quoi?*"

"My gowns were paid for by my father," she insisted through gritted teeth.

"I doubt that Madame Estelle would have made such a mistake in where to send the bills."

"Madame Estelle . . . ?" Horrified, she remembered the name emblazoned on the huge box that had arrived yesterday afternoon.

"On Royal Street." Dufaure reseated himself and adjusted his glasses. Dipping his pen into the inkwell, he began to write.

"But of course, mademoiselle. The rose pink shot with gold. I remember it well, as I do all my gowns."

"A s-sapphire-blue velvet."

The old woman glanced at her sharply. She lifted her chin, the powdered crepey skin rising out of the delicate froth of lace. "I consider that dress to be one of my finest achievements. It was a special order made in great haste. The young man paid double for it, but the craftsmanship was exquisite nevertheless."

Judith thought the pain would rip her to shreds. She swayed where she stood, her eyes closed tightly.

"Mademoiselle!" Madame Estelle struck the floor with her cane. "Irma. Irma. Come help her to a seat."

The assistant hurried from the back of the shop, but Judith caught herself up instantly. "No. I'm all right. Believe me." She waved the girl away. "Madame, you are absolutely sure that a young man paid for those

173

two gowns."

"And for a third as well, more magnificent than the other two. Green silk, *Eau du Nil*, most delicate stuff, very expensive. It requires great artistry to sew correctly. The cost of the gown is . . ."

Judith waited to hear no more. Spinning on her heel, she left the modiste talking to thin air. Outside the shop in the bright sunlight, a terrible pain struck her behind her eyes. The pain in her head was nothing to the pain in her heart.

"Did you care so little about me that you'd let another man buy my clothes?" Judith had to clench her hands tightly to still their shaking. Her heart was pounding in her chest and perspiration wet her upper lip.

Beau could not meet her eyes. "Why not? He owed you," he blustered out.

Judith drew a deep breath, trying to will the pain to go away.

"It wasn't that I didn't care about you. It was just that he insisted."

"He insisted! He's a pirate. A common felon. Even if New Orleans regards him as sort of Robin Hood, I don't find him so entrancing. How did you think I'd feel about that?"

"You didn't say anything about it when he met you on the street," Beau countered.

"You knew about that?"

"Hell, yes, I knew about that. He came to me and apologized. Most abjectly, I might add." Smiling one of his most endearing smiles, Beau looked hopefully at his younger daughter. Judith was staring at him as if at a stranger. Beau hurried on. "He begged to be allowed to replace what he had destroyed."

"My God, Beau. You don't let criminals pay you back for robbing you."

Inwardly, Beau cursed her analytical mind. There was

174

a lot of her mother in her. Neither Celeste nor Laura ever talked back to him as she did. "Judith," he began, striving for patience, "he didn't rob you. He accidentally —accidentally—damaged your clothing."

"Accidentally damaged? Beau, he and his crew systematically tore everything I owned to pieces. They even destroyed the trunk I was carrying it in."

Beau whipped out a handkerchief and wiped the sweat from his upper lip. "He explained how it happened. It was all a misunderstanding."

"And you believed him?"

"I had no reason not to. He is a gentleman and my friend."

Judith shook her head. "Beau. Let me understand you. You know this pirate personally. He raided your ship and took a man and wife off it, perhaps to hold them for ransom. Perhaps to kill them. And you consider him a gentleman and your friend?"

Beau poured himself a pony of whiskey and took a large, steadying swallow. "He is my friend."

"Would you care to explain how this can be?"

Beau Talbot bowed his head. "I can't, baby."

She could not believe her ears. "You can have secrets with a pirate that you keep from your own daughter."

"You don't need to know." He all but whispered, glancing furtively at the door.

"I'm not Laura nor Celeste. I'm not sheltered and frail. I work in your business, Beau. I had hoped to—" She clamped her mouth closed on her words. Now was not the time to tell him of her hopes and dreams. Perhaps the time would never come.

"Hoped to what?"

She turned away in some confusion. When she thought of a way to finish her sentence, the ending made her voice break and quiver. "To be part of this family. To be accepted."

"My God, Judith, you are."

She hurried on, struggling for control. "I didn't expect

love. I can understand how when you don't see a person for years and years, you don't feel anything for them except a sense of responsibility."

"Judith, baby . . ."

She stepped close to him, looking up into his face. She could feel the years roll back. She was pleading again, but this time with no hope. "You didn't have to spend the money for fancy clothes. I didn't need them, nor want them. I was pleased to be allowed to live here in your house and go to work for you every day."

"Judith. I would have bought you the clothes if he hadn't insisted that he was going to buy them."

She pressed her fingertips to her temples, massaging the throbbing pain. "For God's sake, Beau. Don't lie. If you were going to buy the clothes for me, where are they? He ordered my gowns less than a week before the ball. Madame Estelle told me he paid double the price so they could be finished."

Beau Talbot flushed angrily at being accused of lying. "Now, just a minute. Celeste took your measurements and ordered everything, but when Tabor came along and wanted to replace what he had destroyed, I was happy to let him. I didn't cancel the orders for the other things. You'll have twice as many beautiful clothes. Everything worked out for the best."

In that instant she hated her father. Hated him with all the strength in her body. Was there no one in this whole world she could depend on? No one she could trust? Worse. Was there no one who would do her a kindness?

She spun away from him, giving him her back so he would not see the look in her eyes.

"Judith . . ." He reached out to her bowed shoulders.

"Don't! Don't dare touch me!" Each word was perfectly spaced.

He snatched back his hands as if from a hot stove. Frowning heavily, he retreated to the liquor cabinet to replenish his whiskey. "I . . . I didn't think you'd mind. I thought you'd be pleased."

176

"Didn't think! No wonder he sought me out at the ball. He was the man I met, wasn't he?" Beau looked wary. "The man in the silver domino. The man in black."

Miserable, he nodded. "I wanted you to have a good time. I thought you would. You did, didn't you?"

"Is that all you think is important? My having a good time?"

"You've never had a good time. I thought—"

She screamed at him then. "If you wanted me to have a good time, why couldn't you have introduced me to someone nice. You let a pirate pick me off the wall and occupy my time both evenings."

"Judith . . ."

"At least *Grandmère* would have taken me to Almacks and let me meet an honest man."

"Tabor *is* honest."

She laughed hysterically then. "He's a bloody pirate with a fearsome reputation. The men on board the *Portchester* were terrified. They recognized his battle flag and struck sail immediately."

Beau leaned forward earnestly. "Judith, that incident was not what you think."

"Are we back to that again? But, of course, you can't tell me what I am supposed to think."

"No."

She steadied herself. Hurt and hate had turned to icy rage. Her father was exactly as she had characterized him in her mind. Failing her when she needed him. Had her mother felt this way? Alone, having to shift for herself, dependent on a man who did not provide. "Then I'll leave you. There's no point in continuing this discussion."

"Judith. What are you going to do?"

She turned eyes, hard and glittery as gemstones, toward him. "Why, I'm going down to the docks, Beau, and sign the manifests for the *White Cloud*."

"You don't have to do that. I'll do it for you. You need to get ready for tonight."

"I'll have plenty of time."

177

He looked at her closely, unable to fathom her mood. "This is Violette de Beauvaliet's *bal masqué* tonight."

"I remember. Her mother reminds me of *Grandmère*."

"You shall have a ball too, Judith," he promised softly.

She raised an eyebrow, as scornfully as her grandmother had ever done. "So Celeste said, but I believe she has been too ill to take up the burden of the arrangements."

He looked around him wildly, presenting the perfect picture of a man at the end of his tether. "That shall all be rectified."

"But not this winter, Beau. Lent is almost upon us." She might have been discussing the most mundane of affairs.

He swore, then shrugged helplessly. "Then in the spring."

She looped the strings of her reticule around her wrist. "I must go. I mustn't keep Georges and Emil waiting."

The *bal masqué* to announce the debut of Violette de Beauvaliet was to be preceded by an intimate gathering of some fifty guests in the family house on Dauphine Street. Since the distance was only a matter of around the corner and down a couple of streets, they would walk rather than join the line of carriages waiting to get through the narrow streets and pull up under the *porte cochère*.

The family had already assembled in the salon when Judith came downstairs swathed from head to toe in an enveloping domino.

Celeste's smile of welcome was dimmed by curiosity. "But what is your dress like, *chère* Judith? You should not have put on your cloak until you have shown it to us."

"Yes, Judith, let us see it," Laura urged. "Is it as beautiful as the other two?"

Her sister did not smile. "Every bit. Madame Estelle informed me that watered silk is especially delicate. It

178

requires great artistry to construct a dress made of it. It is very expensive." She looked straight at her father, who winced.

"We'll all be surprised by it at the ball," he suggested heartily. "Come, ladies, let's be off."

The streets were well lighted by lamps as well as by the lights of carriages rattling and rumbling over the cobblestones. The narrow sidewalks were also crowded with walkers, mostly masked, their elegant costumes concealed beneath flowing cloaks. Everyone in New Orleans was going somewhere that night.

Before they reached the door of Maison Beauvaliet, Judith had managed to lag behind. As the door opened to admit Celeste, Laura, and Beau, she stopped at the foot of the steps to slip off her shoe and shake it.

"Baby?"

"I'll be right behind you," she called sweetly. "I've got something in my shoe."

Although Beau threw her a doubtful look, the butler was already ushering them into the house. Judith waited a full minute before she, too, mounted the steps.

Thank heavens for Celeste's predilection to arrive fashionably late. Inside, the party was at its height. No one would notice her. A maid escorted her up the stairs to a dressing room.

Staring at herself in the mirror, she clasped her hands to her hot cheeks. Far from exhausting her, her fury had fed itself until she was fairly trembling with outrage.

Stripping off the elegant green and silver mask, she flung it contemptuously on the dresser. From the pocket of her domino she drew a strip of black cloth that she had fashioned for herself. Careless of the hairdresser's best efforts, she tied it in place over her face. A stranger stared at her. A stranger with flushed cheeks and glittering eyes.

Clutching the domino around her, she started down the stairs.

She spied him immediately, stubbornly refusing to consider the emotions involved in finding one man

179

unerringly in a room full of masked people Did he sense her too?

He ended his conversation and bowed himself out of the group. She could see his head turning from side to side, his neck stretched to look over the heads of the crowd. He was searching for her.

From her vantage on the staircase she regarded him dispassionately. He was dressed in a midnight-blue coat of superfine dove-gray trousers and black patent leather pumps. His vest was silver. He wore a blue mask as well.

A betraying warmth began at the bottom of her belly. How she hated him for arousing that feeling in her. It signified the end of innocence, the end of purity she had not known she possessed until it was lost forever to this monster.

She continued down the steps, her eyes never leaving him. Her hands relaxed around the domino, allowing it to fall open, revealing the plain black wool dress beneath. A half-dozen risers from the bottom she came to a halt.

He turned at that moment, recognizing her. His mouth beneath the mask curved upward in a wide smile. He started threading his way through the crowd toward her. At the bottom of the stairs he saw the black dress. His eyes darted upward to her face, clearly reading the expression in her eyes. Abruptly, he stopped, then came on more hesitantly.

She did not move, but held him with her eyes. At the foot of the stairs he stopped.

"Tabor O'Halloran," she said clearly.

His smile disappeared. He held out his hand. "Judith," he whispered urgently. "Let me explain."

"Tabor O'Halloran." Her voice was louder this time. Several people looked around.

He leapt up the steps to take her arm and draw her down the stairs, but she threw him off, hanging on to the banister.

"Tabor O'Halloran!"

Across the room, where the receiving line was formed,

180

the hostess faltered in her conversation with Celeste and Beau.

"Judith . . ."

With a glance toward heaven as if imploring its intervention, Beau excused himself hastily and started toward them.

"Pirate! Thief! Kidnapper!" Her voice rang clear across the room, startling the guests into an uneasy silence.

Celeste's face turned white. Madame Beauvaliet snapped open the fan that dangled from her plump wrist and began to cool herself vigorously. Laura's eyes widened in alarm at the sight of her baby sister struggling on the staircase with a man.

Couples leaned toward each other, whispering, muttering, pointing. Tabor hunched his shoulder as if to shield her from the sound. Judith shuddered. "Come away with me," he begged. "I can explain everything."

"Can you really? Can you really! Oh, I'm sure you could have if I had not been warned about you."

"Who warned you?" His eyes narrowed intently.

"I would never tell you," she sneered. "Even if you tortured me. That's something I'm sure you're capable of doing. Likewise, a bloodthirsty *pirate* would be only too eager to get revenge."

Beau came up beside them to take her arm. "Judith. Let me take you out of here. You're obviously distraught."

"Oh, I'm distraught, Beau. I've been distraught for hours. All afternoon I've been planning how to *kill* this monster."

The word rushed through the assembled guests like a squall from the gulf. Their hostess, who had made her way to the edge of the circle that had formed around the foot of the staircase, uttered a shriek and fell fainting into her husband's arms. Every other eye was trained with avid interest on the little tableau.

"I can explain," Tabor insisted between clenched

181

teeth. He stepped onto the same riser as she and tried with his body to shield her from the ballroom. His head rose above Judith's so that she had to cling to the banister to keep from toppling backward.

"Then do so!"

"Not here."

"My reputation is shredded here with these people," Judith sneered. "Mend it."

"Your reputation."

"Tell them the truth, Beau," she prompted.

Her father backed a step, shaking his head.

"Tell them the truth."

"Judith, please. You're making a scene. Celeste . . ." He looked over his shoulder for his wife but could not locate her in the sea of curious faces.

"By all means, go take care of your wife," his daughter shouted.

Beau's head snapped back around. Tabor looked from one to the other in astonishment.

Beau seemed to shrivel in the light of Judith's steel-blue glare. "You are exactly as I expected you to be," she informed him.

Beau backed down another step.

"Will you let go of that banister and come with me?" Tabor gritted out.

"No. I shall stand here until you tell them that I had no idea that you had bought those dresses for me. Nor did I know who you were when"—she gulped in embarrassment and raised her voice—"when you seduced me."

"My God!" Beau reeled back. His face was white with shock, then his eyes narrowed. Fists clenched, jaw set, he climbed another riser to confront Tabor.

"Who is that girl?" a woman's voice shrilled.

"Hard to say," a man replied in a bored tone. "But Talbot and that new fellow O'Halloran seem to be at daggers drawn over her." He raised one eyebrow critically. "Strange garb for a mistress. Mourning black. But who can understand the English?"

182

At the word *mistress*, a muffled wail from the crowd revealed all too clearly that Celeste had overheard. Beau Talbot roughly pulled Tabor around until they were facing each other. "Is she telling the truth?"

"Of course I'm telling the truth."

"Judith!" Tabor spat out furiously. Flinging off Beau's hand, he caught her around the shoulders and pressed his hand over her mouth.

Her eyes blazed at him between the slits of the black mask. She opened her mouth and bit down hard. His curse was music to her ears.

"Do you know who this is?" she yelled, struggling around his figure, clinging to the banister with both hands, leaning over their surprised faces. "This is a pirate. A pirate! A robber and murderer, a kidnapper and vandal, and God knows what else!"

"Shut up!" He grabbed her around the waist and tried to carry her away with him, but she had fastened like a limpet to the polished wood.

"Stand aside, sir," Beau demanded. "You'll not hurt her."

"Dammit. I'm not going to hurt her." At that instant Judith kicked his shin. "Ooof! Damn you. She's hurting me."

"Shall we all go into the dining room for a light refreshment?" M'sieur Beauvaliet called nervously. Between him and a servant, his wife hung supported, her face sickly pale.

"No!" Judith screamed. "Listen to me!"

Far from moving off through the archway, the guests edged closer, their avid faces upturned. "He robbed my father's ship and tried to ruin me. He's bought me clothes and wanted all of you to think that I've become his mistress. You all think you know about me because your dressmaker told you so."

At the word *dressmaker* Beau closed his eyes. In pain he put out a hand to lean against the wall for support.

A wild cry followed by a small confusion occurred in

183

the middle of the room where Celeste had fainted. The guests in her vicinity parted to give her air, but the rest of them were listening in horrified fascination.

"Shut up!" Tabor thundered.

"No!" Judith twisted around, still clinging to the rail. "I'm not your mistress!" she screamed in his face. "Tell them. I'm just some poor stupid girl that you seduced. Tell them!"

"Be quiet!"

"Tell them! You tore up my clothes. Everything I owned in the world, you destroyed. When you boarded the *Portchester*."

He pried one of her hands loose and then the other, and tried to lift her into his arms. "Come with me!"

She kicked violently. Her heel landed on his kneecap. He cursed again as his leg gave way, dropping him down on his knee. He had to grab for the banister to keep from falling backward. "He's a pirate! He's Tabor O'Halloran of the *Banshee!*" She doubled up her fists and struck at his head. One caught him on the ear.

Cursing fervently, he ducked his head under her flailing arms. His arms opened to catch her around the knees and hoist her onto his shoulder.

"You'll answer to me, sir," Beau Talbot gritted out.

"At your convenience," Tabor acknowledged over Judith's kicking legs. Grimly, he marched down the stairs.

"Help me!" she screamed, twisting and squirming, trying to grab hold of something, anything to stop his progress. "Help me," she beseeched the faces, but they registered a mixture of shock and amusement. "Help me."

Past the amused, the puzzled, the horrified, he strode. At the door he halted and faced the room, his arm locked firmly around the back of Judith's knees. "I beg your pardon, Madame and M'sieur Beauvaliet and you, dear Violette. My mistress has done this to me in a fit of jealousy. She is very demanding."

184

"Liar! Pirate! Monster!"

He spanked her smartly on the rear. "When I get her home, I intend to beat her. Your servant, M'sieur."

"Pirate! Damn you!"

He executed a sketchy bow, as competent as her violent struggles would allow. As he turned, she caught hold of the drapery that masked the arch. As he carried her through it, the fabric and rod ripped away behind them.

Beau laid Celeste tenderly on the chaise lounge in the upstairs dressing room.

"Can I get something for madame?" the footman asked from the doorway.

"No—yes. A little sherry."

"That would be good." Celeste's lips barely moved. Her eyes remained closed.

The footman bowed his way out. Celeste's eyes opened at the sound of the door closing. "Beau," she whispered.

He dropped to his knees beside her and took her hand between his. "As God is my witness, dearest heart, I would have given all I possess to have spared you this night."

She smiled. "Don't be too upset, *mon cher*. They will work it out between themselves."

"But the shame, the embarrassment. The stains on your good name."

"Don't be ridiculous. The Devranche name has survived more escapades than this. In the past both women and men in my family have fallen prey to strong passions. And so have most of the rest of those people below. All is forgiven for love."

"But . . ."

She put her finger over his lips. "Don't worry about me, dearest Beau. Worry about your unhappy daughter."

Beau climbed to his feet, his initial worry about Celeste replaced by anger at Tabor O'Halloran. "I'll call the scoundrel out."

Celeste uttered a faint cry and pressed her hand to her forehead. "Oh, do not. Do not," she whispered.

He dropped down instantly, taking the hand, kissing it, kissing her forehead where it had rested. "Celeste."

"I could not bear it if you were injured. Oh, dearest Beau, your daughters are young and impetuous. They are good girls most of the time. But they cannot be perfect. Let them work out their mistakes for themselves. I beg you."

"Celeste . . ."

"I beg you." Her dark eyes were drowned. Crystal drops trickled down her magnolia cheeks.

He thought her the most beautiful person in the world as he kissed her again and rested his forehead on her shoulder. She stroked her palm across his thick wavy hair. It was streaked with gray.

"I want to return to *Ombres Azurées*," she whispered at last.

He shivered beneath her touch. "Celeste . . ."

"Tomorrow," she said firmly.

"Celeste, I have the press of business . . ."

"Just so you return to me at night. I must have you beside me, Beau."

He sighed. "I promise."

Her heartbeat steadied at his whispered words. The days were for business. Only the nights would mean danger, but at *Ombres Azurées* he would be safe.

Outside on Dauphine Street, Tabor did not set Judith down immediately. Like a man astride a tiger, he feared the claws when he should dismount.

The walk was still crowded with merrymakers hurrying to their parties and balls. Carriages crept along the narrow thoroughfare, many with tops down to take the warm night air and display their passengers' magnificent costumes.

Tabor brushed by a group of promenaders, who stared in amazement, then turned and laughed and pointed at

Judith as she punched ineffectually at his waist.

Their laughter made her slump. All the righteous indignation went out of her. Far from punishing Tabor O'Halloran, she had succeeded only in punishing herself.

And no one in New Orleans would help her. She raised her head again. Among the crowds of people, no hero leapt forward to save a lady in distress, no minion of the law ordered him to halt and unhand that woman. Nothing. Merely laughter.

She should have known. *She should have known.*

"Put me down." Her voice was low and tight, but it reached his ears.

He stepped into an archway and warily set her on her feet. Then, holding his hands placatingly in front of him, he stepped back.

She did not look at him. Not that she could have seen his expression in the depth of shadow. Instead, she straightened her black dress and adjusted the mask on her face.

"Judith . . ."

She tried to brush by him. He put up his arm to bar her way. She stared at it, still not looking at him.

"Judith, why in the name of all that's holy would you do such a thing?" His voice carried equal parts of anger and disgust.

She flinched, then straightened and put her hand on the bend on his elbow. "Let me pass."

"No. Not until we've talked."

"I can't talk tonight." Her voice broke. "I really can't."

She sounded as if she were about to cry. He quickly stepped aside and allowed her out of the archway. "I'll see you home."

"Thank you. It isn't far." She picked up her skirts and hurried along Dauphine. He had to increase the length of his stride to stay beside her.

When she turned into Conti, he put a hand on her arm. "I can explain," he began.

"Explanations aren't necessary." She could see the *porte cochère* up ahead.

He took her arm as she climbed the steps. At the door she reached for the knocker, but he caught her arm. "I'll see you tomorrow."

She did not acknowledge his statement. Instead, she spoke through clenched teeth. "Please let go of me."

He stepped back. "Don't push Beau into a fight on this," he warned.

The door opened and light spilled out onto her. "I wouldn't think of it." Her face beneath the black mask was white as chalk. Even the lips were white. "Whatever is to be done, I'll do myself."

She stepped inside and closed the door behind her.

Interlude III

Judith froze as the knock sounded at the door. She threw a nervous glance over her shoulder. The movement tipped her sideways on the small stool. Off balance, she dropped the shoe she was trying to pull on her foot. Again she glanced unhappily at the door. She very much feared the knock signaled the death of her hope to dress and leave the house before the others awoke. With a sigh she righted herself and reached again for her footgear.

The knock sounded again, a little louder. Then Laura, her nightrobe belted tightly around her, pushed the door open. Her eyebrows rose as she saw her sister already dressed. Then, her voice quivering with angry disappointment, Laura hurried to her sister's side. "Judith Claire, why did you do this?"

Unable to look up, unable to face her sister's accusing green eyes, Judith kept her head ducked, her whole attention centered on crossing the grosgrain ribbons about her ankles. "I don't know," she murmured awkwardly. "I really don't know. I thought I was doing the right thing. For everybody."

"You announced your seduction from the staircase! If only you had told me . . ." Laura stood above her sister, reflected in the cheval mirror, her silk robe drawn tight around her, her hair down her back.

Feeling at a disadvantage on the low stool, Judith gave

189

the ribbon a last hard tug and rose hastily. Laura's face in the mirror accused her of awful things. Judith's rebellious spirit countered with a question. "Is that any worse than your getting into a brawl with a voodoo priestess in a saloon?"

Laura's green stare flickered, then she lifted her chin. "I was fighting for *Ombres Azurées*."

And I have nothing at all to fight for. Holding on to the mirror's frame, Judith bent and tugged on her other shoe with unnecessary force. "You weren't thinking of your reputation when you got into that fight." She lifted her foot onto the low stool and bent to tie the ribbons.

"I couldn't help it. She attacked me."

"I couldn't help it either, Laura." Judith straightened and stared into her sister's face reflected in the mirror. To her surprise, she realized that Laura's eyes were not angry. Unfortunately, the sympathy in them hurt more than condemnation would have. "Perhaps I wasn't fighting for something as noble as *Ombres Azurées*," she whispered, still to the reflection in the mirror. "But my cause was no less just. I was deceived and tricked." Nervously, she cleared her throat and continued in a stronger voice. "I wanted to set the record straight. I wanted to expose Tabor O'Halloran for what he was."

"Instead, you exposed yourself." Laura turned her back to the mirror and walked away. "I don't know if New Orleans society will ever forgive us for this."

Suddenly, conscious that she had been holding her breath, Judith let it out on a sigh. She reached out to touch her sister's shoulder, then thought better of the gesture and dropped her hand. "They'll forgive *you*. And what they think doesn't matter to me."

Laura shook her head. "Of course it does." Her answer came a little fast; her voice sounded a little shrill as she turned back.

"No. I don't care," Judith contradicted flatly. Her own voice shook as the memory came flooding back. "An entire roomful of men and women stood and laughed while I was swept up and carried off against my will. It all seems like a nightmare. All I wanted was for everyone to know what he was and what he had done to me. I was the one hurt by him." She spread her hands in a plea for understanding, then whipped them away into the folds of her skirt. "It all seems like a nightmare now," she repeated.

Her voice broke. *Oh, God! Don't let me cry.* Crying would be like an admission of guilt. And she didn't feel guilty. At least not about that.

Did Laura's furious expression soften just a bit? But no. Her voice sounded different when she spoke. "Oh, Judith, if only you had told me what you planned to do, I could have advised you."

Judith could feel her eyes smarting with unshed tears. "I don't know that I would have listened, Laura. He had done so much that was wrong and was getting away with it. I got so mad I couldn't stand it." Blinking rapidly, Judith turned away to fumble in the drawer of her dressing table for her black gloves.

Laura gravitated with her sister, peering intently into her face. "At least I would have stayed and been there to stop him."

One glove was on. Then the other. Eyes no longer prickling painfully, Judith lifted her head. "Would have stayed! Where were you?"

Laura hesitated. Bright color rose in her cheeks. "I was at the Golden Fleece."

"With Clay Sutherland?" Judith could feel a tight knot begin to form in her stomach. *What had Laura done?*

"Yes."

"Do Beau and Celeste know?"

"Not yet."

Judith hesitated, then managed a disdainful shrug. "I don't know why they would be upset about your taking a gambler for a lover when they allowed a pirate to buy gowns for me."

"They probably wouldn't care so long as I handle the

affair discreetly. That's the key in society. Discretion."

With head lowered to smooth the fine kid gently over her fingers, Judith could still detect the bitterness in Laura's voice. When she was satisfied that her gloves were perfectly smooth, she spoke. "I'm not going to live a social lie. That's why I warned you that society was not for me. I told you I didn't want to go to the ball."

She turned to leave, but Laura caught hold of her elbow. "The ball has nothing to do with this. All you want to do is check cargo on the docks with Georges holding your parasol as if you were queen of the Nile. Your decision to work on those damned docks precipitated this."

Revivified anger flooded through Judith's veins. "I had no control over that either. Maurice Dufaure refused to have me in the office, and Beau didn't want to stand up to him. Besides, it's honest work and I'm learning the business. And this didn't begin on the docks. Tabor O'Halloran boarded my ship in the middle of the Atlantic. He ruined everything I owned. And when I saw him . . ."

"You wouldn't have seen him if you hadn't been on those docks."

Judith felt the barb sink home, but she managed to keep her face impassive. So much would not have happened if she had not been working on the docks. So much that her sister knew nothing about. "When I saw him, I tried to have him arrested, but nobody would pay any attention to me."

Lifting her chin, Laura crossed her arms tightly across her chest. "Yes, M'sieur Dufaure has told us how you behaved in the streets."

"Damn him. He had no business to tattle on me."

"He wasn't tattling. He's as interested in our reputation as we are. The business of Talbot Shipping depends upon goodwill and a good reputation. Besides . . ." She smiled briefly for the first time during the painful interview. "He's worried about what could

192

happen to you."

Judith gave an unladylike hoot of laughter. "Laura, Maurice Dufaure would be overjoyed if I walked off the edge of the dock and sank like a stone to the bottom of the Mississippi. Besides, he's not your friend either. He's the one who told me that you had gone to the voodoo ceremony. I didn't tell on you because I'm not a sneak." She tried to edge her way to the door. Her hand reached for the knob. A quick twist and she would be away. "I never wanted to be a part of this anyway. You and Celeste forced me into it."

Laura laid her hand flat against the door facing, keeping it closed. Her voice was low, intense. "No, Judith. We didn't. You agreed."

With a sigh Judith let her hand fall. "I tried," she whispered. "I really tried. Even though I didn't want to."

Laura stepped back. "I thought we were ready to take our place in New Orleans society. You and I—the Talbot sisters. We could have dazzled them. As it is, neither one of us has exactly covered herself with glory."

At the sadness in her sister's voice, Judith felt as if a heavy hand were constricting her chest. "Oh, Laura, we really have made a mess of this, haven't we? Just like our mother before us. What are you going to do about your masquerade with Clay?"

"I don't know."

"A gambler isn't eagerly welcomed into the ranks of the finest Creole families."

"I know. I know."

Judith made a dismissive gesture. "On the other hand, you can have a discreet affair, as Celeste wants. Even though he isn't invited, he knows he's welcome just as pirates like Tabor and even Jean Lafitte know they can come to the balls. This is the city where everyone wears a mask."

"Not Clay. He wouldn't come where he's not invited."

"Since when do men like him need an invitation? He's like Lord Lythes. He doesn't care whether he's invited or

193

not. He goes where he wants to."

Judith saw Laura's jaw tighten. *Now what did I say,* she thought. Suddenly, she realized she was weary of the whole ludicrous conversation. Prey to the most violent emotions ever since the dressmaker had confirmed Maurice Dufaure's tale, she could regard the fiasco as serious no longer. She gave a helpless giggle.

Laura stared at her, color rising in her cheeks. "I'm not going to listen to you criticize him, Judith Claire."

But Judith giggled again. "Oh, yes, you are, sister dear. You started this conversation. Clay Sutherland is a man like any other. He's no better but no worse. You have to face a few home truths about him. Laura, listen to me." She managed to stop the giggles and straighten her mouth into sober lines. She put her hands on her sister's shoulders. "Every time someone says something you don't want to hear, you run away."

Laura pulled out of Judith's grasp. "I do not."

Again the urge came to giggle. "You do too. And every time something goes wrong around here, you blame me when you're just as guilty as I am."

"I don't. How dare you say that!"

Judith shook her head in amusement. "I denounce a pirate at the Beauvaliets' *bal masqué* and I've ruined the family. You have a secret affair with a gambler, and that's all right."

"You didn't denounce a pirate, little sister. You made public your indiscretions."

Judith stopped smiling. Once more she would try to make Laura understand one very important fact. "Why has it become my indiscretion and not his?"

Laura drew back. She started to speak, then paused. Her smooth forehead wrinkled. "Because it's a rule of our society. A society that caters to the male. A gentleman does not carry the responsibility of proving his virtue. A lady does."

"But that's not fair."

"No, it's not. Society's rules are frequently not fair,

but they work for the majority. Judith, surely you can see the fight in the Golden Fleece is altogether different from the scene that you created."

Judith shook her head adamantly. "I don't see how. There were just as many people present in the saloon as in the ballroom. And probably many of them saw both scenes."

"I told you I was fighting to protect *Ombres Azurées*. I couldn't have the workers rebel against authority because of voodoo."

"So making a spectacle of yourself is all right for you because it's good and right, but when I do it, it's bad and wrong. Laura, can't you understand? I was trying to make a point? Tabor O'Halloran is a lying, thieving pirate. I had to denounce him, or at least make an effort to."

Laura pressed her fingertips to her temples as if the new idea were painful. "We've ruined everything."

Judith made a rude noise. "If everything is so easily ruined, it must not have been worth much anyway."

Dropping her hands, Laura shook her head sadly. "I just feel so bad about tearing down everything we've worked for ever since Papa came to New Orleans."

"I thought you said that marrying Celeste was the way Papa and you were accepted into society."

"That's the way we were accepted into society, but not the way we have stayed in society's good graces."

Laura seemed so truly upset, Judith felt sorry for her. "Lord Lythes told me once that society is fake. The people in it are all liars in one way or another. No one shows his true colors. Everyone hides behind a mask of some kind. I didn't believe him until those men and women stood there as they did."

Laura sank into a chair and rested her palm against her forehead. "You're right, Judith," she whispered in a voice that trembled.

"I am?"

Shocked, Judith dropped to her knees in front of her

195

sister. The pale face looked drawn. Dark smudges showed beneath the green eyes. Judith took both Laura's hands and squeezed them tight. For the first time she was ashamed of hurting Laura. For the first time she saw her sister as a friend and possible ally. Perhaps they really could be the Talbot sisters.

Chapter Nine

"I've come to return these." Judith clasped her hands tightly around her reticule. Behind her stood Georges, three long boxes stacked in his arms.

Tabor scowled furiously. The events of last night had upset him much more than he cared to admit. He rested his hands against the door facings, filling the opening with masculine arms, chest, and shoulders.

Only by dint of willpower did she keep from falling back a step. She tightened her mouth and her grip on the reticule. "I've brought you your property. You bought and paid for them."

"You could have thrown them out in the street. You didn't have to come here," he replied without a glance at the three huge boxes Georges carried in his arms.

Judith kept her eyes firmly fixed on a spot just to the left of his ear as she stepped to one side and motioned to her footman to carry the boxes through the door.

"Don't bring that stuff in here," Tabor objected. "What am I supposed to do with three worn dresses?"

"Only two of them are actually worn," came the frosty reply. "I would suggest that you give them to your mistress, whoever that unfortunate woman may be. It would be a shame to waste such beautiful materials and such exquisite craftsmanship."

"I don't have a mistress."

"You could have said that last night," Judith replied coldly. "Instead of lying and further defaming me."

The black man looked anxiously from one to the other. Tabor shrugged, then dropped one arm to his side. Instead of stepping back into the room, however, he came outside into the hallway of the dockside hotel. There he leaned against the wall, his arms crossed over his chest. "Did you think they were beautiful?"

Judith met his eyes, then sniffed and tossed her head. "I thought they were beautiful. They were the most beautiful dresses I have ever seen. They were the most beautiful dresses I have ever w-worn." Her voice broke. "They are still beautiful. That is why I am returning them to you."

"But you won't accept them?"

She shook her head. Her eyes fell to his chest. He wore a white cotton shirt, open at the neck, revealing the strong tanned column of his throat and a curl of black hair. Its full sleeves had a discreet ruffle that fell over the backs of his hands. His trousers made of dark broadcloth with stirrups under black half-boots fitted his long body to perfection. Even dressed casually, he caused a small ache in the pit of her stomach. If she allowed herself to think about the intense pleasure of their two nights together . . .

Her mouth tightened. "I'll never knowingly accept anything from you."

Tabor remembered the purse of gold. He ducked his head and ran a hand around the back of his neck. She was dressed as he had first seen her, as he had always seen her—in unrelieved black. Even the white piqué bonnet had been discarded for an imposing black felt with no trace of ornamentation. To a man who had seen her dressed in sapphire velvet and rose silk, who had known the delights of her willowy body, the ugly clothing was a tragedy. He felt himself stir at the brief memory of her breasts when he had freed them from the clasp of her bodice to kiss and fondle them.

"They were not intended as anything but reparation," he sighed lamely.

"I don't accept reparation from thieves. Georges!"

"Coming, Maîtresse."

The black man came out into the hallway. Judith turned to lead him down the stairs, but Tabor caught her arm. "Dismiss him," he demanded. "You and I have things to discuss."

She flashed him a look of intense dislike, then stared down pointedly at his hand on her arm. "I don't think . . ."

"Dismiss him."

"Georges. Wait in the landau."

The black man threw him a disapproving look. "I can wait at the bottom of the stairs," he suggested.

"A good idea."

Tabor drew her back into the room and closed the door. She faced him warily, her hands clutching the string of her reticule. After a couple of hesitations he finally began. "Last night I was going to tell you who I was. I swear."

"When I was lying under you, helpless," she suggested nastily.

His teeth flashed in a brief grin. "As good a place as any and better than most."

"I will leave you now," she exclaimed haughtily. "We obviously have nothing to say to each other."

"Hold on." He grabbed her arm as she tried to move past him. "We have a lot to say."

"Take your hands off me. Never touch me again. Never."

"Never."

"Never."

He removed his hand and bowed formally. "I beg you to accept my most humble apology, m'lady."

She waited, her back straight, her chin up.

"I . . . this is very difficult for me to say. I didn't mean to . . . that is, I didn't set out to seduce you."

"Am I supposed to feel better because your act was unpremeditated?"

"You can if you like. I was going to dance with you a couple of times, to get you circulating among the young men, then step back and disappear into the crowd."

"How very noble you make your intentions sound."

"They were. I swear. But when I danced with you you were so sweet. I wanted to dance with you again. And again. And then when we kissed—" His voice had deepened. He leaned toward her. One hand rose; its fingers brushed gently against her arm.

"Please." She shivered violently. "Don't remind me."

He did not change his tone. "But I want to remind you, and me too. The feelings between us were very special. Unique. I've never been so powerfully attracted to a woman."

"No."

"Yes. It's true." His hand dropped to his side. He straightened formally and bowed low again. "M'lady, I could love you. I was half in love with you before we ever went to that room. When I found you were a virgin and the daughter of one of my best friends . . ."

"You're lying," she contradicted him fiercely. "You knew I was Beau's daughter, and you knew I was unmarried before you took me into that room."

He continued as if she had not spoken. "You wanted to come with me," he reminded her. "You loved everything I did to you. Everything. You positively bloomed under my touch. I've never seen a woman so responsive. I was special to you."

"Having never had a man before, I have no basis for comparison," she snarled. "You might be like every other man in the world for all I know. Or every other man in the world might be better."

His eyes sparked dangerously at her words. "Do you intend to go and find out?"

She flinched in horror. "No! Never again. I find myself shamed unutterably by my attraction to a man who lies and steals and seduces from behind a mask. If I can't control myself any better than that, I can't trust myself again. Not with any man."

His mouth turned up at the corners. "Coward," he murmured softly.

"A burnt child fears the fire."

He put out his hand to touch her cheek. "You don't have to be ashamed of yourself."

She allowed the caress for only a second before jerking her head away and stepping back. They stared at each other for a moment before she assumed a hopeful tone. "You profess to have a special feeling for me, but you embarrass me and destroy my reputation in the town where I'm making my home. If you were any kind of friend to me, you'd make a public declaration in my behalf."

He sighed then and shook his head. "I can't."

She nodded as if she expected no more. "Then you're lying to me. About everything," she declared flatly.

He crossed his arms on his chest. "You embarrassed yourself," he reminded her severely. "You destroyed your own reputation. I didn't make a spectacle of myself on the staircase in the Beauvaliet mansion."

"No! You lied."

"There were reasons. You should have confronted me alone. You were a fool to bring it all out in the open. If your reputation is in ruins, it's your own fault."

The look she threw him was pure malice. "I beg to differ with you. I tried desperately to save it. Or at least lessen the damage you had done it."

"I hadn't done it any damage."

"I'm leaving."

He jumped in front of her and leaned his back against the door. "We haven't finished our conversation. There's still the matter of your feelings and mine."

"I am handling my feelings, Mr. O'Halloran. I did not want to come into this room. You dragged me in here."

"I can explain about the reputation thing. If you had

kept your mouth shut, no one would have known where your gowns came from."

She pointed at the striped boxes on the bed. "Madame Estelle counts among her clients the very best Creoles in this city. She knows all their secrets, and if she doesn't tell all, her shop assistants certainly tell the clients' servants."

"As long as no one admits to anything, it's only gossip."

She would not be put off. "Gossip is what destroys reputations. Not truth. My mother was destroyed by gossip, forced to retire to a gamekeeper's cottage and left to die. Her own mother wouldn't come to her funeral."

He shook his head. "You just won't see reason."

"Tell me what your reason is," she pleaded suddenly. "Tell me why you didn't tell everyone that I wasn't your mistress."

"A man does not marry his mistress."

She gaped at him, then raised her eyebrows. "Are you proposing marriage, Mr. O'Halloran?"

He hesitated. He had not meant to say anything about marriage. The parson's mousetrap was not for a seafaring man.

She flushed angrily as the silence grew between them. "It doesn't make any difference anyway. I should have said no. And anyway, I shall be returning to England as soon as I can."

"What? Your family lives here." Suddenly, her words brought his suspicions surging back full force.

"My father and sister live here. They have lived here for many years." Her pride made her draw herself up tall. "I am an Englishwoman. I am a Harrow of Harrestone. Judith Claire Talbot-Harrow. My grandmother has promised me a beautiful come-out."

"Why did you come here in the first place?" The question was rapped out with more force than necessary.

"I came because my father and sister begged me to

202

come and because—" She bit her lip hard. She had no wish to remind herself of Lord Lythes and his threats.

"Because . . ." he prompted.

"My reasons can have no interest to a pirate."

His anger had been building. She had admitted she would be returning to England very shortly. Why should she go if not to take back the information she had collected? She admitted, even boasted about being a member of peerage. She must be the spy. Her connection with Beau Talbot had presented the British War Office with a perfect opportunity. The thought of her debut, doubtless financed by the British government, made him inordinately angry.

He ground his teeth. "Bloody hypocrite."

She gaped at him. "I am not a hypocrite."

He could see her in the rose silk dress, making her curtsy to the bloated Prince of Wales, smiling at him, while British troops escorted Irish landholders off their property. "You and your whole kind are," he choked. "You tell yourselves that the world belongs to you. You come in and take over land that people have worked and bled and died for."

"I've never . . ."

But he would not be stopped. "You think you can have America. That's what this bloody war is all about. You think that any man that's American was born British. Any man under an American sail is a British sailor. Any land that's owned by an American is British land, and you have the God-given right to it."

"Mr. O'Halloran."

"That's what you did in Ireland. We weren't strong enough to fight there. Too bloody many of you. But here in America you're outnumbered. And we'll win." His face had turned dark with passion. His fists clenched to do battle with British foes. "In Ireland there were too many . . . too many for Timothy and Thomas and . . ."

"Tabor," she said. "Tabor!"

He caught himself up. His eyes cleared, but the furies

still looked out of them. "You expect me to crawl to you," he sneered. "You expect me to apologize for spending a fortune on your clothes and satisfying that big itch you've got between your aristocratic—"

Her fury no less than his, she struck him across the mouth with all her might. A shaft of pain lanced up her arm, and her hand stung with the force of her blow. "I do not expect you to crawl!" she lashed back. "I did not ask for clothes or for your attentions."

The blow stopped his flow of words but fueled his anger. Suddenly, it was directed particularly at her. "Damn you."

"Stay away from me." She stumbled back too late.

He caught her by the shoulders, dragging her forward again. "Damn you!" His fingers sank into her tender upper arms, bruising, punishing.

She cried out, but he did not hear.

"Damn you!" She was everything he hated and everything he wanted. Beautiful, proud, well-born. English, enemy, lover. Like a doll he lifted her and shook her until her head snapped forward and backward on her shoulders. Tears spouted from her eyes as the pain shot up her spine.

As suddenly as he had grabbed her, he flung her from him. She staggered and fell to the floor, stunned. He stood over her for a moment, gasping for breath.

She looked up at him. The expression in his eyes made her fling up her arm to protect herself.

The pathetic gesture stopped him dead. What was he doing? He had almost hurt her. Had hurt her, he corrected himself. The anger faded from his eyes. He raked his fingers through his black hair, then wiped his palm across the lower half of his face. "Forgive me," he said. "I'm sorry. I didn't mean to hurt or frighten you, but you provoked me."

Warily, she scrambled to get her legs under her and climb to her feet. "You did the same to me," she whispered hoarsely. "I'm sorry I struck you."

"I can take it." He reached for her, running his hands

204

over her, ascertaining that she was not seriously injured. "Are you all right?" he inquired, his voice shaking.

She stood for his handling, then stepped away quickly when he had finished. "I'll be going."

"It would be best."

"I should never have come."

"No. But you should never have gone with me that first night."

"No." She clutched at her reticule. Her hand hurt. She could see the imprint of her fingers beside his mouth. She closed her eyes against the pain in her heart.

Suddenly, he groaned. With a violent movement unavoidable in its speed, he caught her to him and kissed her. Her lips were cold and lifeless no matter how he tried to warm them. At last he put her from him. "Don't let pride rule you," he warned.

"Pride is all I have. I won't let a thieving pirate . . ."

He laid a gentle finger on her bruised lips. "This is America. Things are not always what they seem. One man's traitor is another man's hero."

She stepped away from him. "I'm an Englishwoman and I'm going back to England just as soon as I can."

He opened the door for her. His face like stone, he waited while she walked through. Outside, she turned to face him. "You needn't worry about my continuing to harry the authorities about your piracy."

"You relieve my mind."

Her lips twitched coldly. "Maurice Dufaure told me that pirates are quite the thing here in this primitive frontier. Probably Jean Lafitte was at the masquerade too."

He waved his fingertips out to the side of his face in mocking imitation of a dandy dipping snuff. "We're very cosmopolitan here, y'know, m'lady. All nationalities, all trades."

She lifted her chin a notch. "I am merely warning you."

He straightened alertly. "Warning me?"

"I don't intend to ask for help. But someday . . .

205

someday I will have an opportunity to pay you back for this. And when that time comes, I will take it. I swear it."

He cocked his head to one side. "Let me know if you have a cargo stowed in the hatch. We'll talk more reasonably then."

At first she did not understand him. While he watched, his meaning flooded her innocent mind. The color washed from her face, leaving it pasty white. One fist—clenched so tightly that the knuckles showed white—pressed hard against her mouth. Then dropped. She spun on her heel and ran down the stairs.

He shut the door behind him and leaned his forehead against it.

God! What a bloody mess! What had possessed him to cut up her peace like that? If she were pregnant, she wouldn't know for weeks. Now, thanks to his mouth, she would have to live with the fear of that in addition to her other problems.

But she knew the way to tear a patch off him. He whistled thinly. Like a blue-steel blade cutting through butter, her words had sliced through his own peace. Shamed, was she? By her uncontrollable attraction for a man who steals and lies and seduces from behind a mask?

He grinned ruefully. He hadn't realized what a very devil he was.

Her come-out in British society would be considerably dampened by a pregnancy. And if she were pregnant? Carrying his child?

The thought stopped him in his tracks. All vestiges of masculine ego were wiped away by the thought. What would he do? Marry her. A lady. There was an earldom somewhere back in her family. Beau Talbot himself was from a fine old family. What would he think about his daughter marrying a pirate?

Damn! The whole situation was a disaster. Everyone was angry and upset at everyone else.

Dufaure. He was the informer here. He had told Judith the identity of her midnight lover. His name had not come up in this investigation. What could Maurice

206

Dufaure have to do with this? Where had Talbot picked up such a partner? Money had to have been the reason. But the old French were notoriously poor. Where had Dufaure gotten the money to buy into Talbot Shipping?

If, by some remote chance, Dufaure were a spy for the Napoleonic faction, then the less Judith knew the better. Perhaps that was why Dufaure had not wanted her in the office. Beau had said that she was working on the docks because his partner had requested that the business not be interrupted by a woman's incompetence.

But he would bet his life that Judith was not incompetent about anything. Her mind was a lance, driving straight to the heart of every problem.

Could she be the British spy and Dufaure the French one? Both working at the same office, both spying on the Americans and each other. The thought tickled him.

He must see Reynolds. A man like Dufaure at the heart of a prosperous shipping line could move information, money, men around the world at will. The investigation must turn in his direction.

Maurice Dufaure was standing at the counter when Judith walked in. His mouth rose at the corners in an expression reminiscent of a carnivore scenting the blood of wounded prey. "So, Miss Talbot-Harrow. Your little affair has rocked New Orleans society to its foundations."

The look of dislike that she threw Dufaure would have stunned a lesser man to silence. It elicited only a bark of laughter from him. "I heard that poor Celeste fainted dead away and has since removed from the city to the peace and seclusion of *Ombres Azurées*."

"My stepmother has gone to the plantation but not because of anything that happened here. She is simply very tired after so many afternoons and late nights. Her health is delicate."

"*Mais oui*. But of course. I knew that."

"Of course you did. Now, where is the ledger?"

"Under the counter in its usual place."

To get to it, she had to practically push him out of the way. His body smelled of rank sweat, reminding her powerfully of Lord Lythes. In more ways than one he reminded her of her nemesis in England. Like Randolph Carew, he sneered and mocked everything that was good. With a feeling of relief she found the ledger and hurried back around the counter, eager to quit the place as soon as possible. Beau should have exercised more judgment in his choice of a partner.

"I take it that the pirate is soon to sail." The grating voice followed her to the door.

The idea brought her no pleasure. She froze with her hand on the knob, then shrugged lightly. "I cannot say. When I saw him last, he didn't share his plans with me. Nor should I have wanted to know them."

"But of course. He is nothing to you, after all. He deceived you and left you to face whatever must be faced alone."

She swung around, her face a mask of anger. "M'sieur Dufaure, you will take care never to mention Tabor O'Halloran again, or you will very much wish you hadn't."

The man drew back in mock alarm. "But of course."

"I mean what I say. Either you cease this baiting, or I shall inform my father."

The black eyes glittered with anger. "And what will your father do, Miss Talbot-Harrow?"

"He will find a way to be sure that you cease baiting me. He is not without power or influence. And he protects his own." With that she jerked the door open and strode out into the street, slamming the door so hard that the glass rattled in the window.

"Now you're talking, Captain. Go after a man. I'm thinking you've been wrong about that girl before and you'll be wrong again."

"I'm not giving up on her, Pinky. She's still the most likely suspect even if she didn't have the money. Those

208

other two could have been working as decoys to let the real spy slip through."

Mr. Pinckney sighed. Tabor O'Halloran was nothing if not a stubborn Irishman. "This Dufaure y' say is in a perfect position."

"Perfect. Perfect to see and hear everything that goes on in New Orleans, and he's old French."

Mr. Pinckney forebore to point out that almost any shipping office along the Mississippi could boast of several men with exactly the same set of circumstances.

"I need to report my suspicions to Reynolds immediately. He can put every man he's got on the fellow."

"How many do you think that might be, Captain?"

Tabor shrugged. "I can't imagine. I don't need to know that. Probably plenty. Madison wanted to be sure that New Orleans was secure."

"And are you going to tell him about your suspicions about Miss Talbot-Harrow?"

This question stopped Tabor in his musings. "No," he said instantly and with unnecessary force. "I don't need to tell him anything about her. I know where she is. She's on the dock every day in front of the hotel and within sight of the *Banshee*. She can't make a move without my seeing it. I don't need a spy to help me keep track of her."

"No, sir."

"She probably can't gather any more information anyway. She won't be going out socially anymore." He shook his head, his voice grave. "She ruined herself."

"That's good, then, Captain," Mr. Pinckney remarked sagely.

"Yes, good. Very good." Tabor muttered as he pushed open the door of the dry goods shop.

Reynolds started at the sight of O'Halloran with a stranger. Hastily, he shoved something underneath the counter and came toward them. "What can I do for you gentlemen?" he inquired politely.

Tabor's nostrils dilated as he smelled Reynolds's breath. He raised one eyebrow.

Reynolds chuckled uneasily, then coughed. He wiped

his mouth. "This blasted climate. Terrible. Terrible. The dampness and the heat get to me. Give me terrible headaches. Headaches simply blinding. I'm from Connecticut m'self."

When the two men made no comment, he coughed again, loudly and deeply, then cleared his throat. "Er . . . I have that special order ready, sir, if you wish to step right this way?"

Tabor grinned slightly. "This is my mate, Mr. Pinckney, Reynolds. He knows everything I know."

Reynolds stared hard at Pinckney, his head thrust forward on his scrawny neck. "The fewer who know about this operation, the better," he cautioned with some severity.

Tabor shrugged. "A captain has few secrets from his crew. It's damned hard to take the ship anywhere without their knowing about it."

Reynolds gaped. Then coughed and chuckled. "Right. Right. Come along. Come along." He led the way to the back of the shop. "Now, report." He lowered his voice to a whisper, as he had done before.

Standing a few feet behind them, Mr. Pinckney snorted, but Tabor shrugged off his mate's derision. "I'm suspicious about the people working at Talbot lines."

Reynolds took his spectacles down off his nose and polished the lenses. "Talbot lines. Talbot lines. Office on Front Street close to the Toulouse Street wharf."

Tabor nodded, a modicum of respect dawning for the little man.

"Whom do you suspect?"

"It could be something. It could be nothing. But Maurice Dufaure is a strange one to be a partner to Beau Talbot."

"Oh?"

"He's from an old French family. What's he doing buying into a business with a relative newcomer to New Orleans society? And where did he get the money to do it? He practically runs Talbot lines now that Beau's time is divided between there and the sugar plantation. He's not the same type of man as Beau Talbot."

"In what way?" Reynolds asked skeptically.

Tabor swallowed uneasily. "He likes to stir up trouble."

Reynolds shrugged. "A lot of men are like that. Doesn't make them spies."

"Could you . . . er . . . put someone to work investigating him?"

Reynolds drew back, affronted. "You want me to assign valuable men to watch some Frenchman because he's unpleasant. That's insane. Absolutely insane. Don't you care about your country's welfare?"

"Wait a minute." Tabor sought to stem the tide of irritated jabber. "This man could be the spy you're looking for."

"And what do you base this idea on? That he's unpleasant." Reynolds shook his head angrily. "Go back to the wharves, Captain. Listen and watch. Listen and watch. Bring me more good stuff. Like that stuff about Lake Ponchartrain. Good stuff. Passed that up the line." He bustled from the back of the store, motioning Tabor to follow.

Tabor felt his irritation growing. "I think you're missing a good bet with this man," he insisted.

"Not close. Not close. Look for someone who's recently come to the area. Someone recently from England. Don't worry about the French. They're a sinking ship. A sinking ship." He held open the door of his shop. "Good day to you, gentlemen."

Tabor did not look at Mr. Pinckney as he allowed himself to be ushered out the door. They were halfway down the block before the mate caught up to him.

"Captain."

"Yes, Pinky."

"Crazy as a loon."

Tabor walked faster.

211

Chapter Ten

The *Banshee* swung gently at her anchor, the muddy waters of the Mississippi swirling and eddying around her hull. The squall with its thunder and lightning had pushed on toward the bayous of western Louisiana. The downpour had slackened to a gentle shower that continued to soak her decks topside. The furled sails dripped; every line was a sluice down which the silver rivers streamed. Just as suddenly as they had blown up, the clouds rolled by; moonlight limned every mast and spar.

The watch rearranged himself in his oilskins, mildly cursing the Gulf storm that had wet him through only minutes before he was due to be relieved. Another half hour and he would have been below in his hammock, and another man would have to wonder how to dry himself out through the morning hours.

The wind dropped; the rain subsided to mist. Flapping strongly to keep its heavy body aloft, a pelican sailed across the river, disturbed from its roost on the pilings along the wharf. The watch flung his head up, searching the night sky in an effort to locate the source of the sound, so unusual at night. The movement tumped the water on his hat down the back of his collar. He groaned. His oilskins were already clammy and cold.

Damnation! He stood and began to pace up and down,

swinging his arms and blowing on his hands. Only a few more minutes and he could go below. No chance that his relief would come early. Not if he'd heard the thunder and rain. More likely he'd be late.

Something floating in the Mississippi bumped against the portside of the *Banshee*. The watch did not bother to investigate. The river was full of snags. Floating debris thudded and scraped against the hull all night long.

Then he heard a creaking as wet rope rubbed against hardwood. Alert, he crossed to the portside, leaned over the bow, and peered down. A boat hook whistled out of the dark and struck the back of his neck with a squishy thud. Its pike pulled him over the side without a cry. The frigid waters received him with hardly more splash than a fish jumping.

"Got him," a voice exclaimed.

"Keep your mouth shut, you fool. D'you want to wake everyone on board?" came an angry whisper.

"He's dead. The rest of 'em are dead asleep. It'll be like walkin' into church." The speaker hooked his lethal weapon over the railing and set his bare foot on the hull. Hand over hand he walked himself up the side until he could grasp the railing and haul himself over onto the deck. Slinging the ten-foot pole over his shoulder, he turned and waved to his fellows. "Come on up. Nothin' to it."

At that moment the replacement for the watch came up on deck. "Seamus," he called.

The intruder spun around.

"Hey! Who're you?"

Again the boat hook whistled through the air. This time it missed the head and caught the second man on the shoulder. He staggered sideways, then dropped backward into the companionway. "Hey! 'Ware, boarders! Boarders!"

Mr. Archer heard the shout. Rolling from his bunk, the first mate fumbled on his pants and reached for the horse pistol he kept loaded and primed.

Below in the pirogue, the intruders abandoned all efforts at silence and swarmed over the brigantine's side, grabbing whatever handholds they could. A half dozen strong in seaman's jackets with stocking caps pulled over their foreheads and mufflers wrapped around their chins, they grouped themselves on either side of the companionway door.

"Damn fool, Lejaune. Now you've turned it into work."

"It was always work. Just a little more fun now." The one called Lejaune grinned widely. He took one step toward the quarterdeck. Mr. Archer opened the cabin door and shot him dead.

The first mate had no time to reload. Three men leapt toward him. The first took the barrel of the empty pistol on the temple. With a grunt he dropped to his knees and fell forward on his face. The second came in low, his knife extended like a sword. It caught Archer in the belly. Gasping, he clutched at the hilt with both hands before a belaying pin above the ear bashed out his brains.

"Damn! That shot'll carry across the water."

"Keep watch. Keep the rest of 'em down below. Splash the deck with oil. Be quick about it."

A couple of barrels were hoisted from the pirogue, and the bungs knocked off. Two men trundled them down either side of the deck, spilling the oil.

"Splash it good over the hatches."

When the oil came coursing down the companionway, the skeleton crew below deck stared at each other in horror.

"They're gonna burn the *Banshee*," a boy screeched. "For God's sake. We've got to get away. We've got to go over the side."

"Into the Mississippi. Are ye daft? The current'll drag ye under for sure. Ye won't come up till ye're in the open Gulf."

One of the barrels ended at the foot of the mainmast, the other against the helm. "Strike a light there, lad.

214

Let's be done with it."

"Burn 'em alive?"

"You'd rather beat 'em to death," came the sarcastic rejoinder.

The spark jumped into the oil. The tongue of flame darted along the oil trail, spreading out as the flow widened, leaping upward in a coil of rope, rising into the ratlines. The cover of the hatch and the ladder of the companionway blazed.

"Over the side, men. Get away before we're spotted. She'll really light up the night in a minute."

Smoke billowed into the night sky, concealing the flames, but the strong winds that drove the squall away carried it into the docks and wharves, into the dockside hotels, and through the jalousies of the fine homes on Bourbon and Royal.

A night watchman caught up the hammer, and the brazen alarum bell clamored deafeningly. Seamen of all ranks tumbled into the streets. Ships officers to a man trained spyglasses on the river, searching their respective anchorages for the cause of the trouble.

Tabor spied the flickering flames rising from *Banshee*'s deck. Bellowing for Mr. Pinckney, he sprinted for the docks, where the fireboat with its brigade of rowers had already set out. As the harbor master pulled away, O'Halloran and Pinckney ran together and jumped for the deck of the cutter.

"Here now . . ."

"That's my ship!"

"Then welcome aboard. We can't waste a minute."

As they rowed steadily closer, the pilot remarked, "It looks bad, sir."

Tabor cursed virulently. "Where the hell are the crew? I've got a dozen men aboard her. I don't see any sign. Ahoy! Ahoy! *Banshee!*"

"They might be trapped below."

215

"Mr. Archer would never allow a deck to go unwatched," Mr. Pinckney declared.

Alongside his ship, Tabor looked up into the billowing smoke with occasional tongues of flame leaping up through it. "My God! How did it start?" Even as he said the words, horrible suspicions flooded his mind.

"Impossible to say. Lightning's a good guess. From the squall."

"Of course." Even as he agreed, Tabor knew the watch would have put out any stray fires caused by a lightning strike.

The crew of the fireboat pumped water steadily onto the blaze. As the harbor master pulled alongside, Tabor pounded on the hull. "Mr. Archer! Mr. Archer!"

"Cap'n O'Halloran!" A crewman stuck his head out of the hawser port. "Glad to see y', sir. We was gettin' desperate."

"Oren Magrath?"

"Aye, Cap'n."

"Where's Mr. Archer?"

Magrath shook his head. "He may be dead, sir. We heard a shot."

"Blast!" Tabor turned to the harbor master. "This wasn't caused by lightning. Can you grapple onto her side so I can get my men off?"

"The deck's still afire," the man objected.

"It's beginning to die down. Thank God everything was so wet. Get me a grappling hook and a ladder."

"On your head be it, sir."

Scaling the side to the quarterdeck, Tabor found it untouched. From there he was able to direct the streams of water from the fireboat until the last flames were extinguished. The fortuitous squall had wet everything so thoroughly that the oil had consumed itself with relatively little damage. Although the deck itself was blackened and pitted, the heart of the timber was not touched. Likewise the mainmast and foremast had charring around their bases, but seemed sound. The fire had burned through the ratlines rather than run up them, so the sails were untouched.

With a feeling of almost painful relief, Tabor estimated that the *Banshee*'s damage was minimal. Only when the smoke began to clear did he find the body.

Cold horror grabbing at his stomach, he went down on one knee. The man lay on his side, his back against the housing beneath the quarterdeck, his hands laced at his belly. Shuddering, Tabor dragged him out into the air and turned him over on his back. Two things he ascertained before he had to leave off or vomit. The man was too young and thin to be Mr. Archer, and he had been shot in the belly.

He rose and hurried to the other side of the deck just as the harbor master climbed aboard.

"Captain O'Halloran, what's the situation?"

Tabor pointed to the body. "The storm didn't do that."

The other man inspected the corpse. "Shot through."

A crew from the fireboat came aboard, tearing open the hatches, wetting down the companionway, helping the *Banshee*'s crew out into the fresh air. "Mr. Ribodeaux . . ." one of them called.

The harbor master rose from beside the stranger's body.

"There's another dead man here."

Tabor started for the companionway just as Oren Magrath emerged from the hatch. "Cap'n O'Halloran, we was boarded."

Tabor nodded. "There's a dead man in the companion-way."

Magrath cursed fervently. "Is it Mr. Archer?"

His question chilled Tabor. The rest of the crew gathered around them, smoke-stained, shaking with reaction.

"They was gonna burn us alive."

"If that squall hadn't soaked the *Banshee* early on,

217

we'd have been fried sure."

"We was gettin' ready to go over the side."

"They must've got Seamus," one man supplied solemnly. "He wasn't on deck when I come up to stand my watch."

Tabor heard their nervous accounts with half an ear. His concentration was trained on the companionway, where the fire crew was bringing out the second body and arranging it on the deck beside the first. Steeling himself, he walked over to stare down. The blistered, blackened face was recognizable as Frank Archer. Dark clots of what could only have been blood matted what remained of the hair on the back of the head.

"This man's been murdered too," Ribodeaux declared. "Bad night. Bad night. Are these men yours?"

Tabor pointed solemnly. "That one's Frank Archer of Bristol. He's—*was* my first mate. A good man. One of the best. The other one must have been one of the boarders. Mr. Archer always kept a loaded pistol beside him when we were in port."

"Sure sorry about this," Ribodeaux apologized as if it were his fault. He raised his voice. "Anybody know the other one?"

The crew of the *Banshee* shook their heads to a man, but one of the fire crew stepped forward. "Looks like what's left of Chanfrey Lejaune." He shrugged off-handedly. "No great loss. He's no sailor. Hangs around the wharves unloading cargo when he ain't drunk."

"A longshoreman?"

"'Bout half the time."

Tabor felt his skin prickle. "Worked for Talbot Shipping, did he?"

Both the harbor master and the crewman looked at him alertly. The crewman shrugged. "Might have? Sometimes. He'd work for anybody who'd pay him enough to drink with."

A heavy silence followed. Then the harbor master looked down solemnly. "Somebody doesn't like you, sir.

218

Do you perhaps have some idea who he is?"

"I think I know very well who she is."

"A fire in the river?" Judith stared up and down the crowded wharves. Everything seemed as usual. "A Talbot ship?"

"Luckily no," Dufaure replied. "A brigantine. I mention it only because I know how happy it will make you—or how sad."

She continued to stare at the wharf, presenting him her profile. The next time she spoke with her father she resolved to discuss Maurice Dufaure's hostility. To be opposed to her working here was one thing, but to continually harass her was quite another. "Are you going to tell me what you want me to know, or are you going to ask me to guess?"

He raised one eyebrow. "Perhaps I shall not tell you. You might be upset and then you would not be able to do your work today. Then cargo would not go aboard the *White Cloud* efficiently."

"I doubt that anything that anyone said could keep me from doing my work efficiently. But you must suit yourself." Judith clenched her jaw to keep from screaming at the man. The more she knew the man, the less she understood the reasons that Beau had gone into partnership with him, or why Dufaure had approached her father in the first place.

His heavy lids drooped over his eyes. A muscle twitched in the hollow of his pock-marked cheek. He did not exactly smile. "I'm sure you will hear from other sources before very long."

"I'm sure I shall." She swept up the manifests and ledger.

"On the other hand, perhaps you might wish to rush to his side. Although I did not hear how many were hurt, I know one man was killed."

Judith frowned in irritation. "Tell me what you want

219

me to know, M'sieur Dufaure. I'm tired of waiting."

"Why, the brigantine that caught fire last night was the *Banshee*. I'm surprised you did not hear the alarm and smell the smoke. It raised quite a stench. The fireboat went out and finally put it out. I saw them bringing the body back in."

Judith slammed the door behind her. Once outside, her knees began to tremble and her hands to shake. She hated Tabor O'Halloran. He had seduced her and lied to her. She had threatened desperate revenge, but never had she had any idea of how to go about it. Nor what such a venture would entail. She knew only that she hated him.

Blindly, she stumbled to the landau. Georges found her hand and guided her up. Emil closed the door. She sank back against the squabs and covered her eyes.

Her mind whirled, then steadied on a reassuring thought. Tabor could not be the one brought in by the fireboat. If he had been, Dufaure would have told her. Filled with malice, he would have taken pleasure in scrutinizing her face for signs of grief and pain.

But if Tabor had been aboard when the fire started, he would have fought it. He might be seriously burned. His crew might not release their captain's body to the New Orleans harbor master. A tiny whimper escaped from between her fingers at the thought of his magnificent body hideously scarred. Panic gripped her. She must hire a boat and go to the *Banshee*!

She sat up excitedly, then fell back. More likely, if he were badly injured, he might be taken to a hospital. But which one? Furthermore, if she hired a boat to take her to the ship and he were unhurt, then he would know that she cared. He would mock her.

The landau drew up onto the quay. Emil and Georges performed their duties, and she seated herself at her portable desk with the sheets arranged in front of her. Within minutes the loading began.

For the first time since she had arrived in New

Orleans, Judith did not feel the heat or the dampness. Cold radiated out from the center of her body. Sometimes during a lull in her activities she would wrap her arms tightly across her midriff in an effort to stifle the chills that racked her from head to toe.

What if he were dead? And she pregnant with his child? The baby would never know its father. She shivered again. Poor little fatherless mite. Tears prickled at the corners of her eyes.

Sternly, she caught herself up. She was surely losing her mind. Grief and worry were making her maudlin.

Georges bowed at her elbow. "Would Maîtresse like a cool drink?"

She looked up, startled. Between his brows was a deep line; his dark face registered kindness and concern, emotions she had never seen there before. Had she really been so obvious in her preoccupation? She took a deep steadying breath. "Yes, thank you. A lemonade would be most welcome."

"I will fetch it myself."

Somehow the day passed. She remembered neither drinking nor eating any of the things Georges served her. Neither did she rise from her desk but kept the cargo moving up the gangplank and into the merchantman's cavernous holds with such efficiency that the bosses shook their heads.

Only by focusing totally could she keep to her work. Once during a lull she had an impression of a horrible shadow hovering at the edge of her mind, threatening to blot out her sanity. Instantly, she directed her pen and her mind to the column of figures before her. Finally, when the last bale of cotton was loaded, the hatches battened down, the signatures in place on all the manifests, she rose stiffly, looking around her in some confusion. Georges offered his arm to guide her to the landau.

221

The drive through the streets seemed to take an inordinately long time. Once she leaned over the side of the carriage to see if a slow-moving vehicle might be blocking their way. The street was empty before them and the horses moved at a good clip.

In the town house she went straight to her father rather than hurrying up the stairs. "I must speak to you, Beau."

He raised his head from his book. His eyes surveyed her coldly. Neither had spoken of the night at the Beauvaliets' masque. He had carefully avoided the subject as he had avoided her. He had thought by his aloofness to bring her to him begging for forgiveness.

Judith, who had dealt with ostracism for most of her life, retreated into the world that she had built within herself. With work and books she had no need of companionship. Talbot lines required a great deal of time and energy. Beau's extensive library contained many works on business, on sailing, and on banking, subjects Judith never tired of reading about. When she came home, she bathed, ate her meals from trays in her room, and retired early, oblivious to her father's attempt to punish her.

Determined as he was to wait her out, Beau was irritated by what he considered to be her stubbornness. Laura and Celeste always came to him in tears when they had committed some small error. A woman was supposed to admit she was wrong and apologize after she had pouted for a while. Although Judith had tried him sorely with her behavior at the Beauvaliets, he was prepared to chasten and then forgive her. By spring, when the scandal had died down, he would give her a ball. She would meet some nice young man.

He lowered his head to hide his smile as he carefully marked the place, then closed the book. "I am waiting, Judith."

She did not know how to begin. If her father asked her too many questions, she would embarrass herself with

222

her answers. Nevertheless, she had to know, had to ease her mind of its terrible fears. Otherwise she would not be able to sleep. "I heard that the *Banshee* caught fire last night."

He stared at her. "Yes," he said at last. "I had heard that also. In fact, I heard the alarum bell and went out to investigate."

She leaned forward, her face strained, anguished. "You heard all that and you didn't waken me? Beau, how could you have let me sleep?"

He blinked. Truthfully, he had never thought to awaken her. She was, after all, a woman. The wharves were dangerous enough places in broad daylight. He told her so.

"But a Talbot ship might have been aflame," she argued. "The owners should be there."

"Fortunately, it was not a Talbot ship. However, should one catch fire, I will certainly wake you up to tell you if you insist." It was a laurel branch, but she was too distraught to recognize one.

She cleared her throat. "Was . . . was anyone hurt?"

"I believe that two men are dead and another missing."

Feeling the blood rush from her head, she sat down abruptly. Her eyes filled with tears. She could not bear this. If two men were dead, one of them had to be Tabor. He was the captain, the leader. He would be in the thick of the fight against the flames.

"Judith." Beau hurried forward to put his arm around her. "Baby."

She shook her head, trying to stifle the sobs. "M'sieur Dufaure told me about it before I left the office this morning. I've worried about it all day. Was Tabor O'Halloran one of the men killed?"

"I didn't hear their names," Beau replied stiffly. The mention of O'Halloran's name reminded him of his anger.

"You didn't hear?" She looked up at him in horror.

"Didn't you care enough to find out?"

Beau drew back. "Not at two o'clock in the morning. There was little or nothing I could do about it. Furthermore, if the scoundrel is dead, I shall be saved the trouble of calling him out."

"You wouldn't have fought a duel over me."

"He impugned your honor."

"You didn't bother to fight a duel with any of Mother's lovers," she reminded him.

"My daughter is a different matter." He looked at her curiously. "But I thought you hated him."

"I do." The last was so low that he had to bend to hear it.

"Then why are you crying?"

"I don't hate anyone enough to wish him dead. Not by your hand. And certainly not by f-fire." She pulled a handkerchief from her sleeve and pressed it to her eyes. "I didn't know ships caught fire," she murmured after a minute.

"It's not a usual thing, but lightning can strike the mast. Oil can spill from a lantern."

Judith remembered the noise of the storm. "Is that what happened?"

"I don't know."

"Would you please find out?" She caught his hand. "Please, Beau, would you find out what happened? Find out who was hurt? And who was k-killed?" Ashamed that she had given so much away, she dropped her head again.

He looked down at her bowed shoulders. "Of course, baby. But I don't think O'Halloran was hurt."

Her head shot up. "How can you be sure?"

"Because he's too important a person for news of his death to be dismissed. If he'd been killed, the whole city would have heard."

"A pirate is important."

Beau raised one eyebrow. "To the English he may be a pirate, but to Americans he's a patriot."

"But you're English."

224

FREE BOOK CERTIFICATE

4 FREE BOOKS

ZEBRA HOME SUBSCRIPTION SERVICE, INC.

YES! Please start my subscription to Zebra Historical Romances and send me my first 4 books absolutely FREE. I understand that each month I may preview four new Zebra Historical Romances free for 10 days. If I'm not satisfied with them, I may return the four books within 10 days and owe nothing. Otherwise, I will pay the low preferred subscriber's price of just $3.75 each; a total of $15.00, *a savings off the publisher's price of $3.00.* I may return any shipment and I may cancel this subscription at any time. There is no obligation to buy any shipment and there are no shipping, handling or other hidden charges. Regardless of what I decide, the four free books are mine to keep.

NAME _____

ADDRESS _____ APT _____

CITY _____ STATE ____ ZIP _____

( )
TELEPHONE _____

SIGNATURE _____
(if under 18, parent or guardian must sign)

Terms, offer and prices subject to change without notice. Subscription subject to acceptance by Zebra Books. Zebra Books reserves the right to reject any order or cancel any subscription. 029002

FREE BOOKS

4

TO GET YOUR 4 FREE BOOKS WORTH $18.00 — MAIL IN THE FREE BOOK CERTIFICATE TODAY

Fill in the Free Book Certificate below, and we'll send your FREE BOOKS to you as soon as we receive it.

If the certificate is missing below, write to: Zebra Home Subscription Service, Inc., P.O. Box 5214, 120 Brighton Road, Clifton, New Jersey 07015-5214.

The Publishers of Zebra Books
Make This Special Offer
to Zebra Romance Readers...

♠

He left her then to pour himself a tot of his favorite whiskey. "No, baby, I'm not. I haven't been for a long time. I'm American. I'm married to an American woman. I own an American plantation and an American business."

"You're a nephew of the Earl of Teigh."

"That doesn't change a thing. I'm an American."

"You have an English daughter," she said.

He looked at her almost coldly then. "I have an American daughter too."

His words pierced her like a lance. "And you've had her for a lot longer than your English one."

"Judith, don't take that remark the wrong way," he protested. "I was just using those as examples of why I'm an American."

"I understand." She rose to leave.

Beau looked nonplussed for a moment. A dark frown marred his forehead. "Was that all you wanted to say to me?"

Judith looked at him. Though her eyes remained tear-drenched, their lashes spiky, her face was set and very still. "Why, yes, Beau. I wanted to find out what happened aboard the *Banshee*. Since you're sure that Tabor O'Halloran escaped the fire, then I can relax. I wouldn't want to think even my worst enemy had been injured in a fire."

"You weren't crying as if he were your worst enemy."

"I wasn't crying for that. I shouldn't have been crying at all. It never does a bit of good."

"Judith!" He set his drink down and came to the door. "So long as you're here"—he cleared his throat uncomfortably—"I'd be interested to hear your account of your behavior the other night."

"Would you, Beau? I thought I said everything at the Beauvaliets. I thought I could clear my good name for the sake of your family, you understand, but Tabor O'Halloran lied." She clenched her hands into tight fists. "I'm sorry for what I did. I've already apologized to

225

Laura. Surely, you and Celeste will be forgiven and I . . . Fortunately, I don't have to associate with those people again, so their belief or disbelief is not important."

He gaped at her dismissal of the good opinions of some of the most powerful people in New Orleans society. "Judith, you do have to associate with them. This city is now your home. Everyone was there that night. Governor Claiborne himself was there, and Jacques Villeré and Nicholas Girod."

"Beau, these names don't mean anything to me."

"Then they damn well should. You want to run the Talbot lines. You've got to have the respect of the powerful people of this city and this country. This is your city and your country."

"No, it's not. My home is England. I'll go back there someday." She heaved a sigh. "Beau, I've been wanting to talk to you about a plan I want you to consider."

"What plan?"

"A plan for the Talbot lines—in England."

He looked her over from head to toe. She was practically swaying where she stood. In her face he saw the signs of exhaustion—dark smudges, hollow cheeks, a strained look accentuated by her recent tears. He shook his head. "Not now, baby. You wouldn't make sense if you tried to talk business with me now." When she nodded slowly, he took her arm. "Judith, don't you think you're working too hard?"

"Perhaps. But I've been attending balls too. I won't be doing that anymore."

"Er . . . how did you get home from the Beauvaliets?" Beau could not look his daughter in the eye.

She allowed herself a mirthless smile. "Why, Tabor O'Halloran carried me home. On his shoulder. He put me down at the foot of the steps and left. I'm surprised you even bothered to ask how I got home," she added.

Beau's mouth tightened. "I had the responsibility of Celeste and Laura."

"Of course." Her voice was expressionless. "I think

226

I'll retire for the night. I'm not especially hungry."

He nodded, unsmiling. "Whatever you want, baby." He put his hand behind her head and drew her to him, dropping a light kiss on her forehead. "Will you be all right alone? I promised Celeste I'd come out to the plantation every night."

"I'll be fine, Beau."

Wearily, Judith mounted the stairs and opened the door to her bedroom. The room was dark, a strange circumstance. Usually her maid lighted the lamp. Perhaps it was out of oil. She started across the room for the bellpull beside the bed.

Suddenly, a hard hand closed over her mouth and a long arm snaked around her waist.

"Not a sound," came a familiar whisper. "Not a bloody sound. You and I are going out of here the way I came in."

She did not struggle. Instead, she felt a wave of relief so strong that it shook her from head to toe. Tabor O'Halloran was safe. He held her in his arms. In an ecstatic dream she leaned back against him, feeling the familiar hard length of his body, inhaling the scent of him.

And her body responded too. In that instant she acknowledged that wherever she might go, whatever she might do, she would never be completely free of her desire for this man.

Chapter Eleven

With recognition came a flood of desire that left her weak in the knees. She could feel tears start in her eyes. The pounding of her heart made her dizzy. If he had died, she would never have known the wonder of his beautiful body again. His hands would never have caressed her. His mouth would never have sent chain lightning through all the parts of her body again.

Tabor. Her mind screamed his name, but she could make no sound. *Tabor. Oh, Tabor.*

His hand covered her mouth so tightly that she could not move her lips. His arm around her midriff crushed her ribs. As the shock of his presence lessened, she became aware of the discomfort he was causing her. She pushed against the constraint. She wanted to turn in his arms, to kiss him, to hold him tight, to tell him how thankful she was that he was alive.

But when she tried to move, he clamped her even tighter against him. "Don't give me any trouble. I can make this easy, or hard."

She spoke his name against his palm, but the word was unintelligible.

"Quiet, I said." Roughly, he pulled her head higher onto his shoulder, dragging her up on tiptoe. His arm came away from her waist. Instantly, she caught his wrist and tried to tug his hand away from her mouth. For a minute she had no success, then suddenly she was free.

"Tab—"

He replaced his hand with a handkerchief stuffed between her jaws. Her angry protest was immediately extinguished. When she reached for it, he caught her wrists and twisted them behind her. Ignoring the furious sounds coming from behind the gag, he tied her hands behind her with a length of common line brought for that purpose.

Her protests became more frantic. She shook her head vigorously.

He paid no attention to her protests. When she was securely trussed, he spun her around. Her face was only a blur in the dark, but he could hear her protests, feel the furious tremors that raged through her body. With a mirthless grin he stooped and lifted her onto his shoulder.

The muffled protests increased in pitch but not in volume. She kicked violently, almost throwing her body off his shoulder. He clamped his arm around the backs of her knees and steadied himself. She kicked again, trying to bring her toes into his stomach.

"Stop that!" He spanked her—swift, punishing, insulting blows on her upturned buttocks.

She only redoubled her efforts, squirming, twisting, rearing herself up.

"Damn you, Judith!" He hit her again, counting himself lucky that he could not understand what she was saying.

He crossed to the window. "Judith!" He struck her buttock again to get her attention. "Judith, be still, or you'll make me drop you. You'll fall to the cobblestones in the alley on your behind. And then it'll really be bruised."

Her protests and squirming seemed to increase. He stooped and set her down again. The light of the streetlamp fell across her face. "Are you going to cut that out?"

Her eyes flashed. Violently, she shook her head, furious unintelligible sounds streaming from behind the gag.

He doubled up his fist and pushed up her jaw with it. He felt her swallow against the back of his hand before she fell silent. He bent again to lift her on to his shoulder and stepped through the window.

She bucked powerfully, throwing herself upward against the wall in an effort to drag herself from his arms. The window sash caught her on the back of the head just at the top of her spine. She slumped forward a dead weight.

With Judith only semiconscious and still, Tabor easily carried her across the roof of the kitchen and down on top of the high wall. There a coach waited for them. Swiftly, he passed her into the interior and swung in beside her. Mr. Pinckney whipped up the horses, and the conveyance clattered away down the Calle di Conti.

Aware almost immediately of the vibration and sway, Judith lay as he had set her down, feeling hard-used. For several minutes she concentrated on marshaling her strength. Violent emotions distracted her; chief among them, equal parts of gratitude and outrage. What could he be doing with her? Where could he be taking her?

Suddenly, the answer flashed through her brain. At first it flabbergasted her. As she considered it, she felt a warm flood of delicious anger.

Marriage!

Of course! He's kidnapping me to force me to marry him. The horrible man. He knew I'd never speak to him again, but he won't give me up. He's taking me to a priest. I'm a Protestant, and he's a Catholic. But that won't make any difference. He loves me. He wants to marry me.

Despite the discomfort of the gag, she smiled. She would be married against her will to a pirate. An American patriot, her father had called him. Tabor O'Halloran. Mistress Tabor O'Halloran.

Her mind raced over the ramifications of the match.

Where would they live? Would he sail ships for the Talbot lines? How many children would they have? Would they have red hair or black?

The coach had left the cobblestone streets and now thundered along the high road. Dust began to sift up into her nostrils. Her bound hands began to tingle painfully. She tried without much success to shift over to her side without rolling off the seat of the carriage.

He was carrying this kidnapping to extremes.

Watching her squirm and sensing her discomfort, Tabor pulled her over onto the seat beside him and propped her up against the squabs.

Immediately, she tried to speak to him through the gag.

"Stop that!" he growled, nudging her roughly with his elbow.

Resentfully, she subsided. She would have to think a long time before she forgave him for this high-handed behavior.

Through the window she could see nothing but inky blackness. No moon or stars could penetrate the tall, dense trees festooned with Spanish moss. She eased herself into a more comfortable position and leaned back. Suddenly, her stomach rumbled, making her remember that she had had nothing to eat all day. Likewise, she was painfully thirsty. The sizing in his handkerchief seemed to draw all the moisture from her mouth. Much longer, and he would not need to keep the gag in place. Her mouth and throat would be too parched to make a sound.

Still, she felt unexplainably content riding beside him. The knowledge that someone cared for her enough to kidnap her against her will made her very happy. She would have turned to him and kissed him if she could. Since she could not, she rested her body against his side and laid her head on his shoulder.

Tabor stiffened at the contact and glanced down, but the carriage was too dark to see Judith's expression. If she expected to get off lightly after what she had done,

231

she was going to be sadly mistaken. She shifted slightly and sighed. Before he thought, he put his arm around her to steady her against the sway of the coach. Within minutes her head grew heavier. Her body cuddled against him, then relaxed.

He cursed under his breath as his other arm went around her. He despised her. She was a spoiled, vengeful monster who had hired men to burn his ship. In the act she had been responsible for the deaths of two good, innocent men. He cursed as he remembered Frank Archer.

Her soft hair rubbed silkily against his jaw. She moaned softly.

He tightened his arms to keep her secure.

Mr. Pinckney finally drew the coach to a halt and swung down off the box. At the same time, Tabor shifted his burden to the seat beside him and opened the door. "Can you see the lights?" he called.

"Aye, Captain."

"Then give them the signal."

The recently appointed first mate hesitated. "Captain O'Halloran," he protested gruffly. "I think you're makin' a big mistake."

"Damn it, Pinky. When I want your opinion, I'll ask for it."

"Yes, sir."

"Give that signal."

"Yes, sir." Mr. Pinckney threw his cap over the carriage lamp, concealing its light. Then again. And again.

An answering light flashed from a ship in the river. "They've seen us, Captain. They'll be comin' in."

"Good."

Tabor climbed back into the carriage and lifted Judith into his arms. Her head fell against his shoulder, but she only moaned faintly. He wondered a little that she was still deeply asleep. Had that blow to the back of her head done more damage than he thought?

Frowning, he pressed his mouth to her temple. The

pulse beat strongly against his lips. She could not have been injured too badly.

"They're comin', Captain."

At first he did not answer, lest he disturb her. Warm and soft and relaxed as a baby, she lay lightly in his arms. Before he thought, his lips moved against her smooth temple. Angrily, he shook himself. "Take her!" he growled to Mr. Pinckney.

Judith awakened as Tabor passed her to Mr. Pinckney. Her eyes blinked open, she moaned and tried to open her mouth. In that instant she remembered. Furious, she twisted about.

"Here, now." Mr. Pinckney almost lost his hold on her. "No need to pitch and heave so, lass. You've nothing to fear."

Tabor snorted unpleasantly. "Maybe not from you, but she does from me."

Judith craned her neck around to look at him, but his hat shadowed his face. She felt the first stirrings of uneasiness. If he were going to marry her, why did he not release her? At least he could take the gag out of her mouth.

Mr. Pinckney thought the same thing. "Shall I pull that handkerchief out of her mouth, Captain? Must be gettin' fearful uncomfortable."

His suggestion made Judith nod her head hopefully as Tabor shook his.

"Don't touch it. You won't want to listen to her. Besides, sound carries over water. She'll make herself heard all the way back to New Orleans."

A skiff pulled in to the riverbank. Tabor took Judith back from Mr. Pinckney and carried her toward it.

Judith's thoughts spun around and around as she tried to see his face in the darkness. Where were they going? To some pirate stronghold? Was Tabor taking her to someplace like Barataria?

As they rowed through the swirling water, she became increasingly uneasy. Perhaps he did not intend marriage

233

after all. Perhaps he intended to kidnap her and hold her for ransom. She was not consoled by the thought that given Beau Talbot's frame of mind when she left him, he would be most likely to pay Tabor not to bring her back. He and Celeste and Laura could probably live happily ever after without ever seeing her again.

She could see the bulk of a ship rising before her, running lights marking her bow and stern. A couple of lanterns also lighted her amidships. As they rowed by the prow, she saw dimly the figurehead of a woman with wind-tossed locks, her mouth open in a silent scream— *the Banshee.*

Just before the skiff bumped against the hull, Judith smelled the smoke. It hung heavy and overpowering in the air around the brigantine. She had forgotten about the fire. Though she strained her eyes in the darkness, she could see no damage.

A rope ladder dangled over the side. "Captain O'Halloran," a voice called.

"Here, Mr. Magrath." He turned to his prisoner. "Now I'm going to untie your hands. You can climb up that ladder yourself, or you can go over the side and try to swim against the current in the river."

She nodded her head and gave him her back for him to untie her. Her shoulders felt strained and her hands were so numb she could not feel her fingers. When finally he pulled the line away, she made a little whimpering noise as she eased her arms around to the front.

"Up you go," he commanded, not giving her time to catch her breath but taking her under the arm immediately and raising her to catch the ladder.

She shook her head helplessly as her hands refused to obey her.

"For God's sake." Impatiently, he swept her up again and threw her over his shoulder. She could feel his chest heave as he drew a deep breath and set his booted foot on the ladder. The deck was ten feet above the waters of the Mississippi, but Tabor lifted her with him, agile and strong as a great cat.

Once on the blackened deck, he stood her in the center of a circle of men. By the lanterns she could see their expressions, grim and forbidding. Fear gripped her. Despite the sharp pains shooting up from her wrists, she dragged down the handkerchief that he had tied around her head and pulled the other one from her mouth.

Holding herself stiffly to keep from trembling, she tried to speak. The sound was no more than a dry rasp. "Why?"

"Why have I brought you here?"

She nodded, pressing her hand to her throat.

"I'll show you."

"Captain O'Halloran!" Mr. Pinckney protested.

"Stand aside, Pinky." Tabor took her under the arm. The ring of sailors parted for them, then closed and followed as he led her down the deck.

She looked around her at the grim faces, looked at him, looked where he was taking her. A lantern illuminated a long, still object on the deck. With a start of horror she recognized the shape.

When Tabor felt her pull back, he tightened his grip. His fingers dug into the soft arm beneath the black wool dress. "Oh, no, m'lady. You're going to look at what you've done."

She swallowed, trying to will moisture into her mouth. Smoke-tainted air scraped harshly across parched membranes. "What I've done?" she rasped painfully.

"Yes." He knelt on the charred deck, dragging her down to her knees. "Look!" Ruthlessly, he pulled back the canvas.

Later, she was to think that the dim light protected her in some small manner from the horror of the thing. It was scarcely recognizable as a man's face. One side was blackened and blistered, the mouth pulled up in a rictus that exposed the teeth in a hideous half grin. What remained of the ear and the skin of the skull looked appallingly like charred meat.

235

A desperate moan rose from the very depth of her being. She twisted violently to hide her eyes from the sight, but her captor was inexorable.

"Look!" he thundered. "Look, you spoiled rich man's daughter. Look at what your stupid revenge has caused."

Her stomach heaved. Frantically, she tried to pull away from him. His grip tightened, punishing her, bruising her. She gagged. Then the convulsions began.

At the first sound of her distress, his grip loosened, then fell away. Shuddering from head to toe, she scrabbled away from him and managed to pull herself to her feet. The circle parted for her. Desperately, she lunged for the rail, where she hung retching for long minutes. Despite the awful sounds and the terrible weakness, she had nothing to give. The long day when she had been too distracted to eat saved her the final embarrassment. After long painful minutes she regained a measure of control.

Then the same hateful hand fell heavily on her shoulder. "Very effective, m'lady. Mr. Pinckney has covered Mr. Archer's face, so your aristocratic eyes won't have to look at what they've done again."

She made a weak mew of protest that he ignored.

"You'll want to be a part of this."

"No." She shook her head positively.

He was utterly merciless. "Yes. I'll be reading the burial service as soon as we've pulled the boat out into the middle of the river. I want you to hear every word of it."

He led her away from the rail to a place not too near the terrible shape and motioned to two seamen. Faces grim, they stepped forward and flanked her on either side.

"Mr. Pinckney."

"Aye, Captain." The first mate, his face reflecting his anguish, turned to the crew. "Hop to it, lads. Up anchor. Foresails set." The foremast had been relatively undamaged by the fire. Its triangular sheets rattled up the halyards. Likewise, the lines attached to the bowsprit had been spared. As the prevailing wind filled them, the *Banshee* responded. Slowly, she came about and moved across the sluggish current into the middle of the mighty river.

By the light of lanterns the sailmaker knelt at the dead man's head to set the last stitches in the shroud. Then six men hoisted him onto their shoulders. The plank on which he lay thudded gently against the rail. Tabor's voice was muted, gentle, reading the burial service.

To Judith's eyes the whole scene became a nightmare. The murmured prayer, the constant motion of the vessel, the odor of smoke, the still, dark men. Then a halo grew around the lights, the figures of the men wavered, the solemn words became a meaningless drone.

When the plank tilted, sliding the corpse over the side, Judith did not hear the splash. She fell sideways against the sailor assigned to guard her. He caught her before she hit the deck unconscious.

She awoke to a raging thirst. Choking, she sat half up in the narrow bunk, gasping and massaging her throat.

"Drink this."

The sound of Tabor's voice brought a rush of memory. Instead of reaching greedily for the drink, she shrank away from it and the man who offered it to her. Their eyes met, his angry, hers defiant.

"It's all right. I haven't poisoned it. Although it's no more than you deserve."

After a minute she took it from him and cautiously sipped it.

He straightened, his face and shoulders out of her line of vision above the canopy of the bunk.

Never had clear, fresh water tasted so good. Judith drained it, then clasped the empty tumbler between her hands and waited.

After a moment he took it from her. "More?"

"Please."

When she had drunk the second, he moved away, setting the tumbler and water bottle down on the table-desk and seating himself. The tilt of the deck told her that the *Banshee* was under way. "Where are we going?"

"Back to drydock in New Orleans. We're making slow progress against the current without our mainsails."

"They were burned away?"

"As you would have liked, m'lady? Sorry to disappoint you. The heavy rain kept the fire from climbing the ratlines. We've all canvas intact. In fact, it's my pleasure to inform you that the *Banshee* has sustained worse damage in a sea battle and sailed away the victor."

The suppressed fury in his voice kept her silent. She shivered beneath her rumpled black dress. Depending upon how long she had been unconscious, she had worn that dress for almost twenty-four hours now. She opened her hand. The palm was black with soot. Considering that she had all but crawled across the deck to get away from the corpse's side, she could guess that her skirt was sooty as well and probably torn in several places.

Fury mixed with anguish in his next speech. "I wish you had damaged my ship irreparably rather than killing Frank Archer and Seamus Killeen."

She struggled to make a sensible answer to his accusations, but her head was beginning to ache harder. Likewise, her body was fast reaching its limits of endurance. Infinitely worse than her physical was her emotional state. Hurt and disappointment made thinking almost impossible. She pressed her filthy hand to her forehead. "I didn't kill anyone."

"Liar!" he snapped. "You vowed revenge, and you took it. You wanted to hurt me. That I could accept. But to damage my ship. To try to burn it with human beings trapped on board."

"I didn't."

"What you didn't do was give a damn about my men." He leaned forward, his eyes burning his head. "They didn't have a part in anything that you imagine was done

238

to you. But that didn't stop you. Did you even think about them? Do you even think of them as human beings?"

What is he talking about? "Of course I think of them as human beings. I don't know what you're talking about. I was angry, and I—I've got a terrible temper. I might have vowed revenge, but I . . . I didn't . . ." She waved her hand helplessly.

He sprang to his feet. His fists clenched at his sides. "The hell you didn't. You took your revenge."

"I didn't. I . . . it was just something to say."

A couple of swift strides and he was hanging above her, eyes boring into her face, searching for some betraying expression. "Perhaps you had another reason?"

"What reason? What reason could I possibly have to burn a man's ship?"

"What if that man were your enemy? If he were getting suspicious of you? If you were obeying orders?"

"Orders? What orders? Suspicious about what? You're crazy."

He caught her by the shoulders. "Tell the truth!" he demanded hoarsely. "Listen! I can understand war. My men can understand it. In war men get killed."

Judith caught at his wrists and tried to push him away from her. He had been grabbing her with his hard hands all night long. Her shoulders, her wrists, her mouth, were all tender. "No! You listen to me! I can't figure out what you're asking me. I don't know what you're talking about."

He let her go and backed away. "Don't lie to me. Don't keep on being a fool. You were a fool when you hired your own longshoremen to do the job. They made a poor job of it. Thank God they were a stupid lot." He began to pace the cabin. "My crew could have been roasted alive if the *Banshee* had burned to the waterline."

She had to raise her voice to break through his diatribe. "I didn't hire anyone."

"Lejaune was your man. He's been identified."

239

"I don't know any Lejaune."

"I doubt that he was the leader. Probably you never talked to him. He was just an underling. His death's on your head too. He was shot by Mr. Archer."

She closed her eyes and prayed for strength and patience. She tried for a slow, rational tone of voice. "Will you please listen to me? I didn't send anyone to burn your ship. I didn't kill anyone."

"You've lied before."

He was back to that again. "I never lied. You're the one who lied."

He lunged back across the cabin and caught her by the shoulders again. This time the pain in her face made him release her immediately. "I had reasons for denying your dramatic, highly public accusations. I've already told you."

"But you consider me too simple to comprehend them?"

"They don't concern you."

"Since they destroyed my good name, I can hardly see how they fail to concern me."

"I'm not going to talk about that night anymore. I just want you to know that if you ever come after me again, I'll make you very sorry that you've done so."

"I'm already very sorry," she whispered, trembling where he had bruised her again.

He stared at her a full minute, taking in the mussed untidy hair, the soot all over her hands and cheeks, the hollows under her eyes, the pinched look around the mouth. Rather than arousing pity, her appearance satisfied his desire for justice. She looked punished and suitably penitent.

Of course, the deaths of two men could never be equated by a night's discomfort. He could almost have forgiven her and taken her home. Almost. But another hurt was still to be assuaged. "I can't believe I thought I loved you," he sneered. "There's nothing lovable about you."

The words brought back vividly her hopeful, almost happy invention during the coach ride. His words were like a knife in the heart. She hunched her shoulders slightly, crossing her arms beneath her breasts. Tears filled her eyes, but she blinked them back. Now as far from a kidnapped bride as any woman could be, she faced her tormentor. "There's no such thing as love in the world. There's lust and pride. What you had was a surfeit of both."

He shuddered violently at the sight of the white face raised so defiantly, the smudged chin outthrust. "You're right. Lust and pride. And you, m'lady, are motivated by pride."

"And you, pirate, are motivated by lust."

"Let's just see." Furious, he backed her against the cabin wall, using the strength of his thighs to push her hard.

The violence of his actions almost paralyzed her. She could not fight him. There was no strength in her hands, nor anywhere else in her body. Exacting its toll was the long day without rest when she had driven herself mercilessly to keep her thoughts at bay. At the end of it, she had had no supper, nor any breakfast. She had been gagged and tied and knocked unconscious. Her sensibilities had been torn apart by horror foreign to her innocent mind. All combined to render her limp in his hands.

Chapter Twelve

Judith's proud defiance infuriated Tabor. She should be kneeling to pray for the souls of the dead men. If she did penance for the rest of her life, she could not pay for their deaths. Instead of being heartily sorry for her monstrous sins, she thrust out her chin and denied any knowledge of them.

His eyes searched her face for some signs of remorse. A gently bred woman, a real lady who had caused such devastation would be overcome with sorrow. Unless—of course—she were also the spy—a spy with a taste for vengeance. And he had come close to loving her.

Even now, with dark smudges under her eyes and her hair in wild disarray around her white face, she had the power to arouse him. Disgusted with himself beyond all forebearance, he gripped her shoulders.

"So I have nothing but lust on my mind," he snarled.

She set her teeth to endure the pain of his iron hands. "Nothing," she whispered defiantly.

He loomed over her, his palms sliding down her arms, squeezing at the elbows. His head with its wild black hair blocked the light. Then he was kissing her on the side of the throat, kissing her with lips and tongue. Finally, his mouth closed over her skin above the pulsebeat.

Despite her hurt and disappointment, his mouth sent excitement through her veins. He sucked gently, then harder, bringing the blood up to the skin. His teeth grazed the spot.

She moaned in pain, but not from the bite. The ache at the bottom of her belly was making her shiver.

Somehow—she was not quite sure how—he had rucked up her skirt. His hand, his familiar warm hand, pushed aside her petticoats, slipped through the slit in her pantalettes, where he pressed then clasped the pulsing mound of her femininity.

A feral cry slid between her set teeth. The gentle sway of the ship tilted her against him. She caught at his shoulders, shuddering with desire, her legs too weak to stand alone.

His hand squeezed her, turned, positioned itself, slid between her legs, finding the betraying wetness.

"Nothing but lust," he gritted mockingly, pushing his second and third fingers into her.

Her frantic intake of breath was a sharp cry. Unable to help herself, she thrust her hips forward. Her head fell back, inviting him to kiss her throat again. Instead of granting her unspoken request, he stepped back from the wall. All her weight hung from his shoulders, her toes dragged on the floor. Disturbed out of her dream, she opened her eyes trying to read his intention.

They widened in shock as she felt him sink lower. "What are you doing?"

"Satisfying your lust and my pride."

"No." The word was totally meaningless. Even as she uttered it, his hard, hot maleness butted against her where his hand had been only the instant before. "What are you . . . ?"

"Shhh, m'lady." He covered her mouth with his own and bent his knees. At the same moment he thrust with his tongue, he guided himself into her moist-satin sheath.

"What are . . . ?" Her question ended in a cry as he straightened his knees, driving himself into her, heaving her up until her toes scraped at the floor, then lost it entirely. Frightened as she realized what he had done,

243

what he meant to do, she whipped her arms around his neck and tried to lift herself off him.

But he would not allow her to leave him. His arms closed around her waist, and he began to move, pushing her down to meet his thrusts, rocking his hips.

"Don't," she moaned fearfully. "Oh, don't. Please let me down. I can't stand . . ."

"You can," he gasped. "Of course . . . you can. You can." His words were paired, rhythmical.

"Oh, God, Tabor." The words hissed out between teeth set on the edge of ecstasy as he pulled himself out of her with deliberate slowness then drove into her, filling her full, dividing her.

She wrapped her legs around his hips and sank down to meet him.

Again he thrust.

She cried out, arching her spine, opening herself impossibly. Her body trembled, shaken by sensations as violent as they were pleasurable. Every muscle quivered.

She tossed her head, tearing her mouth away from his, trying to breathe in the stifling heat of the cabin. Perspiration dampened her clothing and his.

His hands clamped her buttocks, pushing her impossibly tight against him as he thrust higher than before. "Lust," he snarled.

"Yes. *Yes!*" The world exploded. Exploded with slashes of color—red, blue, green, and gold, shifting, rippling, undulating like the river.

Almost unconscious with the pleasure of it, she hung on his shoulders, her head fallen back, her body receiving his thrusts until he shouted his triumph and staggered. The bed received their bodies still locked together.

Tabor stirred, then groaned as a body moved with him. His hand caressed the fine-boned back, the long fall of silken hair. She lay so sweetly atop him. His thumb

244

traced lazily up her spine. She shivered. Her lips moved against his chest bared through the deep V of his shirt.

Then bitter memory burnt away the hazy aftermath of pleasure. Roughly, he shifted out from under her, almost throwing her away from him. Raking a hand through his black hair, he sat up, his back to her.

She murmured, complaining softly. Her body, loose and pliant with love, remained where he left her. She could not draw her limbs together, so weak was she with satisfaction.

"I wanted to deny you pleasure."

When his voice broke through her dream, it uttered damnation for them both. She pushed herself up on one elbow, her eyes wide with shock.

He turned his head, his black brows drawn together over cold, bleak eyes. "I wanted to leave you wanting and burning."

"But you didn't," she faltered.

"I couldn't." He swallowed hard. "I . . . I needed . . ."

The exquisite color drained from her cheeks. Her lips, swollen from his kisses, tightened and pinched together. "Don't bother to explain. I quite understand what you needed."

As if the bed were hot, she sprang off it. Biting her lip against the dizziness she felt from standing up so swiftly, she managed to remain upright and steady while her skirts rearranged themselves. Her eyes searched the dim cabin, steadfastly avoiding the rumpled bed and man sitting across from her. At last she trusted herself to move with steady dignity to the washstand with its tiny mirror. With cold hands she picked up his brush and began to arrange her disordered hair.

The *Banshee* creaked. Once the voice of Mr. Pinckney shouting a command penetrated the cabin. She could feel Tabor's eyes watching her as the silence grew more painful.

Finally, when she could no longer pretend that she

could do anything more with her hair, she laid down the brush and took the chair beside his desk. "What will you do with me?" she asked, not looking at him directly.

"Return you to your father," he replied at length. "I can't punish you as you deserve. The men are dead. They had a certain element of choice in what they did. You can't be held directly responsible for their deaths."

"No." No use to protest that she was innocent. Within her burgeoned a deep and abiding pain. If he believed her capable of such an atrocity as ordering arson and incidental murder, nothing she could say would change his mind.

He stared at her white face, the dark smudges under her eyes, her tightly clasped hands. Uncontrollable, a wave of sympathy swept over him. She was, after all, a very young woman, not yet twenty. She had faced some terrible situations as a result of his interference in her life. And his own temper had once been as hot as hers.

He raked his hand through his hair again. "It'll be a long time till dawn," he muttered. "I need to get topside and relieve Mr. Pinckney at the watch."

She nodded with alacrity. "By all means do so, pirate. No need to remain below to entertain me."

Her sarcasm infuriated him. Would nothing humble her? He rose and buttoned his breeches. "It's many hours till dawn. Best avail yourself of the bed while I'm out. You look quite used up, m'lady."

A bit of color returned to her face in the form of spots of anger on her cheekbones. "Go to the devil!" she spat out. "I wouldn't lie on that bed again if it were covered in satin."

"Suit yourself," he replied, his face stiff with anger. "I'll take you back to your father's house as soon as we dock."

"No."

"What?"

"If I have to walk through the streets in full dark, I'll do it. You'll never take me anywhere again."

"We'll see about that." He closed the cabin door hard behind him.

The *Banshee* grated gently against the pilings of the dock. At the first vibration, Judith had jerked out of her uncomfortable doze and raised her head from her folded arms. With a moan of anguish she straightened her back against the chair and forced herself to her feet.

From topside came the sounds of men moving efficiently about their business. Sick with exhaustion, her head pounding, she walked out into their midst. Pride and will required that she successfully hide her feelings. No one must know that she was in any way discomfitted by the long night's journey. A glance in the tiny glass had assured her that the only sign of her pain was a deep frown line marring her forehead.

While pretending to ignore her, the crew cast nervous glances between the captain on the bridge and the sway-ing female figure among them. She looked incredibly frail and ghostlike, no bigger than a child. Her black garments much the worse for his mishandling of them resembled charitable gifts for paupers rather than the clothing of a well-to-do young woman.

When Mr. Pinckney would have approached her, Tabor caught the mate's arm and shook his head. His own feelings were in turmoil. What had started as an exercise in vengeance and retribution had gone sour. All around him his crew shot him angry looks. The mate's weathered face scowled his disapproval.

Apart and alone, Judith waited while the moorings were secured and the gangplank lowered. Dawn light reflected gold off every droplet in the moisture-laden air. It tinted the faces of the men and gilded the sails.

Judith had no eye for the beauty. Her total attention centered on maintaining her poise until she could disembark and make her way to the Talbot lines office. Surely, an early-arriving employee could be induced to

247

run to the town house for Emil and his carriage. As the plank thudded into place on the wharf, she swayed forward.

Tabor's hand closed over her elbow. "I said I'd see you home."

She tugged at her arm, but his thumb hooked over her, firmly resisting her weary effort to get free.

"Mr. Pinckney, we'll take coffee at morning call. Send a man for a carriage to pick us up there."

"I'll not take coffee with you," she contradicted him fiercely. "Let go of my arm."

"Then wait in the cabin until the carriage arrives."

"No. I'll not stay on this ship one minute longer than I have to."

"I say you will."

"And I say I won't." To punctuate her statement, she twisted her arm with desperate strength.

"Stop that," he hissed. "You'll make me hurt you."

"What do you care about a few more bruises?" Her voice was shrill and pitched to be heard by the crew. "They'll scarcely be noticed among the many you've already given me."

"Captain," Mr. Pinckney began, "don't you think . . . ?"

"This is none of your business, Pinky."

"Let me go." She threw her elbow into the pit of his stomach, then twisted away. When he gave back a step in the face of her ferocity, she slipped from his grasp. When he started toward her again, she sprang for the gangplank. At a speed she had never dared before, she sprinted down.

At the bottom she stumbled and fell to her knees. He cursed fervently under his breath, but she climbed to her feet immediately and hurried off.

Watching her, Tabor grimaced. But when he would have followed her, Mr. Pinckney stepped in front of him. "Let the lass go, Cap'n."

"She can't go home in the dark alone."

"It's not dark. And she's not alone. Me and Oren'll

248

follow her at a distance to see that no one comes near her."

"But . . ."

"Let her go, Cap'n. She's about run to the end of her line, I imagine. Leave her a little pride."

"A little pride," Tabor scoffed. "She's too stiff-necked by half."

"Aye. Just like some others I could mention." Mr. Pinckney motioned to Oren Magrath, who preceded him down the gangplank. "We'll see the poor lass gets home all right."

With a feeling akin to despair Tabor watched the two of them stride off in the direction Judith had taken. This night's work made him sick. He was exhausted both emotionally and physically.

Yet he could not go below for a quick nap. The repairs to the brigantine would begin immediately. He must supervise them. Additionally, he had to find a new mate, make a report to Reynolds, and tender some kind of apology to Beau Talbot before the *Banshee* set sail.

And before he could begin the slow, painful process of forgetting Judith.

"You're useless now. Useless. Useless." Reynolds sighed gustily as he polished his spectacles. "Obviously, someone is aware of your activities on our behalf and has taken steps to get rid of you."

"No need to worry about that," Tabor declared with more optimism than he felt. "It's all been taken care of." Judith had been hurt and angry but not in the least "taken care of."

Reynolds appeared not to have heard Tabor's statement. Instead, he replaced his spectacles and blinked owlishly through them. "Nevertheless, you won't be able to get any more information for us. Too bad really."

"Why not?"

"Because everyone knows about your activities now."

Reynolds gave an irritated wave of his hand, as if brushing away an annoying insect. "You're useless to us. It's a pity. But it's true. Pity."

"Is that all you're going to say?"

"What else is there to say? You've been careless. Pressed too hard, most likely. I'll have another assignment for you that will take you away from New Orleans as soon as repairs can be effected on your ship."

The next instant Reynolds was gasping in shock and pain as Tabor caught him by the front of his shirt and dragged him across the scarred countertop. "Is that all you're going to say?" he thundered.

"My God, man. Let me go. Let me go. What's done is done. Not my fault. You're the one in danger. Next attempt may be successful." Reynolds clawed at the iron-hard arm that held him.

"Two of my men were killed."

"And one of the enemy's . . . Let me down." Reynolds's voice changed dramatically.

"He wasn't the enemy," Tabor said as he let the man back down with deliberate slowness. "He was just a waterfront tough. Hired off the docks. Paid to do a job. No loss to the world."

"Right," Reynolds agreed in an even voice. "They usually are."

Tabor blinked. Before his eyes, the spymaster seemed to take on stature. His shoulders straightened. His chin came off his chest. The nervous mannerisms disappeared as, with purposeful care, he folded the spectacles and laid them aside. "I'm sorry about your men. If you'll give me their names, I'll see that commendations are issued at some future date."

"And letters to their families."

"Of course. Most especially letters to their families."

"Good."

Reynolds cleared his throat. "For now you'll be wise to leave New Orleans as soon as you can make your ship ready."

"It can't be soon enough for me," Tabor replied, lying in his teeth.

"Have the repairs done. Don't pay for anything. I'll take care of them. Then head directly for the Caribbean. The British are massing in Jamaica. The war is almost over for them in Europe. Bonaparte's friends are deserting him. It's only a matter of weeks, even days."

"So now they can concentrate on us?"

"Right. Until now they've mainly attacked along the Canadian frontier with green troops. But when Bonaparte surrenders, they'll have veterans to send against America. And someone's finally realized the strategic importance of New Orleans. They're trying for a pincers movement, and they're giving it all they've got. Wellington's brother-in-law, General Sir Edward Pakenham's in charge of the operation."

Tabor sucked in his breath sharply. "So the British agent in this area *was* responsible for the attack on the *Banshee.*"

Reynolds eyed him sharply. "Perhaps. Perhaps not. Who is the British agent in this area?"

The tension in the air was suddenly electric as each man subjected the other to the most minute scrutiny. Again Tabor watched as the spy's entire body seemed to stretch tighter, although Reynolds made no move.

"She's been taken care of."

"She?"

Tabor swallowed, heartily sorry for his careless tongue. At that moment he decided he was not cut out for espionage. "She's nobility. Recently arrived from England. Looks like an angel. Fights like a tiger."

Reynolds's mouth gaped slightly. He wiped a hand across it. "Do you mean Judith Talbot-Harrow?" Did his voice have a tinge of incredulity?

Tabor studied a spot on the dingy wall behind the man's shoulder. "She went right to work for the Talbot lines on the docks, for God's sake. She's in a position to give and get information of all kinds."

251

"But she can't be more than twenty years old." This time Reynolds's voice cracked slightly. The tension was gone from his voice. He reached for his spectacles.

Tabor felt the heat rise to his face. The man did not believe him. "She's nineteen," he blurted out, then flushed harder. "She wouldn't take money from me," he snarled.

"A spy usually takes money from whoever offers it," Reynolds remarked dryly. "It's a matter of principle. We work for pay."

"I . . . I didn't think about that."

"No matter." The spy hooked his spectacles over his ears, resuming his former personality. "Comes of being an amateur. Many factions at work here. Bonaparte's going to need a place to run to when he runs out of allies. Where better than a huge territory with strong French sympathies?"

"That's pretty farfetched," Tabor suggested skeptically. "The French haven't owned New Orleans for fifty years."

"Tell that to the Creoles. There are a great number of Frenchmen, old royalists, and young Bonapartists, who'd support him."

Tabor remembered the party at the Beauvaliets. Old French themselves, they had invited many people more sympathetic to France than they—Nicholas Girod, for one. Fierce old General Montignac, for another. Celeste Devranche Talbot was old French. Where did her sympathies lie? And Maurice Dufaure. Who owned his allegiance? Both were French who had allied themselves with a British aristocrat.

Tabor rubbed his fingertips against his temple, where a dull pain had begun. Suddenly, the identities of spies and counterspies did not seem such a foregone conclusion.

Reynolds was looking at him strangely. "Something you might have remembered, O'Halloran?" the spy prodded.

252

Tabor dropped his hand. "No. Not really. Just thinking."

"Keep thinking," Reynolds suggested with a brief smile. "You may come to some interesting conclusions."

"I doubt that," Tabor replied a little unsteadily. He shook his head, trying to clear it of a vision of sapphire-blue eyes furious with hurt and disappointment. What if he had wrongly subjected that lovely, gently bred young girl to . . . He couldn't have been mistaken. Even if she were not a spy, she had motive for revenge. "Still, you'd better keep an eye on her."

"Miss Talbot-Harrow!" Maurice Dufaure's surprise was unfeigned.

She rose from behind his desk, bracing herself on the knuckles of her right hand. "M'sieur Dufaure."

"What are you doing here so early?" His eyes scavenged over the desktop. His frown blackened. He pointed peremptorily. "What are you doing here? You have no business to be here."

The fierce pain in her head shortened her hair-trigger temper. "I have plenty of business here," she snarled.

"Who let you in?"

"The watchman."

Dufaure's jaw tightened.

"And before you decide to discharge the man for laxness, let me remind you that he knows me and thought nothing about my arriving early. I've come late and he's let me in to return the ledger and manifests."

"This is my office."

"And mine."

He bit his lips. "Women get in the way. They understand nothing about business."

She waved a weary hand in his direction. "Spare me the argument. I'm too tired to hear it. Just let me borrow your carriage to return to the town house. I find I am

253

decidedly unwell this morning."

What she told was nothing but the truth, but his opaque black eyes narrowed to slits. Then his lips split in a feral grin. "So you've been meeting your lover and using the Talbot lines as a place of assignation. I'll have you know this is a place of business. We have a reputation to uphold. When your father hears about this . . ."

"My father will hear my side of the story long before you have a chance to give him your garbled poison, M'sieur Dufaure." She came around his desk. "I have harmed nothing and no one. Nor have I disturbed anything on your precious desk. And where I came from is none of your concern."

"We shall see," he sneered nastily. "Your reputation . . ."

Fire exploded in her veins. She slammed her hand down on the desktop. "I have heard quite enough of this talk from you. My reputation is as good as any man's, if not better. And I do my job well. What I want to know is why you are so determined to keep me out of this office?"

Dufaure took a step back before her fury. "Control yourself, Mademoiselle."

"What is it that you are guarding so closely in that desk? What is in this office that you don't want me to see? Is there something here that my father and I should know about? Is that why you don't want me in here? Is that why you cover up your papers and close your files . . . ?" She faltered to a stop before the burning hatred in his black eyes. Distinctly, she heard him grind his teeth.

"You will say nothing," he warned. "You will say nothing at all."

Her eyebrows rose; her breath came short. "My father shall hear of all of this," she promised.

"Get out." Shoulders hunched, jaw set, he advanced upon her. "Say nothing at all to your father, or you will be very sorry. Very, very sorry."

"It's you who will be sorry, M'sieur Dufaure."

"Get out!" He raised his walking stick and sliced it through the air only inches from her shoulder.

Paralyzed in the face of such anger and violence, she remained stock still. The door burst open behind her.

"Belay that, mister!" Suddenly, flanking her on either side were male bodies. She threw them a frightened look, then let out her breath in relief. To her left stood a sailor, his face vaguely familiar. He gave her a quick reassuring glance before throwing his shoulder in front of her body. On her right she recognized the familiar face of Mr. Pinckney of the *Banshee*. Instinctively, she moved toward him.

"Are y' ready to be movin' toward home, lass?"

"Yes, sir. I'm ready." She backed toward the door. Her escort backed with her. Dufaure let the tip of his cane rest on the floor, but his angry eyes never left her face. "I don't think I'll be back in today, M'sieur," she called.

"Go to the devil," he snarled.

Tabor O'Halloran presented himself at the town house on Calle di Conti at the end of the week. He watched from the bottom of the staircase as Judith came down. Her flaming red hair contrasted strongly with the translucent skin and somber black dress. A study in contrasts, he thought her—the most beautiful woman he had ever seen.

Halfway down the staircase she halted. "My father is not at home."

"Could you tell me where I might find him?" He seemed to be having trouble keeping his voice even.

"Beau has gone to join Celeste at *Ombres Azurées*."

"And left you here alone." Tabor frowned. If Reynolds's intelligence reports were true, New Orleans could be a dangerous city very shortly. She should have a

255

man's protection. Spy or no spy.

"I am accustomed to being alone," came the cool reply.

"Nevertheless . . ."

"Beau is not here, Mr. O'Halloran. And that's for the best. He's not very happy with you at this time."

"That's what I came to talk to him about."

"And what do you intend to tell him?"

Tabor cleared his throat uneasily. He opened his mouth, then closed it again.

"But do forgive me. Surely that can be none of my business, since it in no way has anything to do with me." She turned to start back up the stairs.

"Wait." Tabor bounded up a couple of steps.

She turned half around on the staircase.

"Wait . . ." He was uncomfortably reminded of the Beauvaliets' reception. "I . . . Judith, are you all right?"

"Do you mean physically? Physically I am quite well. A bit tired perhaps. Too many late nights and unexpected trips."

He grimaced. "Physically is part of it."

She waited.

"Are you . . . all right?"

She lifted her chin. "I'm better than ever."

"I don't understand."

"I still harbored one or two illusions about people before I met you. But not now. Now I harbor no illusions at all."

He flushed. "You're a fine one to talk about illusions."

"I don't know what you're talking about." She shuddered. How could anything hurt so much as the sight of this man? "I wish you'd go away."

"I'm sailing tonight."

"Oh."

He teetered on the riser. The silence stretched barren between them. "There's nothing else to say," he muttered suddenly. "There's only this." He bounded up the steps. Before she could move, he pulled her into his

256

arms and kissed her hungrily. Kissed her face, her cheeks, her hair, her closed eyes. Frantically, she pushed against him, but only when he had finished did he stop the kisses.

Then he steadied her upright and spun on his heel. Down the stairs he thudded. At the bottom he halted to cast one last glance over his shoulder. "Good-bye, Miss Talbot-Harrow."

She watched the front door close behind him. His boots thudded down the steps. Drawn perversely to look upon that which hurt her most, she ran down the stairs and pulled aside the lace curtains at the window.

He had already passed beyond her sight, but still she listened achingly until his footsteps faded.

"Miss Judith, there's a messenger done rode all the way from *Ombres Azurées*." Emil's face betrayed his anxiety as he led the man forward. All around them the business of the docks continued without pause.

Georges stepped back quickly, shifting the sheltering umbrella aside as Judith pushed herself up, her palms flat on the small traveling desk. *Celeste! It must be Celeste. Poor Beau. He loved her so much. He'll be lost without her.* She steadied herself and rose, feeling light-headed as the blood drained from her face.

The man shifted from one foot to the other. His eyes dropped to a spot of tar on the planks between his feet. He crushed his hat in a convulsive grip. Emil exchanged glances with Georges, who closed the umbrella.

"Maîtresse . . ." the man began. He shook his head. "Maîtresse . . ."

"Say what you have come to say," she commanded gently.

"M'sieur Talbot . . . M'sieur Beau . . . He's gone and got himself in a duel. Miss Laura, she says come quick."

Judith could not credit her ears. "You must be mistaken."

257

"No, Maîtresse. He do it. He get angry. Very angry."

Judith blinked. He could not mean Beau Talbot. Not
the Honorable Howard Francis Talbot, who had made no
demur when his wife's betrayal became a scandal that
rocked the *ton*, who had not even cared to follow the man
who had borne away his younger daughter after
destroying her reputation. Beau Talbot would never fight
a duel. "You must be mistaken," she said again.

The man looked as if he wanted to cry. "No, Maîtresse.
Maîtresse Talbot, she say you come quick. Come quick.
You to help her stop him."

"A word from my stepmother should be sufficient,"
Judith replied dryly. Still she motioned to Georges, who
tucked the umbrella under his arm and folded the chair.
Emil followed his lead and folded the table. Together, a
procession of four, they hurried to the carriage.

Emil mounted to the box, and the messenger swung up
behind like a London footman. Georges folded down the
step and held open the door. Just before she climbed the
step, she leaned backward. "Who did he challenge?"

The messenger peered down at her. "That gamblin'
man Clay Sutherland."

Interlude IV

Above every window in the small private parlor hung a swag of black material. Family portraits as well as the oval mirror had been veiled with black-dyed cheesecloth. Every room in the house was permeated with the scents from the candles Celeste ordered kept by her bedside at all times.

Standing beside the drawn drapes, Judith wrinkled her nose in distaste at the odors that came from their heavy folds. Beeswax and vetiver and something unidentifiable but infinitely more potent prickled and tickled at her senses.

Laura sat with her hands in her lap, contemplating the maid as she set down the tea tray on the low table. When the delicate porcelain cups clicked and tinkled against each other, the gentle black face twisted. Smothering a sob in her apron, the maid scurried from the room.

Frustrated almost beyond endurance, Judith lifted one end of the heavy swag, then tossed it from her contemptuously. "I can't take all of this in. It's too much. Papa dead . . . ?"

With the studied motions of a wind-up toy, Laura leaned forward to pour the thick chicory coffee into exquisite porcelain cups. "Will you have cream and sugar?"

Judith spun around. "For God's sake, Laura. I don't

want anything to drink. I don't want anything to eat."

"You might not want to, but we have to. We have to keep up our strength. Remember. Papa's no longer here, so we have to do everything for ourselves." They stared at each other in silence. Then suddenly Laura's tight control broke. She buried her face in her hands. "I don't think I can live with myself. I was the one who caused his death."

Judith threw up her hands in disgust. "No one causes another person's death, Laura, unless he actually murders him."

The older girl raised her eyes, sunken and bruised from crying. So pale and worn was she that she did not look like herself. She had scraped her glorious red hair back from her face in a severe chignon and capped it with a black lace chapel veil. "Papa would never have challenged Clay if I hadn't been such a fool."

"That's silly, Laura." Judith began to prowl around the room, picking up objects, putting them back down again. "When two men decide to fight a duel, there are other things involved besides the obvious. I'm sure that you weren't the only thing."

Oblivious to her sister's restlessness, Laura continued the familiar motions, but when she spooned the sugar from the bowl, her hand began to shake. The grains of sugar scattered across the surface of the silver tray. She put down the spoon with a sob. "I . . . can't do anything right. I can't even pour myself a cup of coffee."

Judith came to her side to put her hand on her sister's shoulder. How hot and feverish she felt! She had probably not slept a wink since Beau had been brought in, his handsome face . . . Shuddering, she turned her thoughts firmly away from the gruesome memories. "Laura, you've always been able to do what was necessary. Remember, we took care of both our parents."

"But I might as well have shot him myself," Laura keened helplessly, turning her face away.

Judith's hand closed tighter. Gently, she pushed

260

against her sister with a rocking motion. "But you didn't, Laura. You've got to stop these thoughts. You of all people. After you've preached and preached: don't be sorry for yourself."

"I'm not. Can't you understand? I'll never be able to put the sight of his wounded body out of my mind. He was so still. I'd never seen him still. He was always so vital, so alive. His eyes were so blue. When Joshua brought him in, his eyes were closed. Oh, Judith, I'd never seen Papa asleep."

Tears welled in Judith's eyes. Despite her blinking fiercely and tilting her head back, they trickled down her cheeks. She pressed her thumb and third finger tight against the bridge of her nose. When the scalding pain subsided somewhat, she spoke firmly. "Stop that, Laura. Stop tearing yourself to pieces."

But the painful memories could not be contained. "They were just as blue as yours. I did it, Judith. *My* infatuation, *my* lack of judgment, *my* lack of control ended his life! Oh, God, if I could only do it over again."

Judith dropped down on the settee and pulled Laura against her. With her own hands trembling, she patted and stroked the back of Laura's head while her sister's tears wet the shoulder of her blouse. "Laura, be quiet. Don't think about it."

Laura would not be quiet. Held inside her so long in her struggle for control, her sobs burst out in deep, ugly sounds. For several minutes she could not be comforted. Her whole body was racked. Still, Judith held her as she had held their mother, murmuring meaningless words until at last the terrible weeping quieted and finally ceased.

When finally Laura seemed steady enough to sit alone, Judith stood up. Pulling her own handkerchief from her sleeve, she walked across the room. Dragging down the black veiling from the mirror, she dabbed at her cheeks and tucked in straying wisps of her own hair.

She had learned long ago that mundane tasks always quieted her. They were especially soothing when she

261

concentrated on them to the exclusion of all else. When she was satisfied that she had repaired the emotional ravages, she turned back to her sister with what she hoped was a serene countenance. "Now, Laura, you're going to have to go on because all the people on *Ombres Azurées* depend on you, just as Talbot Shipping depends on me to step in for Papa. You didn't kill him, but we mustn't let all he worked for during his life slip away."

Laura pulled a fresh black-edged handkerchief from her pocket. "You're right, of course. That's why he left England. To build in the new world and make a success. We're fortunate that he let us take care of some of his things." She pressed the handkerchief to her mouth, suppressing another sob.

If she starts crying again, I don't know what I'll do. "Do you really think so?" she snapped, harder than she meant to. "I think Papa has put both of us in awkward, unpleasant situations."

"Judith!"

Determined to focus her sister's mind on more practical things than the weeping that was making her ill, Judith nodded her head. "Well, he did. He left the fields and the mill to you, but you don't have a house to live in unless you stay in Celeste's good graces. He left the house and the land fronting the bayou to her. He wanted to make sure she was taken care of."

Laura frowned, her weeping forgotten as she concentrated on defending the father she loved. "Yes," she replied positively, "but I don't mind. After all, *Ombres Azurées* was hers to begin with."

Judith snorted inelegantly. "Laura, you and I both know that Celeste would have lost all of this if not for Beau."

"He was such a good man."

No matter what she said, Laura seemed bent on canonizing their father rather than looking at a few hard facts. "You're missing the point."

At that remark the older sister drew herself up. Her

mouth fashioned itself in disapproving lines that reminded Judith of *Grandmère*. "You don't have anything to complain about. Papa left you his controlling interest in Talbot Shipping."

Inwardly, Judith grinned. *Good to see the old backbone, sister dear.* "With Maurice Dufaure to fight with me at every turn."

"You should be glad of Maurice's guidance." Laura cleared her throat in an effort to achieve a more normal tone. "He's had experience in business."

"He hates me." The words fell into a silence that grew between them. *Why did I say that? My sister doesn't know anything about hatred. Until now she's lived in a world of love.*

Laura sounded a little less hoarse. "I find that difficult to believe. Maurice has always been one of our closest friends."

"Maybe yours, but not mine."

Judith watched her sister's hand shake as she lifted the delicate cup to her lips and tasted. Laura wrinkled her nose and set the cup down immediately. "This coffee is cold. I must ring for another pot."

Back to the coffee again. With an impatient sigh Judith turned and walked to the window. Pulling aside the swag and drawing the draperies, she looked out over the acres that Beau had loved. The day was gray with very little sun. She let the drapery fall back, again smelling its pervasive odors.

How she would like to open the windows and let in a freshening breeze, but a blast of cold air, probably the last of winter in the semitropical climate, had complicated living at *Ombres Azurées* the night of Beau's death. For the few days when the temperature was unpleasant, open braziers of charcoal were brought into the various rooms by the servants. To open the house with no more effective heating system than that would undoubtedly disturb Celeste, who was bedridden with grief.

Suddenly, Judith missed her home terribly. There

263

would be snow on the ground and the bushes and trees would be stark, black, and glistening against it. "He should never have brought me here from England. I made so much misery for him these last few months."

Instantly, Laura's face crumpled. Her shoulders slumped. "No, you didn't."

Judith nodded her head. "I embarrassed him in front of all his friends."

Laura studied her hands clasped lightly in her lap. "Maybe a little, but, Judith, having you here made him feel good about himself."

The maid answered the bell. Judith grimaced while Laura ordered another pot of coffee.

Suddenly, Judith's own guilt seemed to bear down upon her. "I said horrible things to him. I always told him that I wanted to go back to England, and I do except . . . I just don't know."

"Well, I do." After Laura filled the two demitasse cups with coffee, she walked to a highboy across the room and opened the door. She returned bearing a decanter of Beau's favorite whiskey, a secretive smile on her face. "I'll tell you what we're going to do," she whispered conspiratorially. She poured a thimbleful of whiskey into each of the cups.

Judith watched with an unhappy expression on her face. Not for the world would she tell her sister that she would rather not drink spirits. Laura's smile was her first since Beau's death.

When Laura extended the cup, Judith came forward and took it off the saucer. Like a man drinking from a mug, she saluted her sister.

Laura returned the salute. "To the Talbot sisters."

They drank together, Judith barely managing to keep from coughing. A thimbleful of whiskey in a demitasse of hot coffee made a potent shot. Through watery eyes she stared at her sister's pleased expression. The Talbot sisters was a dream of Laura's. Judith had her own dream.

To Judith Talbot-Harrow, she reminded herself.

264

Chapter Thirteen

Accompanied by the Devranche family lawyer, Bertrand St. Cyr, Judith pushed open the door to the Talbot lines office. Only two weeks had passed since she had received the message that her father had challenged Clay Sutherland to a duel. Now the Honorable Howard Francis Talbot, nephew of the Earl of Teigh, lay at rest among the Devranches of New France in a pale marble mausoleum nestled beneath spreading water oaks beside the Bayou of Shadows.

And his daughter had come to claim her own.

Clad in a gray suit, his sleeve encased in a black armband, Maurice Dufaure rose from behind his desk. The glowering frown that darkened his face at the sight of Judith was wiped away as the Devranche family lawyer entered behind her.

Despite the lack of necessity, introductions were made, formalities observed. Man and girl eyed each other with open hostility as the lawyer explained the terms of Beau Talbot's will to the electric air between them.

Prepared for a storm, Judith could hardly believe Dufaure's relatively mild response to St. Cyr's stated intent to make known the contents of the will. Only the angry flash of his eyes, swiftly concealed beneath veined, drooping lids, betrayed his antipathy.

By the time the lawyer's voice had ceased, Dufaure's

face was as expressionless as a mask. With almost no hesitation he agreed to hand over the books to St. Cyr at the end of the financial period so that an audit could be made for purposes of probate. Likewise, he made no demur but bowed easily as the lawyer opened the door to the office that had been Beau's.

A shiver scudded up Judith's spine as she stepped over the threshold. Not that she believed in ghosts, nor that she felt Beau's presence. The short time she had lived with him had given her a reasonably clear picture of his work habits. He had been much too active to sit behind a desk. He had been happiest riding a tall horse or balancing himself on the deck of a tall ship. Unless driven by necessity, he had left books and papers to hirelings.

Sadly, she acknowledged the fact that Beau's great loves had been Celeste and *Ombres Azurées*. A member if not a scion of the landed gentry of England, he had embraced the plantation with fervor. The Talbot Lines that had made it all possible was frequently a nuisance and an inconvenience. Much like herself.

The office held no memories of Beau. Instead, it filled her with a sense of ownership and with it the awesome sense of responsibility. Suddenly, she saw herself as St. Cyr must see her, although his face betrayed nothing. In a matter of months she would be twenty years old, and yet she was the majority owner of a fleet of ships.

Determined not to appear overawed, she walked straight to her father's imposing desk of polished cypress. Bigger than Maurice's, it was fully six feet wide and four feet deep. Its tambour top was closed and securely locked. As her lawyer turned to Maurice for the key, she reached into her reticule and drew it forth.

Not for nothing had she and Laura gone through the keys in Beau's leather wallet, trying all the doors at *Ombres Azurées*. Those that fit doors in the plantation, she had left with Laura. The rest she had taken as her own. Back in New Orleans, she had used one to open the town house. Now she recognized the smaller key to be the

266

one to open the desk.

"I see you came prepared, mademoiselle." St. Cyr acknowledged her right to sit by pulling out her chair.

"Yes, m'sieur. I expect to spend many hours here. I did not want to delay."

"We shall have to hire someone new for the docks," Dufaure remarked sourly.

"Perhaps not," Judith smiled wanly. "My father spent very little time in here. I can probably do the work he did and my own work as well."

The lawyer raised his eyebrows in surprise. "But surely you will want to hire an agent to take care of your interests here. If I may suggest . . ."

"Thank you, m'sieur, but I really don't think I shall be hiring anyone." She looked inquiringly at Dufaure. "Unless it were perhaps a clerk?"

A muscle ticked in his jaw. "We need no one."

The lawyer gaped, then addressed himself to Maurice. "But, M'sieur Dufaure, surely there is more work than one man and an inexperienced . . . ?" He shut his mouth over the sentence that might be construed as lack of confidence in his client.

Dufaure shrugged as Judith turned the key in the lock. The desktop slid up smoothly. "M'sieur Dufaure and I have worked together for some months now, M'sieur St. Cyr. Since my father was much occupied with problems at *Ombres Azurées*, the running of the business will probably go on as before." Even as she spoke, she stared at the ledgers and papers piled and stuffed haphazardly inside. Organization did not seem to have been one of Beau's strong points.

Refusing to be daunted, she raised her eyes to the wall behind the desk. There hung a huge Mercator of the world with its fanciful cardinal rose. Attached to its surface by magnets were eight tiny ships in two oceans and the Gulf of Mexico. She felt a surge of anticipation and pride. "Since I have worked on the docks, I am eager to see the other side of the business as well."

The smile put on for the benefit of the lawyer faded as Dufaure shifted impatiently. His hands dropped to his sides, where they clenched into fists. The gesture was not lost on St. Cyr. The partner's attitude had been well detailed by Judith, who, along with her sister, had engaged him on a handsome retainer to handle the complicated legal business of the Talbot estate. St. Cyr's eyes flew swiftly to Judith, whose serene profile indicated that she had not seen the gesture.

He bowed. "I quite agree with you, Mademoiselle Talbot. I always advise people in times of extreme bereavement to make no radical changes for six months to a year. The mind may be clouded by grief; the judgment may not be sound. Decisions made under such abnormal conditions may come back to haunt their maker."

Dufaure cleared his throat noisily. "If you will excuse me, I will return to work. The *Colchester* is in the river and should be arriving day after tomorrow. Shippers must be notified. St. Cyr. Miss Talbot-Harrow." He barely inclined his head before stalking out.

Judith watched him go before meeting St. Cyr's eyes. "I thank you for accompanying me, M'sieur St. Cyr."

"It was my pleasure, Miss Talbot."

"Talbot-Harrow, if you please. To distinguish me from my sister."

He inclined his head again without comment.

"I'll be working here in my father's stead, as I told you. She'll be managing *Ombres Azurées*."

He took from his case several blue-backed documents and handed them to her. "Here are the documents we discussed—your will and your sister's, the powers of attorney. You for your sister, she for you. Madame Talbot's. You must look these over. If they are satisfactory, they should be signed before witnesses. Thereafter I'll keep them in my office."

She took them with a steady hand. "I'll see to them within the next few days."

"*Très bien*. Moreover, if I can be of service"—he

268

paused delicately—"in matters in this office, don't hesitate to summon me."

"I hope your legal services will be all that will be needed."

He raised her hand to his lips. "As do I, Mademoiselle Talbot-Harrow."

When he was gone Judith stared at the interior of the huge desk. The daunting stack of ledgers, the scraps of paper and notes sticking out to mark places, the pigeonholes stuffed with papers. In her left hand she still held the key that would open the desk's drawers which undoubtedly contained more of the same.

When she tried to guide it into one of the locks, her hand started to shake. Clenching her fist around the small piece of brass, she sat back in the chair, her other hand over her eyes. Fear sent nervous rigors to all parts of her body. Fear likewise convulsed her stomach.

So long as her father was alive, she had not had to take ultimate blame for mistakes. He was the boss; he would somehow make it all right. But now she was the boss. If she made a mistake, *she* must somehow make it right.

All around her were people who believed she would fail. Even she had no faith in herself. She needed time to learn the business, to gradually assume the responsibilities. But she had been loaded with the responsibilities with no time at all.

A dark face with burning blue eyes imposed itself on her consciousness. How strange that she should think of him at this time! For what help would Tabor O'Halloran have been? A swashbuckling pirate, a seducer, a liar. If only he could have been someone she could have depended on.

A tiny whimper and then a shuddering intake of breath were the only sounds she allowed herself before she impatiently pulled her hand away and forced herself to open the drawer.

"The *Colchester* is a flute, the sister ship of the

269

Portchester. I'm sure you remember her," he added nastily. At the flash of her eyes he cleared his throat. "Nothing fancy, either one of them. Just good, dependable workhorses carrying goods around the world."

"So we have in all three flutes?"

"Yes, and a schooner that sails around the Florida peninsula. Our newest ship is a merchant ship, the *Laurel,* named for your sister, and, of course, the three merchantmen."

"Of the 'white' fleet."

"Exactly so," Dufaure agreed. "The *White Hound,* the *White Cloud,* and the *White Lady.*"

She looked from the list to the map. The tiny magnets represented hundreds and thousands of dollars in cargo and passengers. More than that, they represented power and independence. She hunched her shoulders against the thrill that shot through her.

"Someone must go down to the docks to meet the *Colchester.*" Dufaure waited for her reply.

She looked at the work on her desk. Nothing seemed of an emergency nature. A potential shipper was coming after lunch, as was a shipper who had used the Talbot lines since Beau had first come to New Orleans. She was eager to meet both of them and impress upon them that the firm could and should carry their goods efficiently.

Still, she would be free tomorrow and the rest of the week. "I can easily continue to handle that end of the business," she agreed, noting how he seemed to relax slightly. "But we're probably going to have to employ a clerk of some sort. I can't see how you did all the paperwork yourself."

"A clerk will not be necessary," Dufaure objected nervously. "Your father met the public. I handled the office work. There is no need to bring someone in here to confuse everything. He will only make mistakes. The papers can all be taken care of if one works steadily."

She looked doubtfully at the stacks of manifests and bills on her desk. What sort of work did Dufaure do if all

270

these things were still to be done?

He caught her look. "Perhaps in the fall when the tonnage of cotton is great," he suggested vaguely.

With a shake of her head she rose. "If you insist. However, I intend to work through these papers. If I find I cannot get everything done and do the work on the docks, I shall hire someone."

Ignoring the glare of antipathy, she collected the appropriate ledger and made her exit.

Georges's smile flashed white as he touched his furled whip to his top hat. Emil bowed ceremoniously as he held the door and assisted her into the landau. Since Beau's death her driver had acknowledged her position and her right to be about her business.

Her footman, however, still retained his coolness. She had noted the way he hovered near Celeste whenever that lady took a drive. His manner toward Beau's lady was affable as well as almost smotheringly protective. With a wry smile she realized that he, the stronger of the two men, had an unremitting sense of propriety. While he would never approve of her, she respected him for his solicitude and for his loyalty to the Devranches.

Georges guided the carriage through the streets and up onto the wharf. The double masts and sheets of the *Colchester* distinguished her from the bigger merchantmen and smaller schooners with their lateen-shaped sails. The morning shower had wet the area down, and now the sun gilded spars and rigging with gold.

Emil sprang down and opened the door. As she alighted, she took a deep breath of the tangy salt air. Even in the short time she had lived there she had come to love New Orleans. Suddenly, a sharp cry of warning rang out. Looking up, she froze in horror.

A huge black man, naked to the waist, his eyes wide and glazed, his teeth bared in a snarl, dashed toward her. A terrible long knife, the kind used to cut cane, flashed in the sunlight.

271

She could not move, could not believe that he was plunging toward her with great leaping strides. His huge splayed feet thudded over the worn boards. From his mouth came a wordless cry.

Emil fell back against the side of the landau, aghast. From his seat on the box, Georges stared as if hypnotized.

The assassin swung the knife in a circle around his head. She heard it whistle, saw its nicked edge catch the light, but could not move to save herself.

A pistol shot broke the trance of the terrified onlookers. The charging man stumbled; his cry changed to a scream. He spun around, clutching at the center of his back as if he had been stung.

A tall man in a planter's hat and butternut broadcloth frock coat dropped a smoking pistol at his feet and drew another from his belt. As he cocked it, the huge black man screamed again, this time in pain and fear at the sight of his own bloodstained hand. As if he were not wounded, he dodged around the side of the landau and dived over the side of the wharf.

Shaking with fright, Judith found her legs would not support her. She sank to her knees on the salt-encrusted planking and buried her face in her hands.

The tall man strode to the spot where the black man had dived into the water, and stared down. Longshoremen, seamen, shippers, drivers of drays gathered around him, swearing, marveling, clapping the hero on the back for his quick thinking, and staring down into the muddy waters.

The captain and the mate of the *Colchester* both hurried down the gangplank to Judith's side.

"I'm all right. I'm really all right," she managed to say in answer to the former's frantic questions. "What could have been wrong with that man? I never saw him before in my life."

The foreman of the longshoremen assisted her to her feet. "Voodoo," he averred darkly. "Probably crocked to the gills with rum and mandragora."

272

"Mandragora?" Judith gasped.

"Makes 'em wild. They'll do crazy things. Get a crazy idea in their heads and can't think of nothin' else."

Judith clenched her hand against her mouth, remembering Celeste and Berthe's potions. Horrible thoughts flashed through her head, but she drove them out and struggled for control. "The man who saved me . . ."

"Quick-thinking chap," agreed the captain of the *Colchester*.

"I'd like to thank him." She looked toward the buzzing crowd milling around the wharf.

"I'll get him," the foreman volunteered.

"Maîtresse?" Emil bowed humbly. "Will you get back in the carriage? Georges and I will take you home."

She took a deep breath. Her shaking had almost stopped. Nothing had really happened. "Nonsense. I'm fine. I just had a little fright after all." She looked around with a shaky smile. "But I do want to thank the man who saved me."

"I can't find him, Miz Talbot." The longshoreman came back, scratching his head. "Maybe he took off after the feller?"

"Strange," remarked the captain of the *Colchester*. "But then he probably didn't want a lot of embarrassing gratitude. Amazing how he could act so fast. I saw the whole thing myself, but I was just paralyzed."

"Bad news, M'sieur Dufaure?" Judith asked curiously as her partner opened and read the same letter for the third time. His face darkened and he passed his hand across his forehead.

With a sharp shake of his head he refolded the paper and thrust it clumsily back into its envelope.

Judith shrugged, then went back to work. Of late, Dufaure had been grudgingly polite and generally uncommunicative. Had she not been too busy with her own work to dwell on his rudeness, she would have been

273

decidedly uncomfortable.

"France has a new government," he said suddenly.

"I beg your pardon."

"The emperor has abdicated. The Emperor of France. The damned British—" He looked at her with pure poison in his stare.

She did not turn a hair.

"They will be onto our ships next," he continued. "Yours and mine. You will see. Talbot flies an American flag."

"We fly the blue flag with the white hound. The talbot," she replied mildly. "My father took it from the Teigh crest. It belongs to him."

He did not reply for a while. She went back to her books again. "The emperor will escape. He only needs a place to regroup his forces. He will be welcomed when he chooses to return," he muttered. "Elba is nothing."

"The British will take steps to see that he has no place to go. They will never allow him to return to France."

"He will always have a place," Dufaure insisted obliquely.

"I'm surprised that anyone would want him," Judith remarked without looking up. "All of Europe was at war because of him."

"You know nothing!" Dufaure spat out. "You know nothing at all about the glory, the prosperity that he brought us all."

Judith stared at the man, noting his extreme agitation. She knew she should not say any more. Yet his fury goaded her to retaliate. "Is that how you had money to buy a partnership in Talbot Shipping?" she asked evenly. "With money that Napoleon gave you?"

He flung up his head, staring hard at her, suddenly conscious of what he had said. His nostrils dilated as if he scented danger. When he met her eye, the malice in his look made her draw back in spite of herself. "Where I got my money is no business of yours," he snarled.

"Of course not," she managed to say. "If Beau was

satisfied, then so I am."

"He was." Standing up abruptly, he pulled the top of his desk down with a clattering bang. "I will be back."

"Please don't hurry," she muttered after him as he slammed the door.

The carriage bounced from side to side on the rutted road to *Ombres Azurées*. Georges could see the road only as a pale ribbon between the impenetrable walls of trees. They had not dared to fill the carriage lamps with kerosene for fear of splashing fire.

Black as the night was, the interior of the carriage was blacker. Judith clung with both hands to the strap to keep from being pitched onto the floor. The team's thundering hooves struck up dust from the roadbed that sifted in and made her sneeze.

Between clenched teeth she cursed the childhood that had deprived her of so much practical training. Laura undoubtedly rode beautifully while she had never even been near a pony. If Charlotte or Beau or *Grandmère* had not been so parsimonious, she could be galloping along easily instead of hanging on to a strap while her body was slowly beaten black and blue.

Bracing her feet against the seat opposite her, she silently vowed that upon her return to New Orleans, she would purchase a horse and take riding lessons.

A particularly bad rut tossed her to the side and bruised her temple despite the excellent padding of the carriage's interior. She cursed fervently, looking upward as she did so, tempted to hammer on the roof to signal Georges to slow down.

But the urgency of Laura's message could not be doubted. Instinctively, she knew her sister would never have summoned her had the matter not been of gravest urgency. With a prickling of her eyes she remembered the message of Beau's death.

When the message, a written one this time, had

275

arrived, she had ordered the carriage instantly. With Georges and Emil on the box, they had set out without supper. And now she cursed the abominable road that prohibited all but the slowest travel in comfort.

On a comparatively flat stretch, she took a deep breath. Celeste had been her first thought. At the graveside, her white face, strained and drawn until she looked twice her age, had shown like a specter through the black veiling. Her stepmother's health must have deteriorated rapidly after their father's death. She had lived in virtual seclusion. And only once in the past two months since the funeral had Laura come into town.

A mirthless smile tugged up one corner of her mouth. If Celeste were very ill, Judith would bet even money that the woman had taken too much of the nostrums that Berthe prepared for her.

Of course, Celeste was only a little younger than Charlotte had been. Perhaps her constitution really was very weak. The strain of Beau's death had undoubtedly undermined her will to live and depleted her frail strength.

Whatever the situation, Laura had seen fit to send an urgent summons.

The carriage rose out of a rut and dropped down on the other side with such force that Judith's teeth snapped together. She uttered a sharp exclamation and glanced longingly overhead again. A knock on the roof of the carriage, and Georges would slow down.

She shook her head and set her jaw. If Laura needed her, she could endure this for just a few more miles.

Suddenly, out of the dark came a sharp crack. A horrible scream followed, and the horses veered off to the side. The carriage rocked and swayed perilously. The strap was torn from her grasp, and she was thrown sidewise on the seat, then slung off onto the floor.

Had a part of the carriage broken? The noise had sounded almost like a gunshot.

Through the impenetrable darkness came the whinnying of horses and Georges's curses. The carriage slewed violently to one side, then came to a halt.

"Climb down from there!" A voice shouted.

Highwaymen!

She scrambled to the door, feeling for the holstered pistol that she knew was there.

"Giddap!" A blacksnake whip cracked in the darkness. The carriage took another violent jump, then sprang forward, throwing her again to the floor and wringing a cry of pain from her as her elbow took her full weight.

Another shot rang out. Georges's shout was almost drowned in the high-pitched scream of the nigh horse.

Again the pitching and slewing to the side. The screaming of an animal in pain. Men's voices shouting unintelligible things.

Breathless, her head aching, her whole body throbbing, she scrambled around and scrabbled for the pistol in the door. Just as her hand closed over it, the door flew open, almost dragging the butt from her grasp.

"Come outa there!"

"No!" She pulled the weapon back against her chest and used her left hand to pull back the hammer. As the man's form filled the doorway, a blacker outline against the starless sky, she fired at point-blank range.

His breath whooshed out of his body as he flew back. The door slammed shut.

"The bitch is armed! She got Squirrel dead center."

"Not anymore she's not. She's emptied her pistol. Get her. Open that door."

"Not me."

"Damned yella belly."

"Maybe so. But you wanta take a chance that she ain't got another one, go ahead."

The wounded horse was grunting and braying in pain. She could hear the jingle of harness. Trembling, she reversed the pistol and pushed herself upward and onto the seat. Her eyes darted fearfully back and forth from one door to the other. The voices came from one side of the carriage only, but she could not tell how many were around her. They might try to sneak around behind and come at her from both sides.

"Run for it, damn you!" The leader's voice commanded.

"You better not hurt Maîtresse." She heard Georges's panting protests. "She's got no money. She's poor."

A curse silenced him. "Git, I said, before I give yuh what I give the other one."

So Emil had been shot. Judith bit her lip and swiped at her face with her free hand. As she did, she heard Georges's footsteps running away.

A chuckle came from outside. "Shore can run."

The leader grunted. "Let's get on with this."

"But, boss . . ."

"We ain't gonna open the door," the leader sneered. She shuddered.

"How yuh gonna get her outa there?"

"Cut that team loose."

Even as she tried to make a plan, she felt the carriage move.

"Put your backs into it!"

The carriage inched forward, rolled up the side of a hump. There the front wheels teetered for a breath, then dropped down on the other side.

"Again!" came the shout. "Heave!"

The back wheels went over the same hump. The floor tilted.

"Give her a shove."

Suddenly, it was rolling forward and downward. Fast and faster. The men's rough voices shouted and cheered. Her hand flew to the door handle, swung it open just as the front wheels hit the water.

A great splash, then the carriage was lurching forward, sinking as the inky water gurgled in across the floor.

She took a deep breath. Horror and fear throttled the scream in her throat. And then she jumped outward from the toppling vehicle into the black night.

278

Chapter Fourteen

Cold, dark water closed over her head. Down she went, and down. Her skirt and petticoats wrapped themselves around her limbs already weighted by her shoes. For a terrifying moment she could not remember the way to the surface, for the whole world was black.

With difficulty she suppressed the scream that would have doomed her, and managed to turn in the water. Then, kicking with all her strength, she broke the surface and caught a breath. Immediately, the weight of her garments dragged her down again.

As she went, one flailing arm slapped against the wooden side of the carriage. Kicking again, she managed to propel herself toward it. Her clutching fingers found the brass lamp fixture. Instinctively, she pulled herself toward it and let it bear her weight as she sucked in a great lungful of air.

Thank God! The carriage was afloat.

But for how long? She whimpered low in her throat. She knew nothing about swimming, had never been in water deeper than a bathtub in her life. Blind instinct had driven her to kick and flail. Without the carriage she would be lost. Beneath her added weight it listed perilously and began to settle. Too much iron and brass was dragging it down.

Sobbing aloud, she threw her head back as her

shoulders sank under the water. She must do something to reach the bank. She must! Clinging with one hand, she twisted to untie one shoe and then the other, letting them fall away. Her legs felt somewhat lighter. Experimentally, she kicked.

Air gurgled out of the carriage. It settled deeper in the water as she cried out in fear.

Another minute and she would have nothing to hang on to. The bank might be two feet beyond her arm's reach or twenty. She had no way of knowing. She could not see the bank in the smothering darkness. She was going to drown if she could not find a way to save herself. *Think!*

The lamp was attached to the front of the carriage beside the driver's box. It had gone into the bayou first. Therefore, the back of the carriage must be closer to the shore. Shifting her grip, she began to pull herself along the top.

Another menacing gurgle, and the vehicle settled deeper.

She cast around her fearfully, encountering only the same impenetrable blackness. *How deep was this wretched bayou?*

The initial terror began to subside. She began to shiver. Her eyes stung as her imagination filled the cold, brackish water with slimy things. Working along the docks, she had seen all matter of creatures pulled out of the river. Huge gars with rows of sharp teeth. Gigantic catfish with spiny whiskers. Water moccasins.

A vision of an alligator swimming toward her, jaws open to crush and rend her, made her hug the carriage tighter.

She began to weep again. To weep like a child. She had no more power to save herself than a terrified, helpless child. She was going to drown in this filthy water. Her body might never be found. Even if it were, she would be unrecognizable.

"Help!"

The word burst from her throat before she could stop

it. Even the knowledge that she might alert the highwaymen to the fact that she was alive could not stifle that cry.

"Help! Somebody please help me!" Her voice sounded pitifully thin and weak. No one could hear it even if someone were there to hear. The carriage settled a little deeper, but only a little. Perhaps its wheels had touched bottom. She pressed gingerly against it. But no! It tilted.

Dear Lord! It was toppling over onto its side. Air bubbled out from under the top.

"Help! For God's sake, help!"

Something slapped the water not far from her. "Grab hold of the rope!" a deep voice called.

Frantically, she clawed at the water. "I can't find it," she sobbed. "I can't find it. Oh, help! I'm sinking."

The water closed over her head again as the carriage fell away beneath her. A desperate scissor kick brought her to the surface. Her hands flailed frenziedly. "Hel—" The water rushed into her mouth.

Then the rope slapped across her face. Her arms and hands clamped about it as she sank again. But her panic was stilled by the tug that dragged her forward. For a tiny space she was underwater; then she was up. Her face cleared, then her shoulders. The rope drew her steadily and strongly through the water that washed away her tears.

She reached the bank before she knew it. Her hands and arms plowed through gumbo mud. She sobbed in gratitude, letting go of the rope with one hand to hook her fingers into the steeply slanting bank of the levee.

"You all right?" came the voice from somewhere above her.

"Yes." She lifted her head to try to pierce the darkness. She could see nothing. "Thank you! Oh, thank you! God bless you!"

Silence was her only reply. For a minute she did not realize that she was alone. Her savior had vanished into the darkness.

"The man on the wharf," she murmured. "The man who shot the Negro." She raised her voice again. "Don't go! Please let me thank you properly!"

But he was gone, vanished into the blackness as swiftly as he had come.

The idea of rising and running after him died a-borning. What if she stood up and toppled backward into the water, or slipped. Hand over hand, she dragged herself up the bank until her legs and feet cleared the water. Even though she shivered in the cool night air, she dared not take a chance until she could see what she was doing.

At first light she continued her climb up the levee. On top at last, she pushed herself to her feet and stared around her. Gray fog rising covered everything in an undulating blanket. Cautiously, she made her way down the other side, trying to follow the ruts left by the carriage.

An errant breeze blew her garments against her chilled limbs and made her teeth chatter. It rippled the ocean of fog so she could discern dark forms. The nigh horse's body lay in the road, still strapped in its harness. She hurried forward, somehow compelled to see to the animal. Its mouth gaped, its tongue lay limp across the bit. A shot had torn a hole in the side of its chest. But a knife had ended its life, slicing cleanly through the throat.

Its blood made a darker stain against the black mud. Instinctively, she knew her rescuer had administered the *coup de grâce.*

With tears in her eyes she looked around her, wishing for a sight of him. What she caught sight of made her shudder. Emil's body lay on the slope of the levee. He had been dragged there and laid out. His limbs straight, his head turned slightly away from the road. Again her savior had been at work.

Staggering to her feet, she approached the body. Poor Emil! He had not wanted her to ride around in a carriage and try to do things like a man. In her heart she knew he had not approved of her starting off to *Ombres Azurées* in the middle of the night.

She bowed her head to take up his cold, dead hand. How he had paid for her stupidity! Sobs tore out of her chest. What had Tabor said? She had caused the death of three men. And now a fourth. Good men! Dead because of her!

She heard the distant rumble of wheels. Someone was coming from *Ombres Azurées*. She prayed that help was coming because Georges had summoned it. Please God that he was alive. Surely he had not lost his way in the darkness and stumbled into the bayou.

The carriage she recognized to be Celeste's pulled to a stop beside the nigh horse's body. Georges jumped from the box, and Laura flung open the door. Judith knew she should rise and go to meet her sister, but for the life of her, she could not bring herself to leave Emil's side, nor to let go of his cold hand.

"You may have an enemy, Mademoiselle Talbot-Harrow. And if you do, I should say a very implacable one." Bertrand St. Cyr leaned forward over his desk. The earnestness in his voice could not be doubted.

"But why? Who would want to kill me? I'm not yet twenty years old. I've never hurt anyone." Even as she said the words, she thought of Tabor. Instantly, she rejected the thought. He had been furious at the death of his men, but if he had wanted to kill her, he could have done so.

"You may not have done anything to anybody. But you are Beau Talbot's daughter. And he is dead."

She stared at him, appalled. "Then Laura is in danger also."

He shrugged. "You are the more vulnerable. She lives a protected existence far from New Orleans, surrounded by her servants, her employees, the overseer of her

283

plantation, her factor, others."

"Whereas I spend many hours a day . . ."

"Exactly."

"But there can't be a connection. My father's death had nothing to do with me. It was a stupid, stupid thing."

"Perhaps. On the other hand, perhaps it was not so stupid."

"My God!" She started up from her chair and began to pace the office.

He held up his hand. "I only suggest. I do not accuse, nor do I presume to prophesy."

She spun back to face him, her skirts swirling around her feet. "I cannot credit this. I . . . I simply cannot."

His shrug was a masterpiece of courtroom theatrics. "Then it was a matter of coincidence. The black man ran amok, mad on rum and mandragora. He passed within arm's length of more than a dozen men and at least one woman. Still he ran straight for you."

"But . . ."

" 'Highwaymen' are lying in ambush beside a deserted road that leads to only two or three plantations. The night is pitch black. The cannon has long been fired. They stop your carriage but make no attempt to rob you. Instead, they shoot your servant and roll your expensive carriage down the levee into the bayou."

"I shot one of them," she reminded him faintly.

"Indeed. You were very brave. I know of no other woman who would have been so brave." He smiled. His brown eyes were warm as he complimented her.

Unused to praise of any kind, she felt herself blushing.

"And the reason you were out in the night," he continued after a moment. "To answer a message from your sister. Which she did not send at that time. No! She sent that message several days before, but you did not receive it until that evening."

Judith hugged her arms across her body.

"Where was that message in the intervening time?"

"You're a good lawyer," she acknowledged with a rueful smile. "You've made a very frightening case."

His eyes darkened as he perceived her shivering figure. His mouth curved tenderly. "I wish it were not so, mademoiselle."

"I do too." Suddenly she was aware that this man was looking at her with more interest than a lawyer should show his client. Flustered by the warmth in his expression, she turned away to stare out the window at the traffic rolling by. "I don't know what to do, m'sieur."

"Mademoiselle . . ."

"Before you say anything, let me tell you that I simply can't go into my house and hide. I have to go on with the work that I have begun."

"But a man . . ."

"My father's business is now mine. It needs my full attention. Matters are in a turmoil. He had been very neglectful for many months. There are debts my sister and I knew nothing about."

He capitulated with good grace. Rising from his desk, he came to stand behind her. "Of course, you must not hide. Perhaps a lesser woman. One who did not rise and go on with the day's work when she was attacked and almost killed. One who did not shoot the highwayman. One who fainted at the sight of her poor footman's body rather than remain beside him, holding his dead hand. She would hide. But you! Never!"

She turned to face him, her eyes searching his kind face. "No," she agreed softly. "Not because I don't want to, but because I can't."

He inclined his head and lifted her hand to his lips in tribute.

She blushed with pleasure. "I do what I have to do, m'sieur."

He nodded slowly. "Of course you do." He stepped back again, very businesslike. "You will allow me to hire two very strong, very big, very tough men to be your bodyguards."

She smiled then in some relief. "Yes, I will."

*   *   *

285

Maurice Dufaure's eyes glittered with special malevolence as he strode into the office. Following close at his heels came a chubby man with the weathered face of a seaman. "That pirate lover of yours has ruined Talbot Shipping."

Judith closed the ledger sharply, making no effort to conceal her anger. "I have no pirate lover."

"Too bad. If he had been your lover, he might have spared our ships."

"I repeat that I have no pirate lover, nor any other lover, for that matter."

He leaned casually against the other side of the counter, his face closer to hers than it had been since she had taken over her father's share of the business. His breath smelled unpleasant. "Perhaps that is a pity. A husband, even a lover, might be extremely useful at this time."

She laced her fingers tightly, as if in doing so she could hold her temper. Her voice, when she spoke, had only the hint of an edge. "I'm sure you plan to tell me something important, M'sieur Dufaure. I am waiting patiently."

A muscle ticked in the corner of his pock-marked cheek. It pulled the corner of his mouth up into a semblance of a smile. "This sailor has just brought word that the *White Cloud* has been lost in the Caribbean."

"The *White Cloud?*" Judith gasped. "Lost in the Caribbean! What happened?"

The little man came forward hesitantly, his mouth working. Finally, he managed to get the words out. "All but lost," he replied cautiously. "Her cargo was taken. Her crew had the choice to join with the pirates or to be put ashore. Me, I would not join with them. I chose to be put ashore."

His French accent was so thick Judith had to listen with special attention. When he had finished, she stared at him for almost a minute while he looked hopefully at her, then at Dufaure, then back at her. Finally, she was able to collect her thoughts. "The *White Cloud* was armed

286

and carried a full crew. I can't believe her captain would allow her to be taken without a fight."

The seaman dragged a crumpled scrap of cloth from somewhere beneath his smock and swiped at his perspiring face. *"Mais oui, mademoiselle.* I do not lie. The pirate's own ship was not seaworthy. One of his masts had a great crack in it. We answered a signal of distress." Here he looked at Dufaure, who nodded grimly.

"And . . ." Judith prompted.

"The captain offered a tow into Santiago. But when the two ships were fast together"—the sailor's shoulders lifted in a Gallic shrug—"he and his armed crew boarded us before we were aware."

"You must have been very busy," Judith remarked dryly.

Again the eyes shifted uncertainly. "It was at night."

"Was no one on watch aboard the *White Cloud*?"

A dark red flush rose out of the sailor's neck. "But of course. We were on watch."

"And still a crew of pirates swarmed aboard and took over the ship?"

"It was very dark," he insisted lamely.

"Where did you find this man, M'sieur Dufaure?" Judith asked impatiently.

Dufaure stiffened. "He came to report to me as a loyal employee."

"Of course."

The sailor looked from one to the other. "I heard that the pirate took her for a debt." He provided humbly.

"So much is true. Do you not agree, Miss Talbot-Harrow?"

"No, I do not agree." Her blue eyes scanned the weathered face. "For an ordinary seaman you seem unusually well informed about some things and totally ignorant about others. M'sieur Dufaure, this man may be giving us correct information about the *Cloud* being taken by pirates—"

"Oui! Oui! I am correct. I was there."

287

She held up her hand to silence him. "But how dare you presume that the pirate was Tabor O'Halloran?"

"So you admit he is your lover?"

She shook her head, her mouth curling in exasperation. "He is no such thing. And he would never take a Talbot ship. He was my father's friend."

"I swear." The little man began to get excited. His fingers crushed his seaman's cap. His forehead contorted as if he struggled to remember. "The black flag had the skull with red hair."

"And the name of his ship. The damaged ship?" Dufaure prodded.

"The *Banshee*."

Dufaure made a broad gesture in Judith's direction as if presenting her the information on a silver platter. "*Voilà.*"

She paid no attention to her partner. Instead, she leaned past him, elbows on the countertop to stare fixedly at the little man. "And how does it happen that you are still alive, sir? When this dread pirate captured the *White Cloud,* why didn't he make the crew members who wouldn't sign on with him walk the plank or some such thing?"

The sailor swung his gaze to Dufaure before appearing not to understand the question. "No. I would not sign with him. He put me ashore and I took a berth on the next ship bound for New Orleans." He indicated a decrepit schooner swinging at anchor in the river. "And here I am."

Throughout his speech she watched him, taking in the twitching hands and mouth, the shifting eyes. "I don't believe it," she repeated.

Dufaure glared at her.

She came around the counter. The little sailor backed away a step. Her blue eyes lanced at him. "He would have no reason—"

Dufaure stepped between her and the sailor. "Perhaps he decided that he wanted his own kind of revenge, Miss

288

Talbot-Harrow."

She nodded. "He had taken his revenge before he left."

Dufaure regarded her narrowly. His opaque eyes fell to her flat belly. One black eyebrow rose.

Swift as thought, her right hand flashed up to slap him with all her might.

His head snapped to one side. He spat out a fierce filthy word. The sailor scuttled out the door, slamming it behind him. Dufaure growled low in his throat. His hands clenched into claws as he made for her.

She dodged away. Hand on the door handle, she stopped. "Lay a finger on me, and I'll scream. Both my bodyguards are within hearing distance."

"You struck me," he snarled, brandishing his fists in frustration before letting them fall to his sides.

"And you insulted me. Unforgivably. Count yourself lucky that I have no male relatives to defend me, m'sieur. Since I have no one to strike for me, I must strike for myself. A woman's slap is much less fatal than a sword point or a pistol ball."

The red mark of her hand stood out brightly on his cheek. "The pirate said you were his mistress."

"And, of course, everyone in New Orleans chose to believe the pirate rather than the young lady of good family."

"Of good family by marriage only. Celeste Devranche is of good family. Her husband was foreign trash."

"Good enough to be your business partner," she reminded him.

He ground his teeth together. "Do not you English have a saying, 'Needs must when the devil drives'?"

She took a deep, steadying breath. As she let it out, she walked away from the door. "We do have that saying, M'sieur Dufaure."

He grunted unintelligibly.

In the heavy silence that followed, she rounded the counter and took up the ledger she had been working on.

289

Dufaure flexed his shoulders under his suit coat and touched the tips of his fingers gingerly to his cheek. At length Judith spoke. "Let us say the *White Cloud* is lost to pirates. What will that mean to the Talbot lines?"

Dufaure shrugged. "I would imagine we would be close to bankruptcy."

"Bankruptcy! With seven other ships on the sea lanes."

"Some are very old. The flutes . . . The *White Hound* was built before the turn of the century."

"But it has always been kept in excellent repair."

"Repairs cost money. So do new ships. We went deeply into debt for the *Laurel*, the new merchantman. I begged your father not to buy it. I preached prudence, but he would ever extend himself."

She felt tears prick at the backs of her eyes as she rushed to defend her father. "He had no reason to suppose that he was going to die. He was young. He should have lived another twenty years—"

"He treated his ships like stepchildren," Dufaure interrupted bitterly. "Nothing was important except his wife and *Ombres Azurées*. Hundreds of dollars in profits he poured into that plantation. The ships worked for him and made their money. And they were treated like stepchildren."

Did he know how his words hurt her? She could feel them sinking like darts into her body. And their poison burning into her soul. The plantation for Laura. The shipping line for Judith. *Ombres Azurées* for his beloved favorite daughter. Talbot's for his "stepdaughter." Salt in the old wounds. She had never felt more as if she had no place.

"What can we do?" she asked humbly.

He raised one black eyebrow, carefully hiding the smile of triumph. "*We* can do nothing. *You* can sell your half to me."

Her head flashed up. "Never."

"You would rather see it bankrupted."

"If you have money, how can it be bankrupted?" she flung at him.

"My money is my own."

"And you would never loan it to me."

He nodded coldly. "Never."

"Then damn you, sir. I will never sell."

He laughed mirthlessly. "Then you will lose it to me eventually."

Judith shook her head. "I shall go to my sister. If the money has been going to *Ombres Azurées*, then I should be able to get all I need to take care of the problem."

With the air of a man trumping an ace, he laughed again. "If it were at *Ombres Azurées.*"

"What do you mean?"

He leaned back against the counter. The marks of her blow were fading to be replaced by a dark flush of triumph. How he was enjoying tearing this English bitch to pieces. "Your stepmother has very expensive habits. Habits that your sister will soon find out about if she has not already done so."

"What do you mean?"

"I shall not tell you."

"You bastard."

"I am not a bastard, but what about yourself?" His expression was almost gleeful.

The question rocked her. For an instant the family's neglect, her mother's expulsion from society, her father's desertion, even the business of letting a pirate buy her clothing, all appeared in a terrible and frightening new light.

Then she rejected it. If she had been a bastard, she would probably have been gotten rid of the day she was born. Her family would never have reared such in their midst. When she had not been born a boy, she had been barely tolerated.

She laughed in his face. "You're grasping at straws, M'sieur Dufaure. You know I'm no bastard. You want me to sell the Talbot lines to you and you will do anything to

291

get it."

The smile was wiped away to be replaced by an expression that would have looked in place on the darkest demon in hell. "You are a fool," he spat out. "And your sister is a fool too."

"Leave my sister out of our conversation, M'sieur Dufaure, or you will very much wish you had done so."

He grinned maliciously. "Women are fools. All of them. Your sister is enamored of the gambler who has destroyed her sustenance. And you are in love with the pirate who threatens your sea lanes."

"I am not in love with the pirate. In fact, I hate him beyond anything else."

"Too bad you did not feel so when first you met him. Now it is too late. You both will soon lose everything. Upstarts, both of you. English parvenues polluting the finest French bloodlines. You should never have come here."

"That's medieval. This is the nineteenth century. Bloodlines don't mean anything."

"You will see," he thundered. "You will see. If you know what's good for you, you will sell this business and go back to England, where you belong."

She clenched her hands tightly over the top of the ledger. "My father—my real true father—wanted me to come, and now that I am here I won't let this business be lost. If he wanted me to take it over to take care of Laura and Celeste, then I'll do it."

"Why would you do so much for a man who never loved you."

"M'sieur Dufaure, if you think you can hurt me by saying that, you are sadly mistaken. There is no such thing as love in the world. A few people who live in luxury have allowed themselves a pleasant fantasy called love, but it's not for the working population. For those of us with responsibilities, there's no such thing as love. I don't believe it ever existed."

"But your pirate lover . . ."

Suddenly, she was very weary. What was she arguing with this wretched ugly man about? Her voice flat, she slid the ledger onto the counter. "A perfect example. I forgot the lessons of my childhood in so far as to allow him to seduce me. When he was through, when he had gotten what he wanted from me, he destroyed my reputation and then deserted me."

He stared at her, awestruck. Such bitterness, such cynicism in one so young threw him off balance. "But still you remain here. Evidently, you do not believe the damage to be so great."

She shook her head. "The damage was total, M'sieur Dufaure. The fact that you are now being so incredibly cruel is testimony to its devastation."

"Miss Talbot-Harrow." He leaned toward her, his face dark. "I advise you to reconsider my offer."

"I have no need to reconsider, sir. I won't take your offer. Nor will I bother my sister, although I'll take care to find out if she is in financial want. If you've lied to me, I'll have the money I need."

"I have not lied."

"If you haven't, then I'll find a way out of my difficulties by myself."

"A way by yourself?" He shook his head, a deep frown creasing his forehead.

"A way by myself," she insisted.

"Impossible."

She smiled mirthlessly. "Nothing is impossible. I'm here, aren't I? M'sieur St. Cyr will find an agent to handle my duties here in the office and on the docks. I will take the *White Hound* myself when she comes into port. If Tabor O'Halloran has taken the *White Cloud* and turned her into a pirate vessel, I'll get her back."

Interlude V

Talbot Shipping Line office
September 30, 1814

Laura's face looked stiff and drawn. Since their father's death, Judith had seen her sister change gradually, then markedly. The Harrow features were more pronounced as the last of the pampered softness had been erased by work and duty.

One glance and Judith led Laura into the office that had been Beau Talbot's. Maurice Dufaure's black eyes snapped with curiosity, but she closed the door tightly behind them.

Silently, she drew up a chair for Laura and hastily began to straighten the clutter on her desk. The older girl took a deep breath. The delicate nostrils pinched tight. "Judith, I'm going to be married."

Judith's busy hands fumbled badly. She dropped into her father's chair beside his desk. "What? To Roussel?" She knew the owner of the plantation adjacent to *Ombres Azurées* had been pursuing Laura for months, but she hadn't thought Laura cared for the man.

"No. To Clay Sutherland." When the words were out, Laura tottered like a marionette into the chair. In the silence that followed, she struggled to pin a smile on her lips. The result was a pathetic grimace. "I hope you'll wish me happy."

"No," Judith whispered.

"Yes."

Judith sprang to her feet, her hands clenched into tight fists. "The man who killed Papa? The man you wished in hell just a few months ago?"

Laura propped her elbow on the chair arm and placed a trembling hand to her cheek. "Don't make this any harder than it is. I know what I'm doing, Judith. I know what I have to do."

Judith stooped and put her arm around Laura's shoulders. She pressed a quick kiss to her sister's temple. "What you *have* to do?" she murmured incredulously. "What could you possibly *have* to do?"

Laura lifted her head. Their faces were only inches apart. "I have to save *Ombres Azurées*."

Slowly, Judith straightened, but she kept her hand on her sister's shoulder. Laura needed strength and encouragement now. Judith would not disappoint her. "Save the plantation? I didn't know it needed to be saved."

"It does." Laura's voice was flat, as if she had reviewed this information half a hundred times. "Clay Sutherland has money to invest in it." She looked around her. "He might even be persuaded to invest some in Talbot Shipping."

Judith returned to her chair. She grasped the arms firmly. "You don't marry your banker, sister dear."

"Women marry for money all the time," Laura scoffed.

"A marriage of convenience? For Laura Talbot?"

"Are you suggesting a marriage for love, little sister?" Laura's eyes were dead. The brilliant green dulled and tinged with gray. Dark circles bespoke many sleepless nights sitting up with dying dreams.

Judith hunched forward, hurting for her. "Yes, Laura. At least for you. Love is important to you."

A brittle laugh and a wave of a black-gloved hand

answered that comment. "Oh, don't be silly. Marriages in name only are all the fashion in our circle. They're more the thing than marriages for love. And much safer."

Judith rose again and caught the fluttering hand. This time she held her sister's eyes with her own. "This isn't like you at all. You're not telling me the whole of this."

Laura nodded wearily. "Clay Sutherland could own *Ombres Azurées* without ever marrying me."

"What are you talking about?"

"Celeste's gambling debts."

"Celeste!" Suddenly, the whole horrible mess became clear. Judith cursed angrily, using some of the choicest language from her job on the docks. "You told me she gambled occasionally, but I thought she'd been too grief-stricken since Beau died even to go out of the house."

"She's been plunging heavily since Papa's death." Laura's voice faltered as she tried to make a suitable excuse. "I'm sure it's the way she exorcised her grief."

"My God. Poor lady."

"Gambling has always been a weakness for her. Even before she married Papa. I think her gambling debts were the primary reason she married out of her church." Laura waved her hand weakly. "Later she really loved Papa."

Judith began to pace again. "But this is all so terrible. How did Clay Sutherland"—she spat the name out of her mouth as if he were something foul—"manage to make this his business?"

"Clay bought up all of her markers."

Judith's comment on Clay's ancestry could not be uttered in polite society. "And now he wants to call them in on you?"

Laura smiled wanly. "It's a simple matter of black-mail."

Judith knelt down in front of her sister and took her hands. "Oh, sister. I wish I could give you the money out of Talbot Shipping. But I don't have enough to give. Is it possible that we could go to the bank? Surely they'll make us a loan on the land or the ships. They're worth more than enough money to cover Celeste's debts. . . ."

Laura freed her hand and placed the icy fingertips over Judith's babbling lips. "Probably so. But Clay doesn't want the money. He wants me—the respectability that I represent—and *Ombres Azurées*."

Judith's already angry flush darkened. "You're going to tie yourself to a man you hate because of your stepmother's gambling debts. That's crazy. This is the nineteenth century, not the seventeenth. A woman has recourse to the law. Laura . . ."

"I can't let Clay hurt Celeste. And she's too wounded to be dragged through the courts." Laura gripped the chair arms tightly and straightened as if she herself were in the witness box. "The law might cancel the debts, but the disclosure coming on top of all she's suffered would kill her."

Judith flung her arms wide. "For mercy's sake, Laura, you love her. You want to take care of her. Beau intended that you should. But you can't give up your plans, your entire life for her. We're talking about marriage. That's supposed to be for life."

"Don't make me out to be a martyr, little sister. I'm doing what I must do to protect Celeste, but also to save *Ombres Azurées*."

Judith sighed. Suddenly the ticking of the clock became omnipresent in the little office. The compromises people made in the name of love weighed heavily upon her. She understood to a degree her own vulnerability to Tabor. Laura must be just as vulnerable to Clay. The marriage would not be a marriage of convenience. It would be something much worse. Laura would love him, desire him, ache for him, and he would know it. The knowledge would give him dominance. She would be totally his to command. To punish if she dared to disobey. Her thoughts frightened her. She shook herself out of her nightmare to feel tears prickling at her eyelids. "When is this slave auction to take place?"

298

Silent tears spilled down Laura's cheeks too. "As soon as I can get ready. My bridegroom-to-be is demanding a huge wedding with all the pomp and circumstance that befits a member of Creole society."

Judith took her hands. "Laura, this breaks my heart."

Laura smoothed her sister's hair and caressed her cheek. "You mustn't talk that way. Just be there to stand by me and help me get through it."

Judith rose. Her next words were the hardest she had ever had to utter. "Sister, I don't think I'll be able to attend."

For the first time in that terrible interview Laura appeared aware of the world around her. "You must. You're my only family. You're my maid of honor. Where else would you be?"

Judith let her eyes wander over the map above Beau's desk. "Laura, someone with the interest of the Talbot lines at heart is going to have to sail on the *White Hound*."

"Sail? A woman on a ship."

Judith shook her head. In her mind's eye she remembered the voyage of the *Portchester*, the ignominious surrender of the captain and crew. She vowed that would not happen again aboard a Talbot ship. "It's not as if I were just a woman. I'm the owner. The *White Cloud* has been taken by pirates. Her cargo was stolen. The crew was threatened. I can't let this happen again."

Laura sprang to her feet and caught Judith's shoulders. By main force she turned her sister around to face her. "You think you can do something about it! You're going among pirates. You'll be raped and murdered. Nothing is worth your life."

Judith shook her head proudly. "Laura, I can't believe that the captains and crews are offering even token resistance anymore. With Beau Talbot dead, they don't have any faith in me as the owner and director of the line. Unless I'm willing to go where they go, to place myself in the same danger, they won't respect me."

Laura turned away and began pacing the office, her own anger kindling. "I can understand your moving into a man's world. I'm in that world myself. I didn't want to be, but I am. But even in a man's world we have rules."

"Yes, and one rule is that the leader must not be afraid to lead. I was on board the *Portchester* when Tabor O'Halloran boarded her. The captain stood aside and let him do what he wanted. He struck sail. He didn't even try to outrun the *Banshee*. Much less fight off the pirates."

"But sailors can't be expected to fight cutthroats," Laura insisted reasonably. "And Papa himself issued the orders that his crews were not to fight. He'd rather the pirates take the cargo and let the ship sail on unharmed."

Judith nodded patiently. "But this isn't a matter of the ship sailing on unharmed. The *Cloud* is lost to us. We've got to fight. I'm hiring extra men, men who won't be afraid of a gang of scurvy pirates."

"Then let *them* go," Laura cried.

"No, Laura, I've got to go with them. To be their leader—if only in name. You're taking care of your problem your way. Tabor O'Halloran is mine and I can't see any other way to handle it than by confronting it."

Laura began to shiver. Her jaw quivered where she clenched it tightly to keep her teeth from chattering. "But you could be killed." Her voice broke again. Judith could see that Laura was near the end of her tether.

Judith sought desperately to reassure her. She had never seen Laura like this before. "Tabor would never harm me. Don't forget. He liked Beau. And Beau liked him."

The name of their father fell like a pall between them. Beau was gone and they were naked to the world. Judith ached for Laura, who had always been the favored one. Sometimes favor was no favor at all. She felt stronger than she had ever felt before.

At last Laura found the courage to speak. "So be it, sister."

Judith held out her arms, and Laura ran into the circle of them. They were both weeping, hurting for each other, hurting for themselves, hurting for the father they had lost, hurting for fear that they would lose each other. Long minutes passed. Judith's sobs stilled. She hiccoughed once, then pulled away, rubbing at her cheeks with the tips of her fingers.

The occasion seemed to call for something beyond words. Suddenly, Judith remembered. She opened the bottom drawer of Beau's desk and extracted a bottle and two small glasses. She managed a watery smile that Laura answered with a nod. "Join me then for a man's drink."

The whiskey gurgled into the glasses. They held them aloft.

"To the new countess of *Ombres Azurées*."

"To the new countess of the Talbot Shipping Line."

Each tossed it down neat. Their eyes watered and the fiery liquid burned.

Judith raised the empty glass again. "To the Talbot sisters."

Chapter Fifteen

The *White Hound* slid gracefully into the harbor of Santiago de Cuba. Beneath her keel white foam flirted off the tops of the blue-gray waves. The morning sun glinted off the water. Drawing the light into its dark-stained stone, massive Morro Castle loomed oppressively at the harbor's mouth.

Oblivious to the view, Judith trained her spyglass on ships at anchor. Legs apart, she absorbed the roll of the ship as if she had trod the decks all her life. The wind riffled her long hair; it fluttered the ends of the scarf tied around her chin to hold her hat in place.

Only a week out of New Orleans she had come to know the pleasure that Beau must have known upon the sea. Harrestone was far, far away—another world fast fading in her memory—obscured by months in the shipping office in New Orleans and finally dispelled by glorious days beside the captain on the quarterdeck of the *White Hound*. Gone forever was the young girl sick at heart who had held her dying mother in her arms when each breath rattled in the emaciated throat.

"Steady as she goes, Mr. Longman," the captain called to the first mate.

"Aye, sir."

Coming up behind Judith, Captain Smithurst rested one hand in the ratlines over her head. "Are you sure you know what you're doing, ma'am?"

She did not remove the spyglass from her eye. "We're searching for the *White Cloud*, Captain. She was taken in the Windward Passage by pirates who put some members of her crew ashore at Santiago."

"If pirates took her, there's not much chance that they'd hang around here," he observed glumly. "We're liable to find trouble ourselves."

She lowered the spyglass to look over her shoulder at him. He was a tall man, thick around the middle, with neatly trimmed gray hair and mustaches. His expression was so bleakly unhappy that she tried to reassure him. "We're not here to cause trouble. We're sailing into Santiago as a private merchantman. When we drop anchor here, we'll find out from the harbor master who else is here and who's been here recently. Maybe we'll find out who'll be docking soon."

He shook his head, his eyes scanning the harbor warily. "Likely, we won't find any such thing. Santiago's not New Orleans. Maybe in Havana they have records. Maybe they have a harbor master, but not this hole."

She frowned. "But surely . . ."

"Look around you, ma'am. I tell you this is no port for the *White Hound*. We don't have any business here. What's more, we stand out like a sore thumb."

Judith lowered the spyglass. The flotilla that stretched before her seemed to contain every type of small craft— schooners and sloops, tiny boats of every description. Only here and there could she see taller masts rising, masts tall enough to be merchant ships or brigantines such as the *Banshee*.

Smithurst tugged at the corner of his mustache. "Every piece of scum with a deck under his feet and a scrap of canvas over his head is taking our measure right now. They're asking themselves what we're doing here and whether they can capture us."

"I'm sure you're exaggerating."

"We don't belong in this harbor. We don't have a

304

thing to trade with Cuba. She grows sugar. We're carrying sugar. We've got nothing in the hold to sell."

"We could report that we've had some trouble. Come into port to make repairs."

"Never." He looked alarmed. "Never tell that we're crippled. Somebody might get the idea that we'd be easy to take."

"I see your meaning."

A heavy silence grew between them as the sails rippled down. The *Hound* slid easily through the calm water, kept moving by its own headway. Smithurst tugged at his mustache again. "This vessel always travels the European and Mediterranean routes," he grumbled. "We're losing money."

His final remark restored some of her confidence. In some measure self-interest was at work here. Certainly, the loss of profits could be leading him to discourage her to give up her search. Smithurst had objected vociferously to her use of his ship to try to rescue the *White Cloud*. A pragmatic businessman, only Judith's reminding him that she owned the merchantman had compelled the captain to take her on this voyage.

Consoled by that thought, she lifted the spyglass to her eye again to scan the forest of masts. Any of the tall ones might be the *Hound*'s sister ship; or if they did not belong to the *White Cloud*, they might belong to the *Banshee*.

A great sheerwater gull flapped swiftly, stilled in midflight, oscillated in the breeze, then dived like a lance. At the last minute it spread its wings, skimmed the water, and forked up a silver fish. The water droplets glittered in the morning sunlight. She sighed at the sight of its beauty. "Make a circuit of the harbor if you please, Captain Smithurst?"

"Very well, ma'am." He spoke over his shoulder to the bosun. "Steady as she goes."

Suddenly, she saw it.

The *Banshee* floated gently at the end of her anchor on the other side of a flotilla of fishing boats. Judith could not conceal her elation. "There she is!" She grabbed Smithurst's arm and offered him the spyglass.

"You're right," he agreed. He swept the spyglass to right and left. "But no sign of the *White Cloud*. She's probably at the bottom of the Gulf. We're wasting our time."

"I don't believe that," Judith declared stoutly. "She's too valuable a ship to have been sunk. Tabor O'Halloran offered her crew a chance to sail with him. That means he wanted her for his own."

"Unless the sailor was lying to you. Where's the captain of the *Cloud*? What does he have to report?"

Judith had no answer for that. Somehow she had expected to see the *White Cloud* as well. Had Dufaure paid a man to lie in an effort to frighten her into selling the Talbot lines? "The deck of the *Banshee* looks all but deserted. Most of her crew must be ashore."

"Shall I pull alongside?"

"No. Drop anchor and put down a boat. I'll go ashore and confront him. He'll—" She stopped at the sight of the black frown that drew the captain's heavy gray brows together.

"You'll not go ashore in Santiago de Cuba," he declared forcefully.

"Captain, I'm perfectly comfortable on the docks."

"Begging your pardon, ma'am. This is not New Orleans."

"I'm sure that with some of the crew to escort me—"

"No, ma'am. I'll send my mate ashore. He'll learn what's to be learned. If this Captain O'Halloran is any kind of man at all, he'll come to meet you, you being the lady. If not, then we may have to persuade him."

"Captain . . ."

He pointed to a couple of ships anchored beyond the brigantine. "Do you know what those are, ma'am?"

She studied them a moment, then shrugged. "Flutes?"

He snorted. "They're flutes all right. Heavy-bottomed floating hellhouses. They're slavers."

306

She stared in horror at the innocent-appearing ships.

"Yes, ma'am. Those sugar planters up in the hills"—he waved his hand toward the Sierra Maestras that rose to the west—"they buy slaves by the hundreds and work them to death." He shook his head. "That's a man's town over there. The Spanish keep their women at home behind *grilles*. You couldn't learn a thing because no one would talk to you."

"But—"

"No, ma'am. When you came aboard, you put yourself in my hands. I'm the captain. And those are captain's orders. You'll stay here. I'll send Mr. Longman ashore. We'll bring the captain of the *Banshee* to you."

Tabor O'Halloran was just as handsome as Judith remembered him. She caught her breath as he looked up from the dinghy. Even with a fierce scowl drawing his brows together over his blue eyes, he still had the power to move her.

Her palms were damp and her heart was pounding as he climbed over the railing and stood before her. "What are you doing here?" he demanded without preliminaries.

She clenched her fists against a sharp stab of disappointment. What else could she have expected? He blamed her for the deaths of his men. He had hurt her in retribution. Still, if he had smiled . . . She thrust out her chin. "I've come for my ship."

"The *White Cloud*? Your father's ship."

"The *White Cloud*. *My* ship. According to the report, you stole her."

He directed a cool glance around him at the stern faces of the men. For their benefit he raised his voice slightly. "I didn't steal her. I saved her."

She raised her eyebrows. "Perhaps I was misinformed."

The heavy frown on his forehead smoothed slightly. "Misinformation is easy to come by."

If he were going to be insulting, she could be insulting

307

in her turn. "I'm sure you see how I could have believed such a report. After the way you came aboard the *Portchester* and—"

He interrupted her quickly. "I had business aboard the *Portchester*."

"So you've said. But I couldn't believe you after what you did to my clothing . . ."

He looked around him at the troop of interested faces. The officers of the *White Hound* ranged themselves around the couple, ostensibly to defend Judith from the cruel pirate. An inordinate number of crew members hung poised on the ratlines, where they seemed to be taking unusual care with the sails. "Is there somewhere that we can speak privately?"

Judith flushed as she realized almost too late that their conversation had assumed a personal tone. "Captain Smithurst?"

The captain inclined his head, his face stern, his eyes flashing a warning to Tabor. "Certainly, Miss Talbot-Harrow. My cabin is at your service."

"Thank you." She inclined her bright head in her turn. Then with a carriage *Grandmère* would have been proud of, she led the way to the cabin. As she negotiated the narrow passage into the captain's cabin, she tried to plan her questions, imagine what he was going to say, anticipate how she would answer him.

Tabor closed the door behind them and crossed his arms over his chest. "Now, what are you doing here?" His bearing and tone accused her of grave wrongdoing.

With her lips fashioned into a smile, she gestured toward the decanter and glasses behind the brass railings in their compartment. "I'm sure that Captain Smithurst would be the first to offer you a drink. Would you like one?"

One black eyebrow rose in surprise, but Tabor nodded in agreement.

She poured the clear brown liquid into the glass with a steady hand. "Here you are."

"Won't you join me?"

"No, thank you. I don't like spirits."

He did not comment but sniffed experimentally, then appreciatively. He swirled the liquid in the glass. "A very good brandy."

She seated herself beside the captain's desk. "I'm glad you approve."

He took a sip, then frowned again as if remembering. "What are you doing here?"

She grasped the arms of the chair. "I've come for the *White Cloud*. She's my ship. I want her back. I have to have her back."

He leaned back at his ease. "First, let's set the record straight. I didn't steal her. I rescued her. If I hadn't boarded her, she'd be docking at Elba right now."

"Elba?" She started in some surprise.

"A small island in the middle of the Mediterranean. Of no importance until very, very recently."

Clear in her memory was Dufaure's impassioned outburst at the news of Napoleon's abdication. Could there be some connection between the two events? Her protest was without conviction. "I know why Elba's important. A Talbot ship would have no possible reason to go there."

He shrugged. "I assure you it was quite possible. You were about to lose her to the greater glory of the 'Corsican ogre.' That's if the British fleet didn't seize her first. They probably had the same intelligence sources that I did. A frigate was waiting for her off Jamaica. I simply caught her first."

She shook her head, unable to take in what he told her. "My ship? The *White Cloud*?"

"If I hadn't taken her, she'd be a British prize right now. Or at the bottom of the sea."

"No. Now I know you're wrong. The British would never have sunk the *White Cloud*. She belongs to the Talbot lines. We're British. My uncle—"

"Your father is an American," he reminded her coldly.

At the mention of Beau, she felt the pain rise in her throat. She bowed her head. "I forgot. You left New Orleans before it happened. You don't know that Beau is dead."

"Dead?"

She nodded. "He was killed right after you . . . left."

"Your father?" he gasped stupidly. "Beau Talbot? Dead?"

"Yes." Her voice quavered. In that minute if he had reached for her, she would have gone gladly into his arms. She had not wept. Not when the terrible news had come. Not when she had stood beside the grave just a step behind Laura, who had supported a fainting Celeste. "Yes."

Tabor turned away, shaking his head. "I can't believe it. How did it happen? Was he taken ill?"

"No. It was a stupid mistake." She still could not bring herself to tell what happened.

Tabor shook his head. "Poor Celeste. How is she?"

Judith had swayed toward him, but at his words she caught hold of herself. Her answer was uttered in an even voice. "She hasn't left *Ombres Azurées* since it happened."

"My God! Her brother and now Beau. I can imagine her state of mind. Poor, dear, delicate lady."

"Yes, she's had a lot of bad luck."

"Bad luck." He turned back angrily. "Her husband dies and you call it bad luck!"

"No!" she blurted out, clasping her hands together in front of her. "I didn't mean that."

He stared at her in disgust. "How could I forget? You're the one who can look down at a dead man whose face has been burned away and feel no remorse."

The color drained from her face at the hateful words. How could she forget that he thought her guilty of trying to burn his ship? She tried to steady her reply. "I didn't mean that my father's death was bad luck. Just that Celeste seems to have had more than her share of unhappiness."

"Of course." His sarcasm was palpable.

"Laura's been taking care of her." Hardly were the words out of her mouth before she regretted them.

He regarded her coldly. "Laura's a brave girl. Celeste's lucky to have her."

Her face felt stiff from her effort to keep it impassive. Her voice was utterly without inflection. "So she's said on numerous occasions."

Tabor frowned, staring more closely at her. She seemed unnatural. Her face was like porcelain in its whiteness. Perhaps she was not so unaffected as she pretended? "I'm sure Laura must be devastated as well."

"Yes. Yes, she is."

"She loved her father very much. He was surely proud of her." Curiously, he watched her, gauging the effect of his words.

Suddenly, she could not stand the conversation any longer. Her own feelings were raw. One trembling hand rose toward her cheek. He caught it. She looked up at him, shocked.

He stared down at her drowned eyes, her trembling lips. "Perhaps you miss him too?" he said softly.

Convulsively, she pressed her lips together, but the whimper would escape. Though she ducked her head, she could offer no resistance beyond that. Easily, he pulled her to her feet and enclosed her in his warm arms.

"Poor Judith," he murmured. His lips brushed her hair.

His words opened a floodgate within her. The whimpers turned to sobs that tore out of her throat. Sobs that hurt, that would be denied no longer no matter how she sought to stifle them.

"It's all right." His voice sounded far off. "It's all right." He stroked her hair. Then he began to rub her back in a slow, circular motion. "It's all right."

In a peculiar way she was conscious of him and not conscious of him. He was holding her in a comforting way, and she clung to his strong, warm body. But in another way the terrible loneliness she felt after her father's death swamped her as never before.

She had swung a curtain of reserve across her feelings, shielding her from Charlotte's death and then Beau's. That curtain once rent now became shredded as the strain of the attempts on her life and the difficulties in dealing with the problems of Talbot Shipping added to her losses and whirled in her disordered thoughts.

She began to fight against him, throw her head back on his arm and try to pull away, to run and hide, to get away from him until the terrible emotion could vent itself.

"No, Judith. No. Cry if you want to. You'll feel better." He would not let her go. Instead, he caught the back of her head and pressed her face into his shoulder. The warmth and tenderness hurt her more, for he offered her a glimpse of what she might have, yet he despised her.

Frantically, she tried to swallow her grief, to concentrate on her grievance against Tabor O'Halloran. She must stop weeping in front of this man. Her whole body shuddered with the effort. Perspiration broke out on her face as she ruthlessly drove the sobs back inside herself.

He must have realized what she was trying to do. "Judith," he said again. "It's all right. I won't take advantage of your grief."

She shook her head against his shoulder and pulled back. "Let's talk about the *W-White Cloud*."

He stared into her pain racked face. "I took your ship," he confessed. "But as I told you, only to save her."

"Then I can have her back?"

His eyes darkened then. "Not till after the war."

He watched the pain and vulnerability disappear from her face. Her trembling lips compressed. One hand rose and flicked at the tears that wet her cheeks. Her eyes turned cold. "She belongs to me."

Dropping his arms, he stepped back. "You'll get her back. In good condition. For now England doesn't need another American ship to bring supplies . . ."

She clenched her fists. "She's not going to be used to transport troops or supplies. She's a Talbot ship. A private merchantman. She'll be used in free trade."

"She will now," he replied significantly. "She's been

taken by Americans. She's a prize of war."

Her eyes were hard as emeralds. "You'd do that to your old friend."

"What do you mean?"

"You took Beau Talbot's ship. Not mine. When you took the *White Cloud,* you betrayed him. You robbed your old friend, your good friend. And you still thought he was alive. Pardon me, Tabor O'Halloran, if I don't believe all this patriotic fervor."

He clenched his fists in an effort to hold his temper. "Beau would have thanked me," he protested. "He couldn't have known that the captain was French. Evidently an admirer of Bonaparte."

"So are a great many people, but they manage to keep at work. They don't flock to Elba."

"Dammit. I know my information was correct."

"Who would give a pirate information?" she scoffed.

An angry flush darkened his skin. "When this is over," he prophesied, "you're going to eat every one of those words."

"Let me ask you a question that has nothing to do with the war."

"All right," he agreed warily.

"If I were Beau instead of his daughter, would you return the ship?"

He hesitated only an instant, but in that instant she read his answer. No matter what he said, she knew the truth. "Beau would have influence"—he chose his words with care—"to demand that his ships be allowed to go on about their business."

"But I have not."

He hesitated, fumbled for words that would soften the blows.

"Don't bother to answer. I wouldn't want you to waste your breath."

"When this is over . . ."

"By *this* I presume you mean the war. When this is over, I shall move the headquarters of Talbot Shipping to England."

Instantly, he was alert. *Spy!* screamed his mind. Evidently, she presumed she was safe in adimtting her British allegiance. "And they'll welcome you with open arms, will they?" he asked silkily.

She shrugged. "They will if I have enough ships to continue the line. I have to have the *White Cloud*. If you loved Beau as you say, you must know that he overextended himself to please Celeste. There were outstanding debts. He didn't expect to die."

"No, I can imagine not."

"I have to pay those debts. I need the cargoes of every one. Don't you understand?"

"I understand."

"Then you'll return the *Cloud*?"

His eyes broke contact with hers. "Just as soon as the war is over."

"But it could go on for years. Aren't you listening to me? I've debts to pay on my father's estate. On Laura's estate and Celeste's."

"I understand that your ship was being commanded by a French captain who was about to use her to aid in the rescue of Napoleon from Elba."

She smiled in genuine approval. "Then I'm glad you stopped her. Europe doesn't need any more of that monster stirring things up. She needs peace and time to rebuild."

"Exactly."

"Then give me back the *Cloud* and I'll swear that no one with Bonapartist sympathies will ever set foot on her deck again."

"Just as soon as the war is over. We can't have her used by the British either."

"You don't like the British, do you?"

"*Don't like* is too mild a condition for the way I feel about the British. America is at war with them. A stupid, useless war that they are waging strictly to try to rejoin us to the British Empire. We will never rejoin, but they won't let us alone."

"I wouldn't let the British take her. Nor any of my

ships, for that matter."

He ignored her protest. "The British forces are massing barely a hundred miles south of here. They could use your vessel and your crew's knowledge of the Mississippi."

She caught him by the shoulders. Her temper blazed in the face of his single-minded conviction to believe the worst of her. "Listen to me, you big fool! I don't have the money or the time to be political. I wouldn't do anything to help them, for the simple reason that I can't without ruining everything my father built. I intend to remain strictly neutral, for Beau's sake."

"Of course, for the sake of your poor dead father."

"And now for Laura. And Celeste."

"How noble of you."

She was getting nowhere in this conversation. She shook her head trying to think of a magic word that would convince him that she told the truth. "It's Laura and Celeste who will suffer most if Talbot Shipping goes bankrupt."

"There's no chance of that," he scoffed. "Beau Talbot left ships, a rich sugar plantation."

"But he left debts! He had just bought a new ship, the *Laurel*. The war had caused problems with markets. He had a"—she swallowed—"a wife who gambled."

He looked at her with distaste, then tossed the last of the brandy down his throat. "I'll say good night, Judith. Thank you for the drink. I'm more sorry than I know how to say about Beau."

"You refuse to return my ship?"

"Just as soon as the British are convinced that this war is over, I'll be bringing her into the harbor at New Orleans. It'll happen within the year."

"I can't wait!" she cried, shaking her fists at him. "Why don't you understand?"

He stepped back. "*You* don't understand," he said mildly. "She's a marked vessel. The British are on the lookout for her. You'll lose her if you try to sail her again."

315

"Something could be worked out," she insisted. "The earl . . ."

The mention of her noble relative finished the conversation. Tabor sketched a bow and opened the door. "I bid you good evening. Have a pleasant journey home, m'lady."

As she flung herself at him, he closed the door. "Damn you, Tabor O'Halloran!" She did not shout the words. They were uttered instead in a voice so low and deep that it might have come from a man's throat.

A few minutes later, when Captain Smithurst knocked on the door of his own cabin, he found her sitting, composed, in the chair beside his desk. The traces of tears were faintly discernible on her cheeks, but other than look a bit closely at her and then clear his throat, he made no sign. "Shall we be casting off at first light, ma'am?" he asked hopefully.

"No."

"No?"

"We shall spend tomorrow here."

"I don't understand."

She placed her palms together and matched the fingertips. "I'm not quite sure I can explain to you right now, Captain Smithurst, but by tomorrow I will have made my plan."

He looked alarmed. "Plan?"

"Exactly. Please sit down, Captain."

Uneasily, he seated himself. "Miss Talbot-Harrow . . ."

"Captain, Tabor O'Halloran refuses to give me the *White Cloud*. He has admitted to me that he has her somewhere. What would you think if someone refused to give you what was rightfully yours?"

"Well, I suppose I'd be mad as blazes, ma'am."

"That's just how I feel, Captain Smithurst. As mad as blazes. That man was and is a pirate."

"If he's a pirate, ma'am, then you should go to the law."

316

She looked at him disgustedly. "Everybody in New Orleans knew about him. They all laughed about it and welcomed them into their homes. My father knew him and called him friend, yet nothing was done to him. New Orleans is proud of its pirates."

"Well, now, perhaps there are some things you don't understand."

"Such as?"

"I can't say for sure, but I've heard tell that he might have a connection with the government."

"How can a pirate have a connection with the government? Unless all of America is as dishonest and thieving as he is."

"Americans come in all sorts of different shapes and sizes, ma'am. They're not like the English."

"I can see that," she said dryly.

"What I mean is that he might have been doing something honest while he was pretending to be a pirate."

"If he wanted to prove honesty and reliability, he should have given me back my ship."

Faced with her implacable attitude, the captain lapsed into silence.

"Would you ask Cook to fix me something to eat?" she said at last.

"Yes, ma'am. I'll send one of the cabin boys down to you immediately. Stay here in my cabin as long as you like. It's larger and roomier than yours."

"Thank you."

He hesitated at the door. "Would you mind telling me what you're planning, Miss Talbot-Harrow?"

"I'll be delighted to, Captain Smithurst. We're going to turn the tables on Captain O'Halloran."

Smithurst tugged nervously at the corner of his mustache. "Ma'am?"

"We're going to steal the *Banshee*."

317

Chapter Sixteen

"Ahoy, *Banshee*!"

Hands on the starboard rail, Tabor grinned quizzically down into the longboat.

"Permission to come aboard."

"Come ahead." He gestured lazily, his loose muslin sleeve swaying in the breeze. Then with some interest he watched Judith negotiate the climb to the deck. An errant breeze caught the skirt of her pale green muslin dress. It billowed up to reveal ruffled and beribboned pantalettes. The man holding the ladder below her grinned broadly.

When she climbed within arm's reach, Tabor held down his hands. Gratefully, she took them and allowed him to swing her onto the deck. Their faces were inches apart as she found her footing and let her skirts fall around her. Light strands of her hair lifted toward him on the breeze that also brought the light floral scent of her perfume. His nostrils flared.

She smiled at him, a little tremulously, he thought.

Stepping back, he made an elaborate leg. "To what do I owe the pleasure of this visit, Miss Talbot-Harrow?"

She tilted her head to one side. "Why, Mr. O'Halloran, surely you can guess? I can't leave Santiago without trying one more time for the *White Cloud*. I'm here to convince you to take pity on my plight."

He stared at the dying sunlight filtering through her

hair, at her smile, the soft flush on her cheek. For a second he did not realize she had finished speaking. Then, regretfully, he shook his head. "Judith, I can't . . ."

She raised her hand. Her fingertips almost touched his lips before she hastily pulled them back. "Don't say anything yet. Let's just be together for a few hours. I have so much to tell you. Can we dine and perhaps talk further?"

He stared pointedly at the delicate fingers, noting that they trembled slightly. His eyes rose quizzically to lock with hers. The moment stretched between them.

She gave him a brilliant smile and tilted her head to the opposite side.

He ran a hand around the back of his neck. If she had come to speak to him, the least he could do was let her make her speech. It would not change anything, but he could be gracious. With an answering smile he swept his arm in the direction of the quarterdeck and the captain's cabin beneath it. "The *Banshee* is yours."

Her eyes widened, their sapphire depths almost trapping him. Then her eyelashes swept down, and she smiled sweetly. "Why, thank you, sir."

"I'm afraid the cook didn't plan on a guest for dinner. May I suggest that we dine late so that he can exercise his talent?"

"Oh, that's not necessary. I'm sure whatever you were going to eat will be fine."

He grinned as he offered her his arm. "Oh, it's no trouble. Riley'll be pleased to get a chance to try his hand at some different things. We're fully provisioned. The crew are ashore taking their last leave before we sail."

She almost pulled away from him rather than have him feel her heart beating so hard against the wall of her chest. What luck! A fully provisioned ship with only a skeleton crew. She dropped her eyes to the deck beneath her feet. Here and there were black scorch marks where the fire had seared it deeply.

319

Hastily, she looked up, only to encounter his bleak stare. He had followed the direction of her eyes and seen what she had seen.

She met his look without flinching, for it restored her resolve. After a brief moment she came to his side and put her arm through his. "Will you show me the rest of your ship, Captain O'Halloran?"

"Little enough to see, Miss Talbot-Harrow," he replied stiffly, a touch of anger in his voice. "The damage was slight and in most cases easily repaired."

"I'm glad," she said sincerely.

His own men—only four of them on deck—continued their duties. The cook would be busy below.

She nodded to her own crew members, a half dozen stalwarts chosen for their size. Their faces bland, two moved to lounge beneath a canvas that provided shade from the Gulf sun, still hot even where it set on the horizon. Two more moved to the waist of the ship. The other two strolled farther toward the bow.

As Tabor led her to the stern, Judith exerted a bit of extra pressure on his arm. "I did not set fire to your ship," she said evenly. "I would never do anything that would put innocent people in danger. I was angry with you. That's true. Furious. I've always had a bad temper. It's my weakness. But my quarrel was with you."

"And still is."

"And still is," she acknowledged, unable to keep an answering note of bitterness from her voice. Inclining her head, she lifted her skirts to climb the steps from the maindeck to the quarterdeck.

In front of the wheel they turned to look back the length of the ship. Tabor put his hands behind him and adopted a parallel stance, the pose of a captain astride the deck in the rolling sea. "The *Banshee* is eighty-five feet long. She weighs one hundred sixty-five tons. She mounts ten cannon, and a full fighting crew is ninety-four."

Judith ran an appreciative eye along the deck. "She's

320

truly beautiful." Placing her hand for shade, she stared up the towering mainmast. With all sails furled, it pointed far, far into the blue.

Tabor's own eyes followed the graceful line of Judith's white throat and the delightful curve where the soft muslin sleeve fell back from her arm. He made no effort to suppress his body's reaction to her nearness. Again he reminded himself that she was there to try to convince him to give her the *White Cloud*. If she were willing to offer some physical persuasion, he would welcome her efforts.

After a moment she dropped her hand, in time to catch him looking at her with eyes that burned hot. She flushed and glanced nervously out over the water. "Do you have a full fighting crew?" she asked as though to cover her confusion.

"Not aboard. No. About a third of them are . . . elsewhere."

Judith flashed him an angry look. She had no need to ask where they might be. The knowledge set her to seething inwardly. She took a deep, controlling breath.

"Would you like to continue the tour?" He bowed, his politeness ironic.

With equal politeness she put her hand on his crooked arm. "Yes, very much."

The meal in the captain's cabin was a treat for them both. Rising to the occasion, Riley, the cook, had prepared fresh fish from the waters beneath them, deliciously seasoned with the juice of lemons and limes that grew in such profusion on the island. With the fish came black beans cooked tender, fresh-baked bread, and slices of melon for dessert. The whole was washed down with orange and lemon juice spiked with potent rum.

Judith sat back replete. "I can't believe how good this all was. The cook on board the *Hound* cooks exactly the same thing every day. I don't know why the crew doesn't mutiny. When I came aboard, Captain Smithurst suggested that the passengers' menu be prepared for me, but I said I wanted no special favors." She gave an exaggerated grimace of distaste.

"Made a mistake, did you?" Tabor took another sip of his drink and smiled appreciatively.

"A big one."

"Riley fixes good food. When we were younger, we helped each other out of some very tight spots. When I decided it was time to leave the old sod, he didn't need much urging to come with me. He wasn't a sailor by trade. Used to get sick as a horse. But he stayed as my cook. And he's a handy man to have at your back in a fight."

She looked at Tabor inquiringly. "The old sod was Ireland?"

"And where else would I be comin' from with a name like O'Halloran?"

"And the tight spots? Did they involve the English?"

"I don't need to tell you the story. You can guess it. It's so much like all the rest. All the people—Irish, Scots, Welsh—that the bloody British have driven out of their homeland have the same story."

"I . . . I've never heard *your* story."

He stared at her speculatively, then took another drink. The rum rolled smoothly on his tongue. "The O'Hallorans were dispossessed."

She sat very still, all ardent sympathy for him.

"My father and his father before him and his before him. As long as there were Irish, there were O'Hallorans on that spot. Then came the English m'lord a-saying that we had not registered the land properly. It was all a matter of paperwork, he assured us. He would take care of it."

He looked at her with eyes dark with pain. "We weren't rich. It was just a small piece of land. Not like what you came from, I suspect."

She thought of Harrestone. Its boundless acres meant

nothing to her. They had never been hers. Nor, for that matter, had *Ombres Azurées*. In her own way she was as dispossessed as he. But even as she shook her head he began speaking again.

"But from the time of St. Patrick, we'd been there. How could they ask us to register what had always been ours?"

"Governments change," she murmured helplessly. "Look at New Orleans. M'sieur Dufaure grinds his teeth every time he thinks about what has happened in just the last fifty years. The city's belonged to three different nations. Its people have had to register their property each time the government has changed."

Tabor took another drink of his rum. "My father didn't believe it. He sent my brother Timothy, who was studying for the priesthood, to find out the right of it."

The black look on his face told its own story. "He didn't find out the right of it," she said positively.

"Ah, no. They threw him into the jail." His hand tightened around the handle of his pewter tankard until she was sure the soft metal would crush to conform to the shapes of his fingers. "Him that was going to be a priest."

"And?"

"In the common cell. With the scum of the earth." He tossed the rum into his mouth as if it had been water. "He was robbed, raped, and murdered."

"Ah, no." She could not comprehend the enormity of the catastrophe. Her own experience was too limited. Still the pain in his voice made her rise from her chair. In two steps she was before him, putting her arms around him, drawing him to her, as if hiding his eyes against her would make the vision of his brother's corpse less real.

He put one arm around her waist and held on to her, accepting the comfort she offered him with her whole heart. "When my father and Thomas came after him, they were told he'd died and his body'd been disposed of."

She felt him shudder.

323

"My own brother—him that was going to be a priest— not buried in the churchyard."

Fiercely, she held him, lacing her fingers through his black hair, feeling the heat rising from him as he struggled with anger years old, yet fresh and horrible.

"They kept my father and Thomas running from office to office for nigh a week. It was all a plan." His teeth clamped together and he rose, tearing himself out of her protecting arms. "My mother and I and my little sisters were herded out of the house and the house pulled down."

He looked toward her with black hatred in his eyes, but it was not directed at her. "A solid stone house, centuries old, pulled down. Thatch thick as a wall set to blazing. I couldn't save it. I was batted away like a fly." The words were almost a groan.

"You were a child."

"I was thirteen. And big for my age."

"You were just a boy."

He glared at her. "When my father came home, he just looked at the ruin and then he looked at me because I'd failed him."

"You didn't fail him. You were alone. You couldn't stop it."

"I'll never forget the look on his face. He thought I should have. He put his arm around my mother and turned her away from me."

Judith remained silent. If Tabor's stubborn nature was inherited from his father, perhaps the old man had indeed tried to place blame.

His back to her, his shoulders hunched repressively, he stared out through the windows in the stern. His conscience flayed him. "I was there. He'd lost Timothy —him who was the smartest and best of the lot of us. And he'd lost his home. So he just didn't care about anything else."

The silence grew in the cabin. The water lapped against the hull of the ship. The rigging creaked faintly. Judith shivered despite the warmth. Her own struggles with guilt came back to her. She laid her hand on his shoulder. "Tabor, are you sure you didn't put this guilt on yourself? Is that your father's accusation or your own?"

He moved from under her hand to drain the last of the rum and set down the tankard with exaggerated care. "At this point in time I'm not really sure. 'Tis all over anyway. My father is dead and my mother after him. Grief and care. Thomas is probably still alive. He married a woman who was willing to help with my little sisters. But I left, and I'll never return."

"Perhaps . . ."

He pulled her into his arms. His eyes blazed bright with anger and with need. "No. Enough talk about that. You came to convince me to let you have the *White Cloud*. Convince me." His mouth came down on hers.

His hot, seeking tongue roughly opened her mouth to his. One arm encircled her shoulders like a rod, holding her tight against his chest. His hand dropped to clutch her buttock and lift her to his manhood.

Shocked by the suddenness of his attack, she was helpless to move or even struggle. His heat and power encompassed her, dragged her in, and made her his willing captive.

Response so intense that her blood thundered through her veins made her open her mouth greedily for the kiss. She found she could not get enough of the taste of him—fierce, potent, male—spiked with rum and citrus. Frenzied, her tongue met his, sliding over the different surfaces of his mouth, feeling the wet, warm edges of his teeth, the smooth satin lining of his lips, the rough texture of his tongue.

"Damn you. Why are you so beautiful? Why do you taste so good?" His whole body vibrating, he growled into her mouth. His hand clamped her buttock tighter, lifted her higher.

He hurt her; his rough, strong taking excited her at the same time it angered her. Without knowing what she did,

325

she bent her leg, sliding her thigh up his flank. The movement opened her throbbing center to him. Layers of material were nothing to the lightning heat that flashed between them.

At the same time, the hard muscles of his chest and the bones of his pelvis bruised her. He took a forward step to steady himself before driving himself hard against her.

Was he going to take her again standing up? Somehow the thought of his doing that seemed the ultimate insult. With a cry she pushed her hand between them, her palm flat against his chest. Her straining fingers found his nipple erect and hard. Viciously, she clawed with her nails.

He started, then ripped his mouth away from her own. His face was dark with heat and passion. His eyes blazing, Irish blue. "What the hell?"

"You hurt me," she gasped. "I just hurt you back."

He let his head fall back, staring at the ceiling, taking deep breaths that hurt her even as his chest swelled against her breasts. "I'm sorry. It's just that I . . ."

"Don't keep breathing like that. You're holding me too tight."

Instantly, he eased his grip but did not release her. His voice seemed to rumble out from deep inside his chest. It vibrated against her breasts. "I want you. The feel of you all warm and giving in my arms got the better of me."

She shivered, alive again to the most devastating sensations now that the pain had eased. Her hands slid up around his neck into his thick black hair. She lifted her lips to his. "I want you too."

He smiled down at her. This time he held her tenderly, turning her in his arms to cup a breast and flick his thumb across the nipple.

She made a soft little mew of pleasure and twisted gently in his grasp. "I . . . I can't believe my own body. I don't seem to have any control."

"Good." His lips slid off her mouth and down the side of her throat, feeling the quickening pulse. "You don't need any. Control is not for lovers."

"Is that what we are?" She caught her lower lip between her teeth as she arched, lifting her breasts to him.

"Isn't it?" The neckline of her dress was low. He pushed the garment down over one shoulder and bared the upper slope of her breast.

She moaned at the prickly soft feel of his chin and mouth. "I thought we were enemies."

His lips stilled, then moved down. Through the thin muslin he found her nipple swollen, ready for him. "Surrender," he groaned.

"I can't help myself."

For a full minute the cabin was silent except for her helpless moans of pleasure as he used his mouth and hands to caress the intimate parts of her body.

Then he pushed her back at arm's length. "Take a deep breath," he commanded, suiting words to action, "and take off your clothes."

She swayed as a blush rose in her cheeks. "Tabor . . ."

He kissed her hard on the mouth. "The dress is very pretty, Judith. It would be a shame to rip it. What's more, I don't have anything for you to wear."

Embarrassed, she dropped her eyes only to encounter the reddened skin where his beard had scratched her. "This is so . . ."

"Practical?" He pulled his shirt from his breeches and reached for the string that drew his sleeve at his wrists. "Perhaps m'lady would prefer if I turned down the lantern?"

She flushed deeper at his mockery. As the evening progressed, she was feeling more and more desperate, as if she were making a fool of herself. She tried to peek at him from under her lashes.

He caught her looking as he pulled his shirt off and tossed it over the back of the chair. He grinned. "If you like what you see, why don't you hurry up so you can touch me?"

Spurred by the mockery in his voice, her fingers found the small pearl buttons at the front of her dress. She unfastened one, then stopped, her fingers cold as ice, disobedient to her will. What did the *White Cloud* and Talbot lines and the whole damn thing mean if she lost her self-respect entirely?

For the twentieth time that day, she thought of Charlotte. Her mother had ruined herself in a pathetic effort to secure her husband's attention, to win Harrestone for herself and her heirs, to find happiness among the vicious tongues of the *ton*. And she had lost so terribly. Lost everything.

Judith felt herself so close to the same sort of disaster. With her fingers on the second button she raised her eyes to Tabor. He had paused, hands on hips, watching her closely, a grim, mocking smile curving his mouth.

He did not expect her to go through with this. He stood waiting for her to break and run, gather her crew and flee the ship.

She would not do so. She would not. She would do anything she had to do to keep him from sailing out of the harbor of Santiago de Cuba. If she could help it, he would not rendezvous with the *White Cloud* somewhere on the high seas and use a Talbot ship for the duration of this wretched war.

Her temper blazed hot. She had come to gamble. She would not throw down her hand, but play her cards to the best of her ability.

Her stiff mouth curved into a falsely bright smile. She held it as she finished unbuttoning the dress. With a steady hand she pushed it and the chemise beneath it to her waist.

Then, imitating his stance and his expression, she doubled her own fists on her hips. "I've taken off as much as you have," she said, her voice strong.

The mockery faded as his eyes were drawn to her white breasts, each crowned with a stiff pink nipple. Her breathing quickened under the impact of his eyes. It

328

stirred them, or did she shiver?

Suddenly, his lips felt dry; he licked them slowly, then dropped down on his knees before her. The action brought his lips even with her breasts. His right hand shaped one while his lips caressed the other.

She gasped aloud, swaying, yet holding her ground.

Gently, then more strongly he sucked her. His eyes closed, he felt her ease the dress down her hips. With a faint whisper of material and a click of pearl buttons, her dress fell to the floor, leaving her standing in her pantalettes.

"These again," he whispered, plucking at the ties. "I've already collected one pair of them. Do you remember?"

"What?" she groaned, passion curling deep in her belly.

"I've already collected one pair of these, silk they were, to match sapphire velvet." The pantalettes fell before his lips as they trailed down her belly to nestle in the soft red curls at its base.

"Tabor," she moaned, clutching his head against her. "Tabor. Damn you."

He did not reply, nor did he desist, but continued his assault.

When she was all but weeping with desire, he pulled his head back out of her clasping hands. Climbing to his feet, he swept her up in his arms and carried her to the bed. There he laid her, her thighs open, her feet hanging over the side. Kneeling between them, he continued to kiss her, hot hands gripping her thighs, holding them apart.

"I can't stand any more," she wept.

He lifted his head, his eyes running up over her quivering body to her face. "Isn't this what you came for?"

"No! Yes! Yes!" She began to weep and writhe and twist, loving the wonderful feeling of his mouth. A torrent of ecstatic sounds poured from her throat. She

329

caught up double handfuls of the sheet in her frenzy.

He sucked hard, laving her with his tongue. Then his teeth grazed the throbbing nub of flesh.

She screamed—not in pain, but in pleasure—and exploded, bucking upward against the pressure of his hands.

He sprang up to watch her, triumphant in the sight of her naked body caught in the throes of the ultimate ecstasy a human being can experience. With sure, eager fingers, he unbuttoned his breeches and pushed them down. He opened her thighs wider with his knees and slid his hands under her buttocks. Without further preparation he rammed into her hot, throbbing sheath.

She screamed in pleasure again. And then her moans and whimpers filled the cabin as he drove again and again to his own climax. In a time incredibly brief lest the human organism die of ecstasy, he cried out, shuddered, and collapsed, his head on her breasts, his hands heavy around her waist.

She lay beneath him, her body bathed in perspiration, as was his. The scent of their union rose strong on the warm air of the cabin. She had never known such pleasure, nor such an aftermath of pain. Tears began to slip slowly out of the corners of her eyes.

The tears were not shame. She supposed she should be feeling ashamed for what she had done, for what she was about to do. But she did not. Instead, she felt regret, sorrow for herself. The feelings he aroused in her were the only true feelings in her life. How ironic that this man could arouse them when he despised her.

What she felt for him must be what the other people called love. How terrible that she had not come for the incredible feelings she had just experienced. She had come with an ulterior motive, one so strong that she dared not abandon it. She pulled her hands away from the broad shoulders she had clasped in ecstasy.

As the throbbing of her body subsided, she tried to marshal her thoughts. One more try. She would ask him once more. Surely, he must feel something for her to have loved her so long and so thoroughly, to have taken such care for her pleasure. She raised herself on her elbows and smiled tremulously. "Why do you make me feel so wonderful and yet you won't . . . won't . . . give me back my ship?"

He rolled off her and laid his forearm across his eyes. "The ship doesn't have anything to do with this. Not a damned thing."

"She's the reason I'm here."

He drew his arm away and stared at her. "If you believe that, then you're lying to yourself. You came because you wanted what I could give you. You came for passion, since you don't believe in love."

She could have cried then. He was so stubborn. But so was she. And determined. So determined that she could now find the courage to play her greatest game of deception. And after his loving came the part that did not come easy for her.

She pushed herself up into a sitting position. "I'll get us both a drink."

He groaned, then raised his arm again. She caught his wrist and brought his hand to her mouth to kiss it. Holding it against her breast, she brought her other hand across her body to stroke his face.

His eyes closed at the gentle sensation. He smiled, turning his head to follow her palm. His lips pressed into its heart. A frisson of pleasure left the skin of her arms rough with chill bumps.

"I'll get us something," she whispered, bending low until her lips were only inches from his ear. Purposefully, she blew a tickling breath into it.

"Minx," he murmured, batting lightly at her.

She drew back with a tiny laugh and slid away. On bare feet she padded across the cabin to the jug of citrus juice.

He hauled himself up into a semireclining position, the better to enjoy the sight of her beautiful body.

She stood with her back to him, where he could admire the graceful curves of her buttocks, the long length of her legs, the small waistline, the perfect skin. Taking up a spoon from the table, she stirred the liquid in the jug, then poured some into the mugs.

When she turned, she took his breath away and hardened him again. As she walked across the room, a pewter tankard in each hand held at a level with her breasts, he thought he had never seen a more beautiful sight.

"You're beautiful," he crooned.

"Thank you. I'm glad you're pleased."

"Pleased!" He took the tankard she offered him. "Any more pleased and I'd be dead." He stretched out his arm. "Come back beside me."

Obediently, she climbed into bed and stretched out beside him, her head against his shoulder. He lifted the tankard to his lips, but she stayed his hand. "Won't you please return the *White Cloud*?"

She felt the tendons strut beneath her fingers. He lowered the vessel to his chest. "Don't ask me . . ."

"It's my ship. I need it desperately. My sister and my stepmother both depend on the Talbot lines." She slid her fingers gently down the back of his hand and over his wrist. Beneath the caress, beneath the fine black hair, beneath the smooth skin, the muscles remained rigid, taut as rigging in a gale. A wave of hopelessness swept over her. "Please."

The arm did not relax. "No," he said.

She drew her hand back.

Eyes wintry, he raised the tankard to his mouth and drank thirstily. When he had drained it, she took it from him and rose from the bed. He did not notice that she had not drunk.

Back straight, buttocks tight, she walked back to the table. The drink left a bitter aftertaste in his mouth. He shivered faintly and swallowed. She set the tankards down with exaggerated care, arranging them on the tray beside the jug. He supposed she was pouting or thinking of the argument that she might use next. He took a deep breath. "Come back to bed," he called.

She did not turn. "No, I don't think so." Instead, she

bent to draw her pantalettes from among the articles of clothing on the chair.

"Leave that," he commanded. He slid a little farther down on the bed, rolling over on his side. The movement made his head swim dizzily. He took a minute to bring his eyes into focus. When he did so, he was disappointed to see that she had already stepped into the pantalettes and was tying the drawstring into a bow at her waist. "You're not going to be mad, are you? I promise you can have her back the minute the war's over."

"Thank you," she said. Reaching for her other garments, she pulled them on one by one.

"Where're you going?" His tongue felt thick.

"Just out on deck. I have some orders to give to my crew. And you're getting sleepy anyway." She crossed to the bed and pulled the sheet up over his shoulder.

"Not . . . sssleepy . . ."

"Yes, you are."

"Why . . . not . . . you . . . ?"

"Because I've drugged your drink." She managed to smile as his eyes flared in sudden recognition, then lost focus and closed, shutting out light, sound, and sense.

For a full minute she stood staring down at him. Her lips curved in a tender expression as she noted the boyish looks, the thick black lashes protecting the tender hollows beneath his eyes. His skin was dark from the sun, in the American way. Not pale like the skin of an English nobleman.

Impelled by passion and emotion, she laid her hand on his shoulder and traced the contour of his body, his chest rising and falling with his slow breathing, the indentation of his waist, the hard muscle of his hip and thigh. He was so beautiful. She stroked his shoulder once more, then turned away.

Closing her eyes tightly, she drew a deep, shuddering breath. Did she dare go through with this plan? The thought of Tabor's rage when he recovered consciousness was daunting. Yet, everything was at stake. She could not falter now.

333

Chapter Seventeen

Tabor woke briefly as the crew from the *White Hound* lowered him in a sling into the longboat. The swing through the fresh air and the rough handling of his body loosened the grip of the laudanum.

"Be careful. Oh, be careful."

He heard her voice above him. All but paralyzed, he felt the crewmen of the *Banshee* receive him and stretch his inert body on the thwart. His face was turned toward her.

The black lashes swept up, revealing the blue stare illuminated by flaring torches that lighted the transfer operation. Their eyes met. His registered his anger; hers shone with concern that instantly turned to defiance.

She clenched her hands tightly on the rail and leaned toward him. "I've taken your ship."

He could not answer, but the expression in his eyes made her shiver.

She swallowed heavily and cleared her throat. "I'm sailing the *Banshee* home to New Orleans. The only way you can have her back is by following us in the *White Cloud* and trading ships. If you don't follow us, then we'll use the *Banshee* to make the China run that's scheduled at the end of December. She can't carry as much as the *Cloud,* but she's faster."

"Bitch." His lips formed the word, but no sound came.

He could feel himself fading, the laudanum taking possession again, his body slumping across the thwarts, lulled by the lap of the water.

She read the word and closed her eyes for a pained moment. When she opened them, the men of both crews were looking at her. "Make for the dock," she commanded.

His crew unshipped their oars.

"Take him carefully," she called.

His eyes opened once more, desperately trying to focus. Then the lids fell closed despite his will.

Captain Smithurst pulled at his mustache with quick, nervous tugs. "I cannot like this entire episode, Miss Talbot-Harrow."

Her eyes red-rimmed from tears, Judith stared at his imposing figure and disapproving face. The hour was well past midnight. She knew that they should be ready to sail on the morning tide. Furthermore, she was tired of arguing with him. Her head ached, and her body felt drained of all its energy, yet nervous and upset.

Deception was not her forte. Her senses still vibrated faintly with the pleasure Tabor had brought her. His body had been hot and strong, arousing her to incredible heights, taking the tension from her and leaving sweet release in its place. She could still feel the effects of the journey in her limbs.

Likewise, guilt left her nauseated, conscience-stricken. She had betrayed him in the most contemptible way a woman could betray a man, and the knowledge of her act was making her ill.

"You took a ship from its captain." Smithurst's voice rumbled on. His chest swelled with righteous indignation. "You took it and set him off in an open boat."

"I put him down in the harbor of Santiago, Captain Smithurst," Judith reminded him dryly. "And then, only after I had exhausted every argument I could think of to

335

persuade him to return my ship. Which he took!"

"Still . . ."

She pressed onward. "And he had no right to take the *White Cloud*. He might claim that he took it to prevent it from falling into the wrong hands, but as far as Talbot Shipping is concerned, his hands are the wrong ones."

Smithurst tugged at his mustache again, then swung about and began to pace the length of the cabin. "To take a man's ship is piracy," he said, gesturing nervously. "You could find yourself in very serious trouble with the United States government."

She shook her head angrily. "How can it be piracy to take a pirate's ship? Especially after he stole ours?"

"Perhaps he thought he had good reason to take ours." He stopped and frowned at her severely, but she tossed her head.

"Oh, I'm sure he could come up with a reason . . ."

"And if his reason is sound enough, then what you've done is piracy," Smithurst continued stubbornly. "You mark my words. President Madison is only waiting until the war is over to commission a fleet of pirate hunters. They'll clear every one of the filthy, thieving murderers out of the Gulf and the Caribbean. If they find out you've committed an act of piracy . . ."

"What he did was piracy," she tried to point out.

". . . it could go hard with you and Talbot Shipping."

Judith sighed in despair. Realistically, she could not be too angry with the man. He was strictly honest, and he was deeply prejudiced against women at sea. She should not be here, much less make a decision that smacked of dishonesty. She tried once more. "If I hadn't taken this ship, the Talbot lines would have no chance to survive the war."

"If she had been taken by a real pirate, the blackguard would have murdered the crew, stolen the cargo, and burned the ship to the waterline. Did Captain O'Halloran do that?"

Judith stirred uncomfortably. "No."

336

"No. Captain O'Halloran merely kept the ship from falling into the hands of the French. He did you a big favor, if you ask me."

"That's what he said."

"And you repay him by taking his ship, taking away his livelihood—"

Judith interrupted him angrily. "Captain Smithurst, I have done it and I will be the one to take full responsibility for my action!"

His mouth snapped to. He took a deep breath and tugged at his mustache distractedly. At length he shrugged. "Very well, Miss Talbot-Harrow. Then let's not delay. The *Hound* will escort you home."

She thought of his disapproval, of his frustration at the delays this rescue mission was causing. "That won't be necessary."

He gaped at her, rocking back on his heels, head thrust forward.

"If you can spare me Mr. Longman, your first mate, for this trip, he can command a skeleton crew to sail the *Banshee* back to New Orleans for me. You can be on your way."

"Miss Talbot-Harrow, I couldn't allow—"

"I know you'll miss Mr. Longman, but . . ."

"I'll miss him, yes, but that's not my concern. I am responsible for you," he reminded her stiffly.

"I thank you, Captain Smithurst, but the voyage across the Gulf to New Orleans should be easy. I promise to pay Mr. Longman for his time in port until you return."

Captain Smithurst shook his head. "I'm sure Longman would be glad of the shore leave. He has a family in New Orleans. But, ma'am, a storm can blow up anytime. And it would be the least of your worries."

"But I believe that the time for hurricanes has passed."

"These are war times. The sea lanes are full of ships from one country or another looking for targets. There

337

are pirates . . ."

"We saw nothing on our way out," she reminded him. "I'm sure it would be a safe voyage home."

He hesitated, then shook himself visibly. "I won't allow it, Miss Talbot-Harrow."

"Think of how you would hate to delay another two weeks." She smiled persuasively, her words a temptation. "One week into New Orleans, and another week to get back out to the Gulf. This way you've lost only two days. Three at the most. You must go, Captain Smithurst. It's only good business."

Smithurst wavered. His eyes lighted. He tried unsuccessfully to hide the look of relief that spread across his face as he bowed to her sweet reason. "As you wish, ma'am."

When he had closed the door behind him, she crossed her arms on the desk in front of her and dropped her forehead onto them. Somehow she must find the strength to still her whirling thoughts. Unfortunately, closing her eyes failed. She could see only the body and face of Tabor O'Halloran, and in particular his furious, accusing eyes.

She raised her head to stare around her at the captain's cabin of the *Banshee*. It was to be her cabin for the next week. Here Tabor O'Halloran faced her again. He filled it. His books lined the shelf above the head of his bed. His sea chest stood at the foot. His papers stuffed the cubbyholes of the desk. His logbook undoubtedly lay inside the drawer.

Rising, she wrapped her arms tightly across her body and walked to the table where they had eaten together. She stared miserably at the jug, nearly empty, and the tankards, his empty, hers full. Her hand was cold that she slid into her pocket to draw out the tiny laudanum bottle.

Sudden rage boiled up in her. What had she become? How could she coldly and calmly make love to a man, then drug his drink to steal from him? She was Judith

Claire Talbot-Harrow, the great-granddaughter of a belted earl, but it seemed she was also Charlotte's daughter. And she had proved to be no better than a whore. If all else failed, perhaps she could apply to Lord Lythes . . .

With a wild swing of her arm she swept the objects off the table. The tankards went flying, landing with a horrible clatter. Their contents spattered across the floor. The heavier jug fell with a resounding crash, breaking into several pieces.

Instantly, she was sorry. The mess made her feel no better. And she shuddered with embarrassment to think of calling in a crew member to clean it up. How could she have been so stupid?

Wearily, she retrieved the tankards, now dented. Going down on one knee, she began to pick up the shards of thick pottery. A sharp edge where the glaze was thickest sliced her finger. The unexpected pain drew a shocked gasp from her. How could she have cut herself on this poor stuff? Lifting her hand to the light of the lantern, she watched a drop of blood well from the wound.

The pain was nothing, the wound nothing; yet, tears began to slip down her cheeks. She had just gotten the better of her pirate nemesis. He, who had robbed her, seduced her, lied about her, shamed and humiliated her, ever and forever believed the worst of her, was now brought low. She should be laughing in triumph—and she could only weep.

Tabor leaned back against the wall of the *taberna* to let the hot coffee drive the dullness from his brain. Sweat trickled down his temples and soaked his clothing. "We'll hire horses, Pinky," he said without opening his eyes.

"Horses, Captain?" The mate scratched his head.

Tabor took another swallow of coffee and sucked in air

339

to cool the scalding liquid. More sweat stood on his forehead. "We'll hire wagons and ride to Guantánamo. We'll follow her in her own ship. She won't get far. If Miss Talbot-Harrow thinks that she can just sail into a harbor and take the *Banshee* out from under my nose, she's much mistaken."

"Unless I'm mistaken, that's what the lady did," Pinky observed to no one in particular. The corners of his mouth quirked upward.

Tabor's face flushed darkly. "She drugged me," he muttered.

"How did she do that if Riley fixed the food?" the mate asked with a show of great interest.

"She put laudanum in my drink, after . . . after . . ." His voice was bitter as the taste in his mouth. "She was like some whore rolling her customer for his money." His hands clenched the cup tightly. He opened his eyes to pour himself another cupful from the pot and toss it off.

"You took her ship, Captain," Mr. Pinckney reminded him mildly.

Tabor ignored the last comment. Instead, he turned to Mr. Magrath. "See to hiring us some horses."

"Yes, sir." The younger man straightened away from the wall.

"Hold on," Mr. Pinckney protested. "Let's think this over for a minute."

"What's there to think about?" Tabor demanded belligerently. His pounding head made his temper shorter than usual.

"For one thing, I can't ride," Mr. Pinckney protested. "And neither can most of the men. We're sailors, Captain."

Tabor's mouth curled in disgust. "We'll hire a wagon, two wagons. A couple of teams. The crew can ride in the wagons. I'll take five men who can ride. We'll go ahead and get the *White Cloud* ready to sail. When you come along behind us, there'll be no delay weighing anchor."

Mr. Pinckney swung his head in the direction of the

growth-covered mountain range that rose behind the town. "Those are mighty big hills, I'm thinkin'. The road between here and there may not be fit to travel on. In the long run, we'll probably make better time hiring a boat."

"Too slow. It's less than fifty miles. We can be under way within hours. We'll catch her before she gets out of the Caribbean." Tabor wiped the sick perspiration from his face and took another swallow of coffee. "See to it, Mr. Magrath."

"Aye, sir." Magrath hurried out through the door of the *taberna*.

A short silence followed, then Mr. Pinckney spoke. "And what will you do with the lady when you catch her?"

Tabor smiled unpleasantly. "I'll take the *Banshee* back."

"And then . . ."

"I'll take the *White Cloud* too." Tabor set his teeth hard. A muscle jumped in the side of his jaw.

"And what about the poor lady?" Mr. Pinckney prodded. "Will you be setting her adrift in an open boat?"

Tabor's brows drew together in a fearsome scowl. "Of course not."

"What then?"

The question stopped him with the coffee halfway to his mouth. "I'll not let her get the better of me," he declared sullenly.

"Captain, she's not much more than a girl."

Tabor shook his head angrily. A violent oath burst from him. "She's not a girl. She's a woman. She tried to burn the *Banshee*. Mr. Archer's dead because of her."

Mr. Pinckney made a dismissive gesture. "Captain, she said she didn't have anything to do with that."

"Of course she'd lie. Nobody would admit to doing something that terrible."

"Aye, it was a terrible thing. So terrible that only a bloody cutthroat could have done it. So, how could she

341

have done it? She doesn't seem a bad sort at all. Suppose she was telling the truth."

"You heard Reynolds. The British War Office has spies in the area."

Mr. Pinckney threw back his head and hooted. "They've never sent young girls."

"She would be the perfect spy. All the right connections. And she worked on the dock." He set his mouth stubbornly. "Don't forget that."

"I'm not forgetting. But that doesn't make her a spy. Remember, you were wrong before. We didn't find anything in her cabin. The other people were the couriers."

Tabor stirred uneasily at the memory of his cold-blooded, systematic destruction of Judith's personal possessions.

Mr. Pinckney leaned forward earnestly. "You've done enough to her, Captain. She's not got your sail. She's not got your tonnage. If you can't forgive her, at least forget her. Follow her back to New Orleans at a fair distance to see that she doesn't meet with any trouble. After she's safely berthed, the two of you exchange ships. And no one gets hurt."

"And what about the French sympathizer? What about him?" Tabor growled the words out. His headache was easing, but his conscience began to prick.

"You've warned her about him. She'll handle it if she can. If she can't, what with her father being dead and all, it's the way of the world." The mate shook his head sadly. "The innocent suffer and the guilty prosper."

"Just spare me the sermons, Pinky."

"Aye, Captain."

Tabor donned his most aggrieved expression. "You might give me a little credit for knowing what's best for her and her shipping line. I was really doing my best for her."

"By taking her ship?"

"By keeping it from falling into enemy hands. What's more, if she's spotted in the Windward Passage in the *Banshee,* it could go hard for her with the British Navy. They could very well shoot first and ask questions later."

Mr. Pinckney nodded sagaciously. "That's just what I was thinking, Captain."

Tabor sniffed righteously. "And if she's taking the *Banshee* home by the quickest way, she'll sail her right by Jamaica. That part of the Caribbean is crawling with British frigates. They can recognize that brigantine as far as they can see her. The ship'll be blown out of the water before Miss Talbot-Harrow has a chance to let them know who she is."

"Aye, Captain. If that pretty lady comes to harm, it'll be your fault."

"My fault!"

"Aye, Captain. You're the one who drove her to this desperate voyage."

Tabor looked as if he were going to rise out of his chair and strike the mate, but he was too weak. Instead, he cursed tiredly. "That's why we need the horses. We need to get after her as fast as we possibly can."

"To take the ship back?" Mr. Pinckney pressed him for an answer.

"No." Tabor shook his head. "To escort her home and trade vessels with her."

"Aye, Captain. Since you're so determined, I'm sure the lads'll be glad to ride if we can find enough horses in this town for the whole crew of us. I'll put it to them like it's a matter of life and death."

Tabor looked at his mate's grinning face with ardent dislike. "Which it may very well be. Right now, just leave me in peace to sweat this damned stuff out of me. Go round up the crew. Tell them what the plan is. Find out which of 'em can ride. And call me when Magrath gets back."

When the mate's footsteps had died away, Tabor

slumped forward, resting his elbows on the table and leaning his forehead on the doubled fists. The movement increased the throbbing in his temples. He groaned and rolled his head back and forth.

The entire enterprise had gone sour. Damn Reynolds anyway for getting him into this. Damn James Madison. Damn the United States. If he'd stayed a pirate, he'd know what to do.

What?

He'd capture her ship and take her prisoner and take her away with him. He'd keep her safe until he could make her fall in love with him.

And then?

He'd take her back to Ireland. No! He'd take her with him when he left the sea forever and settled down on land. With a good priest to marry them and baptize their children. A faraway look came into his eyes at the thought of her carrying his child.

He could be with her right now. They could be sailing back to New Orleans on the *Banshee*. This damned war! And besides it, she'd lost both her mother and her father within a year. No wonder she was desperate enough to steal his ship when he'd refused to give it back.

What if Pinckney were right? What if she had told the truth? What if someone else had sent the men to burn the *Banshee*? What if he had punished her when she'd done nothing? He groaned aloud.

And still she'd come to him, begging him for a favor. And he'd denied her. And he knew himself to be in love with her. She had not been pregnant with his child when he left New Orleans. The memory of the previous night stirred a groan of pleasure from him. God! She might be now. She had loved him with such passion. Surely at least that much was the truth.

She hated him enough to steal his ship. Damn! His thoughts were traveling in circles.

All he knew was that he had to go after her as swiftly as possible for none of the reasons he had given Mr.

344

Pinckney, but for the reason that he wanted her to be his forever.

The *Banshee* drove on smoothly by dead reckoning. The masthead disappeared into grayness so thick it was virtually impenetrable. The helmsman could not see the end of the bow, much less the tip of the bowsprit.

Judith shivered in her oilskins. "How can we sail through this, Mr. Longman?" she asked. "We can't see where we're going."

"We sail by the compass, Miss Talbot-Harrow." His thin voice had a disembodied quality coming out of the grayness. The mate's slender, stooped figure was a silhouette in the glow of the lantern.

"But what if we should"—she hesitated fractionally—"run into something."

Longman's shoulders flexed under his oilskins as if he were shrugging off her fears. "We're not likely to do that, ma'am. We're past Cabo Cruz. Nothing lies between us and the Yucatan Channel. If we keep steady as she goes west by northwest, we'll sail out into the Gulf of Mexico."

Judith blinked. The movement was involuntary. The fog was so thick and wet, it felt like film over her eyes. The moderate wind filled the sails, the swells rocked the ship gently and foamed from beneath her prow. The rigging creaked. Yet Judith had no feeling of motion. The atmosphere remained utterly the same and utterly gray.

Longman cleared his throat. "Why don't you go below, miss? Catch a little sleep. The night's more than half gone. This may lift anytime, or we may sail along in it for hours. Fog's a tricky kind of stuff. But better it than a storm, I can tell you."

"I suppose you're right." Judith rubbed her wet face. Besides her tired eyes, her back hurt and her feet ached to the knees. She had spent the day and night pacing the deck. Unable to sleep, she had worried ceaselessly about

Tabor and what she had done to him and his ship.

Over and over in her mind she reviewed the wisdom of her course. What had seemed at first a sensible solution now seemed insane. She had made an implacable enemy who would come sailing after her with all speed and take back his ship without returning hers. She had to grit her teeth to keep them from chattering.

"I'll call you at first light if you like?"

She considered his offer. Although her nerves simmered and jumped, her body was completely exhausted. Surely sleep would come as soon as she drew the covers over her. "Thank you, Mr. Longman," she murmured at last. "I'll go below."

"Good night, ma'am."

A British frigate hove out of a fog bank just before dawn, sailed like a giant ghost across the *Banshee*'s path, and disappeared as if she had never been.

The watch on the bow gaped in horror as the phantasm slid by him, then backed off his post in alarm. Almost falling over his own feet, he scampered down the deck to the mate's cabin. Mr. Longman came running, his shirttails flapping. "Hardaport," he ordered. "We'll run parallel to them."

"Aye, sir."

"Did they see us?" was his next question.

"I don't know, sir."

Longman stared at him. "Are you sure of what you saw?"

The watch ran his hand across his eyes. Chills skittered up and down his spine as he struggled with doubts. "No, sir," he muttered at last. "Not entirely. I might have dozed for a minute. But I don't think so."

In the cabin below, Judith stirred, then hoisted herself up on her elbow in Tabor's bed. Something was wrong. The ship had taken too hard a swing. She could not have told how she knew. Perhaps preternatural instincts had

346

been awakened. Perhaps her own nervousness had made her sleep unusually light, but she found herself wide awake, her senses alert. She listened intently. All the sounds of water and creaking timbers were the ones she had become accustomed to. Yet, she was sure something had happened.

Feeling slightly foolish, she pulled on trousers of the type she had worn outward bound from New Orleans, and a seaman's smock. Throwing her oilskins over them, she left the cabin. Her query coming out of the night startled the three men at the helm.

Mr. Longman started. "Miss Talbot-Harrow . . ."

"Is something wrong?" she asked again.

"The watch reported seeing a British frigate."

She looked around her unbelievingly in the impenetrable fog. "He saw a frigate?"

"Aye, ma'am. The British have a fleet less than a hundred miles south of us in Jamaica."

Judith shivered in the chill, damp air. "Are they looking for us?"

Mr. Longman shook his head. "Not much chance of that. They're looking for whoever they can find."

"Would they c-capture us?"

He shrugged. "If we were the *White Hound,* they might board us and line up the crew. See if they could find a 'British' citizen or two that they could press into service. Damn 'em!" He hesitated.

"But we're the *Banshee.*"

"Aye, ma'am."

"The ship of a notorious pirate."

"We've already taken a turn, ma'am."

"And now?"

"We're running parallel with them."

"Wouldn't it have been better to continue on our course?"

"Might have a collision. The watch saw only one ship. But there might be more."

Judith made no effort to control the chattering of her

347

teeth. "You mean we might be in the middle of a British squadron?"

Again the lift of the oilskins at the shoulders. "Impossible to say, ma'am. But chances are when the fog lifts they'll be nowhere in sight."

"And if they are."

"Then you'd better run up that set of Talbot flags and hope they believe us about how we came to be sailing the *Banshee*."

"Will the fog hold?"

"Certainly till dawn. The sun might burn it off. It might not. It may last until midday. May last for a day or two. Or we may sail right out of it at any minute. Tricky stuff, fog."

It lay like a thick gray blanket around them, but somewhat lighter than before. "It's almost dawn," she observed shakily.

The deck and the railings were wet beneath her feet and hands. She could see nothing, hear nothing except the tossing of the waves, waves that she could not see. The *Banshee* glided on slowly under headway.

Suddenly, Judith heard the sound of voices. She snapped her head around to the starboard. "I must be going crazy."

"No, ma'am." Mr. Longman's voice had a hollow sound. "It's the fog. It plays tricks on you. Sometimes you can hear things far away. Sometimes you can't hear things close up."

"My God. We *could* be in the middle of a squadron." She lowered her voice. "They could be hearing everything we're saying."

Mr. Longman lowered his voice. "You can hear what they're saying, but can you understand it?"

She listened intently. "No."

"They can't understand us either."

"But . . ."

"I don't think they saw us," he said softly. "Leastwise, we didn't hear an alarm. If they hear us talking now, they probably think it's one of their own."

Judith listened again. She could hear nothing more. At length she sighed. "If the frigate wasn't alone, and they did hear our voices, then they won't know we're not one of their own. But we don't know she wasn't alone. In which case, she'll know someone is near her."

She thought the mate chuckled. "If they heard us," he agreed.

"Shouldn't we be trying to steer away from the sound?"

"We might try it, but we don't know exactly where the sound comes from. Sometimes the fog throws back echoes. The frigate the watch saw could be ahead of us by now, traveling faster than we are. Another could be coming up behind us."

She pressed her fingers to her temples. "This is all too much for me."

"And for me, Miss Talbot-Harrow." He touched her arm. "We're not going to figure this out. Why don't you go below and have a cup of coffee?"

She looked up at him. The light was strengthening. She could make out his features in the paling grayness. "Whatever's going to happen will happen soon," she said with a certainty that defied contradiction.

He sighed. "Probably, ma'am."

"Then I'll stay on deck."

Chapter Eighteen

A sudden wind lifted the sails and blew the fog away before them. Beyond the bowsprit the sea stretched gray and blessedly vacant.

"Where's the frigate?"

"Probably somewhere to the starboard." Mr. Longman scrutinized the widening expanse of water with a worried frown. "Where we need to be."

"Back into the fog?" Judith gasped.

"Right. Where we can't be seen."

She stared around her at a world without horizon. The sea on all sides disappeared in gray banks of drifting fog. "Perhaps it will close in around us again."

"Maybe," the mate said skeptically. "Leastways, we'll get back on course." He took the helm himself, sending the helmsman below to his rest. Eyes on the compass, he swung the wheel slowly. The jibs caught the breeze and filled, turning the ship around smoothly in a wide arc.

The *Banshee* headed toward the fog that seemed to disappear as she approached it.

Judith clenched her hands tightly in the rigging. A sense of urgency swelled from deep within her. She leaned forward, teeth set, willing the brigantine to reach the safety of the fog. Below her on the main deck, shadows of sails and rigging began to appear as the morning sun, still unseen, mercilessly burned away the protecting cloud cover.

"Sail! Sail dead ahead!" The watch in the bow shouted the words, his voice cracking in fear.

As the fog bank thinned with miraculous swiftness, the tropic sun broke through the clouds. Coming dead at them, bowsprit like a lance, was a British frigate.

"Holy Mary!" Mr. Longman swung the wheel hard. The *Banshee* heeled like a highly bred horse, instantly responsive to commands.

The lookout on the frigate shouted the warning at the same time, and the H.M.S. *Implacable* slid by with less than twenty feet to spare.

With a sense of horror Judith stared at the ship. Its gunports on the lower gundecks were closed, the black portlids in place creating the famous checkerboard pattern on the bright yellow bands. However, on the main deck the mouths of the cannon yawned ominously. As each one slipped by, it was aimed at the occupants of the *Banshee*.

She had taken Tabor's ship into deadly danger. Could she get her out unscathed? Whatever she did must be done immediately.

Behind the nets strung up around the quarterdeck to protect against flying splinters stood a group of officers. Two of them trained spyglasses on the brigantine. Smiling sweetly, Judith pulled off her seaman's cap and waved it over her head. Her long hair streamed free in the freshening breeze. The sun caught it and turned its waves to fire.

The spyglasses dropped as one, then were hastily repositioned. One uniformed officer leaned toward another. Another man lifted a horn to his mouth. "Heave to!" The words boomed out across the water.

Judith looked helplessly at Mr. Longman, who had already dispatched a man to bring the ship's horn. "What do they want?"

Angry color darkened Mr. Longman's face. "If they don't recognize this ship as the vessel of a known pirate, they probably want sailors."

"Our sailors?"

"They consider them *their* sailors if they were born in England. Press gangs can't work fast enough to keep the ships manned, so they take 'em off any American ship that happens to come by."

"But that's kidnapping or something."

Mr. Longman shrugged.

"Heave to!" came the next command.

"Don't do it," Judith ordered, outrage in her voice. "We're nothing to the British Navy."

The color drained from the mate's face. "Please, Miss Talbot-Harrow," he begged, "if man holds a gun to your head, you don't just keep on running."

"Then hoist up the Talbot flag and the Union Jack. They'll see who we are as we disappear into the fog."

"But there isn't any more fog."

She looked again. The sun had worked its miracle; the waters of the Caribbean had turned aquamarine to the blue horizon line.

"Heave to!" came the next shout. "Or we will fire." In a flurry of movement, gun crews wheeled a couple of twelve pounders into position on the quarterdeck.

"Miss Talbot-Harrow?" Mr. Longman's thin voice rose in a squeak of protest.

She felt a surge of rebellious anger at the high-handed commands. By what right did they think to stop a private merchant vessel. Her jaw tightened mutinously, but the cannons were trained on the quarterdeck where she stood. "Very well. Heave to."

Half a dozen seaman scrambled up the ratlines to reef the sails. Immediately, the *Banshee* lost headway.

The spyglasses left the quarterdeck to follow the flags up the mast. The red and blue bars of the Union Jack snapped out in the breeze above the Talbot flag, a white hound on a field of blue. Judith felt a thrill of pride at the gallant sight. Her father's flag was now her flag.

The *Implacable* came around in a tight turn and

maneuvered alongside the *Banshee*. "Identify yourself."

Judith exchanged wry glances with Mr. Longman, who stepped forward with the horn to his mouth. "We're the *Banshee* bound for New Orleans."

A couple of men on the quarterdeck conferred. One spoke at length. A third snapped a smart salute. The expected request came immediately thereafter. "Request permission to come aboard."

Judith took over the horn. "We're a peaceful merchantman!"

She might have saved her breath. "Stand back there!" came the call. Grappling hooks flashed across the space and the crew of the frigate brought the lighter ship in tight. A gangplank bumped into place amidships. A squad of British Marines ran onto the *Banshee* and formed a double line.

The frigate's second officer strode across. As Judith came down from the quarterdeck, he stared in open-mouthed disbelief at her red hair and youthful face. When she arched an inquiring eyebrow at him, he blinked rapidly. "This ship is the ship of the notorious pirate Tabor O'Halloran," he announced loudly. He stared at each crewman in turn as if he expected to recognize Tabor. "This is the *Banshee*."

Mentally cursing her shabby seaman's attire, she advanced with all the icy presence she could muster— *Grandmère* at her best. "Was," she declared in her most British voice. "Was, sir."

The captain of the *Implacable* followed his junior officer. Hands behind him, he stared her up and down, his face disapproving. "What do you mean, was, young woman."

She smiled in what she meant for a beguiling manner. "I mean was, sir. Do I look like a notorious pirate?"

"No, of course not." He cleared his throat noisily. His already ruddy cheekbones grew a little redder. "But see here. You did not heave to when ordered. We could not allow this ship to proceed unchallenged."

"Challenge away, but she flies the Union Jack, as you can see." Judith gestured toward the masthead. "And beneath that she flies the White Hound, heraldic symbol of the Earls of Teigh. I'm sure you've heard of the present earl. My father, Howard Francis Talbot, is his cousin." Surely word of Beau's death could not have reached England. "You have made a very grave error, Captain . . . ?"

He cleared his throat. "Captain Exton Rollings, Lady . . . er . . . Talbot."

"Talbot-Harrow, sir. I maintain the name of my maternal grandmother as well. She is the Countess of Harrestone."

He frowned heavily at her clothing, her unkempt hair. "Miss Talbot-Harrow."

She nodded graciously. "I'm sure you are wondering about my presence on board this ship. The truth is that my men and I captured her and are taking her back to New Orleans. There she'll be overhauled and refitted ready for service on the China run for Talbots. La, sir! Quite a coup, wouldn't you say?" She batted her eyelashes for all they were worth and smiled her most winning smile.

The effect was all she could have desired. He glanced incredulously around him. "You, milady? You captured this ship?"

"Indeed. As you can see, I have only a skeleton crew. Captain Smithurst and almost the entire crew of the *White Hound* are on their way to England with a cargo of cotton and sugar. Must keep to the schedule, you know."

The captain looked dazed.

"I'm sure you understand why we didn't heave to when you so peremptorily ordered us to."

"Well . . ."

"Surely you realize the situation, Captain, a man with your experience at sea. We couldn't spare a man. Captain Smithurst could only allow me these few—to escort me home, as it were. I do so love the idea of bringing my prize

354

into port." She laughed richly, as if she were enjoying a lark. "Mr. Longman"—she waved in the direction of the mate, who had left the wheel and come down from the quarterdeck to stand some distance away, his face perfectly white—"Mr. Longman, dear man, was terribly peeved with me because I wouldn't stop, but I thought we'd just lose headway."

The captain of the *Implacable* harumphed loudly. His face turned redder.

"That is the word, isn't it?" she asked with a giggle. "I get all these nautical terms so confused. I really need to get home. Papa will be so concerned about me."

"Miss . . ."

Another man, this one in civilian clothing rather than a naval uniform, had come amidships in the *Implacable* and was staring at her intently; but since every man on the deck was too, one more made little difference. "Papa's going to be so proud of me, bringing home this ship and all. I mean she's just a little ship compared to your big warship, but he'll be impressed."

"I'm sure he will be." The captain looked doubtfully around him, seeing the few men that comprised the crew.

Judith nodded. "I'm so glad. We really need to get under way."

The man in civilian clothes came across the gangplank. "Why, Judith Talbot-Harrow, you naughty girl. Telling lies again."

The malicious voice froze the blood in her veins. She stumbled backward into a stalwart marine. She looked up fearfully into a dark figure silhouetted in front of the sun. "I . . . I do not tell lies."

The figure chuckled. "Captain Rollings. My congratulations. You've caught a traitor."

The captain's embarrassment vanished instantly. "How fortunate you were aboard, Lord Lythes. I knew something was wrong here. The *Banshee* is the ship of a notorious pirate."

Randolph Carew, Lord Lythes, climbed down in front

355

of Judith. His mouth was twisted in the leering expression that had haunted her for months after Charlotte's death. When he spoke, ugly insinuations fell from that mouth. "Come down in the world, have you, little Judith? A pirate. Tsk! Tsk! What would the dear countess say?"

Incensed at his suggestion, she righted herself to snub him angrily and address the captain. "The *Banshee* belonged to a pirate once. But not anymore. Captain Rollings, I am a British citizen and no traitor. I must ask you to leave my ship. You have delayed me long enough."

The captain placed his hands behind him and thrust his head forward pugnaciously. "How did you come by this ship?"

"I told you. I took it from the pirate. He took one of the Talbot ships. We were lucky to find him. In fact, we set out purposefully to find him. And we did."

"And where did you leave him?"

The question stopped her cold. She could not tell that she had left Tabor ashore without means of transport in Santiago de Cuba. They would be sure to sail back and capture him. "We . . . er . . . put him and his crew over the side in a boat."

"She's lying," Lythes sneered.

Judith shot him a look of hatred. "I tell you again. I do not lie."

Captain Rollings was not convinced. "Miss Talbot-Harrow, you'll have to come back on board the *Implacable* with us. We must get to the bottom of this."

"I'll not leave my ship."

"Your ship?"

"Of course, Captain Rollings. This is my ship. Mr. Longman is my mate." She motioned the man to come forward. If only he appeared more prepossessing, instead of quaking in his boots. Captain Smithurst had probably been glad to be rid of him.

Captain Rollings barely glanced at Mr. Longman. "He

can take over while you are on the *Implacable*."

"No."

Rollings drew back, clearly upset by her refusal and reluctant to force her. "Miss Talbot-Harrow. I must insist."

"Captain Rollings, you have no right to insist. I have done nothing wrong. I have harmed no British ship. I am on my way back to New Orleans."

"May I remind you, Miss Talbot-Harrow, that a state of war exists between the United States and Great Britain?"

"But I am a British citizen. A private citizen. Talbot Shipping has offices in London as well as in New Orleans. I . . . I was just making for the nearest port."

"Nevertheless. You must come aboard and make a full report."

"I have made a full report. There is simply nothing much to report."

"When a notorious pirate is robbed of his ship by a private British citizen, the War Office would like to know the circumstances," Lord Lythes inserted smoothly. "If for no other reason than to issue a commendation."

Rollings looked relieved. "That's correct."

Judith's mouth thinned dangerously. "I don't want a commendation from the British War Office."

Rollings took a deep breath. His jaw jutted stubbornly. "I must insist."

She looked around her at the worried faces of her crew, the determined face of Captain Rollings, and the leering face of Lord Lythes. "Very well." She acquiesced with chilly dignity worthy of a countess.

"Then allow me to escort you." The captain reached for her arm, but she quickly lifted it out of his reach.

"However," she said, "I must be allowed to go below and change into something more suitable for a luncheon. You did mean the invitation for luncheon, did you not?"

The captain looked surprised, then nodded in some relief. "Of course. Luncheon in an hour."

She fluttered her hands helplessly. "I'm afraid it will have to be at least two hours, Captain Rollings. A lady requires time."

He bowed then, his eyes raking her costume. "Of course."

"Miss Talbot-Harrow, what's going to happen?"

"If I knew that, Mr. Longman, I wouldn't be down here in the cabin trying to figure out what to do."

The mate actually wrung his hands. "None of the men want to serve in the British Navy."

She stared at him, then turned away with a faint shake of her head. "Mr. Longman, I'll do everything in my power to persuade Captain Rollings to allow us to continue on our way. He seems a gentleman. He also seemed impressed when I mentioned *Grandmère* and the earl."

"Yes, ma'am."

She chuckled. "It's the first time either of them ever did me the least bit of good. What's more, I'm sure they'd both be furious if they knew about it."

Mr. Longman allowed himself a wan grin. "If you say so, ma'am."

"Ask Cook to bring me some coffee. I'm going to make a couple of entries in the logbook. In case the captain thinks he might want to read it."

The first mate could not conceal a horrified look. "You're going to make entries in the captain's log, ma'am?"

"Who has a better right? I took this vessel. That much is the whole truth. Now get out of here and reassure the men. They work for Talbot. And whether Captain Rollings likes it or not, he will be in serious trouble when he gets back to London if he gives me too much trouble."

Alone she could not stifle the whimper of terror that slipped through her tightly compressed lips. She had never been so terrified in all her life. Not of Captain

Rollings, to be sure. The captain seemed a fair man.

But what was Randolph Carew, Lord Lythes, doing on a British ship? His presence on the frigate that sailed out of the fog toward the *Banshee* made her believe in nemesis.

What was she going to answer about Tabor O'Halloran? What story was she going to tell? She could not betray him even though she doubted seriously that he would remain in Santiago. Unless, of course, she had left him with no choice. The idea of Tabor ashore without a ship made her very sad. Tears prickled behind her eyes.

A knock sounded at the door of her cabin. Hurriedly, she blinked the tears away and called, "Enter." The cook had brought her coffee.

When he had gone, she opened the logbook, determined to write an account that reflected well and honorably on both Tabor and herself.

The effort proved harder than she could have imagined. She quickly realized she would have to make a rough draft, then copy the entry from a separate sheet of paper. The time involved left her with barely half an hour to dress.

If the log had presented a slight problem, her wardrobe presented a much bigger one. She had brought no lovely, fashionable dresses of the type that would dazzle the captain and detract him from his intent. Only the soft green muslin with which she had seduced Tabor could be called attractive. But she could not look at it, much less wear it. The rest of her trunk contained only serviceable dark colors chosen with neither fashion nor provocation in mind.

Now, when she needed to look feminine and elegant, when she needed to play the social game she had so much despised, she had no counters. The irony of her situation was not lost on her. Laura would have enjoyed saying, "I told you so," and *Grandmère* would have nodded disdainfully.

One dark blue faille was not too bad. She had chosen it

in case she was ever called upon to attend a dinner at some port they might have visited. It was cut rather low with a net and lace insert filling in the neckline. Ruthlessly, she ripped out the insert. The effect was good given her white skin.

But then a critical look at her hair in the mirror wrung a groan from her.

Now that she remembered, she had not dragged a comb or brush through it for forty-eight hours. How could she have neglected herself so? Worry and unhappiness were no excuse for bad grooming.

For the first time since the voyage began, she stared at herself. She did not look at all the same. Her face was thinner, the skin golden tanned. Thank heaven she had not freckled. But the mouth and jaw were firmer than ever. She did not look like a girl anymore.

Of a sudden, she stared at the logbook. The date on the page dawned on her as if she were remembering something long ago forgotten. She was twenty years old. Today was her birthday. The twenty-fifth of November.

The thought did not make her sad. Instead, she laughed. Birthdays did not matter. They were just like any other day. Twenty years old and she could pass her birthday completely surrounded by strangers.

She made a face at the mirror, then pulled out her brush from her small trunk. A pair of small, needle-sharp scissors had caught in the bristles. With a grin of inspiration she bent to her dress. From the seam beneath the skirt she cut two long strips of material. One would be a ribbon for her hair. The other she would tie in a small bow around her neck. It might not be red *à la victime,* but it would take the place of the jewels she did not have. At the same time, it would serve to control her hair since a coiffure was impossible to achieve without a maid.

Draping the ribbons of cloth over the towel rack on the washstand, she set to brushing her hair with rough, vigorous strokes. *À la victime* fitted her mood. The thought of Lord Lythes made her feel like a victim going to the guillotine.

The luncheon table was set for eight. Captain Rollings sat at its head and Judith at his right hand. Across from her sat the captain of the marines with Lord Lythes at his right. The other guests were the rest of the ship's officers.

Under other circumstances, Judith realized she would have been flattered, excited, even complimented. Eating lunch with seven men who paid her pleasant compliments and seemed to hang on her every word would have been a dream of any young girl of the *ton*.

Instead, she found herself unable to taste the few bites of food she put into her mouth.

"I say, tell us about the ladies in New Orleans," one young lieutenant asked from down the table. "Are they as beautiful as you?"

The question snapped her out of her mood. She smiled. "Oh, much more beautiful than I. The loveliest ones are French Creoles with dark hair and pale magnolia complexions."

"Sounds marvelous." He nudged the fellow next to him in the ribs. "Beauty and booty, eh, what?"

The other man laughed and nodded. "That's what the Old Cock promised. Beauty and booty."

Judith lowered her eyes, remembering suddenly that the men that sailed frigates were mostly volunteers on board for the promise of prize money. And they were headed for New Orleans. She shivered as she thought of the peaceful city of merchants and tradesmen.

"I can hardly wait," the first went on, seizing his mug and lifting it high. "To a strong wind and a clear sea."

"Are there many Indians?" another man asked. "I've always wanted to see an Indian. Are their skins bright red and covered with feathers?"

Judith shook her head. "You'll be disappointed. The Choctaws who work around New Orleans are dark-skinned and wear the same clothing that Americans do. Some of them wear a sort of turban, but I've never seen one wear feathers."

"I've heard they have big ballrooms with parties where everyone wears masks. You can dance with anyone as many times as you like. Can you really?" a young marine commander wanted to know.

Judith flushed, remembering her own experiences at the two balls she had attended. "Yes, that's true," she managed to explain. Her eyes lowered to her plate, where she carefully selected a bite of food.

"Imagine that." He thumped the table. "Beauty and booty."

"What were the Americans planning when you left New Orleans?" Captain Rollings asked when the cheese and nuts were brought.

Startled, she looked up from her plate. "Why, I have no idea. No idea at all, sir."

He glanced swiftly at Lythes, who raised his eyebrows. "But surely . . ."

"Captain Rollings, permit me to enlighten you as to what my life is like. I work. Every day that a Talbot ship is in port in New Orleans, I work on the docks. I am in charge of the cargo manifests. Everything that is unloaded from a Talbot ship or loaded onto a Talbot ship is my responsibility. I do not have time to consider what the Americans may be planning."

A murmur of disbelief rose from the assemblage.

She looked around her with what she hoped was a demure smile. "Truly. I am not the usual sort of lady of quality. When my father, Beau Talbot, did not have a son, he allowed me to become his son. He places great trust in me and I . . . I must work very hard to assure him that his trust is not misplaced."

"You? Work?" The marine captain was staring at her critically, as if she were something strange.

"I would never allow such a thing if you were my daughter," an older man down the table from her declared angrily. "Women aren't strong enough to stand such rigors. This will injure your health, my girl. Permanently damage it. The sun—"

"I assure you that I never felt better," she interrupted him. "I cover my skin with veils and gloves—in deference to the fashion—but I do the job well. Talbot captains are pleased with my work. Everything is handled honestly and efficiently."

"It's the fault of that Wollstonecraft woman," another man declared. He looked at her sadly. "You'll ruin your health, Miss Talbot-Harrow."

"Nevertheless, I intend to continue especially now that—" She stopped. No need to tell them that Beau was dead. His name and presence was strong protection. ". . . now that I have taken the *Banshee*."

"And how did you come to do that?"

She had rehearsed her story over and over while she wrote in the logbook and during her toilette. "It was ridiculously easy. I cannot think why it is not done all the time." Here she giggled girlishly and leaned toward Captain Rollings. "Of course, I knew about ships and the way of things around the docks. We were lucky to come into the harbor just before the *Banshee* was about to sail. The crew and the captain were taking their last shore leave. The ship was fully provisioned with a skeleton crew aboard. It was easy to sneak on board with my own crew. The pirates were a cowardly lot when they were faced by strong, well-trained men. They surrendered. We put them over the side in the ship's boat and sailed off."

"And what harbor was this, Miss Talbot-Harrow?" Captain Rollings's face registered neither acceptance nor disbelief.

"Er . . ." She paused as if considering, trying to remember. "You know, I can't remember. It was a Spanish word. And I don't speak Spanish. Not a bit."

He frowned. "Have you been at sea long?"

363

"Oh, quite a few days," she replied vaguely. She reached for her glass of wine and took a tiny sip.

"How many days?"

"I can't remember."

"Gentlemen, you may leave us."

"With your permission, Captain Rollings, I will remain," Lord Lythes put in. "I'm sure that what Miss Talbot-Harrow has to say will be of interest to the War Office."

"Quite right."

Judith clutched the stem of her wineglass as each man bowed to her in turn and left the cabin. Alone she faced Rollings and Lythes.

Rollings rose from the table. Hands clasped behind him, he paced the length of the cabin and back. Suddenly, he turned. "Now, Miss Talbot-Harrow! We want the truth."

"Captain Rollings, I assure you I have told the truth."

"No, ma'am. You have not. I am convinced that you came in possession of the *Banshee* by some means other than what you have told us. Intelligence tells us that the ship is not a pirate at all, but a privateer commissioned by the United States Navy and that Tabor O'Halloran, her captain, being a British citizen, is therefore a traitor as well as a pirate."

A shock went through Judith's body, but she concealed it by taking another sip of wine. Could Rollings's intelligence be correct? Could Tabor be a patriot rather than a pirate? If he were, it would explain so much. Aloud she feigned irritation. "My goodness, Captain Rollings, you can't have your story going both ways. He's either one or the other. Since pirates owe no allegiance, he can't be a traitor, or, conversely, he can't be a traitor, since traitors must be citizens of the country they've betrayed. You're not making sense."

The captain's face darkened. "I am not amused, Miss Talbot-Harrow. Where is Captain O'Halloran?"

"I don't know."

"If you refuse to tell me, I shall have no choice but to place you under arrest and take the *Banshee* as a prize of war."

She pushed back her chair and rose abruptly. "How dare you, sir? Are you impugning my honor. I captured the *Banshee*. She belongs to me. I need her for the good of the Talbot lines. Her captain stole my ship the *White Cloud*. We have sustained several losses—as who has not during wartime. I need that ship."

"Then tell us where Captain O'Halloran is and you may continue."

"I can't tell you what I don't know."

"Miss Talbot-Harrow."

"My uncle and my grandmother shall hear of this."

"Neither of whom care a fig for you." Lythes had kept strictly in the background until that minute. Now he advanced, his leer firmly in place.

"You are an American," Captain Rollings insisted. "You are sailing a pirate ship. I would be within my rights to hang you from the yardarm and sink the ship."

Judith felt the color drain from her face, but she persisted. "Don't be ridiculous, Captain Rollings. I may live in New Orleans temporarily, but I can assure you I have not lived there even a year—as Lord Lythes can attest." She shot him a look of loathing. "I was spending only a few months there after the death of my mother. I have always intended to return to England."

"Then you should have no problem giving us the information we need."

"I would give you whatever information you need if I had any to give," she cried.

"We are getting nowhere," Lord Lythes interrupted. "I say clap her in irons. A few hours with manacles around her wrists will convince her of the seriousness of lying to the British Navy. She'll be ready enough to cooperate."

Captain Rollings still hesitated.

"You can't do that. You wouldn't dare. I have done

absolutely nothing wrong." She started up from her chair and marched haughtily to the door of the cabin. Flinging it open, she was met with a stern-faced marine who presented his weapon across his chest.

She spun around, staring furiously from one to the other.

"I'll take full responsibility," Lythes said, his dark brown eyes gleaming with anticipation.

Rollings looked from one to the other. The nobleman's words gave him the authority he needed while the girlish temper tantrum had merely irritated him.

"Miss Talbot-Harrow, as the self-proclaimed captain of an enemy vessel, I have no choice but to place you under arrest pending a hearing before an authoritative board. You will remain on the *Implacable* until such time as we make port in Jamaica or meet with another British ship of the line returning to London."

Chapter Nineteen

"Two sails on the horizon, Captain."

"Two, Pinky?"

The mate lowered the spyglass from his eye, then lifted it again. "One's the old *Banshee*. I'd know her anywhere."

Tabor took the glass. "You're right, by God." He threw back his head in a mirthless laugh. "One's the *Banshee*. Caught her the second day out." He trained the glass on the other ship. "She's hard to make out. The *Banshee*'s between us and her. She's bigger."

"Probably the merchantman the lady came in."

Tabor lowered the glass, the frown lines smoothing from his forehead. "Probably so."

"Shall we catch up to them, sir? I doubt those merchant seamen would have the stomach for a ruckus."

"Yes. No! They might fight. And if they did, you can bet she'd be the one leading them." Tabor grinned at the memory of the fight she had put up in the cabin. Then the grin disappeared. "No, Pinky. If shots were exchanged, she'd be in the line of fire. No. Hold this course. Close up just at dusk. We'll travel without lights."

"They might too, sir."

Tabor shook his head. "I'm betting that they won't. The captain of the merchantman was a conservative. He was bristling like a bull walrus from the minute I came aboard his ship. No, Pinky, he plays by the rules. He'll hang a light out by the beakhead and one off the stern because that's the way it's supposed to be done."

"This sort of solves your problem, doesn't it, sir?" Mr. Pinckney suggested hopefully.

"What problem?"

The second mate cleared his throat ostentatiously. "Of what to do with the lady. You could put her aboard her ship and let them take her back to New Orleans."

Tabor shook his head. His grin spread wider from ear to ear. Suddenly, he realized he was enjoying this whole thing. "Not on your life. I'll take her with me. I should have done it the first time I saw her."

"Captain?"

Tabor gripped the rail, shoulders hunched, blue eyes trained on the distant sails. "Hell, Pinky. She's the woman for me. But I can't convince her if she's in New Orleans and I'm at sea. I need to have her with me for a while to show her that I'm the man for her."

The mate scratched his head. "Are you sure that's the way to make it work?"

"Of course I'm sure. Keep her with me. She can't do any more harm. The war'll be over soon. Then she'll turn her mind to other things." He stared fixedly at the distant sails. "Just follow at a distance. At nightfall we'll close up and take the *Banshee*. That merchantman will be unprepared. He'll never break open the arms chest."

"Captain Rollings, I suggest you think again about the risk you are taking when you take such an action against me. You may not always want to remain a captain on a frigate. You and your wife . . ."

"I am not married."

"You and the wife you will have someday will want to be accepted into polite society. Doors. Important doors will be forever closed to you if you . . ."

Rollings's already cool demeanor changed to ice in the

blink of an eye. He opened the cabin door and spoke to one of the men standing guard, then turned back to face her. His words were noticeably more clipped. "Madam, you are under arrest."

"But my ship . . ."

"Your mate will be informed that so long as he keeps the *Banshee* within hailing distance of the frigate, he will be allowed to perform his duties. Should your vessel fall behind or try to take a separate course, he will be shot as though he were a criminal attempting to escape."

Judith clenched her fists within the skirt of her dress. "Captain, you're making a mistake."

"Be thankful, Miss Talbot-Harrow, that I do not take the *Banshee* as a prize of war or simply sink her summarily."

One guard marched into the cabin and saluted smartly. The other followed after a moment. They arranged themselves on either side of her. A man in sailor's garb hurried in behind them. He nodded, then edged forward with the manacles to close over Judith's wrists.

Instantly, she knew panic so great that it threatened to suffocate her. But she could not break before them. At all costs she must maintain her composure. *Grandmère. Concentrate on* Grandmère. The proud, stern countenance of the dowager countess of Harrestone rose before her eyes. Judith steadied. At that moment she was conscious of Lythes watching her, his leer lifting the corner of his mouth. Determined on control, she forced the fear down and focused her eyes straight ahead.

As she lifted her chin another notch, she heard his deep chuckle quickly concealed behind a cough. He was a monster. Her voice quavered only slightly when she delivered her last warning. Even as she spoke, she knew her speech was wasted. "You will regret this, Captain Rollings. I promise you. You stand to lose much."

"I am of the opinion, ma'am, that I stand to gain much. I have apprehended a pirate. If not a pirate, then certainly a traitor to the Crown. I might receive a commendation for this. Proceed." With those words he turned his back on her, staring out the windows, his hands firmly clasped behind his back.

When the sailor knelt to put irons on her ankles, Lord Lythes waved him away. "Not necessary m'man. She's got nowhere to run," he joked.

"Yes, take her out of here. To the brig," came Captain Rollings's tight-lipped command.

The remaining color drained from Judith's face. She swayed where she stood. The lower decks of ships were horrible places. Filthy, wet, steamy, always rat-infested, stinking of the waste that trickled and oozed its way down from the decks above.

Correctly reading her fear, the captain nodded. "Perhaps you would like to tell us where we might begin to look for Tabor O'Halloran?"

She shuddered. A few words were all that were needed to set her free. Tabor O'Halloran was probably miles from Santiago now. He might be anywhere in the Caribbean. He might be through the Windward Passage and out into the Atlantic. He might be on his way to the Gulf of Mexico.

She closed her eyes. He had been so angry, so hurt when his ship had been burned, his mate murdered. Likewise, she remembered the terrible story of his family's destruction. She could not chance betraying him. He had suffered enough at the hands of the British. A few days of discomfort would see the end of her captivity. If he were captured, his story would end in tragedy. She shook her head. "I have nothing to tell you."

Rollings shrugged. "To the brig, then."

"Not just yet." Lythes moved to block the door. "I think I might be able to learn more information from her. We know she hasn't told us anything. Her father is an influential man in New Orleans. She's probably privy to important information."

Horrified, Judith looked from Lythes to Rollings.

"That's ridiculous. I don't know anything. Not a thing except the shipping schedules of the Talbot lines. All I want to do is get home to New Orleans and get on with the business. For heaven's sake, Captain—"

"I don't hold with torture," Rollings interrupted stiffly.

Lythes nodded smoothly. "No, of course not. Never considered it. Never for a minute. That's really what I was thinking. The brig's a terrible place for a young and tender lady." Here his leer grew more pronounced. "She's proud too. High in the instep. She'll come round in a bit now that she realizes you mean business."

Still, Rollings hesitated. "We should turn the matter over to Admiral Cochrane when we rendezvous. He'll know how to act in this matter."

Lythes frowned. "But then you'll get little of the credit. Think what a feather it would be in your cap if she told where she left O'Halloran and you could capture him."

Rollings frowned. "Our orders are to proceed to New Orleans."

"But if you could capture a pirate, a Yankee privateer who might be of aid to the Americans, you could be sure of a commendation. Perhaps a promotion to a fourth or even a third rater."

Rollings's eyes lighted. He turned back from the window. "Whatever you wish, Lord Lythes. I leave the manner in your hands."

"Nooo."

"Now, Judith, m'dear, you mustn't thrash around so. Iron manacles take the skin right off, don't y'know?"

Grinning like a demon out of Dante's *Inferno*, Lythes took up the short chain between her wrists and pulled her toward the door of the cabin. Her temper, the only stop against her rising panic, erupted. She pulled back heedless of the pain. Over her shoulder she shot a furious look at Rollings.

"You'll never have a chance at a fourth rater. When

this is settled, you'll be back to mate on a sloop."

"Come along, m'dear," Lythes chuckled. "Don't annoy the captain with idle threats." He pulled her through the door and the marine guard followed.

Down the companionway and out onto the deck, Lythes led her. British sailors paused in their work to stare at the spectacle of a young woman, beautiful and well-dressed, being led in chains. Amidships, Judith stubbornly dug in her heels to watch as the gangplank was hauled back aboard the *Implacable* and the *Banshee* allowed to drop away. A squad of marines had been deployed at intervals on the deck in guard positions.

Mr. Longman saw her from the quarterdeck and stepped forward, his face agonized. His mouth opened to speak, but she shook her head. He lifted his hand in silent salute.

Lythes's cabin was much smaller than the captain's, long and narrow. Fitted only with a bunk, a washstand, and a locker at one end, its bulkheads were meant to be removed at the call to battle stations. A twelve-pound cannon tied in place before the closed port filled the second half of the room.

Lythes dropped the chain and turned. He spread his arms expansively. "Welcome, Judith, m'dear, to my cabin. Please to take a seat. Perhaps the massive black one behind you. You really should, y'know, since I owe all these luxurious appointments to you."

"To me?" She did not fail to understand his meaning. "You did this to yourself, Lord Lythes. I had nothing to do with your being aboard a British frigate."

He struck the pose of a gentleman of fashion, drawing his snuffbox from his pocket and inserting a pinch in each nostril. She stared at him as he meant her to, noting for the first time his condition. His delicate skin was no longer white, but red and peeling from the nose and cheekbones. A myriad of crow's feet spread from the corners of his eyes. The superfine broadcloth coat had spots of soil on the lapels and cuffs.

He sniffed noisily; his eyes watered. Then he flicked the lid of the snuffbox closed and replaced it in his pocket. "I've often thought of those last hours with you, m'dear. You obviously were badly spoiled."

"I have often thought of those hours too, Lord Lythes. I can remember the screams of my mother when she tried to run after you and broke her hip."

"Poor Charlotte. She was ever the fool." Not a flicker of emotion showed in his face. "You will call me Randolph, Judith. Or Rand, as you come to know me better."

"I have no wish to know you better."

"But you will, m'dear. You will." He reached out almost lazily to touch her cheek.

She jerked her head aside. "Don't!"

"Do you still not like to be touched, Judith?" He grinned delightedly. "Has no man taught you the pleasures and pains of the flesh?"

"Don't touch me," she repeated angrily. She backed a step. "My family."

He drew back his hand in a fist and dropped down on the bunk, lifting one foot up onto it. His boot had not seen polish in many a day. "Your family has already done everything to me that it can do."

"I had nothing to do with—"

"Ah, but you did, m'dear. When you left me with a knot on my head on the library floor and ran screaming to your grandma, the old bitch took her revenge."

"*Grandmère?*"

"*Grandmère?*" He mocked in a falsetto voice. "Yes, *Grandmère*. The estimable Countess of Harrestone let it be put about that to accept me into society was to exclude oneself from her circle of friends and acquaintances as well as from the circles of the present Earl of Harrestone and the Earl of Teigh. Suddenly, it wasn't the thing to be seen with me. And after all I'd done for Charlotte too."

373

He took on an air of wounded dignity.

Judith shook her head in amazement. She could not believe that *Grandmère* had done such a thing. The full realization of what he was saying dawned on her and with it the irony of the situation. She had not needed to leave England after all. She had followed Laura to America as much as anything to escape Lord Lythes. But he would have posed no threat to her had she remained. She would never have seen him again in polite society.

Suddenly, she felt nauseated. She had suffered so much emotional pain, had struggled so hard to find a place among strangers in New Orleans. Now all the effort appeared to have been for nothing. She could not think about it now in the face of present peril. For now she spoke sarcastically. "Yes, indeed. You had done so much for Charlotte."

"Don't adopt that tone of voice with me, Judith," he warned.

"What tone would you like, Lord Lythes? Whimpering and pleading." Her temper flamed as she remembered the terrible wreck of Charlotte's life.

His grin would have caused a demon to draw back. "Why, yes, m'dear. That'll do for the present." Almost lazily he reached out to wrap his hand around the short chain between her wrists and twist.

The terrible grinding pain caught her unprepared. She cried out as the rough iron scraped the skin from the delicate bones of her wrists.

"Whimpering and pleading before me," he snarled. His fist came up under her chin as he stooped and brought her down, hands twisted at her breasts, palms out. He forced her to her knees in a mockery of prayer.

Sure enough, she whimpered at the pain, then bit her lip to still the sound. But he had heard it. He smiled, his lips curling back from his stained teeth. She could see the dark brown stains of snuff on his mustache, smell the odor of his body. If once Lord Lythes had been careless about his grooming, he was now filthy. "Rand, Judith,"

374

he prompted. "Call me, Rand."

She gritted her teeth. "Monster."

He twisted the chain until she cried out. The manacle on her right wrist cut the skin. Blood welled from the point of the bone. "Rand."

"R-Rand."

Instantly, the pressure lightened. His smile widened. "That's right." He bent still closer. His mouth came down on hers.

She pressed her lips tightly together. Not for anything would she allow that foul creature to intrude.

The chain twisted.

She gasped at the pain. Her mouth opened and he drove his tongue into its interior. The taste of him was acrid—tobacco and sour wine and decaying food. The kiss went on and on as if he raped her, enjoying her squirming and her little grunts of pain and revulsion.

At last he drew out and straightened. His knees creaked.

She swung to one side, crying out again as two thin streams of blood trickled down her wrists. When she was completely off balance, he let go, deliberately allowing her to drop to the floor with a thud.

He stared down at her for a minute, then swaggered to his locker. He withdrew a bottle, uncorked it, and took a healthy swig. Returning, he knelt and held it to her mouth. "Here, m'dear. Always offer a drink to a lady."

The pain, the ill usage, the fall to the floor on the point of her shoulder, had dazed her. She swallowed it gratefully, not knowing what she was offered. Neat rum burned into her mouth and down her throat. She choked and gagged, tears pouring from her eyes.

He laughed again, then toasted her with the bottle. "To us, m'dear. I have just seen my luck change." He drank again, then flopped down on the bunk to stare at her huddled on the floor.

Gingerly, Judith moved her hands back into a normal position and pulled them into her body. Her wounds throbbed painfully. **Salt and rust** had crusted the manacles so that the **tiniest abrasions** burned like fire. With shaking hands **she pushed** the cuffs up her arms away from her wrists. For the first time she saw why convicts were forever branded by the iron they were forced to wear. She **realized** that tears were drying on her cheeks. Furtively, **she tried** to lift a shaking finger to wipe them away.

Lythes chuckled. "It's **been** quite a long time since I've had a beautiful woman in **my** hands."

She clenched her fists. Her eyes blazed steel-blue defiance. "If you **harm me,** the world will not be wide enough for you to **hide in.**"

He rolled his eyes in **pretended** boredom. "Fine threats for a girl lying in **chains at** my feet."

"The next officer **we meet** will not be the fool that Captain Rollings is. **He will recognize** my name and know with whom he is **dealing. I am a** Talbot, and Talbot ships go everywhere."

He appeared to **contemplate her** statement. "Why, so you are. And the **granddaughter** of a countess. I had not considered that from **the profit angle.** Perhaps it's not too late. Perhaps you can **do more** than I first suspected. I might not have to **spend the** rest of my life as a minor functionary. You **could be** my ticket out."

"What are you **talking about?**"

"Simply that I **had not considered** that I might have more than a woman in **my hands.**"

She sat up abruptly. **"You should** consider letting me go."

"Oh, no. In my **hands you'll** stay, dear Judith."

She closed her eyes **tight for a** moment, then opened them with a resigned **expression** on her face. "I can pay you."

"Can you? That's nice, but I want more than pay."

"I can't restore your place in London society."

His eyes narrowed. A flush of anger mottled his neck and cheeks. "No, you can't. And I mean to see you suffer for it. If you'd been nicer to me back when I wanted you to be, I might have been willing to say something to the eager captain, but you weren't."

"You're a monster."

"Tsk! Tsk! M'dear. Words like that will come back to haunt you."

She shook her head tiredly. "I had nothing to do with your misfortunes."

"As it turned out, you did. Since Charlotte was of no use, you were my last chance then. I needed some fast money. You could have provided that, but you didn't. I called in my last chit. From quite a minor official. So here I am, aboard a frigate bound for some outpost on the frontier when we shall take this savage village from the Americans. It was either this or a lengthy stay in debtors' prison." He looked around him critically. "Can't say whether I made the best choice yet."

She leaned forward a little. "Lord Lythes . . ."

"Rand, please."

"Rand, then. You might have a chance if you would aid me now. I could speak to someone in New Orleans on your behalf." Remembering New Orleans society as she did, she was certain Lythes could find a place there. "My stepmother is not without influence."

Lythes leaned up on one elbow. He took another drink of rum. "M'dear. You don't fool me at all with your offer. Waste of breath. No. No. You'll never speak to another official, m'dear. Except in a business capacity." His eyes slitted as he ran an appraising eye over her figure.

She drew back angrily. "I'll not whore for you."

He grinned unpleasantly. "Unless you tame down to my hand, you might very well die of a strange malady. A jungle fever. After all, we are in the tropics. Yes, a jungle fever might sweep you away."

"You wouldn't dare!" Her defiance was weak. She was beginning to feel nauseated again. The rum had not set well in her stomach. The cabin was hot and odorous. Only inches from her head, Lythes's booted feet stank powerfully.

Lythes laughed—a short, high-pitched bark—and slid back down on the bunk. "Do you think Rollings cares about you? You were right about one thing. The man is a fool. He has already forgotten you. He has no imagination. For myself. I wonder how you came by the pirate ship."

"I stole it from a better man than you."

Lythes sat up on one elbow again, a cynical expression on his face. "And how did you get it, m'dear. Seduce him for it?"

She flushed.

Lythes's mouth dropped open. "My God! Charlotte's daughter to the very life." He chuckled, then laughed.

Hastily, she tried to disavow him of his notion. "I . . . I drugged him and my men took over the ship. They put him and his crew over the side in an open boat. It happened just as I told Rollings."

"No, I don't believe it. You seduced him." He laughed again and took another swig of rum. "Show me how, Charlotte's daughter. Show me how."

She thought she would die. "No. I have nothing to show you. You'd best call for the crew to put me in the brig."

He swung his legs over the side of the bunk and sat up. At that moment a knock sounded at the door.

He grimaced. "Wha'd'y'want?"

"Captain requests your presence in the ward room."

"Tell him I'm busy."

"It's urgent, Lord Lythes."

"Oh, very well." He rose and steadied himself against the locker while he took another drink, then put his rum bottle back. He turned and stared down at her, a pleased grin on his face as he towered over her supine body. He nudged her breast with the toe of his boot. "Lie there for a bit, little Judith. And don't think futile thoughts about talking to anyone about your sad plight. You'll be wasting your time. Instead, think about how you seduced the

378

dread pirate captain. Remember it in every detail. For tonight."

As the door closed behind him, she struggled to her feet, looking wildly around for some means of escape. Piece by piece, seam by seam, she inspected the bulkheads with trembling fingers. When she was certain they were all tightly battened, she began a search of Lythes's locker for something she could use as a weapon.

Again she was disappointed. Lythes carried no pistol, nor even a razor. She recalled that his chin was prickly with pale blond stubble. Doubtless he availed himself of the ship's barber—although not too often.

Sinking down with a sigh, she selected two of the least grubby of his linen stocks from his locker to pad her wrists under the cruel chafing of the manacles.

At length, when he still had not returned, she made herself as comfortable as she could. Not for a piece of gold would she stretch out in his rumpled, odorous bunk and risk the chance of his finding her there. The space between the bulkhead and the cannon was tight but sufficient. She could stretch out her legs, lean her back against the hull, and rest her cheek against the cannon's cool iron barrel. There she closed her eyes, striving to control her racing thoughts, even dozing a bit through the heat of the afternoon.

Each time someone came near, she started out in fear, but when the footsteps passed on by, she settled herself again. She was safe for a few more minutes. When he came, she must have all her strength to face him.

At full dark Lord Lythes returned to the cabin, his lack of experience at sea betraying him. Judith heard him even before he touched the door. He shuffled down the companionway, the gentle sway of the ship making him stagger from side to side. The only other feet that had come down the passage had been bare, placed surely, as sailors walk when they are more used to the deck than

379

the earth.

She heard him curse mildly, heard the scrape of the key against the metal plate, heard it fall. She heard him curse again more viciously as he stumbled against the door. The sound of his body bumping around, undoubtedly bruising itself, wrung an hysterical giggle from her. That he sounded drunk and virtually incompetent boded well for her that night.

At last he managed to fit the key into the lock and open the door. She slid down as far as she could behind the cannon, her back pressed to the bulkhead.

"Judith," he called mockingly. "Judith. Is it too much to hope you're waiting in my bunk, m'dear?"

She did not answer. She would not assist him in his quest.

"Judith. Judith. Damn!" He stumbled against the end of the bunk. "Judith. Where are you?"

She heard the sound of flint striking. The light caught in the oil lantern. He held it high and stared around him. His unsteady swaying made grotesque shadows leap about the cabin. "Where the hell are you?"

She shrank as far down behind the cannon as she could squeeze.

His bark of laughter ended in a gusty belch. One hand slipped the lantern onto its hook, the other fumbled at the opening of his trousers. "Little mousie in the hole. Come on out of there, little mousie. Come see what I have for you."

She did not move.

The *Implacable* lifted on a billow. His shadow swooped across her. The tone of his voice changed from teasing to irritated. "Come now, Judith. Don't make me drag you out. If you make me angry, you won't like it."

She shuddered.

He ducked his head, no longer staring at her. His hands were busy at his front. His voice became deeper, huskier. "Show me what you can do for me. Show me how you stole the ship from the big, bad pirate."

380

Suddenly, he took a couple of unsteady steps forward. His toes scraped against the gun carriage. His fervent curse covered her gasp of revulsion. The obvious bulge in the front of his trousers gave evidence—even in the poor light—of his arousal.

Grinning, he covered it with one hand, rubbing himself roughly while the other braced against the cannon. "You're going to like what I have for you, Judith," he grunted. "And when we're through, you're going to tell me how much you enjoyed it."

"Get away from me," she whispered. "Get away."

The *Implacable* sank into a trough that toppled him forward so that he had to use both hands against the cannon to stand. She could smell his breath as it fogged out in another belch. "Come on, Judith," he demanded, his voice angry. "Don't make me drag you out from behind there."

The ship climbed again, teetered on the edge, then dropped. Its motion gave him impetus. He leaned forward. His reaching hand caught in her hair. With a grunt of laughter he staggered back, pulling her forward, determined to drag her out. She screamed in pain and anger. He laughed again. She twisted her head around and bit his wrist.

Cursing, he shook her violently as a dog shakes a rat. His superior weight inexorably dragged her out of her corner and across the cannon. Struggling blindly, the pain squeezing tears from her eyes, she wrapped her hands around his arm to take some of her weight off her scalp.

Suddenly, he laughed. "I always said I'd punish you, Judith. I've been waiting a long time to do it."

Her eyes flew open. She blinked frantically, clearing her eyes in time to see him tug a long snake of leather free from his shoulder. It rippled across the cabin floor. "No. Oh, no."

He clenched his fist even tighter in her hair, holding her face down against the gun carriage. Her body

381

sprawled helplessly across the long metal barrel. "This time there's no dying mother upstairs to put a damper on the proceedings. No ancient butler to come in and spoil the fun. There's just you and me."

"You're crazy."

"No. Vengeful. I remember the contempt in your eyes. You despised me. You thought you were better than me. But you're not. And I'm going to teach you that you're not. You're going to learn to do exactly what I tell you to do. You're going to help me get back up in the world." He shook out the whip. It slithered across the floor, hissing and slapping against the furniture in the confined space.

"No! I'll scream."

"No one will come and help you. No one cares."

"Rollings cares. He told you . . ."

"Rollings is drunk tonight. They're all drunk tonight. Why do you think it took me so long? I don't intend to have my pleasure interfered with. I've waited too long for revenge."

He leaned into the carriage, the front of his body scant inches from her. "Now," he drawled, tugging at her hair and wringing a little cry from her. "Let's lift up that pretty face. I want to see all those pretty tears."

Chapter Twenty

Her terror rising, she could no longer choke back a scream. He laughed, then cursed as she pulled her head away despite the pain in her scalp. How she hated the thick curly mass of hair that made his grip so easy to maintain.

"Stop struggling, m'dear." Lythes grunted the words from somewhere above her. "You'll not get away. Oh, no! Not this time! And your lovely cries make it more exciting."

Instantly, she willed her lips sealed. With a deep moan of agony she twisted frantically on the cannon and finally managed to worm her body over it. She dropped to the floor in front of him with a thump and began to scramble. Her breath burning in her nostrils, she managed to get her knees under her—and then one foot.

He laughed at her clumsiness, then jerked her hair violently, dragging her head back on her neck. The muscles and tendons strutted; she arched to avoid the tearing pain. The chain clanked as she clawed viciously at his arm and wrist.

"Stop it!" He swung the whip. It lashed through the cabin, then came down across her back. She could not help herself. The burning stroke tore a scream from her.

"That's right. Scream. Beg me to stop and take you." He swung the whip again. This time the force of it fell on the cannon, but she began to whimper. Nothing in her young life had ever prepared her for an experience like this. Like a small animal in the jaws of a carnivore, she could not react except with terror. The tiny sounds disappointed him.

He prodded her with his boot. "Damme, but you're a spiritless wench. Hardly worth the trouble." He prodded her again. "So much for bloody English aristocrats."

The insult inflamed her. She might be afraid, but she would not disgrace her family. With a wild cry she drew back her legs and kicked at him with all her strength.

He sidestepped with a laugh, then hit her again. The whip tore down the length of her spine. She screamed, a long, gurgling wail of agony.

The *Implacable* rose on a billow. At the same time, Judith lunged up. The combined movements overbalanced him. They fell together. He released his hold on her hair to catch himself.

The moment of freedom was all she needed. High above her head she swung her manacled wrists. A cry of pure hatred on her lips, her hands locked together, she brought them crashing down into his face.

Hot blood splashed her fists. A gurgling howl of pain burst from his throat as his nose splintered. He bucked beneath her, throwing her to the side, but she scrambled back a-straddle of him and slammed the manacles down again. This time they struck his temple as he tried to avoid the blow and banged his head against the cabin floor. He went limp beneath her.

She raised her hands above her head again, but the stillness of the body between her thighs halted her. She waited, her pounding heart shaking her whole body, her chest heaving jerkily as she panted in pain and fear.

Slowly, infinitely slowly, she lowered her hands. As she did so, she became aware of dampness. Hot tears flowed down her cheeks, perspiration coated her body and trickled down between her breasts. Her thighs where she clasped his body were wet with sweat. And her hands

384

and arms were spattered with blood. Sour vomit rose in her throat, but she knew, once begun, she would never stop. A terrible feral groan tore from her as she sought to control the heaving of her stomach.

She pulled one knee up under her and leaned her arm on it. Not once did she think that she might have killed a man.

Finally, the ringing in her ears quieted enough for her to hear his stertorous breath bubbling through the ruin of his nose and his slackly open mouth. At the same time, she became aware of other things. Her position appalled her. She slumped astride the hips of that despised unwashed body.

Galvanized by the thought, she made a mad scramble to get away across the cabin from him. Catching onto the side of the locker, she climbed to her feet.

The pitch of the ship had nothing to do with the drunken swaying of her body. She had never felt so weak or so ill. More tears trickled down her face. She lifted her manacled hands to the lantern's flickering light. Dark spots and streaks of red mottled them from fingertip to elbow. Staggering away from the locker, she sat down hard on the edge of the bunk, where she waited for her breathing to even and her heart to stop its terrified pounding

For a minute only, she held her hands at full length from her body, her fingers curled like claws afraid to touch for fear of smearing the blood. A shudder coursed through her. She swallowed convulsively and pushed off the bunk. Lythes lay on his back, his arms and legs sprawled wide. Blood spattered his clothing and trickled in a dark stream from beneath his head.

One step. Then a bubbling snort came from the figure on the floor. She started back with a high-pitched scream of pure terror.

His hand closed around her ankle, and he reared up braced on his other arm. Above the bleeding ruin of his nose and mouth his eyes sparked madness. Unintelligible sounds poured from his lips. He jerked with insane strength, toppling her backward. She fell onto the bunk, the wooden edge catching her in the small of the back. Unaware of the pain, she twisted and clawed frantically to escape.

He jerked again, pulling her half onto the floor. Another pull and she would lie alongside him. His loathsome body would cover hers, weigh her down, crush her. With a shriek of rage and revulsion she drove her foot into his face.

He howled his agony and clapped both hands to his nose. Again she scrambled around, gathered her legs under her, and rose above him. Chained hands high above her the third time, she brought them down with all her strength on the top of his head.

He wavered, grunted, shook his head as if to clear it. His bloody hands reached for her.

Shuddering with revulsion, she struck again. Her manacled wrists came down with all her might on the back of his skull. He crumpled to the floor. As he fell forward, she leapt back out of his reach.

Tears and horror blinding her, she pushed herself up the side of the cabin wall. Her heart pounded so hard against her ribs that it shook her body. On her feet at last, she braced her legs wide and prayed they would hold her. Through the haze of tears she watched Lythes's body for the slightest movement.

None came. Her breathing steadied; her heartbeat slowed. Her eyes flickered to the door. She feared to step across Lythes. Yet she dared not stay where she was. She must get out of the cabin. She must find someone to help her. Surely among all those men must be one to save her.

The hopelessness of her plight dawned on her. No one would listen to her appeal. The first person she met would take her to Rollings. And he would bring her back to Lythes.

She stared again at the body. It lay so still. No sound came from it. No movement. The dark red pool beneath the head began to spread. Thick streams of blood crept across the floor toward her. He lay facedown in his own blood. He could not breathe. And then she knew!

He would never breathe again.

She had killed him. Never mind that he had beaten and tried to rape her. Never mind that he had planned the degradation of her body and the damnation of her soul. She had done murder. Still, she felt nothing. Nothing at all except fear. She had to get off the ship before one of its officers found her.

If she were found beside his body, they would ask no questions. They would hang her. Hang her from a spar. And they would sink the *Banshee* or make her a prize of war. Turn her into a British ship. How Tabor would hate that! She could not let them take the ship. Somehow she must escape. Her men on board the *Banshee* would be impressed into British service. They would hate that. And Laura needed her. She could not repair the Talbot fortunes alone. Tabor would never know what happened to her. He would sail back to New Orleans looking for his ship, and she would not be there. He would be furious. When he caught up with her, he would . . .

"Stop!"

The cry tore from her. She must stop her whirling thoughts and act. She was not mad! She would not lean helplessly against the wall of the cabin with blood on her hands. Nor would she sink to the floor and cower in the corner, waiting for someone to come and find her.

She had killed to defend herself. Lythes would have killed her. Or hurt her so badly that she would have begged for death. But he was the one who was dead and she was alive.

With a spurt of energy she pushed herself off the wall and stood erect. She wanted to stay alive. To do that she had to escape—from a British frigate in the middle of the Caribbean Sea.

If she could somehow get aboard the *Banshee* . . .

Lifting her skirts high, she stepped over the body and

pushed the door open a crack. The companionway was
dark and empty. In a flash she was out and the door shut
behind her. For a second she chided herself. She should
have brought the key and locked it. Too late now. Not for
anything would she return to the cabin and search her
victim's pockets.

Her head popped up onto the main deck. The watch
looked out to sea. The helmsman's face was lighted by the
lantern before him. He would be unlikely to see a dark
figure creep across the main deck amidships.

Somewhere off within hailing distance ran the
Banshee. Judith darted to the rail. The brigantine sailed
no farther astern and starboard than thirty yards.
Lanterns swung from a foremast spar and from its
bowsprit, illuminating the figurehead's carved demon
face split in a silent scream.

As she stared, she detected movement on the deck.
Confusion, a scuffle, men struggling. Longman must
have organized the men to overpower the marines. A
thrill went through her. She must get to them. She must.
But how?

Most of the hammocks were down, but a few remained
stowed in the netting. Could she snatch one free and
jump into the water with it? She hated the thought of the
water. The memory of the bayou made her shiver with
dread. Again she vowed to learn to swim whenever she
should find the time. The chain between her wrists
clanked softly as she tugged at the makeshift life
preserver.

On the *Banshee* two figures moved to the prow. They
stared toward the frigate, toward her. She waved her
chained hands frantically. The *Banshee* seemed to move a
little closer, or did the *Implacable* give ground? One
figure leaned toward her. He fumbled with the light at the
beakhead, held it aloft. Light illuminated his features.

Her heart stopped. Tabor O'Halloran. She could not
believe her eyes. He stared at her across the short
expanse of water.

388

Would he pick her up if she should go over the side? Desperately unsure, she hesitated.

The helmsman, the watch, paid her no attention. They must be mistaking her for an ordinary seaman. When Lythes's body was discovered, she would have no chance. Surely Tabor O'Halloran would pick up a person in the water.

Clumsily, she slid her arms around her hammock. Holding it against her, she climbed to the top of the rail.

She shot him one quick look. Could he see her face? Did he recognize her? Would he help her if he knew who she was? Then she launched herself out into space.

The air tore past her ears. The black water rushed up to meet her. From the rail of the frigate to the surface of the Caribbean seemed but the flickering of an eye.

She hit with terrible force. If not for the chain, the hammock would have exploded from her hands and been lost. Only the sense of keeping her breath as long as possible kept her from opening her mouth and swallowing a mouthful of the dark, cold water. Down she went and down. Immediately, she kicked, pushing herself upward, dragging the hammock with her, or did it drag her? She could not tell. She could not tell which way was up.

Panic exploded in her when she could no longer tell whether she was sinking or moving upward. She opened her eyes; the saltwater stung like fire, but she could see. But what? Nothing but blackness. No air. No light. She clutched the hammock tightly and kicked with all her might. The hammock and her head broke the surface at the same instant. She had not sunk far at all.

She tossed her head to clear the water from her face. The wake of the *Implacable* rolled her aside. But where was the *Banshee*?

Something was thrashing toward her. She thought of the huge fish she had seen dragged out of the river at New Orleans. Gar with huge teeth, alligators with great jaws.

Again the terror. She tried to look around her. A wave washed over her, washing her long hair into her eyes. She gasped and sputtered. The splashing came nearer. The hammock bobbed, dragged down by the weight of her clothing and the chains around her wrists. Another wave lifted her, then dropped her into a trough. Saltwater slapped her in the face. She blinked rapidly and tried to kick. She must get alongside the *Banshee* and scream for help before the ship passed her by in the night.

The hammock slid forward in the water, not propelled by her kicking. She clutched frantically, gasped, swallowed water, then an arm slid around her.

"Got you."

"Tabor . . ."

He gave three quick tugs on the rope attached under his armpits. And they were drawn through the water at amazing speed.

"Tabor . . ." She moaned again and began to cry.

"Let go of the hammock."

She tried, but her chains had somehow tangled in the lashings that rolled the heavy canvas up. "I can't."

"Let go, dammit. No sense dragging it aboard."

"I can't," she sobbed again.

They had come to the side of the *Banshee*. Tabor clung to the towline with one hand and to her with the other. "Let it go. You're safe."

A wave threw her against the side of the brigantine. Her head bumped against the wet wood. She groaned. "Help me. I can't swim."

"You can't swim?"

"No. Help me. Please."

"I will, you stubborn woman, but you've got to help yourself. I can't climb the side of this brigantine with you and the hammock. Let it go."

"You won't let me sink."

He cursed fluently. "I won't let you sink."

She gave a wiggle and a squirm. Her struggles increased, but she could not free her arms. "The chain's caught," she sobbed.

"Chain?"

"It's caught in the rope."

He cursed. He let go the rope and felt along the hammock. The first thing he encountered was her arm, then the manacle around her wrist. He cursed again, then pulled on the chain. She cried out at the pain, but the hammock slipped from beneath her. Suddenly she was suspended in water at the mercy of Tabor O'Halloran.

A terrified cry escaped her as the hammock bobbed away.

"Put your arms around my neck," he commanded.

While he held her around her waist she looped her arms around his neck. He brought his arm up through the loop and clasped her against his side. "I . . . are you sure you can carry me up with you?"

"Probably not, but your crew ought to have enough strength to pull us both up." He tugged on the line again. They rose out of the water. He set his feet against the side of the ship and walked up as the crew pulled from above.

Her feet swung free of the waves as the water poured off her in streams. Her arms felt as though they were being jerked from their sockets. And the pain in her wrists made her faint. Her dress and all the water in her clothing seemed to weigh a hundred pounds. "Tabor." Her face was pressed against the hard muscles of his back. "Oh, Tabor."

He did not acknowledge that he had heard her. His own efforts were taking all his strength. Once his foot slipped and he banged his knee against the side of the *Banshee*.

Then they were at the rail. The mate of the *Banshee* leaned over the side, his hands reaching down.

"Careful," Tabor warned.

She was caught by the wrists. The manacles sank deep into the abused flesh.

"Sweet mother of God!" Mr. Pinckney exclaimed.

The pain smote Judith on top of all the others. It seemed to streak down her distended arms and into her

391

brain. The darkness of the Caribbean night became deeper, and she knew nothing more.

She awoke to pain. Her right wrist felt as if it were being broken.

"Be careful, damn you. That's a tender, delicate girl. Her wrist's no bigger than three of your fingers."

"I'm doing the best I can. But she's so swollen . . ."

She cried out as the pressure increased. She heard a harsh, metallic snap, then she heard nothing more.

When Judith awoke again, she was in the big bed on board the *Banshee*. She stared at the ceiling, then out the windows in the stern. The sun shone brightly through them. She lifted her hand to shield her eyes. Her wrist was heavily bandaged. With a moan she lowered it gingerly and turned her head.

"Awake, m'lady?" Tabor O'Halloran bent over her, a growth of black beard on his chin, his eyes deepset in his skull.

She started to speak. Her voice came out in an unintelligible croak.

"Drink this." He held water to her lips.

She drank thirstily, then lay back. "Thank you," she breathed. She lay for several minutes waiting for the liquid to take effect. When she tried to speak, she was able to marshal up clear sounds. "The frigate?"

"We lost her. Or, rather, she lost us." He grinned faintly.

"Good."

"Mr. Longman has told us how you happened to be aboard but not how you came to be chained"—he paused angrily—"and whipped."

She wanted to be strong and tell him none of what had happened to her was his business. He was a pirate and she might very well have leapt from the deck of the

392

Implacable into worse trouble, but she could not speak. A huge, hard knot of pain swelled in her throat, and before she could swallow, a harsh sob forced its way out from between her lips.

"Judith."

She tried to curl away from him, to hide her face until she could recover, but he put his hand on her shoulder. "Judith."

"Leave me alone."

"Judith." He turned her back over gently but inexorably, and lifted her into his arms. "Shh. Don't you be taking on so."

The sobs were unstoppable. They flowed out of her mouth, and the tears streamed down her cheeks. She felt hot and terrified, as if the water had been very cold and her body needed to build a fever to rekindle her life. She tried to cross her arms to hug her body, but her wrists and arms hurt so much that she felt cut off from her hands.

"Judith." His voice was warm and deep as he kissed the top of her head, her temple, her cheek. "Judith."

She shivered under the caress of his mouth, uncontrolled by the softness and gentleness in his voice. "Tabor."

He held her for a long time, until her sobs stopped and her body began to cool again. "Feel better now?"

She tried to wriggle away and sit up, but the movement caused a tightening along her spine and she moaned.

"Why don't you just lie back down and tell me what happened?"

"Why do you want to know?"

"I want to know who to hunt down and kill." His voice was calm and deadly.

She shrugged painfully. Looking down at herself, she realized she was wearing one of his shirts with frills of lace on the sleeves that covered up the bandages on her wrists.

"Mr. Longman said everything seemed to be all right until this man dressed like a gentleman started talking."

"It was." Judith plucked at the edge of the covers. "His name is Randolph Carew, Lord Lythes. He was a . . . 'friend' of my mother's." She could not meet his eyes.

"Wonderful friend."

"He lied about me. The captain of the *Implacable* would probably have let me go after he searched the ship, but Lythes . . . er . . . had a grudge."

"So the captain ordered you chained up and whipped. I can't believe even the bloody British would go so far as to whip a woman."

"Not the captain. It was Lythes. The captain was going to just put me in the brig, but Lythes offered to . . . question me." The shamed flush rose in her cheeks. How she hated to tell him this. She wanted to hide forever the humiliation of being tortured.

Tabor made a grinding noise with his teeth. "What could you possibly have known?"

"Your whereabouts, for one thing."

"So you told them you'd left me in Santiago harbor," he grinned wolfishly.

She lifted her chin. "No."

"What?"

"I didn't tell them anything. That's why Captain Rollings was so angry."

Tabor stared at her in disbelief. "Go on," he said finally.

"Lord Lythes promised to get the information from me." Her voice was low. "But he really wanted revenge."

Tendons strutted in the brown column of his throat. "Did he rape you?"

"No." Her cheeks felt as if they were on fire. "He planned to. Perhaps. I don't know. He was awful. He wanted me to do terrible things."

"Bloody perverted swine."

"Oh, no. He had a score to settle," she said honestly. "When he came to see my dying mother, he saw me and wanted me to become a . . . someone who would provide

394

him with an entree into wealthy fashionable homes. He was very . . . insistent. With the help of my butler I managed to get away. After I told *Grandmère*, she used her influence to ostracize him."

"No more than he deserved."

"He saw a chance for revenge. With my hands chained he planned for me to provide him with what he called fun." She managed a mirthless smile. "He tricked himself though. He spent the early part of the evening getting all the officers drunk, so they wouldn't come to help me when I screamed."

"You screamed and no one came to help you."

"They were all drunk, you see. But when he screamed, he had no one to help him. That's why I was able to get out of the cabin and across the deck."

"I couldn't believe it. When I saw you wave, I couldn't believe that you were really there. And when you jumped . . ." He shook his head. "I couldn't get the line around me fast enough. I didn't know how well you could swim."

She laughed shakily. "I can't swim."

"That's what you told me." He looked at her incredulously. "You really can't swim?"

"No."

"I'll be damned." He jumped to his feet and began to pace the cabin. "Let me get this straight. You dived over the side of a frigate in mid-ocean with nothing but a sailor's hammock to keep you afloat. You're crazy." He threw back his head and laughed.

She shook her head. She had to make him understand. "Please believe me. You don't know what he was going to do. You can't imagine. I had to get away from him."

He stopped his pacing. "Death before dishonor."

"Infinitely worse than death. Infinitely worse than dishonor."

He stared at her as if seeing her for the first time. "I guess you really mean that."

The silence grew in the cabin. He stared out the stern

windows. She slid back down in the bed. "What happens now?"

He shrugged. "Now we sail like mad for the coast of Cuba, dodge in and out of the bays and inlets, and play hide-and-go-seek with the *Implacable* and any of her sister ships that might be in the area."

"We probably don't need to do that," Judith said quietly.

"What?"

"The *Implacable* is bound for New Orleans. She was only making a sweep before she headed in that direction. If the fog had lasted a few minutes longer, I'd have lost her."

His brow creased. "How do you know that?"

"I was being entertained at the officers' mess when—"

"At the officers' mess!"

"Captain Rollings was at first impressed with my forebears. The Dowager Countess of Harrestone is a very famous woman."

Tabor's voice had turned nasty. "I'm sure."

The silence grew between them.

"What else did they tell you while they were entertaining you?"

"Nothing much." She drew her eyebrows together, trying to remember the bits and pieces. "They said something about beauty and booty. They said it several times. Someone had promised them 'beauty and booty.' Someone they called Old Cock."

"That'd be Admiral Cochrane. His password the night before a battle is supposed to be 'beauty and booty.'" Tabor was glaring at her now, fists clenched on his hips. "They certainly told you a lot for a captive," he sneered.

"I don't think they expected me to escape to pass the information on," she faltered.

The eastern sun had risen higher in the sky. Judith looked out the stern windows. "The *White Cloud*," she whispered.

396

His scowl blackened as if he had forgotten the merchantman. "Yes. I came up in her."

"Where was she anchored?"

"At Gauntánamo."

"That was to have been our next port." She bowed her head.

"I will return her to you."

"When?"

"As soon as you are able to take command."

She managed to lift her wrists before her face. "Am I badly hurt?"

"The greatest danger is infection, but Pinky thought the dip in the Caribbean probably washed that all away. Saltwater works in an almost magical way."

Again the silence. The mention of the officers' mess had turned him cold and distant. The man who had held her in his arms while she had sobbed out her physical and emotional hurts had been replaced by the cruel Captain O'Halloran, who had kidnapped her and brought her on board the *Banshee* to witness a funeral. "I want to thank you for diving in after me. I don't think I could have climbed the side of the ship."

He looked uncomfortable. "You were making good progress for a girl who couldn't swim. Probably we could have thrown you a rope in another few yards. You could have passed it around your waist—" He stopped, thinking of her chained wrists caught in the lashings of the hammock.

"You saved my life," she murmured.

He shrugged offhandedly. "Don't think about it."

"How can I not?"

"Just concentrate on getting well, so you can be away." He strode to the door. "Now that you're all right, I've got to go out on deck. Time to relieve Pinky. He's taken double watches for me to stay here with you."

She nodded. "Tell him I thank him too." But he had closed the door behind him. She rolled over on the bed and stared at the graceful sails of the *White Cloud* through eyes blurred with tears until she fell asleep.

"It's time to wake up and eat something."

Tabor's voice seemed to come from a long way off. She stirred and turned over. The room was dark. Judith felt him set a tray beside her on the bed. "Can you sit up?"

"Yes."

He went away and lit the lantern.

"If you'll wait outside for a minute," she suggested.

"What for? Oh . . ." He nodded curtly and stepped outside.

When she had used the jar in the bottom of the washstand, she returned to bed and called to him.

His face impassive, he came back in and arranged the tray on her lap. "Cook fixed you his best fish stew tonight."

"It smells good."

"Can you eat it yourself?"

"I think so. I'm not entirely helpless."

While she ate, he worked over the *Banshee*'s log. "You wrote these entries," he accused her.

"I wanted them to believe that I had really taken the ship from you. I didn't want to lose your ship. You must believe me."

"Oh, I do." He closed the logbook. "If the *Banshee* had gone down, you would have lost the *White Cloud* too."

She lifted her chin angrily. "Of course. But why don't you believe the absolute worst of me? I hoped they'd take me aboard their ship and sink the *Banshee*. Then I could go back to England with them. Lord Lythes could beat me until I agreed to become one of his prostitutes. I could spend the rest of my life as a plaything of high government officials."

"Judith, that's not necessary."

"No, it's not, but neither are your accusations necessary."

He smiled slightly. "Truce."

"Truce."

He took the tray away and then returned, looking her over. "You seem better," he said decisively. "Would you like me to brush your hair?"

She raised her hand self-consciously. "Oh, would you? I'd forgotten about it. I probably look like a witch."

He took the brush and began the task of unsnarling the mare's nest of her hair. At first the task was painful for them both, but gradually, as he worked out all the tangles, she began to sigh with pleasure. He brushed through it as it lay in long, shimmering waves in the lantern light.

His voice was hoarse when he finally laid the brush aside. "There."

She looked over her shoulder at him. "Thank you."

He felt himself drowning in her eyes. The lantern danced in them and the ship rocked beneath them. "Judith . . ."

Her blood clamored in her veins. Passion and a terrible need curled deep within her. She held out a trembling hand. "Tabor, please. Drive away the shadows."

He put one knee on the bed and kissed her long and deeply. "I'm afraid I'll hurt you. You're somewhat the worse for wear." He rubbed his thumb gently over the bandages on the back of her hand.

"You can be gentle," she whispered. "I know you can."

He drew back off the bed. Never taking his eyes off her, he pulled his shirt from his waistband. She watched him gather it up over his bronze chest. The beauty of his body drew her eyes like a magnet. Involuntarily, she reached out. Her fingers slid through the black curling hair to touch the flat nipple. He quivered. Roughly, he pulled the garment over his head and flung it aside.

"Be careful," he whispered throatily. "You'll get more than you bargained for."

"I doubt that I will."

399

Slowly, his jaw clenched around a tight smile, his eyes slitted, he pulled at the buckle of his belt. When it, too, dropped away, he pulled at the drawstring on his loose seaman's trousers.

Both of Judith's hands clasped his rib cage, her fingers fitting into the slight indentations between the ribs. Holding him lightly, she leaned across the bed and placed her mouth to the nipple she had caressed before. It hardened under the flick of her tongue. As his gasp of pleasure expanded his chest, she sucked hard.

"For God's sake, Judith."

"It's been so long, so long, Tabor. I can't wait . . ."

"At least let me get my boots off."

Trembling, she sank back against the head of the bed. Instead of sitting down beside her, he bent and caught the heel of first one and then the other and pulled them off. The trousers fell and he stepped out of them.

"You're beautiful," she murmured.

"A man's not beautiful," he protested as he put one knee on the bed and bent over her.

"You are." She put her hands on his ribs again and raised her mouth to his chest. "You are. And I have a basis for comparison now."

He tossed the bedcovers aside to expose her long, slender legs. "I'm just glad you didn't have more than a look."

She shuddered. Her teeth scored his breast. "Please," she breathed.

Without further preliminaries he parted her legs, running his hands over the insides of her thighs, spreading them so they lay loosely sprawled. He knelt between them and parted her still farther, exposing the most private and secret parts of her body.

She stared up at him, her eyes liquid, while his fingers worked their magic. "I should be ashamed."

"No, you shouldn't be. Not ever. You're beautiful." His voice groaned out of his throat as he knelt to kiss her and take his time caressing the sensitive bud, the delicate

400

folds, the secret niche.

Her pleasure was so acute that she clenched her legs involuntarily, then let them fall open again. A deep breath swelled her chest and arched her spine. "No more. Don't. No more. I can't stand . . ."

"Don't you want your pleasure this way?" he whispered, his tongue never still. "You wanted me to be gentle. This is the gentlest way I know."

"Nooo. No!" She felt the sweat break out on her body. The cabin was unbelievably hot. "No. I want you."

"Me?" he laughed. "Me? A pirate. A Yankee."

She set her teeth against the pounding waves of pleasure. "Please, pirate, please!"

He laughed again. "As you will, m'lady."

He pulled away, then guided himself back until the veriest tip of him was seated in her niche. His mouth hovered over hers. "Now kiss me," he urged. "Taste the flavor of your passion."

Throbbing, flaming, her mind awhirl, she thrust up to clasp his mouth and draw his lips within her own. He drove into her, sliding deep, unimpeded, into the hot receiving folds and exploded even as she screamed her own ecstasy into his throat.

Chapter Twenty-One

Tabor pushed open the window and let in the soft sounds of the Caribbean night—the creak of timber and rigging, the slap of the water against the hull, the foaming of the wake as the *Banshee* moved surely onward. He leaned against the ship's great frame, staring out at the white phosphorescent spindrift and the midnight-blue water.

Judith lay perfectly still, drinking in his beauty. The moonlight glided lovingly over the muscles of his arms, the angularity of bone across his shoulders, the corded neck. Below the crossed forearms a dark lance of hair ended in a thatch that surrounded the heavy male organ. Relaxed now, emptied of potency for the moment, it lay against his sleekly curved thigh.

She must have sighed or drawn in her breath sharply— or perhaps he felt the caress of her eyes. He looked in her direction. His eyes peered intently into the darkness of the bed.

"Judith, are you awake?"

"Yes."

"We're almost into the Gulf of Mexico."

"Good."

"We'll be home in three or four days depending on the wind."

She pulled the sheet up to her chin and sat up. "Tabor,

what will we run into when we try to go up the Mississippi? The British may have it blockaded."

He shrugged, staring back at the water. "We'll soon know."

She hesitated. "They should let the *White Cloud* through."

He ran a hand through his tousled hair. "Perhaps. If the right captain is in command. One who recognizes your flag and your name."

She groaned at the bitter note in his voice. "Tabor, do you still think that I'm a spy?"

He refused to answer. Pushing himself away from the window, he strode idly to the desk, where he moved objects around. The grayness of early dawn began to lighten the sky. The *Cloud* glided astern, a black silhouette on the horizon.

She threw back the covers and came to him on swift naked feet. "Even though you saw the marks on my back? Even though I was chained?"

"Mr. Longman said you had them convinced, and then this Lythes stepped in. Bad luck that you met him. Everyone makes enemies."

She caught his arms and turned him to face her. Both stood naked, their bodies inches apart, yet no sparks leapt between them. Instead, intensity of another kind, just as searing, held them still. She stared up into his face. Even in the dark she could feel his expression. "Wouldn't the captain have protected me if I were a valuable spy?"

"They didn't mind talking in front of you," he reminded her stonily. "You could tell me where the British fleet was bound, who the commander was."

"The words meant nothing to me."

"So you say."

She spun away from him. "Oh, for the love of heaven! Do I have to be killed by a British marine to convince you that I'm innocent?"

"I don't want you to be killed, m'lady."

"Thank you for that, pirate." She flung herself on the

403

bed and presented him with her back. He stared at her for a minute, then sighed wearily.

"I'd better get up on deck and relieve Mr. Pinckney."

"Perhaps you'd better."

As if by mutual truce they said no more about the British. Judith remained coolly aloof. Tabor brooded on deck for hours at a time. When finally he would come to his cabin, he would lie beside her, rigid, listening to the sound of her breathing in the darkness. His body hardened until it ached with wanting. Every inch of his skin felt the warmth radiating from her.

The closer they sailed to New Orleans, the cooler the weather became. Judith sifted through the clothing in her trunk to find that nothing was heavy enough. In her haste to make this voyage into the Caribbean, she had failed to pack for the return trip. With a sigh she rummaged through Tabor's clothing, hating to borrow it but finding the prevailing wind too daunting.

Usually, Judith paced the cabin as he paced the deck. He had chosen to keep her with him on the *Banshee*. Her plea to be transferred to the *White Cloud* had been met with a fierce frown.

When he sat down at his desk to write or even entered the cabin, her nerves started to tingle and a faint ache began to curl at the base of her belly. She wanted him, but she vowed she would never touch him again knowingly. She would not receive pleasure from a man who thought her guilty of the most damnable of all crimes. Still, the sight of his body as he stood stripped to the waist before the shaving mirror, or turned in sleep, or dressed in simple garb drove her wild with frustration.

Tabor steered the *Banshee* into the main pass at the mouth of the Mississippi. The sails spilled cold rain down his face. "This doesn't feel like Louisiana," he complained to Mr. Pinckney.

"It'll turn warm soon, I'm thinking," came the answer. "I'd guessed you'd ordered this just special."

"Me? Order this weather? Why, for heaven's sake?"

"To keep the lady in the cabin and you up on deck."

Tabor hunched his shoulder away from his mate's disapproving gaze. His face reddened.

Mr. Pinckney was not to be silenced by a mere turn of a shoulder. "What happened to that man who was going to take the lady away with him and teach her to love him? Make her his wife?"

"Shut up, Pinky."

"Ah, Captain, you're a fool."

"I'd be a worse fool to fall in love with a spy."

Pinckney laughed dryly. "Spies don't jump off ships in the middle of the Caribbean with chains around their wrists. The lady could have sunk like a stone. You know that yourself. If that hammock had been improperly tied, or just a little bit smaller, the weight of that iron—"

"Shut up, Pinky. I don't want to talk about it."

"You've never been fair to the lady. You got off on the wrong foot the first time you met. And damn your Irish head. You can't get an idea out once it gets in. You're determined to believe the very worst about her no matter what your own eyes tell you."

Tabor did not answer immediately. The wind filled the sheets as the *Banshee* turned north into the main channel of the river. The sand banks and marshes fell away and the water began to show the muddy stain.

When they were moving smoothly upriver, Tabor spoke softly. "I'm taking her home and giving her back her ship. After that, I'll have to wait until this damned war is over."

"Pray God it'll be soon."

"Amen to that."

The *Banshee* and the *White Cloud* docked side by side at

the quay at the foot of Calle di Conti. Judith could scarcely believe that barely two and a half weeks had passed since she had sailed. Her whole world had turned around in that time, and yet nothing had changed.

Dressed in the same dress she had embarked in, she came down the *Banshee*'s gangplank on Tabor's arm. The landau with Georges in attendance waited for her, word of her arrival having been flashed upriver from Fort St. Philip.

Looking extremely handsome in blue superfine and gray buckskin, Tabor helped her into the carriage and climbed in beside her. "Canal Street," he directed. "The tobacco shop between Royal and Bourbon streets."

"I want to go home," Judith objected angrily. "You may have the carriage after that if you must smoke."

Tabor shook his head. "You'll go home after you talk to a man I know. What you have to report may be of utmost importance to the United States of America, m'lady."

"Oh, for heaven's sake, pirate. I've told you all I know. Every single bit of it. What's more, I'm sick and tired of being shoved from pillar to post by you. Stop this carriage and get out."

"No."

"Then stop this carriage and let me out."

He put his hand on her arm. "I'm going to settle this once and for all."

She looked at him squarely. "And if I'm guilty? If I am a spy? Then what? Will you turn me over to them to be tried and hanged for treason?"

"I . . . I . . ."

Tabor sprang out without finishing his sentence in front of Reynolds's tobacco shop. A quick rattle of the doorknob revealed that it was locked, but an old man answered his insistent banging. "Where has he gone?" Tabor demanded.

"Mr. Reynolds spends most of his hours now around the corner at 106 Royal Street." The old man grinned a toothless grin and nodded as if enjoying a huge joke.

Tabor gave him a penetrating look, then strode back to the carriage. "Pull around the corner."

The sight of the house with its guard of Tennesseans alerted him. "My God! General Jackson must be here in New Orleans."

Judith sniffed. "Then take me home. Everything will be in a turmoil. They won't be interested in anything I might have to say. Especially when it's nothing."

He shot her an angry look and opened the carriage door. "We're going to get to the bottom of this once and for all."

Judith stepped down from the carriage on his arm. When Tabor would have led her in immediately, she turned to Georges. "Is Miss Laura at the town house?"

"Yes, Maîtresse. She come from the plantation as soon as the word was flashed that the ships were in the river."

"Then tell her that I have been taken to the American General Jackson's headquarters charged with"—she looked significantly at Tabor—"spying. Tell her that she should come immediately."

"Judith," Tabor protested. "I'm sure it's not necessary to bring Laura into this."

"And I'm sure that it is. Go on, Georges."

The black man touched his hat and sprang to the box.

As the landau clattered down the street toward the Calle di Conti, Tabor turned to Judith, his expression bleak. "You must really be guilty," he said quietly.

She swallowed hard, a painful lump in the back of her throat. "No. I'm not. I'm not now and I never have been. But if you won't believe me when you . . . once you said you loved me, how can I expect strangers to believe me?"

"I believe that you are doing what you believe is good and right," he replied humbly.

She lifted her chin to keep salty tears from spilling down her cheeks. "You believe that I'm guilty of causing the death of two men for revenge. You believe that I'd actively betray the country my father chose to call

407

his homeland."

"You're an Englishwoman. You haven't been treated well since you've come to this country." He shifted uncomfortably at the admission.

"That's certainly true," she jeered. "I've had my clothing and all my possessions destroyed. I've been demeaned in public and kidnapped. A black man ran amok and tried to kill me. My servant was murdered and my carriage was pushed into the bayou. On the high seas I've been arrested, chained, and whipped. But all that does not mean that I am a traitor."

At the beginning of her recital, he looked shame-faced, but by the end he gaped incredulously. "You never told me you were attacked."

"I've never told you a lot of things for the simple reason that you never asked me. You've been so busy leaping on me, or disapproving of me, or accusing me of terrible things. You've never tried to find out anything about the way I live or what might have happened to me."

"I've tried to find out everything about you," he countered angrily.

"You've tried to prove that I was a spy. I need my sister with me. I need at least one person so I won't be totally alone."

He clenched his jaw tightly. "Then let's see once and for all." He took her arm to lead her up the steps. To confirm his suspicion, she was trembling. "You're not alone," he whispered.

"Yes, I am. Until Laura gets here."

Inside the headquarters they were ushered into an anteroom by a man in military uniform. Instead of asking to see the general, Tabor asked to see Reynolds.

The aide scanned the pages in front of him, then shook his head. "You must have made a mistake, sir. There's no such person by that name on General Jackson's staff."

"I know that, but I'm sure he's here."

The aide looked blank, then brightened. "Major Catesby," he suggested.

"Possibly."

"I'll see if he's available."

Judith sat in a chair. Tabor stood behind it, becoming more and more uncomfortable. What if she were a spy? They shot spies. But she was a British citizen. Surely that mitigated the circumstances.

He would not let them shoot her. As the time dragged, he began to rock back and forth on his heels, then to pace. "What's taking them so long?"

"They have more important things to take care of than a single lady and a lunatic," she told him sarcastically.

He shot her a fiery glance. "I'm not a lunatic."

"Pardon me. A half-wit."

He began to pace the floor again. "I won't let them do anything to you," he promised suddenly.

"Then what are we here for?"

"I have to know," he groaned. "I can't . . ."

The door opened. A tall man in a frock coat and strap-leg trousers walked in. He extended his hand. "Captain O'Halloran."

"Yes, sir."

"I'm Lieutenant Larkin."

Judith had glanced at the man when he entered; now she stared at him fixedly.

Tabor did not notice but continued his conversation. "I need to see Mr. Reynolds immediately. I've important information for him."

"Major Catesby is in conference now with General Jackson and Governor Claiborne. They can't be disturbed. However, how may I help you?"

Tabor cleared his throat. "I have a report that the British frigate *Implacable* is on its way to New Orleans and may in fact be in Lake Borgne right now."

Larkin raised his eyebrows. "You've obviously been at sea for several days, sir. The British are massing at Cat and Ship Islands in the Chandeleur Sound. General

409

Jackson has just arrived and is even now planning the strategy to defend the city."

"I know you," Judith said suddenly. She rose from her seat and came forward with hands outstretched. "Don't I know you?"

Larkin took her hands and looked down into her eyes. He smiled and bowed. "Mistress."

Tabor scowled from one to the other. "Miss Judith Talbot-Harrow."

"Lieutenant Newell Larkin at your service, Miss Talbot-Harrow."

Judith searched the man's lean face. "You're the man who saved my life." She came forward and took both his hands in hers. "Oh, I've been wanting to thank you for so long."

"I did very little, ma'am." A flush rose in Larkin's tanned cheeks.

"No, you did quite a lot, I believe. You shot the man who ran at me with a knife."

"I just happened to have a pistol handy."

"And you were there the night my carriage was rolled off into the bayou, weren't you?"

"On a dark night, Miss Talbot-Harrow, who can say?" He pressed her hands a moment, then stepped back.

"I would be dead twice over if not for you."

"You can't know that, ma'am."

"I'm eternally grateful to you."

Larkin smiled at last. "My pleasure, ma'am. A fellow in my business doesn't have much opportunity to play knight to a lady in distress. I was glad to be of service."

She smiled in return. "My door is always open. If ever I can be of use to you . . ."

He nodded. "I'll remember." He stepped back and addressed Tabor. "I can't say when Mr. Reynolds will be free. If you'd care to wait, I'll have some refreshment brought."

Tabor struggled with his impatience and a sudden dart of jealousy. So Judith was grateful to the man, but did she have to go on and on about it? A simple thank-you would have been sufficient. Suddenly, he wanted to send Judith home. "Perhaps we should go and come back another time?"

Judith raised her eyebrow. "Oh, no, I don't think so, Captain O'Halloran. Lieutenant Larkin will be pleased to help us, and we can get this situation resolved once and for all. You will, won't you?"

"My pleasure, ma'am."

When Larkin had gone, Judith returned to her seat, her eyes shining. "At least I got to thank him."

"He's right, you know," Tabor remarked sourly. "He just happened to be there at the right time."

"I'm not going to try to convince you of anything."

Laura Talbot, closely escorted by Bertrand St. Cyr, strode up the steps of Jackson's headquarters. "I'm here to see General Jackson," she demanded.

"The general is ill and quite fatigued," the aide said. "He's just ended a long and difficult meeting of utmost importance."

"This won't take long."

St. Cyr stepped forward. "May we speak to the next in command?" he requested soothingly.

"Do you wish the person in charge of military affairs or domestic affairs?"

St. Cyr looked at Laura. She looked uncertain. "I would say domestic, wouldn't you?"

He shrugged. "Perhaps. Certainly your sister is a civilian."

The aide reseated himself at the table set up in the foyer. "Perhaps I can help. Is your sister missing?"

"No. She's here in this building. She's being held here."

The aide shook his head. "No one is being *held* here. This building has been commandeered for General Jackson's headquarters."

St. Cyr bent his head toward Laura's. "Perhaps Georges got his information confused."

Laura shook her head impatiently. "Georges wouldn't make a mistake like that. He knows New Orleans like a book. If he says he took my sister here with Captain O'Halloran, then he took them here. May we speak to Captain O'Halloran?"

The aide consulted his list. "We have no Captain O'Halloran on the staff."

"He would have arrived only today," Laura said.

"Still, he would be on the roster. It's brought up to the minute." The aide stabbed his pen into the inkwell to punctuate his final statement.

Laura felt her agitation boiling up inside her as he started to close the book. Since Beau's death, she had dealt with all kinds of people. The sheltered existence he had provided altered irrevocably. In its place was a world that did not always bow to her wishes. She did not like it.

She could not face it alone. Judith had become increasingly important to her. Something inside of her snapped. Stepping forward, she caught the ledger and pushed it back open. "I insist that you look again, sir." Her voice rose shrilly. "My sister, Judith Talbot-Harrow, is in this house. She should be home with me right now, safe and sound. Instead, she's being accused of spying. The charge is utterly ridiculous. What's more, it's being made by that damned pirate Tabor O'Halloran."

The aide reddened furiously. Rising from his chair, he pushed her hand off his book. "Ma'am, there is no one here by the name of O'Halloran or Talbot-Harrow. And you cannot see General Jackson."

"Miss Talbot." St. Cyr took her arm. "Perhaps there is some mistake?"

"Who is in charge of spies? Someone must be in charge of them." Laura raised her voice and directed it up the stairs at the back of the entrance hall.

"Madam, control yourself." The aide shot a worried glance at the closed double doors to his right. "I tell you,

412

we have no one officially in charge of spies. If you do not leave, I'll summon the guard. I have been most polite."

"Miss Talbot." St. Cyr tugged at her sleeve.

Laura shrugged him off. "Damn you, sir," she snarled at the aide. "I demand to see the person who would question spies, then. Who is in charge of . . . of special services?"

St. Cyr threw a pleading glance at the aide, who reluctantly opened the book once again. He grimaced at them both, then ran his finger down the page. "That would be Major Catesby."

"Then call him."

"He's with General Jackson. I can't disturb him."

The last fragments of Laura's control broke. The calm, the cool, the collected Laura Talbot slammed her fist down on the desk. "I demand to see him. My sister is not a spy. You will not hold her against her will for even an hour."

"Miss Talbot . . ."

"Ma'am . . ."

"Damn you both!" she screamed. "Find my sister!"

The double doors of what was the parlor of the house opened. A short man with wire-rim glasses in the dress of an impecunious clerk peered through them. At the sight of the three combatants, he stepped through and closed the door tightly behind him. "What seems to be the trouble?"

"Major Catesby . . ."

"So, you're Major Catesby," Laura interrupted what the secretary might have said. "You must release my sister. There's been a terrible mistake."

"I'm sure there has been, ma'am. Who is your sister?"

"Judith Talbot-Harrow."

"Ah, yes. Tabor O'Halloran was concerned about her."

"Yes. And now he's brought her here. But she's not a spy. She's the daughter of Beau Talbot, who founded the Talbot Shipping Line here in New Orleans. He owned

413

Ombres Azurées. His wife, Celeste Devranches Talbot, belongs to one of the oldest families in New Orleans. Judith would never spy."

"At least not for the British."

Laura gaped. "Not for the British. Then for whom?"

"For the French."

Laura managed a hysterical laugh. "That accusation is more ridiculous than the first. She doesn't even speak French."

"A Talbot ship was about to be given over for the personal use of Napoleon Bonaparte."

"Judith had nothing to do with that. She deplores what that monster has done to Europe as much as the rest of England."

"Follow me." Major Catesby led Laura and St. Cyr along the hall to a room at the end. He opened the door. "Please enter."

"Judith."

"Laura."

Laura flew across the room to embrace her baby sister. "Are you all right?"

"You came for me." Judith's eyes filled with tears.

"Of course I came for you. The minute Georges came with the message, I got Bertrand and we came together. We almost thought they weren't going to let us see you. Have you been hurt?" Suddenly, Laura became aware of Tabor. "What do you mean bringing her here and accusing her of spying?"

He stirred uneasily. "I wanted to clear the charge once and for all," he muttered lamely.

"What did you find with regard to the French thing?" Catesby asked.

"She knew nothing about it. In fact, she gave every indication of being appalled that a Talbot ship might be used for the purpose our intelligence suggests."

Judith spoke from Laura's side. "The man in charge of that particular operation was Maurice Dufaure, my partner. I believe that he bought into the line with that purpose in mind. Our father was deceived into believing he was an honest business man."

"There, now you see." Laura turned to Tabor triumphantly. "You were wrong." She linked her arm in Judith's. "Come home at once, baby sister. You must be exhausted. I've missed you. And I want to spend this time with you. You will let her go, Major Catesby. All charges dismissed."

"There never were charges, Miss Talbot. Only unproven suspicions."

"Then we'll bid you good day and take up no more of your time." Bertrand St. Cyr opened the door for them and the two sisters sailed out.

After a moment's silence Tabor turned angrily. "Reynolds, I want to talk to you."

"I'm sure you do, Captain O'Halloran. I'll be at your service as soon as I've escorted the two lovely ladies to their carriage." Catesby hurried down the hall after them.

As she climbed into the carriage, Judith begged, "Go with me, Laura. I want to confront Dufaure, to tell him that his little Napoleonic plot failed."

Laura shuddered at the thought. "For heaven's sake, sister. You're back and safe. Don't stir up trouble."

"I can't let this go, Laura. My father's business partner is determined to ruin the line."

Laura pressed a hand to her temple. Now that they were away from Jackson's headquarters, she felt a headache beginning. "We've both been left with terrible problems," she sighed. "At least leave it for now. It can wait till morning. Tonight you're going to rest and we'll talk together."

Judith opened the door to the shipping office with Mr. Longman at her elbow. She had brought the mate from the *White Hound* with her as a protective shield.

"Miss Talbot-Harrow." Maurice Dufaure did not

415

bother to rise from behind his desk. His expression for welcoming customers changed to one of derision. His smile slid into his more familiar sneer. "Welcome back. Your trip did not take long. Giving up so soon?"

"No, M'sieur Dufaure. I was very fortunate. Captain Smithurst had suspected that the *Banshee* might have made a call at Santiago de Cuba. He was correct."

Dufaure closed the ledger with a snap, his look incredulous. "You! You found the pirate. But what happened?"

She made no effort to conceal her triumph. "Why, I did as I said I would. I captured his ship."

"You? Then he is dead?"

"No. He is not dead. We reached an agreement of sorts. He returned to New Orleans with me. In fact, we brought each other back. He came in the *Banshee* and I in the *White Cloud*."

"The *White Cloud*!" Dufaure started up from the desk. "Impossible. She was reported lost. You heard the report of the sailor. I heard it too."

"The sailor was correct insofar as he knew."

Dufaure ran his hand over his mouth. For once his usual sneering expression was replaced by one of amazement. "The *White Cloud* is here in New Orleans?"

"Yes."

He sank back down at his desk. "I cannot believe it. This is beyond anything I have ever heard of. I was sure that O'Halloran must have taken her cargo and scuttled the ship."

"Tabor O'Halloran is many things, M'sieur Dufaure, but he is not a fool. No one would scuttle so valuable a ship as the *White Cloud*. I believe she is the newest of the 'white' fleet, isn't she? A pirate knows how to value a good ship."

Dufaure's face brightened. He placed both hands palm down on the desktop. "Then the *White Cloud* is in New Orleans. And she is ready to sail again?"

Judith watched his expression closely. "Just as soon as

416

we can employ a new captain and enlist a crew."

"Yes. Yes. Of course." He pulled another ledger from a drawer beside him. Opening it, he flipped through several pages. His frown deepened. "A new captain. Such a man may be very hard to find. Very hard."

"The *White Cloud* is a fine ship. We shouldn't have a problem finding a captain to take her out. If we need to look." She nodded toward the mate who had been lounging against the counter. "And, Mr. Longman, the first mate of the *White Hound*, has his captain's papers. Part of the crew from the *Hound* will enlist immediately."

Dufaure frowned at Longman as if at some particularly unpleasant specimen. "The captain of the *White Cloud* must be experienced," he said curtly. "He must be someone familiar with European ports."

"Particularly Mediterranean," Judith suggested.

He gaped at her, then lowered his eyes. "We will not choose a captain immediately. We must find the right man."

"And while we do, Talbot Shipping loses money. Didn't you tell me that we were in danger of bankruptcy?"

He shrugged. "I may have perhaps exaggerated the situation. Although it is very grave, with the *White Cloud* returned we should be in no danger."

"How very fortunate!"

"I congratulate you, Miss Talbot-Harrow, on your success. Now, do not worry about finding a captain for the ship. I shall take care of that. It is the least I can do." He stood up and came around the desk. Smiling, he tried to usher her toward the door. "You've done an extraordinary job. You should go home and rest."

She avoided his arm. Standing her ground, she spoke firmly. "I think we should send the *Cloud* on the China run with Mr. Longman in charge."

"The China run?"

"Yes. That way there can be no danger of her winding up in the Mediterranean. You see, Tabor O'Halloran told me that he had intercepted the *Cloud* as her French

417

captain, a close personal friend of yours, I believe, was about to sail her into the Mediterranean."

A muscle ticked in Dufaure's face. He coughed heavily. "To the Mediterranean? It is true that the captain was my friend. But . . ."

"When I spoke with Bertrand St. Cyr about this problem, he thought that Governor Claiborne would want to hear why a Talbot ship was sailing into the Mediterranean. When the present danger of British invasion is over, of course. I will also want to know why the *White Cloud* was bound for the Mediterranean."

"Perhaps there was some mistake?"

"The captain must have been completely ignorant and unable to read destinations. Captain O'Halloran said he was bound for Elba."

Dufaure regarded her steadily for a minute, then drew himself up proudly. "So he was. I admit it. I admit to everything. I am proud of my patriotism. I will deny it no longer."

Judith stared back, amazed at the man's lack of embarrassment at being caught out. "You planned to use the *White Cloud,* a Talbot ship, to bring Napoleon Bonaparte off Elba. Did that seem particularly honest to you?"

"*Certainement!* The *Cloud* should have been mine to do with as I chose. I had spent many long hours at this desk. I had put my own money into the line. Beau Talbot was a fool. He wanted the ships for cargo and passengers. He had not a patriotic bone in his body. All business. Damned *bourgeoisie!*"

The man's insufferable attitude confounded Judith. "I'll thank you not to speak ill of my father, M'sieur Dufaure. He is dead and cannot defend himself."

"When he died, the business should have come to me. Women do not understand business. However." He faced Judith squarely. "I should have been honest with you. You would have seen rewards from this as soon as the emperor was brought to America. From here he will

418

return to France."

"Not on a Talbot ship." Judith spoke between clenched teeth. "He will not be brought off Elba on the *White Cloud*. Nor will he return to France on her. The Talbot ships are not political."

"You." Dufaure's face reddened. "You are just like your father. He never cared about anything but making money. This is my line too. I shall do with it as I choose."

Judith drew herself up very tall. "But I am the senior partner. And I have the final say. I understand you've chosen not to bring the books to Bertrand St. Cyr as you were requested to do. What are we going to find when the books are examined by court order, M'sieur Dufaure?"

"You!" Dufaure's temper exploded. "You have ruined everything. You would have the books examined. They are my books." He came around the desk toward her, his shoulders hunched, his breath coming short and heavy.

Mr. Longman stepped between them. "Settle down there!"

"You will leave!" Dufaure stormed. "You will leave now."

Judith stood her ground. "I want those books," she insisted stubbornly.

But Mr. Longman caught hold of her arm and all but dragged her out the door. "Send the lawyer for them" was his succinct advice.

Chapter Twenty-Two

The cannons boomed at two in the afternoon.

Citizens of New Orleans stared at one another in varying degrees of wonder and horror. Tabor and Reynolds exchanged looks of understanding. From somewhere close at hand, snare drums began their rat-tat-tat call to arms.

"It appears the British have arrived," Reynolds said unnecessarily.

The two men joined the group of officers milling around General Andrew Jackson in the parlor of the house on Royal Street.

Old Hickory, with his mane of iron-gray hair, stood tall among them, waiting for their silence. When he rode into New Orleans, he had been a frail old man, gaunt from his illness. Now the call to arms had created the god of war.

Streaks of hectic color stained his cheeks, which had been pale only hours before. Even standing still, his posture radiated a fierce tension that communicated itself to every man in the room. Energy flowed from him to the others, who read in him a spirit like their own, but greater. The rattle of drums had stripped away his humanity and turned him into a spare blade of Toledo steel, incredibly strong and incredibly deadly.

His voice, which had been hoarse and weak, gained strength through its own hoarseness. His strained vocal cords vibrated with a peculiar penetrating timbre. "The British have made their way through the swamps. They are pitching their tents on the east bank of the Mississippi above the English Turn."

His announcement cued a roar of comments and questions.

He did not wait for them to quiet. Instead, his voice rang out above them. "We march within the hour. General Coffee, you will lead my Tennesseans." He smiled fondly at his old friend. "Not exactly horse troops this time, John."

The general grinned. Although he had shaved since arriving in the city the week before, he still wore his hunting shirt and coonskin cap. Looped in the deerhide belt around his lean waist were a hunting knife and an Indian tomahawk. The others waited while he moved a chew of tobacco to the other side of his mouth. "No need for them, Andy. The distance is so short, we'd be there before we got the horses saddled."

"Shouldn't we wait until . . . ?"

Jackson's hawk profile swung around. His eyes drew together. "And give them time to get entrenched? Never. Never give the invader a minute's peace. He must be fought this very evening."

"This very evening!"

"My God!"

"What the hell with?"

"Who's going to fight?"

Their exclamations of disbelief as well as their furious questions were soon answered as Jackson began deploying his units. The marines, the regulars, the squadron of Mississippi dragoons that had come with Coffee and the Tennesseans, the militia of French and Spanish Creoles formed by Major Plauché, Major Daquin's battalion of Negro refugees from Santo Domingo, and, of course, the Choctaw scouts. The military genius that was Andy Jackson, the victor in the Battle of Horseshoe Bend, the destroyer of the mighty Creek Nation, now turned its full

421

attention against the invading British Army.

Tabor listened with half an ear. His own position ambiguous in the extreme, he watched, but thought of Judith. Where was she? She had heard the guns. She knew their meaning, perhaps better than he. Would she be safe in a city now under martial law? She had no one to protect her. The other Talbot women were safe for the present at *Ombres Azurées*, but Judith would be virtually alone.

He glanced at the mantel clock. It was somewhat after two. He knew her. She would be in that shipping office, stubbornly continuing her business, as if her world were in no danger of coming to a crashing end in a matter of hours.

He tightened his jaw. Before he could find a place for himself in this battle against his most hated enemies, he had to be sure that she was safe. No matter what their differences, she was his responsibility.

Humbly and happily, he assumed it with his whole heart. No matter who or what she had been, she was his love for the rest of their lives. As a pair of officers left the room to carry out their commissions, he slipped out the door with them.

Halfway down the hall he was halted by Reynolds's angry call. "You can't leave now, O'Halloran. We need you on the river."

Tabor waved a casual hand. "Just tell me where to report. I'll make it as fast as I can."

"As fast as you can! Report now! Patterson needs you aboard the schooner."

Tabor shook his head. "I've got business to attend to first." He selected his hat from the many in the hall and set it firmly on his head.

"Dammit, O'Halloran. We're in the middle of a war. Your business can wait."

Tabor grinned stubbornly as he opened the front door. "That's the trouble with recruiting pirates, Major. You can't order them around." He strode down the steps without a backward glance.

Reynolds sprinted after him and caught his arm. "Listen, O'Halloran. You've got to report to Commodore Patterson on the *Carolina*. He's slipping her down the river."

"When?"

"Probably at nightfall."

Tabor glanced overhead at the gray, overcast sky of midafternoon. The north wind blew in frigid gusts, sharp as a whetted knife. "He won't move then for a couple of hours."

"Dammit, O'Halloran."

"I'll be there, Reynolds, or whatever your name is. Don't get yourself all lathered up."

Dufaure scowled when Judith walked into the office. "I thought you had decided to remain at home, as you should."

Judith shook her head. "Surely you have heard something of what's about to happen, M'sieur. The British may appear at any moment. We must make arrangements to get the *Cloud* down the river. I have already sent Mr. Longman to take command." She pulled the manifest ledger from its place beneath the counter.

"What!" Dufaure rose from behind the desk. "Leave that alone."

"I beg your pardon."

"Leave that alone. That ledger goes nowhere. And neither does the ship."

Judith clasped the ledger before her like a shield. "I'll not leave it alone. The cargo must be checked against the manifest. I'm going to do that now. Then Mr. Longman can take the *Cloud* . . ."

Dufaure made a rumbling sound deep in his throat. Stooping, he felt for his walking stick beside his desk. "You will do nothing of the sort. Nor will that American sail with my ship. You were a fool to come here." He rose to his full height, the gold-headed stick clenched in his right hand.

"M'sieur Dufaure!"

The office door opened and Tabor walked in. Instantly, he felt rather than heard the conflict. Thick as the gathering storm was the atmosphere between the combatants. Judith stood, one hand clenched over the top of a ledger that she held in front of her like a shield. A menacing Dufaure, positively red with rage, appeared about to leap over the top of the desk to attack her.

"What's going on here?"

Judith turned at the interruption. "Tabor! What are you doing here?"

"Get out." Dufaure dismissed him with an impatient gesture. "Get out, or I'll have you arrested."

Tabor assumed an air of nonchalance as he rounded the counter. "You'd have a hard time finding a man to do it today. I've come to get you, Judith."

"To get me!" Where she had not retreated from Dufaure, she now backed a step away. "I don't need anyone to get me, pirate."

His smile unchanged, Tabor followed her. Gently, he held out his arm. "But you do, m'lady. Don't you hear the drums? In a matter of hours this city may very well be under siege. Or in British hands. You need to be barricaded in your home."

"I have to protect . . ."

He took the ledger from her. "You don't seem to realize that you can't protect anything. You need protection. Women in a conquered town are fair game."

She shook her head, even as she allowed him to lay the book down on the desk.

Dufaure snatched it up with avidity and thrust it into the desk drawer. "Good! Now get her out," he snarled savagely. "She never belonged here in the first place. The both of you go!"

Judith started to argue, but Tabor put her gently behind him. "Oh, no. She belongs here," he said firmly.

424

"This is her shipping office. She'll return as soon as it's safe. And she'd better find everything as she left it, or you'll hear from me."

Flecks of spittle gathered at the corners of Dufaure's mouth. "You . . ." He slammed the desk drawer with explosive force. "Get out! Get out!" In a fury he rounded the desk, hands doubled into fists. "You should have left when Lejaune set fire to your ship."

Tabor did not retreat, but his jaw hardened. A muscle ticked. "Lejaune?" he queried through clenched teeth.

Judith gasped at the name. Tabor had accused her of hiring Lejaune to destroy the *Banshee*. Her eyes flew from one man to the other.

Dufaure backed a step, then rallied. "Everyone heard the name of the man who set fire to your ship," he declared defiantly. "Everyone."

Tabor's face darkened with anger. "You . . . you're the one who hired them. You're the one who tried to sink my ship. But why?"

"You can prove nothing. Nothing!" spat Dufaure.

"Maybe not, but I'm not intending to take you into a court of law," Tabor retorted meaningfully. "I suggest you get the hell out of here."

"You are the one who should be taken into a court of law." Dufaure drew himself up haughtily. "Pirate! Spy! Sneaking mercenary who sells information to this rabble of upstart barbarians. I am a loyal Frenchman. I work for the safety and security of my emperor."

"Emperor?" Tabor frowned.

"Napoleon Bonaparte." Judith supplied the information. "He's convinced that Napoleon is going to come here from Elba and lead a return to France from New Orleans. He's also convinced that Louisiana is going to return to French rule."

"The city is filled with loyal Frenchmen," Dufaure declared.

Tabor shook his head. "You're crazy. This is America. Your 'loyal Frenchmen' are lining up right now with

425

Andy Jackson's men from Tennessee to fight the British. If the Americans don't keep Louisiana, then the British will take it. But it'll never belong to France again."

"You do not know," Dufaure spluttered. "Napoleon will come here and we will . . ."

"So you and that French captain planned to bring him here on a Talbot ship." Tabor shook his head. "You're both out of your heads. Napoleon's stuck on Elba in the middle of the Mediterranean. He's got more problems than he can handle in Europe without adding Louisiana."

Dufaure shook his head stubbornly. He took a belligerent step forward. "You will see."

"No, you're the one who'll see." Tabor stepped forward as well. The distance between them narrowed dangerously. Judith held her breath. "There's still the matter of my ship and my men. Mr. Archer and Seamus Killeen."

"Spies!" Dufaure cried. "Pirates! Aboard a pirate ship." He snatched his walking stick from under the counter and swung it with all his strength. Tabor flung himself backward to knock Judith out of range.

His elbow drove into her chest, and she fell against the wall, banging her head and shoulder. Her cry of pain brought him around to drop to one knee. He caught her in his arms and supported her.

Dufaure glared at the couple, then darted out the door to lose himself in the confused crowd of dockworkers.

Tabor slipped an arm under Judith's legs and lifted her in his arms. He pressed his cheek to her forehead. "I didn't mean to hurt you. I swear. I couldn't let you get hit. That gold-headed walking stick could have killed you."

She slid her hand up his cheek. "I know."

He gathered her closer. "You were innocent. You didn't set fire to my ship and kill my men. I hurt you. Kidnapped you. Made you look at . . ." He shuddered. He kissed the top of her head.

"Tabor."

"I'm such an idiot. Such an idiot. I never once considered that I might have other people who would be after me. My God! I've been making enemies since I was thirteen years old. My God!" He kissed her forehead.

She slipped her arm around his neck. "You couldn't have known. I did threaten revenge."

"I was obsessed with you. I loved you so much, I was wild with fury. All I could think of was you and punishing you for hurting me so badly. All I could think of was that I loved you and you'd betrayed me." His chest heaved against her. A harsh sound tore from his throat.

She pressed her lips against the pulse throbbing there. "You love me?"

He sank back on his heels, cradling her in arms. His rueful chuckle was a little shaky. "I've never denied that I loved you. I tried to put you out of my mind, but I couldn't. And now I want you so badly. I can't imagine that you'd forgive me. I don't have the right to ask after what I've done to you. Kidnapping you. Putting you in danger. You'd never have been on that British ship in the first place if I hadn't . . ."

She pulled his head down to her and kissed his open mouth. Her tongue slid over his, stilling his confession. He stiffened, determined to refuse the benison. His tender conscience would not allow him to accept her forgiveness.

Judith remembered the youth who could not forgive himself for the death of his brother or for the destruction of his family. As determined as he, she closed her lips and began to brush his mouth and cheeks with little soft, feathery kisses, feeling the salty moistness of his tears. "I forgive you, Tabor. I forgive you. There's nothing to forgive. I swear you didn't hurt me. I forgive you. Forgive yourself."

For a time he remained still as a stone, holding her gently, close to him. The tears slipped out from beneath his thick black lashes.

"Forgive yourself," she whispered again.

He shook his head. "I'll take you home," he said simply. As if he did not feel her weight, he rocked back slightly, then lifted them both to his feet. He hugged her once again, very tightly, then set her down.

She did not move out of the circle of his arms. Gradually, the world outside intruded. Shouts and the confusion, the rumbling of wagons over the cobblestones, the clang of steel-shod hooves began to din on their ears.

He put her from him, looking over her shoulder through the windows where even the cold, gray light was beginning to fade. "I'll see you home. Get your cloak, m'lady."

She nodded, suddenly afraid as she had not been before.

The landau was waiting with Georges struggling to hold the heads of the nervous horses. With alacrity he sprang to the box and guided them up Conti. The ride was remarkably short, given the panic and rushing around in the streets.

Once he had her safe inside the house, Tabor would have gone without another word, but she caught hold of his arms and made him face her.

"Where are you going? What are you going to do?" She could not control her voice. It trembled and broke.

He shrugged. "I have the *Banshee* to see to. And I suppose the *White Cloud.* Mr. Pinckney and Mr. Longman will need to take them farther upriver. No sense risking damage from cannon fire."

She shivered. "Pinckney? You're not going with the *Banshee*?"

He managed to evade her eyes. "I have other things to do."

"Oh, Tabor, what?"

"The *Carolina* needs men who know how to fight as well as men who know the river."

She turned away, her hand pressed to her forehead. The sudden pain was terrible. "Tabor," she began, "this isn't your fight."

But he was gone. Out the door, down the steps, back along the street in the gathering twilight and the heavy mist that had just begun to turn to freezing rain.

"Glad to have you aboard, Captain O'Halloran." Commodore Patterson extended his hand stiffly. "Major Catesby said you'd be coming along. Get your detail completed?"

Tabor nodded smoothly, wondering who Major Catesby was and what detail he had been assigned to. "Glad to be of service."

"We need your expertise on the river."

"I'll give you what I can, but surely one of the more experienced pilots would have been preferable."

"Not necessarily. You're a fighting man, O'Halloran. I need a pilot who's not going to faint on me at the sight of a little blood."

The last of the light was going as the *Carolina* with ninety-five men aboard her cast off her moorings and drifted out into the middle of the black water. Her lateen sails rattled up, the north wind caught them, and she immediately began to make headway.

Standing beside the helmsman, Tabor looked portside. Over on his right, unseen behind the sheltering trees, Andrew Jackson led an army of some two thousand men marching toward the British encampment.

The Mississippi's shores were dark walls, the river a stretch of lesser darkness. The men on board the *Carolina* went about their business in silence. The only light came from the glowing coals in buckets between the fourteen guns on the schooner's deck.

"Can't see a blasted thing."

"Do we know what we're looking for? What if we sail right past 'em in the dark?"

"They're human, ain't they? They'll put up a camp. They've got to eat. There'll be cookfires. We'll hear 'em or see 'em."

"Might not. Might keep quiet, lay low. Not let anybody know where they was. Just keep movin' right up the river toward New Orleans. They'd march right past us. They could be over there right now, moving along quiet like. We'd never see them."

"Belay that!" Commodore Patterson commanded the men on the gun just below the quarterdeck. He trained his spyglass on the bank.

Beside him Tabor O'Halloran did the same. Privately, he wondered, too, if the British forces might even now be slipping by them under the dark trees.

The north wind filled the schooner's sails and the Mississippi carried her smoothly.

At that moment, all questions were answered. Neither man needed a spyglass. The British camp was suddenly in sight. A glow bright as a town itself lighted the darkness off the port bow. As the *Carolina* swept down, the glow became the cookfires of the British camp. Each one was a beacon around which dark figures of men could be seen moving.

"They're crazy" was Patterson's succinct comment as he closed up the spyglass. "Anybody'd think they just came out on maneuvers. They're having a damn picnic."

Tabor chuckled grimly. "Just like the British. All for glory. They've probably been told they can just march right in tomorrow without a shot being fired."

"Is the river deep enough here for us to bring the schooner in close?" Patterson asked.

"You should be able to take her in as close as you want," Tabor said. "Too close and we'll be within range of their muskets."

"Not afraid of a little small-arms fire, are you, Captain?" Patterson sneered.

"I'm not afraid, but there's no need to risk the men's lives. The cannon have a much longer range."

"The more havoc we can wreak on that camp, the fewer Old Hickory'll have to mop up when he attacks" was Patterson's reply. "Steady as she goes."

430

Tabor raised his face to the north wind. It blew south southeast, driving the schooner easily and swiftly in to the shore. But how would they get her out of harm's way? He stared at Patterson's broad back. The man was daring. Too daring.

He tried once more. His final warning came between tight-clenched teeth. "Unless the wind changes, you'll trap the ship against the bank."

Patterson shook his head irritably. "We need to get in as close as we can. Make them feel they're surrounded. We can always tow her out under cover of darkness."

"But, think, man. You can't put your men in an open boat with British sharpshooters on the bank. Haven't you heard about sitting ducks?"

"Then we'll just simply let her drift on down the river. We can bring her back when the wind changes."

Tabor looked at the hundreds of campfires. The British numbers could quickly dispatch the small number of men on the *Carolina* as the ship moved along the bank. Furthermore, the presence of one lone schooner was scarcely going to give that army of trained men a trapped feeling. Helplessly, he watched as the *Carolina* headed for the bank.

Patterson looked at him once again and smiled grimly. "General Jackson's going to win this battle," he predicted. "You're working yourself up over nothing."

"Nobody but a fool cuts off his own escape route."

Patterson's smile disappeared. He glared at Tabor, then turned his back to bark an order with unusual ferocity.

Soon they were so close that Tabor could clearly make out the figures of the huddled men. He knew within reason that the schooner must have been seen by lookouts.

"Why don't they give the alarm?" Patterson asked out of the side of his mouth.

"They don't think we're important," Tabor replied. "Small boats have been scooting up and down this river all day long. What's one more?"

431

"But they're in enemy territory. They're an invading army. Why aren't they suspicious?"

"Because they're British and they believe the world's in holy awe of them," Tabor observed bitterly.

"Gunners, load with grapeshot." The soft command was passed down the line.

"Ready."

"Aim for the cookfires."

"Aim."

"Fire!"

Seven cannon on board the *Carolina* spoke as one. As the seven recoiled to the length of their lines, their crews leapt to clean and reload. The other seven cannon, primed and ready, slid forward, their muzzles just over the bulwark, and fired at the campfires of the confused, frightened men.

Looking through a spyglass, Tabor watched the British commanders trying to get their men to arms and form up their lines. Among the deafening blasts of the cannons could be heard the rat-tat-tat of drums assembling the men and the hoarse shouts as officers made themselves heard above the din.

Man-made thunder shook the houses of the French quarter.

Judith threw on her cloak and dashed up the stairs to the top of the house. Letting herself out through an attic window, she crawled onto the roof. After a shaky few moments she found her footing on the narrow widow's walk. Its ornamental iron railing offered her some stability on the slippery tiles. Despite the wind cutting through her like a knife and the passionate entreaties of Georges, she braced herself and trained her own spyglass eastward.

At first she swept the horizon, unable to make out anything, but suddenly, then in swift succession, lights began to flash far, far away. The faint explosive glows

432

coincided with the thunder of the guns.

As she strained her eyes in the icy darkness, she became aware that all around her people were doing the same thing. Mostly men were standing on their rooftops or on their balconies looking toward the east. Of course, the entire exercise was futile. She could see nothing but the faint distant flashes, but her heart beat faster at the thought that Tabor might be creating one of them or worse that he might be falling before one.

The British rocketeers returned the salvos almost immediately. As their glare lighted the sky over the *Carolina,* British soldiers knelt in squads to fire. The first salvo tore across the deck, wounding several men.

Tabor felt the blow low on his side, stabbing in just above his hipbone. It knocked him off his feet and drove him against the mast. The helmsman, too, screamed and spun away to fall unmoving to the deck.

"Fire!" Patterson bellowed at his men, dashing down the deck. "Keep firing."

One man, a bloody hole in both cheeks, reached out toward the commodore as he passed, but Patterson ignored him. "Fire!" he bellowed again. "Fire!"

Tabor pulled himself upright, his arm around the mast. "For God's sake, Patterson," he yelled. "Take the schooner out of here. Your crew'll be cut to pieces."

"Fire!" came the command.

A British guncrew loaded and aimed their three-pound cannon. Face-to-face across the narrow strip of water they fired at each other. Firing low, as the British loved to do, they drove both balls through the schooner's hull at the waterline. The grapeshot of the *Carolina* decimated the British gunners, but others were quickly in place. The second command to fire was never given. A fusillade of shots came from the bank upriver. The British squadrons wavered. As the light of the rocket died, they could be seen turning away.

"It's Jackson," Patterson bawled. "It's Old Hickory, boys. Keep firing. Aim for the campfires. Give him everything we've got."

But the campfires were being extinguished. Cooks overturned the food and drink into them. Soldiers smothered them with blankets or canvas. The barrels of the cannon were leveled at where the gunners remembered the fires to have been or toward plumes of gray smoke that swiftly streamed away on the wind.

In the darkness of the Mississippi banks, the two armies came together. Beneath tall, wide-leaved oaks festooned with Spanish moss and dripping with icy moisture, they cut and thrust. Friends could not be told from foes.

The British officers tried desperately by drum and voice to form their men into some kinds of lines. Unfortunately, as soon as they were formed, they became distinguishable from the fierce men who knew no rules except to kill as swiftly and efficiently as possible with musket, knife, and tomahawk.

"Cease firing, you idiot!" Tabor flung himself off the mast and caught hold of Patterson as the man dashed by him.

Patterson looked at the other man as if he did not recognize him. Then he shook himself. "Right. Cease firing, boys." The *Carolina*'s guns fell silent.

In the darkness they waited, the schooner swinging peacefully on her anchor while less than a hundred yards away the noise of the battle continued unabated.

The sounds of hell carried over the water. Cries, groans, orders, curses. The bark of rifles. Commands to fire. The screams of terrified men attacked in the dark. The battle calls of attackers screwing their courage by yelling as they made their kills.

Gradually, the shots grew fewer and fewer. The shouts came less frequently. Then began the pleas for help. For aid. For God.

The *Carolina*'s men lay under canvas, their wounds

434

bound up, their bodies warm and reasonably dry despite the steady drizzle and the miserable cold.

Tabor shivered where he lay, his pain tearing him apart. He felt on fire from armpit to hip. He could not move, only tremble in shock.

A man knelt beside him and lifted his head. "Here, mate. Take a drink of this."

It was corn whiskey. Raw grain alcohol so terrible that it made his eyes water and his breath catch in his throat. But he welcomed it. The last things he knew were the sounds of men moaning beside him. Soon his own voice joined them as he tried to breathe, but his chest did not seem to move properly.

Chapter Twenty-Three

"Judith! Judith!"

Judith sat bolt upright in bed, pushing her tousled hair back from her forehead. She could swear she had heard Laura call her name.

"Judith! Get up." A quick knock on the door and Laura burst in without waiting for an invitation.

"What are you doing up at this time of the night?" She glanced toward the window, through which the palest gray light shone faintly.

"I've come to get you up, silly. Clay's here. He's come to take me out of the city. You have to come with us to *Ombres Azurées*. You'll be safe there. And besides, don't you remember? It's Christmas. Happy Christmas."

Judith stared at her sister. "Christmas?"

Laura halted in midstride. Her face twisted as if she were going to cry. "You didn't even remember Christmas."

Judith stiffened. She did not want pity. "There's been too much to think about. With the city in such turmoil and the British soldiers just eight miles from here. You know what a terrible time I've had getting to the office every morning. What's more, Talbot's has a ship at the dock that can't move."

Laura nodded. "All the more reason for you to come back home with us. You can't do anything here. Clay's been so

436

worried about me. So he's come to take me home."

Judith stared at her sister. Laura had changed markedly from the unhappy white-faced woman who only two months before had announced that she was going to marry Clay Sutherland. "You look so happy, Laura," she said suddenly. "You're beaming. I can believe you now when you say your marriage is happy."

"Yes, it's happy. So happy." Laura looked down at her clasped hands. "I'm happier than I have a right to be."

Judith slid from her bed and came to her sister. She put her arms around her and they hugged each other close. "I'm glad, then. Really glad for you."

Both stepped away, uneasy, their eyes bright with tears.

"Get dressed now." Laura continued to talk briskly as she opened Judith's closet. "We've got a long drive ahead of us and the roads are terrible."

"I'm sure of that. How did he get into the city? What time is it anyway?"

"Five o'clock in the morning."

Judith slumped back in the bed. "Five o'clock! I thought we were locked in tight. Every night. How did he get in?"

"Oh, Clay has ways," Laura rejoined airily.

Judith pushed herself up again on her elbow. "Then he's perfect for you," she said seriously. "Beau always had ways."

"Yes, he did." Laura smiled mistily as she opened the wardrobe door and pulled out a garment. "Come on, sister. Why don't you wear this? It'll be warm. I can't remember when we've had a cold spell this long. Every green and growing thing will be ruined. All the plants will freeze down. It's terrible."

Judith gently accepted the black wool dress Laura spread across the bed. It was one of her heaviest and had been repaired after Tabor's depredations on board the *Portchester*. How long ago that seemed, and yet not even a year had passed. "I can't go with you," she said with a sigh. "I'd love to, and maybe I'll follow you in a few days. But right now I can't."

"Whyever not?"

"Because I can't leave the city."

"You're not giving me a reason. This is crazy. You're crazy."

"No. I . . . Tabor O'Halloran saved my life. He's on the *Carolina* downriver."

Laura looked at her strangely. "But you can wait for him just as easily as at *Ombres Azurées*. He'd want you to wait out of danger, I'm sure."

"Probably so, but I can't be too far away." She paused, avoiding Laura's penetrating green stare, too like *Grandmère*'s. "He might need me."

"Tabor O'Halloran! A pirate need a lady! Never!"

"I'm sure you're right. Nevertheless, I can't go with you."

"Little sister, is there something more here that you're not telling me." Laura looked directly into her sister's face.

"Yes, there is." She held up her hand to halt the flood of questions. "But I don't know what it is myself."

Laura smiled. "Perhaps you're in love."

Judith laughed mirthlessly. "In love. Me! A lady with a pirate? Never!"

Laura put the heavy black wool dress back into the closet and pulled out a lighter blue. "Put this on, then. We'll wait downstairs. At least we can all have Christmas breakfast together before Clay takes me back to the plantation."

"That's all!" Incredulous, Judith stared at her sister's back. "You aren't going to try to argue with me?"

"No. You don't sound the way you did before you went off in the *White Hound*. You're . . . I don't know . . . softer."

Judith flung back the covers and stood up briskly. "Don't be silly. I'm just the same as I always was."

* * *

438

"Elevate the guns. Put a couple of shot into them every half hour" was Patterson's command to the *Carolina*'s crew.

"Aye, sir. Give 'em lots and lots of presents for Christmas, boys."

Patterson regarded the empty bank of the Mississippi with satisfaction. The British had pulled their camp inland away from the schooner's fire. "That's the ticket, boys. As long as they have to think about us, they can't concentrate on General Jackson."

"Aye, sir."

Patterson strolled down the deck to duck beneath the canvas stretched to shield the wounded. Tabor managed a weak whisper. "Has the work crew come down from New Orleans?"

Patterson frowned. "Still afraid we're going to be trapped, Captain O'Halloran?"

"We can't move with two holes in our hull and the rudder out of commission."

"So far we haven't needed to move."

Tabor stared at the harsh, stubborn set of the commodore's mouth. "But if the British come at us, we'll need to move fast."

"Yellow streak, Irishman?" Patterson hissed contemptuously.

Despite the pain on his bad side, Tabor reared up on his elbow. His right arm shot out. The fist fastened in the man's lapel and brought their faces close together. "Call me a coward if you will, Patterson. But I call you a fool."

"See here . . ."

"No, you see here. You're in a position to lose your ship with all your guns and ammunition that your beloved Jackson needs so badly. If that's the way you want to die, then so be it. Every war has its share of glory-hunting fools, and every cemetery too. But your men are good men. Some of the finest I've seen. They've done everything you've asked of them. And you're risking their lives needlessly."

The speech was long, but its righteous wrath was

quickly extinguished as Tabor swiftly exhausted his spurt of strength. Instead of ending as a fierce denunciation, it became a whispered plea.

Deliberately, the commodore grasped Tabor's wrist and twisted it away from his lapel. Face like a thundercloud, he watched the wounded man sink back onto the crude pallet. Then he rose to his feet and strode away down the deck.

Except for an occasional shot when an American sharpshooter would try to deliver his own "Christmas present," the British had seen no signs of Andrew Jackson's troops. The shots from the *Carolina* had done some damage, but had inflicted few casualties. Still the British troops became more and more nervous as each half hour approached.

Then, the day after Christmas, the Americans, dug in behind the earthworks on the Rodriguez Canal, exchanged puzzled looks.

Loud cheers echoed from the British camp. A few guns went off and a drum rolled. More cheers followed. Lieutenant General Sir Edward Pakenham, the brother-in-law of the illustrious Duke of Wellington, rode into their camp. Almost the first order he issued after calling together his staff was for the destruction of the *Carolina*.

At dawn on the twenty-seventh, hot shot fell on the schooner. Flaming coals of fire and heated iron sprayed out of the mouth of the British three-pounder. Wherever they struck they set the deck to smoking. The canvas over the wounded caught fire in the first salvo.

Beside Tabor a man screamed in mortal agony as a triangular piece of red-hot iron sliced into his belly. A couple of men near the edge rolled themselves out from under the blazing canvas. The others could do little but shield their faces with their arms while the hot ashes and burning strips of material trailed down across them.

Hearing their cries for help and screams of pain, two of

440

Patterson's crew abandoned their gun to rip off the blazing canvas and hurl it into the Mississippi.

"Where are they?" Patterson bellowed as another shower of red-iron peppered the deck. "Damnation!"

"To the right, in the trees . . ." The voice of the sailor on the masthead rose in a terrible scream as fire ran up the lines engulfing his feet. In agony he flung himself out as far as he could away from the mast and fell headfirst into the river.

His comrades below jumped to the bulwark to throw him a line, but he did not come to the surface.

"Get back there! Swing that cannon 'round!" Patterson screamed. Viciously, he kicked one man who had cowered back as a flaming line dropped across the barrel. "Get on with it, you cowardly bastard!"

The *Carolina* answered the British guns with a salvo that fell to the right in a field.

Patterson raged up and down the deck. "Damnation! Find the range before they cook us! Stupid idiots!"

Another volley came smashing in. To a man the crew ducked behind whatever they could find. Tabor managed to pull himself over and shelter against the bulwark.

"They've got our range, sir," the lieutenant cried. "They've got us down to a point."

"Then find theirs," Patterson bellowed.

Tabor managed to pull himself to his feet. "Warp around that tree!" he shouted, pointing to a huge water oak that draped its branches out over the river almost to the *Carolina*'s masthead. "Drag her into shore."

"I'll give the orders around here, Mr. O'Halloran."

"Then give them. You've lost your ship. The next shot could hit your powder magazine. Then we'd all be blown to hell in a second. If one doesn't, we're sunk already. She's afire. She'll burn to the powder in no time, and that'll be the end. At least give your men a chance."

"My men"—Patterson raged—"will obey my commands."

"Then give good ones."

The commodore winced as a burning ash from the sail blistered his cheek. Still, he hesitated. Another man screamed as a sheet of flame that had been the lateen sail fell over his back. "Warp onto the oak!" Patterson yelled. "Grappling hooks and lines. Two of you, over the side to make fast."

Tabor hung on grimly to the bulwark as the *Carolina* began to move. Her sails were gone. Flames ran along every line, giving her masthead the macabre look of a blazing Christmas tree.

When the next round came from the British artillery, part of the shot fell into the river, but the effort by the *Carolina*'s crew was still not enough. Already the schooner's shallow draft had found the rising bank of the Mississippi. She could go no farther.

The deck blazed in several places. The crew could barely function in the thick smoke that not even the prevailing wind could carry away.

"Drag her on over," Patterson yelled. "We'll unload her."

"But, sir . . ."

"The cannon must go to Jackson. Boy." He caught one of his powder monkeys by the shoulder. "Jump for the bank. Run along it as fast as you can. Find General Jackson. Tell him to send some men double quick. Go!" He caught hold of the boy's wrists and swung him over the side. "Jump!"

The youth managed to land on his feet and dashed away to disappear in the trees.

"Get these wounded over the side!" came the next command.

As the wounded men were helped to the relative safety of the riverbank, Tabor shrugged off the sailor who came for him. "I'll stay with Commodore Patterson," he declared.

Patterson overheard the remark. "As you wish, Captain O'Halloran. However, you have been proved right in this."

"I hope you believe that I wish I'd been proved wrong."

"I believe it."

"She's goin', sir. We ain't got a minute."

A glance told Patterson the lieutenant's estimation was correct. The deck above the powder magazine was blazing fiercely. "Abandon ship!"

The men needed no urging. Almost to a man they leapt from the bulwarks. Some landed in the river, but most made the jump safely onto the muddy bank.

"After you, Captain O'Halloran."

"Thank you, Commodore Patterson." Tabor crawled weakly over the rail. Because of his wound, he could not summon the strength to leap. Instead, he clung to the side of the ship, then stepped out as far as he could from the side. The gray-brown water was barely chest high, but he would have slipped beneath the surface had not two men sprung in and dragged him ashore.

Behind him Patterson spared the dying schooner one quick look, then leapt onto the bank.

Once on the bank, the commodore did not hesitate. "Come on, lads. Form up. Double time. We've got to get out of here. Jackson needs us."

With his two rescuers on either side, Tabor was dragged along between them. Fingers of fire worked their way beneath the deck and touched the flannel-covered cartridges in the powder magazine. The force of the explosion lifted the *Carolina* out of the water and disintegrated her. Pieces of blazing wood rained on her escaping crew.

"The *Carolina*'s been sunk," the harbor master told Judith in strictest confidence. "Things aren't going so well for Jackson. I've heard it said that he was sleeping when the British blew the schooner right out of the water." He clicked his tongue self-righteously.

She caught hold of the side of the landau. "Mr. Ribodeaux, were there . . . ?" She could not ask the question. "Have the survivors been brought back to town?"

443

"I haven't heard that they have. Indeed, I think they probably haven't. Poor devils. Probably lying out under a cypress tree somewhere freezing to death." He snuggled more deeply beneath the many collars of his great cloak. "Ah, war is a terrible thing. So many young men. And for what reason? Later no one can even recall."

"You mean there are wounded men lying in a field somewhere." Judith felt a stab of pain at the thought of Tabor lying under this gray and dripping sky.

"Probably. No one goes out there to pick them up. The trip is very dangerous. Besides, the Americans guarding the road might shoot someone by mistake."

"But not the river."

"Well, no, Mistress Talbot-Harrow. Not the river. But . . ."

She did not wait to hear what reservations or objections he might have had.

Judith pulled open her reticule. "I want to hire you and your flatboat," she said bluntly. In answer to her knock, a short, bearded man had come to the door of the boat house. A slow grin spread his features until they defined an almost perfect circle.

"Well, she's sure fer hire. Wantin' t' hold a fancy tea aboard 'er?" He chuckled hoarsely at his joke.

"No, I want you to take me downriver a few miles and bring back whatever we can load up."

"Y' want t' hire me fer a salvage job?" He tilted his head to one side, staring at her—a beautiful and obviously well-to-do woman. All that red hair and clear white skin. He had never seen a woman like her up close. He scratched his groin area ruminatively.

Behind her Georges rolled his eyes toward heaven. Then he made so bold as to touch her sleeve. "Maîtresse."

Judith paid no attention to her man's obvious distress, nor the lack of manners on the part of the flatboat captain. "No. I want you to pick up men for me."

444

He looked at her speculatively from beneath raised eyebrows. "There's sure plenty of men around here. Y' don't need t' go downriver for 'em, perty gal."

"I want you to pick up wounded men. From the *Carolina* and anyone else who may be wounded."

"Y' want me t' take my boat and my mules int' the war."

"I'll pay you."

"Hell, perty gal, pay's no good to a dead man. I could get myself kilt."

She shook her head. "You'll fly a white flag. No one will shoot you then. The British honor a truce."

He thought about that for a minute, then eyed the purse speculatively. "Let's see the color of yer money."

She pulled a handful of coins from her reticule. They lay bright gold in the palm of her black glove. He gaped at the sight of English guineas, then grunted, "Who'd I be workin' fer?"

"I'm Judith Talbot-Harrow. Of the Talbot lines." She jerked her head in the direction of the line office. "I can pay."

He nodded. "I guess y' can by the look of y'. Why don't y' use yer own boats?"

"Their drafts are too deep. We need to go in to the bank. Will you go or should I try to hire someone else to take me?" She made to pour the coins back into her reticule.

He shifted his heavy body in alarm at the sight of the money disappearing. "Y're goin' along?"

"Yes. And my man, if he will?" She turned to him. "Will you go with me, Georges?"

The black man looked at her in surprise. "Are you asking me, Maîtresse?"

"Of course. This could be dangerous. I wouldn't order you."

He smiled slowly and with quiet dignity. "Then I will go."

*   *   *

On the left bank of the Mississippi, Andrew Jackson had originally set up an earthwork rampart at the Macarté Plantation behind the Rodriguez Canal. After the destruction of the *Carolina,* he had extended the line a quarter of a mile into the swamp and added eight batteries of cannon.

Commodore Patterson with the men of the schooner was placed in charge of the gun set up on the right bank to fire across the Mississippi. Under a canvas a few yards behind the emplacement lay Tabor, the other seriously wounded members of the crew, and some few of Jackson's men who had been in too severe a condition to transport back to the city in wagons.

The ship's barber, who also doubled as its surgeon, had done what he could for them. What he could consisted of a crude cautery. The pain of the burn to seal the wound had made Tabor so miserable that he drifted in and out of consciousness. For hours he lay in a haze of pain. His entire left side was feverish, his head throbbing so violently that he was virtually blind when he was conscious. Unconscious, he moaned softly as pain pierced even the mind's own attempt to escape.

In the bleak morning, the last day of the year of 1814, he lay on his right side, staring hopelessly at the crushed, stained grass beside him. About midnight the man who had lain there had died when the cautery on the stump of his leg had burst open. Before the surgeon could be roused, the wounded man had bled to death. Now only the reddish-brown stains remained to mark the spot where a man had died within minutes. Tabor touched his own bandage gingerly. The heat of his flesh rose it.

He closed his eyes, then opened them again as a raucous cry disturbed him.

"My Gawd!" yelled one of the Tennessee volunteers. "Lookee what's a-comin'! Damn my eyes!"

"Lord-ee, but ain't that a fine sight," a second agreed.

Tabor opened his pain-filled eyes. Then closed them, sure he could no longer differentiate between dream and reality.

Striding across the fields in her seaman's breeches and a long black frock coat came Judith Talbot-Harrow. Only a step behind at her left shoulder, his big body shielding hers from the river and from any British sharpshooter, came Georges.

The cold wind had blown her red hair completely loose from pins so that it swept to the side, tendrils lifting and tangling like flames. Patterson stepped down from his hastily thrown-up earthworks to meet her. Scowling blackly, he held up his hand as a signal for her to halt. "Ma'am, you'd better turn yourself around and get back on that flatboat."

"Please . . . er . . . Commodore, I'm Judith Talbot-Harrow of the Talbot Shipping Line. I've come from New Orleans to transport wounded Americans back where they can get nursing."

His eyebrows rose at her name. For a moment he hesitated. Then he shook his head. "Miss Talbot-Harrow, this is no place for a lady." He threw a warning look over his shoulder at his gunnery crews, hanging over the emplacement grinning like apes. "You're a good Christian woman, ma'am, to think of us, but . . ."

"I'll be away as fast as I can, Commodore . . ." She smiled sweetly.

"Patterson, ma'am."

"Commodore Patterson, sir. You'll be able to fight ever so much better if you don't have to worry about hurt men." She walked by him and began to climb the earthwork. "Do you have any badly wounded men?"

Hastily, he strode up after her. "Why, yes, ma'am. We've got a couple that are pretty bad." He noticed that she bit her lip. Some of the bright color stirred up by the wind seemed to drain from her cheek.

On the top of the earthwork she paused to locate the bodies stretched out in the grass beneath a dark cypress. "Is one of them"—she took a steadying breath—"Captain Tabor O'Halloran?"

"Why, yes, ma'am. He's about the worst now that—"

"Oh, no. Take me to him, please."

447

Patterson took her by the elbow to assist her down the rampart. "This way, ma'am."

Once down, Judith broke into a run, leaving Commodore Patterson to follow after her. "Tabor. Oh, Tabor . . ."

He heard her voice, sure that he was dreaming. Nevertheless, it was so real that he rolled half over onto his back.

She dropped down on her knees beside him and took his cold hand. "Oh, pirate, what have you done to yourself?"

"Why, m'lady." His amazement was obvious despite the painful rasping of his voice.

Tears starting in her eyes and trickling slowly down her cheeks, she put her hand on his forehead. His skin burnt like a brand. "Tabor," she murmured. "Oh, Tabor, you're so hot."

He dared not close his eyes. She would be gone when he opened them again. And he wanted to keep her with him as long as possible. "Where . . . ?"

"I've come to take you back to New Orleans." Her voice broke.

She bent closer, closer. He watched her, but he was so weak. The pain was so terrible. Just as she was about to touch her lips to his cheek, his eyes closed.

"Tabor?"

She was still there; he could feel their cool softness. "You're still here," he whispered incredulously.

"Oh, yes." She raised her head. A small semicircle of men, with Commodore Patterson at its center, had formed around the tree. "We must move him."

Without opening his eyes, Tabor squeezed her hand. "Others . . ." he managed to say.

"Of course, Tabor. They'll go too. Commodore Patterson, will you allow me a few of your men to carry these wounded to the flatboat?"

He shot a quick glance toward the left bank of the Mississippi. "Well, now, I don't suppose . . ."

448

"I assure you no one will fire upon them. We are here under a flag of truce. The British soldiers should allow the wounded to be picked up from the battlefield."

"Miss Talbot-Harrow . . ."

A gust of icy wind shook the cypress. Droplets of water pelted the canvas. Tabor coughed rackingly and groaned. Judith clutched his hand harder, determined not to lose her temper, but equally determined to have her way. "Georges can get the captain from the flatboat if you cannot aid me, Commodore, but I intend to take these men out of harm's way."

Patterson glanced from her pale set face to the stern black man who hovered over her. To move the men would solve one of his problems, but the commodore did not like officious women. "Where're you going to take them?" he demanded coldly.

"The Ursuline Convent hospital." She looked around her distractedly. What difference did it make where she took them? Anywhere would be better than where they lay. "Georges can ask the captain of the flatboat to send a couple of his men, but that will take time."

Patterson hesitated. "The British sharpshooters . . ."

Tabor coughed again and managed to open his pain-filled eyes. Bitterly, he stared at the schooner's commander.

The commodore bowed his neck stubbornly. "These are sailors and soldiers of the . . ."

A lank Tennessean in worn buckskins stepped forward. With a jerk of his head he brought several of his fellows with him. "We're volunteers, ma'am. We'll be right glad to put these boys aboard that there flatboat so y'all can skedaddle outta here."

Patterson's eyes darted cold steel at the backs of the men who stolidly scooped up their fellows and carried them away.

Georges stepped forward. "Ready, Maîtresse."

Judith looked down at Tabor. "We have to move you now, sweetheart." His eyes were so deeply set in his head

449

that they looked black. The beginnings of a black beard contrasted sharply with the sickly gray of his skin.

"Shall we lift him now, ma'am?" one of the Tennesseans asked.

"No need for them to trouble, Maîtresse." Georges dropped down at Tabor's side and scooped up the man's body.

As the strong arms lifted him, Tabor gave a terrible groan and slumped. His cold hand slid from Judith's grasp. Fear chilled her, so heart-stopping, so agonizing that she had to grit her teeth and clench her fists to keep control of her emotions. For she dared not let them break.

Hastily, she put both sets of knuckles on the ground and pushed herself to her feet. "I'll be going now, Commodore," she said, coolly facing the angry officer. "I assure you, your men will be having the best care available. I will see to it myself." She adjusted the blanket more warmly about Tabor's shoulder. "Take him gently, Georges. . . ."

"You come too, Maîtresse," he insisted.

"Very well. Good-bye, Commodore Patterson." She held out her hand as if they had been introduced at a fancy tea.

"I don't like this, Miss Talbot," he began.

"Talbot-Harrow," she corrected him.

"You're the beatin'est," the captain of the flatboat called as she and Georges hurried toward him with their burden. "I was perty sure y' were goin' to git yerself kilt stridin' off acrost that field."

Judith grinned wanly. "I wasn't too sure I wasn't going to 'git kilt' myself. Let's get this boat back up the river."

"Yes, ma'am. Heave-ho, bully boys. Put yer backs into it." He looked in the direction of the east bank. "We don't want t' be here a minute longer'n we have to."

450

Chapter Twenty-Four

"I'm sorry to tell you this, Miss Talbot. He's a very sick man. Besides his wound, he's undoubtedly suffering from exposure."

Judith clenched her hands around the lamp that she held aloft for Dr. Chatillon. "Can't you do something more?"

"My dear young lady, I wish I could, but I don't dare do anything more. I've cleaned the wound itself as best I could, but there are probably pieces of trash beneath the scab. The fool who cauterized him couldn't have taken the time to clean the area properly. Battlefield surgery is crude at best. Butchery, at its worst. This lies somewhere in between. He's weak. Very weak."

"But what about the fever and the chills? The cough?"

The doctor hunched his shoulders as if to avoid a blow. "You say he's been lying out under a tree for several days. He may very well develop lung fever if he doesn't have it already. Against those types of diseases I have so little that I can do."

She took a deep breath. "Then what do I do?"

He smiled faintly. "Keep him warm. If his breathing worsens, prop him up on pillows so his head is above his chest. If he begins to lose his breath, boil a packet of these herbs in a kettle of water close by the bedside. Give him quinine for the fever."

"And the wound itself?"

He shrugged. "The human body has the most wonderful ability to accept a foreign object and wall it off with scar tissue. If the trash doesn't poison his system, he may have lumps under his skin for the rest of his life, but they won't kill him. I want scars given every chance to form. At all costs, I want to avoid having to open that wound."

He looked at her as if for confirmation. Judith nodded her head vigorously.

He sighed. "Very good."

The lamp was making her arm ache. She set it down and massaged her palm.

The doctor followed her gesture with his eyes. "I say again, you made a mistake in insisting that he be brought here."

She whipped her hands behind her. "The good Sisters were full to overflowing. At the convent he would have gotten very little nursing."

"But I cannot spare a man to nurse him," he warned.

"It's not necessary," Judith replied coolly. "I can tend to his needs."

The doctor gaped in shock. "You're a young gentlewoman. He's a man." He made the statements as if they were accusations.

Judith smiled. "Think of him as if he were my husband."

Dr. Chatillon reddened. He closed his bag with a hard snap. His voice became dogmatic, dictatorial. "But he's not. And even if he were, young married women of good family don't nurse their husbands."

She lifted her chin. "That's ridiculous. Besides, I am used to nursing, Doctor. I nursed my mother for over a year while she slowly died of cancer. I assure you that the suffering human body, whether female or male, will hold no surprises for me."

He stared at her a moment, taking her measure, then nodded brusquely. "You've made your decision and I

452

don't have the power to alter it. Give him quinine for the fever. Laudanum for the pain, but not too much. I've known men to become so dependent on it that when the pain of their wounds goes away, they have a different and more terrible pain. You understand?"

Judith felt a prickling behind her eyes as she remembered Charlotte's terrible cravings for laudanum and brandy. Her answer sounded rough and harsh. "I understand."

The doctor waited a moment. When no explanation of her strangled tone was forthcoming, he continued. "If he begins to toss and turn, he'll most likely injure himself. Maybe tear open the cauterized wounds. He has to be kept still. Do you have someone who can help you with this?"

"My manservant Georges."

He took up his bag. "Then I'll say good evening. I can let myself out. No need to leave your patient's side." He opened the door, then halted. "I don't know when I can return. The reports are that a battle is imminent. I suspect I'll be needed very shortly."

"Take care, Doctor."

Uttering a little prayer for strength, she pressed her forehead against the door. Then, straightening her back, she turned to the bed that had been Beau Talbot's.

Tabor lay on his back. His tangled black hair and stubbled chin starkly separated the white pillow from his equally white face. As she bent over him, Judith felt the heat and smelled the taint of fever. Pain for his pain curled within her, but only a moment, then she sternly tamped it down.

Briskly, she rang for Georges, whom she instructed to bring towels and cold water from the cistern.

While he was gone, she began to strip the ripped and stained garments from Tabor's body. When he was naked except for the wide bandage passed around his middle, she covered him and lifted his head.

"Tabor," she said clearly. "Tabor. You have to wake

453

up and swallow some medicine."

He moaned softly. Her voice seemed to come from a long way off, but hers was the voice of authority. It called him back from the desert of pain and burning brimstone where he wandered, a sheet of fire strapped to his side. His pale lips framed the word, but no sound came. "Judith?"

"Drink this, Tabor." She held a teaspoon to his mouth. "It'll help to bring down the fever."

He swallowed, choked, then barely nodded his head against her arm. "Hot."

"Yes, sweetheart, you're very hot, but we're going to get you cool."

"Don' worr' 'bout me. Pirate . . ."

"Yes, I know you're a dreaded pirate, the scourge of the Atlantic. Now drink some water."

He obeyed her thankfully, taking small sips until the bitter taste of quinine was all washed away.

He was already asleep again when she settled his head on the pillow and smoothed the tangle of black hair off his forehead. Georges knocked softly, then entered without waiting for permission. "Icy water, Maîtresse. Little skin of ice on the cistern."

"Good." She dipped a cloth into it, wrung it out, and laid it across Tabor's forehead.

Suddenly, he coughed deeply. With a cry he tried to roll over away from the pain. She pushed him back, but he swung his arm. Before Georges could catch him, he had struck Judith in the face and knocked her to the floor. She fell heavily on her hip.

Georges finally succeeded in getting Tabor back on the pillows, where he lay as still as if he had never moved, as still as death.

Stumbling in his haste, Georges hurried around the bed to help her to her feet. "Let me get some of the boys to nurse him, Maîtresse," he begged. "He hurt you and not mean to."

She accepted his support until the world stopped

spinning, then touched her jaw tenderly where Tabor's fist had landed a blow. "I'll do it, Georges." She laughed a little shakily. "He doesn't mean to hurt anyone. He's just hurting so badly." She wrung out another cloth and lifted the arm that had struck her. While she washed it, she talked softly, recalling old, sad memories. "Once my mother threw a heavy vase of flowers across the room. It shattered against the door. Poor thing! She was so very sick. She thought she was throwing it at spiders."

Georges nodded unhappily. "I could fetch a conjure woman to help get rid of fever spirits. Plenty of work for them in the bayou."

Judith shook her head. The blow was no longer stinging. It was nothing, she acknowledged. Tabor's life was so important to her that she would suffer a hundred such blows if necessary to make him well. She wrung out the water from another compress and draped it across his throat, where the pulse of life beat strongly.

"What are you doing up?"

Judith set the breakfast tray down beside the door and hurried across the room to catch hold of Tabor when he swayed against the bedpost. "You're still weak. You'll open your wound."

"I can get up. I need to get up. The *Banshee* . . ." He lost his train of thought as black spots began to whirl before his eyes.

"You can be a pirate later. For now, lie back down." She put her shoulder under his armpit and helped him to sit back on the bed. Since he had not been able to put on his boots, she simply lifted his legs and tucked him back beneath the covers.

"You don't want me here," he argued in a breathless voice. His own weakness had surprised him.

"If I hadn't wanted you here, I would have left you on the riverbank, or at the very least, taken you to the Ursuline Convent."

"Jackson . . . ?"

"We haven't heard."

"How long have I been here?"

"A week."

"My God." He pushed himself up, then sank back limply, sweat standing on his forehead. "What about the *Banshee*?"

"So far as I know, she's still upriver."

Judith tried to spread a napkin across his chest, but he pushed it away. "I'm not hungry."

She looked at him appraisingly. "Of course you are."

He stared at the bowl of thin corn meal mush that she set in front of him. "Not for that."

She dipped the spoon into it and held it to his mouth. "Come on. You can't expect to be strong if you don't eat. It won't taste bad at all. I've sweetened it with pure cane syrup." She smiled as if he were a child. "You'll like this. Open up."

He groaned but opened his mouth obediently. It was as she had described—hot and sweet. As he ate it between swallows of strong tea, he stared at her. For the first time he noticed the thinness about her cheeks and the dark circles under her eyes. She had lost flesh and sleep. "Where am I?"

"At my house."

He raised a black eyebrow. "What will the neighbors think?"

"Probably that I'm your mistress. But they've thought that all along."

"You brought me in and put me in your bed—"

"This was Beau's bed."

He grimaced. His hand smoothed the coverlet as if to placate the indignant spirit of his friend.

Judith poked the last spoonful of mush at his mouth. "Finish your breakfast."

He swallowed, his eyes studying her face. "And you've been taking care of me?"

"Georges and I."

456

"When did you sleep last?"

"Don't make this into more than it is!" she told him briskly. "I sleep every night. My room's right across the hall." She unrolled a warm, wet cloth beside the plate and began to wash his face and neck and hands.

He submitted to her ministerings, his eyes half closed.

When she would have risen to go, he caught hold of her hand. "Why did you come after me?"

She sat down. "I came after wounded. Any good citizen—"

"Don't give me that, m'lady. The river wasn't exactly crowded with boats of good New Orleans citizens coming down to pick up wounded."

She looked away irritably. "I own a shipping line. I'd be a logical one to do that."

"Since when has a flatboat been part of the Talbot fleet?"

"I thought you were unconscious."

He shrugged. "Slipping in and out. Enough to know I wasn't on a sailing ship." He waited, staring at her. Then he pushed a little at her wrist. "Why did you come for me?"

"Because it seemed the thing that I must do." She bowed her head, staring at the lean brown fingers where they held her captive.

"Then I must do this." He pulled her gently toward him. His hand slid up her arm and over her shoulder to cup around her neck. "Kiss me," he whispered.

Somewhere in the forest of his whiskers their lips met. Their touch started a shiver that ran through her entire body, right down to the tips of her toes. She made a tiny sound. Her muscles contracted and curled in her belly.

As the kiss went on and deepened, she melted, sliding bonelessly into the circle of his arm. Another shudder racked her as her breasts touched his chest. The heat of their bodies turned the heavy material of her dress into tissue. "Tabor," she moaned. "Tabor. Please stop. We can't do this."

457

His hand clasped her breast, squeezing it, finding the nipple hard in his hand, plucking at it. "Why not?"

"You're weak. You've been hurt. You could scarcely stand." Each short sentence was punctuated by gasps for breath as her desire for him set her heart pounding.

He chuckled softly, nuzzling her ear, biting the delicate lobe. "Don't make me stand. Let me lie here . . ."

"Tabor."

". . . beneath you."

She squirmed helplessly, clasping his leg between hers, rubbing herself against his thigh. Recklessly, unable to resist her own desires, she brought her leg up to rub across his belly.

He was already hard when her thigh covered him. His soft parts had retracted, shaping the entire organ into a lance, hard as metal under velvet, ready for her.

She began to whimper as wanting him became sheer pain.

He squeezed her breast again. "Take off your clothes. You won't hurt me. You'll hurt me and yourself a lot more if you pull away right now."

"Yes," she whispered. Shivering as if the room were very cold, she pushed herself away from him. Her fingers fumbled with the buttons of her dress, then made short work of the ties on her petticoat and drawers.

He stared at her, his face avid with desire. At the sight of the red curls surrounded by the pearlescent white skin, a shudder ran through him. With one quick whip of his hand he flung aside the covers and accepted her on top of his body.

The wound did not pain him. He felt only the sweet pain of desire. His moan as she straddled his hips was pure pleasure.

Judith's body, sternly restrained for the past week, flamed at the sound. Every day she had bathed and cared for his body, touched him intimately, looked at him, learned his shape. Now she released the checkrein she

458

had held on her desire, let it flow into the muscles of her thighs. Bracing herself on his shoulders, arms at full stretch, she rode him.

He watched her. Her breasts were incredibly white, pink-tipped. They moved with her body. Her face hung above his, rapt with desire, seeming to transcend the present, glowing, coated with a fine sheen of perspiration. Her bottom lip showed a white line caught tight between her teeth.

"Come," he whispered. Then, more strongly, "Come with me, m'lady. Let's leave this world together."

His command was all she needed. She lifted herself almost to the tip of his staff and thrust herself back down upon it, clenching her muscles. With virgin tightness she came to the base. The hard, throbbing nub of her desire ground against his pubic bone.

They screamed together. She collapsed, releasing the terrible tensions of her body in the sweet sister of death. He caught her and managed to guide their bodies together and draw the covers over them. The last thing he remembered before sleep was her lips dreamily caressing his shoulder.

"He's gone," Judith announced, amazement obvious in her voice. "I unlocked the office this morning and every scrap of paper was cleaned out of his desk. Every tiniest thing was gone."

"What about your money?" Tabor asked in alarm.

She shrugged. "According to Dufaure, there wasn't any. Of course, I suspect that he had some stashed away, but I know that there was never much in the office at a time. When the ships would dock and their cargoes would be sold, the shippers would pay us percentages. We'd pay bills, make repairs. Sometimes we'd buy cargoes ourselves to bring back here on speculation, but in the time that I've worked at Talbot, I've never seen a huge sum. It was just steady."

"I don't intend to let him get away with this," Tabor insisted darkly.

Judith frowned. "He loaned Beau money to make repairs on *Ombres Azurées*. A large sum of money was spent within the last couple of years for the *Laurel*. If he cleaned out the bank account, he still probably didn't get what he was entitled to."

Tabor clenched his fists on the chair arms. "He was responsible for the deaths of two of my men."

"He shouldn't go unpunished, but if he's gone from New Orleans, if he's going to join Napoleon and return to France, he's exiled himself. He loved this city and this country and now he can never return to it."

"Still . . ."

She bent to lay a gentle finger over his mouth. "When you're stronger, when this whole terrible business is over, we'll go together to Governor Claiborne and get the records set straight. For now . . ." He reached for her, but she backed hastily away with a smile. "Not too much of that either. You slept twenty hours after the last time."

He grinned, but when she turned away, he ground his teeth in frustration. Being in a sick bed was enough to make a man crazy.

"Reynolds." Tabor extended his hand. "Or whatever your name is?"

The spy drew his brows together as if trying to remember. "Reynolds is good. Catesby is nice, too, although it's someone else's." He waited a minute as if for Tabor's smile. When no smile was forthcoming, he shrugged. "Reynolds is someone else's too."

"What does your wife call you?"

The spymaster shrugged. "She calls me dear." They stared at each other in silence. Then Reynolds spoke. "You're looking better than I expected to see you. Dr. Chatillon informed us that it was touch and go with you. But here I find you able to be up."

"I've had personal attention," Tabor replied.

"Yes." Reynolds looked around him at the quiet luxury of the room, the fire in the fireplace trimmed with fine Dutch tiles, the polished furniture, the exotic appointments brought back from wherever Beau Talbot had taken the *White Hound* when he had first sailed to make his fortune. "Yes, indeed. It seems the very best of care."

In the silence that followed, the fire crackled and hissed. Sparks jumped against the fire screen. "Jackson whipped them to a standstill," Reynolds said at last.

"When?"

"It's been more than a week ago now, January eighth. Damn fools! Lined up at dawn in their bright red coats. Marched right at the ramparts we'd built behind the Rodriguez. Kept on coming. God!" The spy's voice shook. "Damnedest thing I've ever seen. They just kept marching, right over their own bodies. We waited till we could count their buttons, then shot them down."

"They still believe we ought to come at them the same way. War is a gentleman's game to the British," Tabor explained dryly. "You didn't play by the rules. Shame on you."

"At least one gentleman won't play anymore." Reynolds nodded in agreement. "Pakenham's dead. We shot his horse out from under him when he rode up to the front to keep the poor devils from retreating. Then he got another and came back. Damnedest thing I've ever seen," he repeated.

"Damnedest," Tabor agreed. "Brave as only a fool can be."

"You don't have much use for them, do you?"

"I don't have *any* use for them," Tabor rejoined. "Except one."

"She never was a spy, you know."

"I know that now." Tabor hesitated. "But it wouldn't make any difference if she were."

Reynolds grinned. "Is it like that, then, Captain O'Halloran?"

"It's like that."

The spy heaved a mock sigh. "It's probably just as well. You had no talent for spying."

Tabor raised an eyebrow. "I told you about the Rigolets, didn't I?"

Reynolds pulled his eyeglasses from his pocket and polished them carefully with a handkerchief. As he did, his posture began to change, his body seemed to shrink.

"Good information. Good. Good. Turned out to be correct. If you ever hear anything more of that caliber, let us know." He hooked his glasses over his ears. They immediately slid down his nose until he could look over them at Tabor. "Must be going. Many things to do. Many things."

"Thank you for the tobacco, Mr. Reynolds," Tabor said with a straight face.

"Don't mention it. Don't. Don't. Don't get up. I can find my own way out." So saying, the spymaster bowed nervously, picked up his hat, and pulled it down tight.

Tabor rose despite the other man's admonitions. "Good luck in whatever war you fight in next."

Reynolds held out his hand. "Perhaps I won't have to fight again. I much more enjoy diplomatic spying. Jackson's the man. Wait and see. He'll be president of these United States someday."

They shook hands solemnly. Tabor watched from the porch until the little man rounded the corner and was gone.

"He's gone, Judith," Tabor called up the stairs.

"Did he tell you anything new?"

"Not really. It was pretty much as you had heard it in the streets. Jackson won. The British have pulled back to their ships on Lake Borgne."

"Then I can send upriver for the *White Cloud* and dispatch her."

"And the *Banshee*."

He could have sworn she winced. "Yes, of course.

You'll be wanting to get back to your ship."

"Can you think of any reason why I shouldn't?"

She shook her head. Two spots of color stained her cheeks. "Not at all. I'm sure the Caribbean awaits your depredations." She started to leave.

He caught her arm and turned her to face him. "I am not a pirate, Judith. I was once, but I haven't been for several years. I'm a citizen of the United States of America."

She searched his face. "Are you really?"

"I really am. And I want you to marry me."

"Marry . . ." Her throat was dry. "You don't want to get married."

"I didn't want to until I met you."

"But I betrayed you. I stole your ship."

"Only when I refused to give back yours." He hugged her to him. "You can ask Mr. Pinckney when he gets back. I'd already planned to ask you to marry me long before I found out you weren't a British spy."

"Why should you want to marry me? You've already had my body. What more do you want?"

He shook his head a little sadly. "Is that all you think I want? I want the whole of you to belong to me forever."

"But we fight."

"That's all right. The Irish and English always do."

"You're not Irish anymore," she reminded him.

He released her and stepped back, retaining her hands but putting distance between their bodies. "Perhaps I'm not what you want. If you marry me, you won't be English. No more Miss Judith Talbot-Harrow. Just plain Judith O'Halloran."

She considered that idea for a moment. "Once upon a time I thought I wanted to return to England, but now that's all behind me. I don't want it at all. I really want to stay in New Orleans." She looked him straight in the eye. "But are you sure?"

"I've never been surer of anything in my life."

She smiled then, her eyes dreamy. "Judith O'Halloran.

I suppose that makes me American."

"I'm afraid so. Even if your grandmother is a countess."

"You don't have to marry me, you know."

He kissed her hands, palms first, then backs in courtly style. "On the contrary. I absolutely have to."

"Why?"

He placed her palms together between his own as if he offered a sacred pledge. "Because I love you, m'lady. Don't you know that?"

She stared at him, her blue gaze wistful, then closed her eyes with a sigh. "I don't think I love you. I swear I don't. I care for you very deeply. I'd do anything for you. But I don't know what love is. I don't know how to give it or receive it."

He closed his own eyes against a pang of sympathy for her long loveless state. When he opened them again, it was to make her a new pledge. "You don't have to love me. Just keep hating me the way you have since you came downriver for me. If that's all I'm going to get, then I can live with it. As for receiving it, believe me, it's as easy as your standing still"—he put one arm around her waist—"and lifting your face"—he turned up her chin with his fingertips—"and holding your sweet mouth just so." He kissed her as a benison and a benediction.

He felt her shudder, saw the tears sparkle on her lashes.

"If you don't want love," he whispered, "I'll give you whatever you want."

Epilogue

Ombres Azurées
Spring 1815

"I feel as though I'm looking into Beau's eyes." Judith picked up the baby and cradled him against her shoulder. She planted a soft kiss on the top of his head. "Michael, you are so sweet. And you smell so good."

Laura grinned equably. "That's not Michael. That's Malcolm."

As Laura picked up her other son and snuggled him into the crook of her arm, Judith stared hard at him. "The very least you could have done is have one with blue eyes and one with green, so I could tell them apart."

"Look at the name on his bracelet." Laura ran her finger across the top of the gold bracelet around the chubby baby wrist.

Judith raised her eyebrows. "So you can't tell them apart either?"

"I can—but Clay can't. He's still annoyed that they look more Talbot than Sutherland."

Judith laughed heartily as she switched Malcolm from her shoulder to the crook of her arm. She put her index finger into his little fist. He gripped it reflexively and pulled it toward his mouth. "I'm not surprised. *Grandmère* would tell him that the English strain is dominant."

Laura's gaze grew speculative. "I've been thinking about taking them to England for her to see. As soon as they're old enough, that is."

"You'll have to take Celeste with you if you do," Judith said lightly. "She couldn't stand for them to be gone for all those months. She'd be afraid that they won't be spoiled enough."

"That's where you come in, little sister. You have to give her something else to spoil. When can we expect another addition to the family?"

Judith was silent for a moment, then capitulated. "Well, as Tabor so poetically puts it, the cargo's been in the hatch now for three months, so sometime in late fall we should be able to unload."

"Oh, Judith." Tears slipped down Laura's cheeks as she managed to embrace both her sister and both her sons in her arms.

Clay opened the nursery door for Tabor. "Looks as if we're being left out, old man."

"Here now. Is this a private circle? Or can a couple more fellows get in?" Tabor asked.

As he came into the room, Laura held out Michael to him. "You wonderful man. Judith's just told me the good news. Here. Get some practice before the actual time comes."

Clay slapped his brother-in-law on the back. "Congratulations, Tabor. Looks like your adventures on the high seas are over for good."

"No more gambling for you either, my friend."

"Right. From now on everything's a sure thing."

Judith smiled sweetly as she handed Malcolm to Clay. "One thing is for sure. His diaper needs changing."

Here's a preview of Emma Merritt's *Masque of Jade,* on sale this spring from Zebra Books. Don't miss the story of Judith's sister, Laura—of her love for gambler Clay Sutherland and the undeniable passion they share!

Wearing a white organdy morning dress, Laura sat at the table in the small dining room and read her latest letter from Judith. The snow had already begun falling, her sister wrote, and the fields were covered in white. At the moment she was sitting in Charlotte's room in front of a blazing fire; her mother was sleeping. Sighing, Laura imagined an English winter—a winter she had not seen in nine years. Their mother, Judith went on to say, was increasingly dependent on pain-easing drugs, and not long ago she had broken the antique Chinese vase.

Laura lowered the letter and looked at a twin vase sitting on the mantel. Tears burned her eyes and blurred the beautiful piece of transclucent porcelain with its delicate paintings. When she had left England with her father, she had taken one of the vases. The other she had left for Judith. She had always felt as if this had created a bond between them. Now Judith did not even have that.

Assailed with a homesickness such as she had not suffered since she left England, Laura refolded the letter and slid it into the envelope. Perhaps it was time for her to consider a holiday. Still, Laura hesitated. While Judith's letters to her were regular and newsy, their tone was polite rather than sisterly. Judith never asked about Beau nor did she invite Laura for a visit. Nor did *Grandmère*. The old woman had never forgiven Laura for sailing to America with Beau.

Laura sighed and slipped the letter into her pocket. She poured a second cup of coffee and began to read the newspaper, looking up only when she heard the soft knock on the door. "Yes?"

"A M'sieur Clay Sutherland is here to see Maîtresse Celeste, mam'selle," said Saloman.

Clay Sutherland! Laura's heart skipped a beat and she lowered the paper to the table. Strange that he wanted to see Celeste. She wondered if her stepmother had run up a gambling debt with the man. "Did he say what he wanted?"

"No, ma'am."

Laura lifted the paper again, but the black print danced before her eyes. "Tell M'sieur Sutherland that Maîtresse Celeste is resting and is not to be disturbed. He may leave her a message if he wishes. I'll see that she receives it."

"Yes, ma'am."

Laura was so nervous, her insides were fluttering. Laying the paper aside, she walked to the window and stared at the back gardens, which were as lovely as the front, although much smaller. Knowing Clay Sutherland was here in the house disturbed her greatly. All too quickly she remembered the feel of his body pressed against hers, the rough sweetness of his lips.

Saloman returned. "Mam'selle, since M'sieur Sutherland cannot see Maîtresse Celeste, he would like to see you."

Laura lifted a finger and ran it down the cool pane. "Inform M'sieur Sutherland that I'm much too busy to receive visitors this morning."

"*Oui*, mam'selle." His expression never changing, the servant disappeared down the hall.

A moment later from the doorway she heard the deep resonant tones. "When would be a good time for me to come see you, Miss Talbot?"

Laura gasped and spun around to see Clay lounging indolently in the doorway, elegantly dressed, as he had been the previous evening, when she first saw him in Dufaure's courtyard. So quiet was his appearance she could almost believe he materialized and disappeared at will. Today a black coat contrasted with gray trousers. He held his hat in his hand, riotous black curls framing a devilishly handsome face.

"You have audacity, M'sieur Sutherland." She composed her voice with greater ease than she did her nerves.

"I thought we were agreed on that last night," he mocked, brown eyes alight with laughter.

He leaned more fully against the door frame and stared at Laura, who was bathed in the fragile glow of morning light. Last night she had been lovely; today she was beautiful. The sun set her auburn hair on fire, and her green eyes, framed with long, dark lashes, sparkled with life and vitality.

"May I come in and talk with you a minute?"

"I run a sugar plantation, M'sieur Sutherland, and am extremely busy. I have no time for frivolous conversations, and since I have never gambled in your establishment, I know you're not here on business . . . if you know what I mean."

Clay reached into his pocket and extracted her fan. "I have to admit my business is more frivolity than business. I wanted to return this to you. Somehow, last night we forgot about it."

Laura was puzzled. "If you came to return this to me, why did you ask for my stepmother?"

The firm lips curved in a dazzling smile. "Last night you seemed to be distressed because I was no gentleman. Today I wanted to prove to you that although I'm not, I have manners."

Laura stepped forward to take her fan. "Thank you, M'sieur Sutherland. Now, if you'll excuse me, I must be

469

going. Saloman, please order my gig to be hitched," she called.

Following the servant's faint *oui*, Clay asked, "Where are you going?"

Laura moved from behind the chair and gave Clay a cold glare. "That is absolutely none of your business."

Clay looked first at Laura's morning dress, sunlight gleaming in the window to silhouette her shapely legs through the thin material, then at her house slippers. He glanced at the newspaper on the table, and while his countenance was serious, his voice was underscored with gentle amusement.

"Are you going out attired in your morning dress?"

Laura glowered at him, despising the smile that tugged at his lips. "How I dress is also none of your business, m'sieur."

"I must disagree with you, mam'selle. Let me drive you, and we shall discuss the point at length. My gig is hitched and waiting."

Laura hesitated only momentarily, then said, "I'll be gone all morning, M'sieur Sutherland. I certainly don't intend to argue with you, and as we don't have any interests in common, I'm sure we don't have that much to talk about. And I wouldn't want to impose on you."

"You might be surprised to find out that we have many interests in common, Miss Talbot." He stepped fully into the room, his boots clicking against the hardwood floor as he moved to stand in front of the fireplace. "My gig and I are at your disposal."

"M'sieur Sutherland—" Laura straightened her back and stepped away from the window, careful to keep the table between her and Clay. "I don't want either you or your gig. First, I own one of the newest and latest models of the English Stanhope gig, imported directly from the Continent. Second, when I want an escort, I shall find one who is worthy of me and my station in life. Now, if you'll excuse me, I have work to do."

On shaking legs Laura turned to walk out of the room,

but Clay's long strides covered the distance to block her exit. Standing directly in front of her, his brown eyes smoldering with anger, he glared into her face. He stood so close, his breath splayed against her skin.

"I don't pretend to be a gentleman, Miss Talbot, and certainly I'm not one of your Creole aristocrats, but I am a person, and as such I demand respect. You can stick your pretty little nose up in the air as much as you like and pretend that I don't exist, but deep down both of us know I do. We know that I affect you in exactly the same way that you affect me."

"If that's true—" Laura took courage in her anger. "Then you abhor me, M'sieur Sutherland. You take advantage of the innocent, luring them into your—"

"Ah, yes," Clay drawled, moving a step closer to her, drinking the sweet scent of her clean body. "I'm the devil, am I? Luring the innocent into my 'den of iniquity.' I believe that's the way you described the Golden Fleece. Did you bother to learn from the city officials that my casino is one of the most reputable in New Orleans? Do you know that I don't use rigged tables or loaded dice or marked cards? Do you know that I hire security personnel to police my establishment and to protect my customers?"

Mesmerized, Laura stared into the indomitable face.

"No, Miss Talbot, you don't know any of these things; yet you point an accusing finger at me. You call me a lowlife without knowing anything about my life."

"M'sieur Sutherland," Laura said, extremely uncomfortable under the heat of his accusations, "leave now. You and I have nothing to say to each other."

"You may think you have nothing to say to me," Clay said, "but one of these days you'll realize you do. I knew the minute I saw you last night in Maurice Dufaure's courtyard that fate had put us together."

"I think greed more than fate is the reason you were at Maurice Dufaure's," Laura said mockingly.

"I was speaking of our meeting, Miss Talbot," Clay

returned, "not my reason for having been at Dufaure's home. I know why I was there, and let me assure you, greed had nothing to do with it."

"No?" Laura questioned, feeling herself on firmer ground now. "You didn't threaten to take Roussel's home?"

"I never make threats. I came to collect money owed me. I was always taught that paying one's debts is good business. If one gambles and loses, one must be prepared to pay the consequences."

In the distance Laura heard a bell tinkle and knew Celeste had awakened and was calling for breakfast. "Thank you again for returning my fan," she said. "Now, I really have work to do, M'sieur Sutherland. Good day."

"Before I say good day, Miss Talbot," he murmured, his eyes lingering on the fiery curls that framed her face, "I would like to apologize for last night."

Laura felt heat rush to her face. His nearness, coupled with the memory of their kiss, unsettled her. As they had done last night, her heartbeat accelerated and the blood rushed through her body quickly to make her head roar. "There's . . . really . . . there's no need."

"Oh, yes," he insisted, "there is." Without her being aware of the movement, Clay hooked his hat over the back of a nearby chair and moved closer to her. "Last night I left you with a bitter taste in your mouth. I kissed you merely to punish you for slapping me."

His fingers tweaked one of the silky curls, the callused tips brushing against the inflamed flesh at her temples. Laura wanted to dodge the touch; she knew she should but somehow her body, running truant, trembled beneath the caress. When Clay took another step, she backed up but found herself wedged between him and the table.

"I accept your apology," she said in a breathy little voice, her gaze irresistibly drawn to his mouth. Slightly parted, his lips were firm and generous, turning up at the corners in a perpetual smile. Visually tracing the shape of

472

his mouth with her gaze and remembering it against hers, she wondered what it would feel like beneath her fingertips. Unconsciously, her tongue darted out to moisten her lips. He had not touched her, but already desire raged through her.

Clay moved that imperceptible few inches that brought their bodies together. He caught Laura into his arms to clamp her hands between them. His grip was strong enough to dissuade any resistance but gentle enough to send her senses whirling, sensual enough to set her afire with desire.

"Today I want to leave you with a sweet taste. I want to show you what a kiss of pleasure can be."

"No!" Laura twisted her head from side to side, evading his lips.

"I must, Laura." A hand fastened on her chin to hold her still. "I can't have you entertain such lowly thoughts of me."

Soft laughter flowed over Laura as firm masculine lips tentatively touched hers. Had the kiss been as savage and brutal as the one the previous evening, she would have fought for honor and integrity. But his gentleness was her undoing. After a night of tossing and turning, of wondering what really being kissed by Clay Sutherland would be like, she abandoned all thoughts of honor and integrity and gave herself to the wonder of discovery. Again and again his mouth brushed lightly across hers.

Laura had often imagined what went on between a man and a woman, but she was totally unprepared for these feelings that Clay was stirring in her. Reason abandoned her; desire and instinct guided her actions now. She pressed herself closer to him, feeling his hardness through the thin layer of organdy. Her hands slid up his chest.

When Clay braced his neck, pulled his head back, and did not immediately meet her lips with his own, Laura's hands twined around the base of his head. Silently begging and unashamed of doing so, she pressed his lips closer to hers.

"Ah, yes, sweet," Clay murmured. "This is the way it should be between a man and a woman."

The last vestige of Laura's resistance fled when Clay's mouth captured hers, his firm touch sending a flash of heat through her body. Though still gentle and inquisitive, his kiss was steadily becoming demanding and proprietary and urgent. His mouth moved back and forth on her supple lips, the insistent tip of his tongue pressing along the indentation that marked the entrance into her mouth.

"This is wonderful," Clay mumbled, his lips moving against hers without releasing her, "but it can be so much more wonderful, Laura Elyse." His warm mouth glided up her cheek, his lips kissing her eyes shut.

"Please, Clay," Laura begged.

Clay bent to claim Laura's parted lips before she could close them on his name. His tongue penetrated the sweet moistness of her mouth to fill it with the essence of his kiss. Laura's lips opened beneath his as she fully received the caresses of his tongue. Freely she allowed herself to be carried into the wild, wonderful world that Clay Sutherland's touch created.

Laura moved her hips restlessly and moaned. Each movement of his tongue inside her mouth nudged and tugged at that secret place in her lower body. Caught up in desire, she responded intuitively. Her tongue tentatively touched his.

"So sweet," Clay murmured. His lips traveled over her cheek to her neck to leave a trail of hot kisses in their wake.

Though his lips on her neck were sending exquisite shivers over her body, she wanted his mouth on hers, his tongue touching hers. Laura moaned softly and arched against Clay. Turning her head, her mouth sought his.

Clay's hands banded around Laura's upper arms, and he set her away from him. She opened her eyes and blinked uncomprehendingly at him. Breathing deeply, he stared into the green passion-glazed eyes. Involuntarily, Laura swayed toward him.

"If we don't stop now," he murmured, "I won't be responsible for what happens next. I may not be a gentleman, but I'm not a seducer of the innocent. Neither do I intend to be seduced."

The words were like a splash of cold water in the face. Laura gasped and stumbled back from Clay. Last night had been excusable; this was not. She had allowed this man to walk into her home, into the intimacy of the family dining room, to take advantage of her. Humiliation raged through her. She lifted her hands to her swollen lips.

"Get out," she whispered, "before I have you whipped for the dog you are."

"If I'm a dog, Laura," Clay said with total disregard for her title and position, "what does that make you? A bitch?"

Laura's hand flashed out, but Clay caught it. "You slapped me once. Not again."

"Get out of my house, and don't ever darken my door again," Laura snarled. "I never want to see you again."

Clay stepped back and picked up his hat, settling it on his head as he walked away. When he reached the door, he stopped. His back to her, he said, "I owe you another apology, Laura. Last night I accused you of being an iceberg. You're not." He turned. "Underneath the icy trappings is a fiery woman begging for release. I would love to be the man to free her."

"Get out!" Laura clasped her hands together, barely hanging on to her composure.

After Clay left, Laura stood in a rage of anger and humiliation. Never had she been so used by a man before, so degraded. Not even George had done this to her. Bitter tears stung her eyes, and her hands shook. Never had she felt so empty and alone as she did when he stopped kissing her. The man would not be satisfied until he had totally destroyed her.

Laura raced through the house, wiping the tears from her cheeks as she ran. Standing in the window behind the gauzy curtains, she watched him climb into his gig and drive down the oak-lined avenue, leaving a cloud of dust in his wake.

Slowly, Laura turned and walked up the stairs to Celeste's room. The drapes were drawn, and sunlight streamed into the room. All the incense and candles were removed. Propped up on several pillows, Celeste enjoyed her breakfast.

"Bonjour," she greeted Laura, lifting a cup of *café au lait.* "Come join me."

"No, thanks," Laura said, moving to the window on the other side of the room. "I just finished breakfast myself. How's your head?"

"Fine. I think I shall be up and about in a few hours. What are you planning to do today?"

"Mandy's grandson fell and hurt his leg yesterday. I'm going to see how he's doing."

"Laura, will you not consider the idea of an overseer?" Celeste set her tray aside and slipped out of bed, pulling her wrapper on.

Laura sighed and arched a brow. "You know how I feel about the running of *Ombres Azurées.*"

"When, Laura, are you going to learn that there are certain privileges to being a woman?" Celeste waved her hand through the air. "You do not have to get out in the sun and work the plantation like a field slave."

"I like earning my privileges because I'm a person, not a woman. I like working the plantation. And I don't like Papa and Roussel conspiring behind my back to hire me an overseer."

"They have not conspired, *ma petite.* Roussel has recommended this M'sieur Donaldson, and your papa has asked that you consider him."

"I did. His previous employers spoke highly of him, and his qualifications were excellent, but I don't want to hire him at the present time."

476

Celeste threw her hands up in exasperation. "Oh, Laura, what are we going to do with you! You are such a stubborn child, determined to make yourself a place in a man's world. Running a plantation. Practicing with swords in Exchange Alley. Why could you not be content to embroider? It is so much more genteel and ladylike." After a moment she added, "I suppose you'll be going to practice your swords tonight?"

Laura laughed at her stepmother's turn of phrase. "Yes, if all goes well today, I will fence tonight."

"And I suppose that means you'll be spending the night in town?"

"If I should finish before the curfew, I'll return to *Ombres Azurées*. Otherwise, I'll stay at the town house." Laura leaned against the window casement and stared in the direction of the fields. After a few minutes in which Celeste fussed with her toilette, Laura said, "Today's going to be a long day. We start the planting."

"And soon the grinding."

"Soon the grinding." Laura warmed to her favorite subject. "I figure this year, Celeste, our grinding will last two months and will produce two hundred fifty thousand pounds of sugar."

"Very good," came the absent reply. The running of the plantation was not Celeste's favorite subject, and she spared it little thought or attention. Using two fingers, she gently massaged the muscles at the corners of her eyes. "Deeding the plantation to your father and turning its supervision over to you were two of my best decisions, I think. Because of you we have more than doubled our production."

"Tripled," Laura corrected her.

"You need not be so arrogant, *chère* Laura," Celeste chided gently.

"Not arrogant," Laura returned. "Just proud."

"And well you might be. Did I hear you talking with someone earlier?"

"Yes."

477

"Must I guess who?" Celeste lifted the lid off the ivory powder box.

"Clay Sutherland," Laura muttered.

The large puff suspended in midair, Celeste's brows lifted in surprise. "What was he doing here?"

"He returned my fan. He found it in the courtyard, where I dropped it last night."

"M'sieur Sutherland is sweet on you, *chérie*, yes?" Celeste discreetly dabbed the powder on her face and laughed.

"It's not funny," Laura snapped.

"Of course not, but it is romantic, *oui?*"

Turning, Laura grinned. "You're an incurable romantic, Celeste."

"I am."

"I didn't think you liked Clay Sutherland. After all, he's an American and a gambler."

"He's an American, but in case you haven't noticed, *chérie*, I'm quite intrigued by foreigners. I married one. And I love gambling."

Laura laughed. "Clay Sutherland is nothing like Papa. He's contemptible."

"Perhaps you think so at the moment. But I'm not so sure. He has a good reputation. People like him."

"Not me. I hate him."

Celeste brushed the curls around her face for a few minutes, then said, "That is a dangerous sign, Laura. It sounds to me as if you might be falling in love with the man."

Laura spun around to gaze in puzzlement at her stepmother. "Whatever do you mean?"

"Clay Sutherland reminds me very much of your father when I first met him. Rather a rogue. A very attractive rogue. Perhaps like Beau, Clay is nursing a great loss." Celeste laid the brush down and stared unseeing into the mirror. "I don't know what I would have done, *chérie*, had I not met your papa." She hesitated briefly. "Had he not come along, everything

478

had would have been lost. He has been so good to me."

"You've been good for him," Laura said softly.

Celeste turned around and large tears rolled down her cheeks. "But I do not know if your father has gotten over his love for your mother or not. Always I am plagued by doubt. Because they are divorced, he and I are not married in the eyes of the church. Always I wonder if one day he will return to England to her. She is so beautiful."

Laura rushed across the room and took Celeste into her arms. "Papa loves you," she said. "You're the only woman in his life. He and Charlotte were not in love with each other; their marriage was arranged. He never loved until he met you."

"At first we did not love," Celeste said. "We married for convenience. Both of us wanted *Ombres Azurées*. He was willing to pay my debts, and I was willing to marry out of the church."

"But you love each other now."

"I love him." Celeste hugged her stepdaughter tightly. Then she pushed away and wiped the tears from her eyes. "Be careful, *chère* Laura. You and I are both victims of the society we embrace. As long as you are discreet, you may have your lovers, but you must make a good marriage. You must marry Roussel Giraumont, *oui?*"

Berthe knocked on the door. "Maîtresse Celeste, you rang for me."

"Yes." Celeste stared at Laura. "I'm ready to get dressed." In a lower voice she repeated, *"Oui?"*

Closing her eyes, Laura recalled Clay Sutherland's soft, mocking laughter and the feel of his hard body pressed against hers.